Le**a Fleming** was born in Lancashire and is married with thr**ee** sons and a daughter. She writes from an old farmhouse in the Yorkshire Dales and an olive grove in Crete.

The Postcard

LEAH FLEMING

**SIMON &
SCHUSTER**

London · New York · Sydney · Toronto · New Delhi

A CBS COMPANY

First published in Great Britain by Simon & Schuster UK Ltd, 2014
This paperback edition published, 2014
A CBS COMPANY

5 7 9 10 8 6 4

Simon & Schuster UK Ltd
1st Floor
222 Gray's Inn Road
London WC1X 8HB

www.simonandschuster.co.uk

Simon & Schuster Australia, Sydney
Simon & Schuster India, New Delhi

A CIP catalogue record for this book is available from the British Library

Paperback ISBN: 978-0-85720-402-8
eBook ISBN: 978-0-85720-403-5

Typeset by Hewer Text UK Ltd, Edinburgh
Printed and bound in Great Britain by CPI Group (UK) Lrd, Croydon CR0 4YY

Remember before God
those men and women of
The European Resistance Movement
who were secretly trained in Beaulieu to fight
their lonely battle against Hitler's Germany
and who before entering Nazi occupied territory,
here found some measure of the peace
for which they fought.

From the plaque in the Cloisters of Beaulicu Abbey,
unveiled 27 April 1969.

Prologue

The summons from the hospital came in the middle of the night. Although it was expected, it was still a shock.

'Your father's asking for you, Melissa. I think he wants to make his peace,' said the concerned-sounding nurse.

Why should I go? Mel's head was spinning. Why should I bother? He's never been the greatest dad in the world. Where was he when I needed him after Mum died? When did he ever give me anything but cheques and empty promises?

Yet something stronger than her anger made her shoot out of bed, ring for a taxi, then throw on her jeans and T-shirt before dunking her face in cold water.

Lew Boyd was all the flesh and blood she had left in the world. Years of heavy drinking had taken its toll on his liver, and all his success in the world couldn't spare him now. Besides, Mel owed it to her mother to hear him out one last time.

The hospital corridors were silent but for her scurrying foot-steps, and Mel's heart sank at the thought of what was waiting for her in the private ward. The one and only time she'd visited, she'd breezed in with a bunch of grapes and a smile to tell him she'd won the coveted Post-Grad Music Scholarship to the Royal Academy in London, but her excitement had been quickly doused by the sight of the once big man reduced to skin and bone. They'd made small talk, but she had been shocked at the change in him and glad to escape.

This was different. This was the last goodbye. With a sinking heart she wondered what he wanted to say that couldn't have been said before now.

Lew sat propped up with an oxygen mask by his side. His tanned skin was now a papery yellow, his cheeks pinched, his hair in sparse tufts from the chemo. He looked a shadow of his former handsome self. At the sight of his daughter he held out a bony hand.

'You came,' he croaked. 'I wouldn't have blamed you if you hadn't.'

'They rang and said you wanted to see me.' Mel's voice trembled as a nurse retreated discreetly from the room. Mel sat down, staring at this frail figure struggling for breath, shocked at his deterioration. How could she have thought of not coming?

He turned slowly, those blue eyes fixed on her. 'Not been much of a dad, have I?'

'You're the only one I've got,' she replied, trying to hide years of resentment. He'd been such a driven man, developing his building empire, making a fortune, and for what?

'Time to come clean, Melissa. I'm sorry for letting you down so many times. I really loved you and yer mom, but when she was killed in the car I couldn't handle it, lost the plot, as they say now. I'm sorry, kiddo. I've always been so proud of you and those lungs of yours.' He paused as if saying each word was agony to him. 'I've often wondered just who gave you that wonderful voice. Not me or your mom, for sure. She was tone deaf, bless her. Must have skipped a generation, I reckon.'

'You didn't bring me here to talk about my voice,' she snapped. 'Sorry, but I don't understand you.'

'Of course you don't. I don't understand myself, but I need to tell you a story and I'm hoping you'll be able to finish it.' He took a gulp of oxygen.

'Long ago I came on a ship from England with Ma, yer gran Boyd. It was after the war. I don't remember why we came or where we went. The truth is I don't know who I am, Mel. You'll not find a birth certificate for me. Granny Boyd was not my mother. You need to know all this in case . . .' Lew tailed off and Mel could see tears in his eyes. She reached out her hand to take his.

'It doesn't matter now, Dad. It's all in the past.'

'You're wrong. I've lived with these blanks all my life. I once saw a shrink in rehab who wanted me to have some hypnotherapy but I wouldn't go there. Now I wish I had. It might have made me face this head-on instead of just drowning my sorrows. I've been a closed book to you with my binges and my moods. I never deserved the love your mom gave me.' Lew stared at his daughter as if seeing her for the first time. 'I sense such a waste of potential in me, love. I worked so hard to blot out bits of my childhood. My folks were kindness itself but they never shared my past and I never asked until it was too late. When I asked your gran about things, she clammed up tight.' He smiled, shaking his head. 'Your mom opened my heart to such loving possibilities but I let you both down. I'm ashamed of how I neglected you. I've messed up on you and your mom big time. I thought if I was successful it would prove I was a proper provider, but it all went too far. I wanted you to be proud of me but no one is proud of a drunk.'

'Stop this! It doesn't matter now.' Mel felt the tears rising.

'If only I knew . . . There's blanks in my memory but there's one thing I do remember when I was a kid . . . One day you'll have kids of your own and they ought to have a proper history to blame for all their failings. I've left some stuff for you with Harry Webster, my lawyer. Promise me you'll go and see him when I'm gone?'

'What are you trying to say?' Mel leaned forward, the better to catch his words.

'When you go to England you might find the places, people who might recognize my stuff. I meant to do this for myself but I was always too busy and now I've run out of time. I just know Gran was not my real mom. There was a lady who once came from England when I was little . . .' He paused, staring towards the wall. 'Would you find out who she was and why she never came back? She may be still alive. Please, Mel, before it's too late. Will you do it for me?'

Panic rose in Mel at the thought of what he was asking of her. 'Why didn't you tell me all this before? We could have searched together.'

'I just never gave it much thought until I got crook, and then with the chemo it went out of my mind.' Lew sank back as if all the breath was leaving his body. 'See Harry – he'll help you – and forgive me for letting you down . . .' Those were the last of his words she heard through her tears.

The nurse slipped back into the room. It was almost dawn. 'You take a break, Miss Boyd. It won't be long now.'

'I'll stay,' she whispered. 'I'm not leaving him alone.'

One afternoon two weeks later, Mel, wearing her black audition suit, found herself walking along the busy King William Street, climbing up the steps to the offices of Harry Webster Associates for an appointment with the senior partner. Having delayed the meeting until she felt strong enough to face this stranger, now she felt nervous. So many questions were racing through her mind and here was someone who might provide some answers.

Webster was a squat little man of her father's age. He looked like a rugby player, with his squashed nose and his arms bulging beneath his jacket sleeves. His cheeks were ruddy as he smiled and ushered her into his office, which was a clutter of files, books and coffee mugs. The walls were covered with certificates stating his legal qualifications, but sports trophies acted as paperweights.

'I'm sorry for your loss, Melissa. Lew was so proud of you – I hear you are in for the Elder Hall Award. We go back a long way, yer dad and me . . . school and that sort of thing. Great man for keeping stuff in order,' he laughed, glancing around his room. 'Not like this. My father knew the Boyd family and looked after their affairs . . .' He looked straight at her, then made for a cupboard and pulled out a shoe box from the bulging shelves, catching the files before they clattered onto the floor. He took the box to his desk, swiping away some papers to make a space for it. Mel sat expectant. She realized she was holding her breath and let it out slowly. At last, some answers were on their way.

Harry tapped his finger on the box. 'Lew came to see me six months ago as soon as he knew . . . He said to open the package after his death so I've opened it. There's a letter for you and some bits and pieces of private stuff. He's made good provision for you. It's all straightforward: the apartment; moneys, should you wish to travel. His will is in order.' He pushed the box across the desk to her. 'I think his whole life is in that box . . . what little he knows of it. The Boyds were not his birth parents. I reckon he meant to follow up on his real history but you know what he was like.' He hesitated. 'He could get easily distracted.'

Oh, yes, full of promises never fulfilled was Lew Boyd: birthdays forgotten, outings cancelled. She'd learned early to take any contact if and when it came, but now he was gone she felt bereft.

'There's been a lot in the papers about child migrants,' Harry continued. 'But I don't think he was one of those poor sods who got shipped out here after the war. He never said much, only that the Boyds saved his life.'

'Do you realize I only found out they weren't my real grandparents at his bedside?' Mel snapped. 'Why couldn't he have shared all this with me himself instead of making it all a mystery?'

Harry sat down and sighed. 'I've met a few guys like Lew, guys with no history. They can't remember and there's no one left to jog their memories. He just didn't talk to anyone about his past. Perhaps he had a bad start. Humankind copes as best it can, but I think this is the nearest we're going to get unless that box holds any clues. I've not opened anything addressed to you. I hope it's all in there – what he wanted you to know, Melissa. I realize he wasn't much in the dad department but he was proud of you.'

Mel took the box from him, shaking her head. 'Thank you. I prefer to open it alone.'

'If I can help in any way, feel free to ask,' Harry said, ushering her to the front door.

She nodded curtly and fled down the steps into the bustle of the busy traffic and the bright afternoon, heading straight back to the Music School to shove the box in her locker, where it stayed for a week until all the formalities of her future studies were confirmed and she took it home.

The box stayed unopened for another week. She just couldn't face what might be inside. One evening, however, curiosity got the better of her, so armed with a bottle of Shiraz and a large block of milk chocolate, she carried it to her father's flat in his apartment block. It was all black leather sofas and glass, the sort of soulless place she'd hate to live in. Now it felt emptier than ever.

This was a private wake between the two of them. She poured herself a large glass of the wine before she sank down to open the letter addressed to her. Her heart lurched to see that familiar scrawl. From out of the envelope a postcard fell to the floor. She picked it up. It had an old British stamp with a King and Queen's head on it and it was addressed to 'Master Desmond Lloyd-Jones c/o Mrs Kane, Ruby Creek, South Australia'.

Opposite, the message read: 'TO DARLING DESMOND . . . from Mummy with lots of love'.

She flipped over to the picture, a sepia-tinted photograph of some village by a lake.

She picked up his letter with trembling fingers.

Dear Mel

Sorry to spring all this on you but I wondered if you were up to solving the mystery I never got round to sorting in my life. I feel I owe you an explanation . . .

I've had this postcard for years. Found it when I was clearing out old Grandma Boyd's effects. It was stuffed in with Pa's love letters. She'd kept it for a reason and when I saw the picture and the name, I just knew it was something to do with me. Don't ask me why, I got a tingle of something, a fuzzy memory that just wouldn't surface, but when I asked Pa he just laughed and offered to chuck it out. He said she liked the picture. It reminded her of her home in Scotland before the war. I knew he was telling fibs so I kept the postcard, and the other bits.

I don't recall much how I came to be in Australia. My memories are like shards of broken glass: fragments, flashes of colours in a kaleidoscope. I recall the taste of the metal of a ship's railings, flaking grey paint, salt spray on my cheeks; these are images that come to me in dreams. Some bits are heavy as lead, dark memories. It's as if I am peering through a hole in a huge wall at a garden full of flowers. I'm not one for flowery lingo, as you know   don't know one plant from another – but I can tell the smell of roses anywhere.

I'm not making excuses, but there are memories and bits of my life I've worked hard to blot out. Perhaps if I could have faced up, I might have made you proud of me instead of ashamed. The Boyds were kind folk but not ones to lavish the praise and affection I craved. It was your mom who opened my heart. I wish things could have been different for all of us . . . I'm handing on the baton to you. You have a right to know what made me the way I am, warts and all. There's a Berlin Wall between me and my past.

I know once you get your claws into a job you see it through, but don't let this interfere with your future. Have a wonderful life. I just hope you are curious. If you can find out who I really am, you'll know where you belong too. The answers are out there somewhere but time may not be on your side.

Remember I never stopped loving you both, so forgive the apology who was your father, Lew.

The room swam around Mel as the tears flowed for all the misunderstandings and arguments they'd had in the past. Now she was completely alone.

Eventually, she gathered herself to see what else the box contained. At the bottom were swimming badges, snapshots, a postcard of some old-fashioned lady in a cartwheel hat smiling up at her, and a medal, its ribbon faded, its inscription in a foreign language.

For one angry moment, she wanted to ditch the whole box of tricks into the bin. What had all this junk got to do with her? Why should she burden her new life in London with a search for mystery ancestors? She knew in her heart, however, that she could not let her father down.

Perhaps fate was taking her to England for a reason.

Darling boy. Mummy is safe and coming home to you soon.

Part One

CALLIE

1923–45

When they being the beguine
It brings back the sound of music so tender
It brings back the night of tropical splendour
It brings back a memory evergreen.

'Begin the Beguine', lyrics by Cole Porter, 1935

1

Caroline came tearing through the wood down the path from the walled garden of Dalradnor Lodge, bent and holding her bleeding knee from climbing the Witch's Broomstick, which Niven Laird said was made by the devil. She knew it was only an old bent branch covered in knots but it had skelped her just the same, and that hurt. She didn't want the twins to see her crying so she shot off home so Marthe would make it better. And she was starving.

It was mid-September and the brambles were fat and juicy so the kitchen was filled with jammy smells as Mrs Ibell filled the old Dundee marmalade jars with ruby jelly. This was no time to stop to collect acorns and beechnuts or look for hazelnuts and wild mushrooms, however, with her hurt knee.

She ran into the hall and almost bumped into a man in tweed jacket and knickerbockers, who was standing admiring the pictures on the wall by the staircase. He turned at the sight of her in her kilt and grubby socks, her thick Fair Isle jumper, splattered with sticky burrs, with a hole in its sleeve.

'Now who is this wearing the clan tartan?' he said, eyeing her with interest.

Just at that moment Mrs Ibell hurried in to greet him. 'Mercy me, look at the state of yon bairn. Whatever will Sir Lionel think? Miss Phoebe's niece is such a harum-scarum.'

'I can see that,' he smiled . 'How old will she be now . . . six tomorrow, by my reckoning?'

'Seven,' Caroline snapped back. 'Sir.' She remembered her manners just in time. Fancy this old man knowing when her birthday was. Perhaps he'd come to bring a present, though she had never seen him before. She hung back shyly, seeing him examining her closely.

'Tall for her age, wouldn't you say? Looks like a tomboy to me,' he laughed.

'You can say that again. Never out of the wood – or the mud. Her aunty always brings dresses from London, but to get them on her . . . well, you'll no' be wanting to hear all this. It's good tae see you back for the Season. How are the family?'

He turned to the housekeeper. 'Just the same as ever. My wife's never got over Arthur's loss and it's hard on his sister, Verity. So few of her old friends made it back but I'm glad to see Dalradnor looking like in the old days. Nothing like children's banter to breathe life into a place. The child looks at home here. You say she's Phoebe's niece . . . Caroline?' He was staring at her again.

'Callie. I'm Callie, and my knee hurts,' she replied, pointing to her bloody knee.

'I wonder there's any skin left on those knees,' said Mrs Ibell. 'Away upstairs and Marthe will clean you up out of those dirty things.' Callie reluctantly did as she was told and Mrs Ibell turned back to the visitor. 'It's good to see you again, Sir Lionel. You've been away awful long. If only things had been different for young Arthur and his bride . . . You're welcome to stay for supper. I've no idea what time Miss Phoebe will arrive from Glasgow.'

'Thank you, but I'll be on my way; just wanted a wee peep at the place for *auld lang syne*. I see your hand is still at the tiller, Nan.'

'I have tae admit to liking wee ones round the place. She's a bright lassie and Marthe, the nursemaid, is good with her considering she's a foreigner. Miss Phoebe is always busy down in London.'

'I'd thought she'd give that up,' he said.

Callie was listening from the top of the stairs, ready to chip in. 'Aunt Phee's going into filums and she's going to take us all to the picture house in Glasgow for my birthday Have you brought me a birthday present?'

'Caroline!' spluttered Mrs Ibell, but the old gentleman just laughed.

'If you don't ask you don't get,' he said, looking up at her. 'I'll see what I can find, young lady.

'In my day it was if you ask, you *don't* get,' said the house-keeper, folding her arms across her chest. 'Away you go and do as you're told or there'll be no birthday for you at all. I do apologize for that wee madam.'

Callie shot up to her bedroom to find Marthe sitting in the rocking chair, mending her torn school shirt.

She'd never known a time when Marthe wasn't there helping her dress, making sure she had a clean liberty bodice, darned stockings, a handkerchief in her knicker pocket for school, telling her stories when she couldn't sleep. Marthe, Nan Ibell and Tam in the garden were her world, Nairn and Niven her best friends, and the only bad thing in her life was that she was a girl not a boy.

Marthe bathed Callie's bleeding knee with such tenderness it no longer hurt, wrapped a bandage around it, washed her all over and put her to bed. 'Time for your nap. You can stay up late if you sleep now until Miss Phoebe arrives.'

Callie was too excited to sleep. When Aunt Phoebe came to stay, there were always presents to open new picture books and sweeties in pretty boxes – and lots of news to tell. Mrs Ibell baked fresh scones with raspberry jam and cream, sponge cake and steak pie. The table in the dining room was already laid out with a lace cloth and silver cutlery and pretty china cups and saucers. Aunt Phoebe was coming for her birthday, as she always did, and Callie was on holiday from school at Miss Cameron's

Academy so there would be lots of lovely days to plan. Tomorrow morning they would go on the train into town, as promised in Aunt Phee's postcard.

Marthe and Nan were her daily bread but Aunt Phee was like iced buns: a special treat, for best only. There was so much to tell her about the owls' nest in the wood, the special flowers she'd pressed, the songs from Belgium that Marthe taught her, the new stitches she was learning at school and how she could write her name neatly in a straight line.

On her wall she had a special book with all the postcards Aunt Phee had sent from faraway places: Biarritz, Paris, Malta before the Great War ended and the church bells rang out in Dalradnor village. There was the Tower of London and a place called Le Havre, after which Aunt Phee had appeared, sunburned, with dolls in costumes – stripy skirts and lace hats – for her display cabinet. They weren't dolls you played with, not that Callie played with dolls. She had a stuffed donkey with a real leather saddle, a real pair of Dutch clogs and a necklace of shiny blue beads.

None of her friends at Miss Cameron's had such a famous aunt who acted on the stage and wore beautiful gowns, furs and hats. She knew this was Miss Faye's home and that her own parents had died before she was born so she must be grateful that this was her home too. Miss Faye had served her country helping soldiers in their time of need, Marthe said, but there was no war now, just a big cross in the village square with names carved in gold, names she could almost read. She was slow with her letters but she could name all the flowers in the walled garden and woods, the birds in the trees. Tam had taught her to recognize their songs. She knew where there were tadpoles and frogspawn in spring, where the blackbird had nested. Marthe would take her to the loch and they had picnics on the pebbled beach: game pie, sandwiches and chunks of fruitcake, with a Thermos of piping hot tea.

Callie hated being stuck indoors when it rained but when it snowed in the winter it was a wonderland of snowball fights, snowmen building and sledging down the brae. Sometimes she helped in the big kitchen with Nan and the maid, Effie Drummond, who was full of tales about kelpies and scary ghosts in the mist. Callie was allowed to lick the baking bowl and cut out pastry tarts or draw with crayons in colouring books, but today she must shut her eyes and pretend to sleep so Marthe would leave the Nursery in the attic, with its barred windows and coal fire with the brass guard rail round it, and let Mr Dapple, the rocking horse, guard the door, which was always left ajar just in case she was frightened in the night.

Callie loved her bedroom, with the brass bedstead and patchwork counterpane. She had her own dressing table with drawers scented with sprigs of lavender in which dresses were layered in tissue paper. Most of the time she wore a bottle-green school uniform, gymslip and gold-striped shirt with a green cardigan piped with gold, and thick green itchy three-quarter socks and a big green felt hat with the school hatband. She couldn't wait to change back into her kilt, handmade in her very own tartan, red with green and blue plaid, belonging to the Clan Ross. Aunt Phee had told her that Rosslyn was her second name, so she could wear the tartan. It came from Lawrie's the kiltmakers in Glasgow.

If only she could wear nothing but a kilt and jumper she could race along with the twins like a boy and not a sissy smothered in the smocked dress with white socks and sandals that she must wear on Sundays. She'd begged for bobbed hair like Aunt Phee, but Marthe said she mustn't have her hair cut before she was twelve. It was bad luck, she warned, tugging Callie's thick hair into ropes before school every morning.

Callie snuggled down under the covers with not an ounce of sleep in her. The last time she'd seen Aunt Phee was at Easter egg time and she'd brought her friend Aunt Kitty to stay. She was a nurse in a big hospital and quite strict. Marthe was so excited when she visited. It was Aunt Kitty's father, the Reverend Mr Farrell, who'd rescued her family and given them a home in the war. She would bring news of Marthe's family. Marthe's sisters and parents were back in Belgium in a town called Bruges, where they were teachers, but one of her brothers had gone to Canada. Callie couldn't bear to think that one day Marthe might leave and join them, especially not just before her birthday . . . Would that old man in the hall really bring her a present too? She reached out for her little toy cat, Smoky, shut her eyes tight and hummed her favourite Belgian lullaby: '*Slaap, kindje, slaap. Daar buiten loopt een schaap . . .*'

2

Phoebe Faye stared out of the carriage window as the view changed from the tunnels and smoke-filled dark recesses of Buchanan Station, to sandstone tenements and the great ship-yard cranes of the Clyde, onwards north to the leafy suburban gardens of Bearsden and Milngavie, then out onto the moors and the rise of the Campsie fells. She never tired of the last part of her journey, knowing Nan, Effie and Marthe would have a warm welcome for her. Tam would be waiting at the station and she had a surprise for him. She'd ordered a new automobile from a garage in Glasgow to be delivered tomorrow, one that he could soon learn to drive and would store in the stables.

Leaving London, with all its glamour and busyness, was never easy, but now there was a telephone at Dalradnor Lodge she could be in touch for any new auditions. The Season was always quiet with everyone out of town for the shooting and school holidays, but the Scottish school year had different terms from the English, with breaks in September, so she would make the most of her visit and relieve the household of their duties towards Caroline. Picnics, outings, treats – she would spoil her for a few days. It was her birthday, after all. It was months since Phoebe's Easter visit and she wondered if the child had grown and if the clothes she'd bought her would fit. She'd meant to come earlier but the play had had a decent run for once, then she'd stayed to audition for a new film, though that had come to nothing.

Watching through the train window as the hills became steeper and the landscape more rugged, Phoebe felt the return of the excitement, anxiety and not a little guilt that always tinged her coming back to Dalradnor. She recalled that very first visit, when she was still reeling from Arthur's death and the reading of the will that had left her this house. The long journey north with Marthe and the baby had felt like an exile. Yet when she opened the large wrought-iron gates and saw the fine house in the starlight she just knew she'd found a refuge. The lamps were lit and the door flung open.

The housekeeper gathered them in with surprise. 'We were awful scunnered to hear of the master's death. So who do we have here?' She peered at the baby swaddled in thick blankets, her face peeping out from the covers. 'I wasnae prepared for a bairn.'

Then came the big lie. 'This is my niece, Caroline. Her parents are dead in an accident. I am her sole relative now. And this is her nursemaid,' she added, pointing to Marthe.

Now she had been living this lie for years but it still didn't sit easy. What the child didn't know wouldn't harm her. Better this than to be labelled a bastard. The deception had given Phoebe the chance to continue her war work. It was a drastic solution but what else could she do to protect them both?

This was Caroline's home and the decision to leave the girl here with Marthe had not been straightforward or easy to make, but it did have much to recommend it. The house stood in open grounds with magnificent views. The village was only half a mile down the road. They had a tennis court and a paradise of grounds for a child to roam in safety. There was clean fresh air.

The first year she had stayed here to recover from her fiancé, Arthur's, death felt like a far-off dream now. Away from prying eyes she'd grown to love the staff, the village folk who admired the Seton-Ross clan and had been so kind when they learned she was Arthur's fiancée, receiving a telegram of his death only days before their wedding.

Then the pull of the greasepaint and limelight began to draw the former Gaiety Girl back south. It began when she made guest appearances at Erskine House, the magnificent mansion turned into a hospital by the River Clyde, a specialist centre for limbless soldiers and sailors. She'd started to entertain the boys in the Great Hall with songs from the shows, taken tea with them on the terrace, watching the great ships slowly gliding out into the estuary. Sometimes she'd taken Caroline to cheer them up until the child became frightened of the disfigured men. Then the call came back to rejoin the YMCA Concert Party tours, and Phoebe knew her duty was to them, not to sit idly in a houseful of women. It was hard to let go but when Caroline hardly noticed her absences, attached as she was to Marthe, she knew she'd done the right thing.

It was only when Kitty had arrived home from Salonika, sick with dysentery, and Phoebe had brought her up to Dalradnor to recuperate that she'd got the hard word from her best friend.

'What on God's earth are you thinking of, leaving that child up here in the wilds?'

'Everyone thinks that I am her aunt, not her mother,' Phoebe confessed, and Kitty looked at her in horror. 'It's for the best,' she continued, hoping she'd understand her motives.

'Best for whom? A lie like this is dangerous,' snapped Kitty. 'The trouble with you is you've always wanted the cake and the bun, Phoebe. She is your daughter – how can you think of deceiving her like this?'

'She's too young to be told the truth. I'll explain when she's older. You can see how happy she is up here. It's a beautiful place to bring up a child.'

'You'll both pay for this one day,' said Kitty with a sharpness that was wounding. 'I can see its charms, and the staff are kind and Callie is happy, but it's all founded on lies. Oh, do be careful. It's not too late to rectify your mistake.'

Much as Phoebe respected her friends' honesty, she wasn't ready to heed their warnings. They just didn't understand. Poor

Kitty was stuck nursing ageing parents and trying to adjust to life back in a London hospital after the freedom of the Scottish Women's Hospitals. Maisie Gibbons, her other friend and flat-mate from those dizzy theatrical years, surprised everyone by leaving the stage to set up a school of dancing and stagecraft in Kensington with Billy Demaine, her co-star. All of them had been there at Caroline's birth, keeping this secret, but none of them approved of her decision.

She hadn't told Kitty that Billy, on hearing about Arthur's death, had written offering to marry her himself to give the baby a name. That would have been a worse disaster than the solution she had found. Billy was a dear friend, but as a husband he was out of the question. She knew he was being generous, but a little careful, too, for his own reputation. As a married man he'd be safe from gossip, although all the theatre world knew of his proclivities. Their marriage would have been a farce.

Maisie adored baby Caroline. 'You will miss all her child-hood,' she warned Phoebe. 'If I had a little girl, I wouldn't leave her with strangers. You are so lucky to have her.'

Phoebe didn't feel lucky; at times she found it a burden to be responsible for everything. She had to be father and mother to the child, making sure they received the right income from shares and funds, running the Dalradnor household from a distance, ensuring accounts were filed and expenditures tallied, while furthering her own career to fit in with everything. As an aunt she could dip in and out of life at Dalradnor with no awkward questions asked of her.

She did love Caroline. She couldn't wait to see the little girl flinging herself into her arms, shouting, 'Aunty Phee, Aunty Phee, you've really come!' She would twirl her around until they were both dizzy and collapsed on the lawn. But always at the back of her mind was the truth waiting to explode one day, and the regret that Arthur Seton-Ross never saw his baby daughter. If she revealed the truth it would label Caroline the illegitimate girl of an unmarried mother. Women were put in lunatic asylums and the workhouse for less.

Then there was the guilt that she had never shared her secret with her own father before he died suddenly of chest complications in the Spanish flu epidemic. She had always kept her humble beginnings in Leeds to herself. She'd used her brother Joe's untimely accident to give Caroline some parents. Her other brother, Ted, who was married, was kept in the dark and she'd lost contact with him years ago. There were so many secrets to hide away and she felt ashamed, but it was better this way. No one needed Society's condemnation.

Now she had a trunk of goodies to distribute, a smart new outfit from Marthe, a tray of exotic fruits for the kitchen, and for Caroline's birthday she planned a perfect present. As Tam drove her slowly up the lime-tree avenue to the turning circle outside the front door, she looked up at the old Lodge, admiring its crow-stepped gables and the red sandstone dormer windows, the French windows opening out onto the stone terrace with its steps down to the immaculate lawns and tennis court. Every time she arrived she thought of Arthur returning for his summer holidays, eager to alight and find his horse, go fishing and picnicking by the loch. I've brought your baby to where you were happiest, she told him in her thoughts. I know she'll have deep roots here. I hope you're proud of me in this, if nothing else. But would Arthur approve? That was something she'd never ever know. His final bequest was to give them this house, much to his family's horror.

'We've kept the lassie up to see you,' said Nan smiling. 'And you had a visitor today, old Sir Lionel Seton-Ross himself. He kent it was the anniversary of his son's passing and came to cast his eye over the war memorial in the square. His son's name is up there now at his request.'

Phoebe felt a stab of alarm at this news. Had he come to see his granddaughter too?

'Was her ladyship in the house?' she enquired as calmly as she could.

'Oh, aye, bounding in, nearly knocking our visitor over. He was quite taken with her and promised to send her a birthday present.'

'That won't be necessary. I hope she behaved in front of him.' Phoebe did not want Sir Lionel coming to spoil the party, or his daughter, Verity, who looked at Phoebe down her long nose as if she was a bad smell. The family had been shocked by their son's revelation that he had a child who must be provided for. Verity had stormed out of the lawyer's office in disgust at this news. Sir Lionel had been the only one to be concerned for her welfare. Now he was coming to check on her.

'So is everything arranged for tomorrow? You've invited the Laird twins, I suppose?' she sighed. 'I'd've preferred to have her to myself apart from Flora from school.'

'It'll just be the boys; there's been a falling-out with the girl. I've made sure Marthe's got her dress ironed or that wee divil will wear her kilt again and it's covered in mud.'

Phoebe climbed the stairs to the second floor, to the Nursery bedroom with its adjoining living room. Caroline was sitting by the fire.

'You're late. I waited and waited.'

'I'm sorry. Come and give me a big hug and let's see if you've grown.'

Caroline jumped up and stood by the door. Marthe found a ruler and placed it over her head and made a mark. 'A whole inch since Miss Phoebe was here last. I think she will be tall like you. Was her mother tall?'

They never mentioned her late brother, Joe, killed on the roads in the blackout, or his fiancée, Beryl Poole, in Caroline's hearing as a rule. It made sense to make them Caroline's deceased parents. They were family, after all. There were no false photographs – she had drawn the line at that – but trust Marthe to keep bringing this up. A girl needs to know about her mother, she had once hinted. But tonight Phoebe ignored her, unwilling to tell any more lies. 'She gets her height from my side of the family, it appears. Come, let me read you a story.'

'Will you tell me the one about Brown Carrie and Fair Carrie? I can nearly tell it in Marthe's language.'

'I don't know that one. I'll find something else.' Phoebe turned to the bookshelf. She didn't like the idea that Marthe and Caroline shared a language, but what did she expect if she hired a foreigner?

'No, I want that one.'

'Where is it then?' she said, feeling tired and hungry.

'I'm afraid it's in my head,' Marthe replied. 'My mother told it to me. It's a famous folk tale in our country. I can tell it to her, if you like.'

Phoebe was disappointed that nothing was quite as she'd hoped about her arrival. She poked the fire, feeling out of sorts. The news of Sir Lionel's visit had unsettled her. Was Arthur's sister, Verity, in the district too? What if they both turned up tomorrow? Now Marthe was taking centre stage, spinning some tale about two little girls, sisters with the same name as Caroline. One Carrie was fair and pretty, the darker sister, plain and pock-marked, so much so that their stepmother wanted to scald the pretty one to make her more like her favourite ugly one. The sisters ran away to a lake and were carried on the back of a swan but grew too heavy for him. He asked one of them to drop off into the water and it was the ugly one who offered to drown.

Then the fair one was left to weep for her sister by the shore until the dark one rose from the water, unblemished and beautiful. When the stepmother caught up with them she was ashamed of her actions and they all lived happily ever after . . . 'She laid down her life for her sister and as a reward she's as beautiful on the outside as she always was on the inside,' whispered Marthe, seeing that Caroline was fast asleep. 'It is always what is inside that matters, yes?'

'Of course,' said Phoebe, feeling strangely challenged by this folk tale. What was she really like this inside, dark or fair?

She watched Marthe put the child to bed and turn out the lamp. 'She likes the curtains and the door open so she can see the hills in the morning,' the nursemaid smiled as she tidied away clothes and toys from the floor.

Phoebe looked away, knowing she wouldn't have done this. There was so much she didn't know about Caroline's routine. Tears filled her eyes, and she was unsure whether they were tears of guilt, shame, love or confusion. Perhaps it was all of these feelings that darkened her heart . . .

The trip into Glasgow next day was a great success They took the train First Class into the city and went to Miss Cranston's tearooms on Sauchiehall Street for soup and cakes. Phoebe always loved to dine here among the startling décor, the tall-backed chairs, the wonderful wall murals and fancy cutlery. The waitresses wore identical outfits. It was like a theatrical production. Nairn and Niven Laird wriggled but managed not to spill anything, and then Marthe supervised them all onto the green and yellow tram as a treat. They went to the Fossil Grove to admire the stone tree trunks, and then it was back to town, to the Argyll Arcade and Henderson's Jewellers so Caroline could choose a pretty gold watch with a white leather strap.

'But I can't tell the time, Aunt Phee . . . Can I have a bangle instead?'

'You'll soon get the hang of it,' Phoebe insisted, hoping she liked the expensive gift. Then they made for the picture house, sitting at a table to watch the latest Charlie Chaplin film and having tea and ices. Chaplin really was a fine actor and his face looked so sad that Caroline sat clutching Marthe, and Phoebe was suddenly overwhelmed with jealousy for their closeness.

As the party arrived back at Dalradnor, Phoebe stiffened at the sight of a large car outside the front door. It was not the one she'd ordered from the garage; she recognized it, though. The two boys jumped out to examine the shiny black monstrosity and the chauffeur offered to run them down the lane when they'd finished looking. Caroline wanted to go with them, but Marthe pushed her into the hall.

'It's time for you to have tea. We have a visitor.'

Phoebe held back to compose herself, wondering why Sir Lionel had come again.

Nan Ibell was bustling round them. 'Tea's laid out in the dining room. Go and wash your hands, young lady, and greet your guest.'

Phoebe walked in, praying he'd be alone and, to his credit, he was. It was such a relief. Lionel had always shown sympathy towards her, and it was close to the anniversary of Arthur's death as well as being Caroline's birthday. Why shouldn't she seek some solace in the fact that he too would see that her child was growing more and more in looks like her father?

'Sir Lionel, it is good of you to call again. I'm sorry I missed you yesterday. As you can see, we've had a busy day in town, but do stay for the cutting of Caroline's cake. Caroline, here is Sir Lionel come to see you again. Isn't that kind?'

'Did you bring it?' She bobbed a curtsy with her smile.

'Bring what, young lady?' He put on a face of mock surprise.

'It's my birthday today,' she said proudly. 'I'm seven now.'

'So you are, and I thought I'd better bring something.'

'Where, where is it?' The minx was searching round the room for a box. 'I got a watch. Aunty Phee gave me this . . . I chose it in a shop.' She held out her wrist so it could be admired.

'Oh, that's a fine watch. Now where did I put that penny whistle for you?' He was teasing her, seeing her impatience. 'Oh, it's there in the basket, I think.' He pointed round the back of the leather armchair by the window to a wicker basket. 'Can you open it for me?'

Caroline rushed to the basket and opened it with a screech. 'Oh, look! Marthe, Aunt Phee, look, look, come and see.' She lifted up a small furry creature, a sleepy little puppy just a few months old. 'For me, it's for me?'

Sir Lionel's face was a picture of gratification as he nodded. 'Now you have to care for him, take him on long walks and teach him how to behave. His name is Cullein, hero of the clans. He's a Cairn terrier so he won't grow very big but he'll be very fast. I think seven is old enough to know he's not a toy but a real living thing. Don't you agree, Miss Faye?'

'Phoebe, please,' she muttered, knowing he was asking her approval after the event. The clever old man had won the child's heart with such a thoughtful gift, so very appropriate for an only child. He'd got it so right and she'd got it so wrong. Who wants a watch when you really want a bangle, when you can have a puppy as a friend and playmate? Why hadn't she thought of that herself?

You don't know your own daughter, that's why you're peripheral to her world here. You are just the aunt who pops in now and again and then disappears. Why are you bemoaning your lot? You chose this for yourself. Now you must pay. Pin on your smile and get on with it. This is Caroline's special day, not yours.

They processed into the dining room by candlelight. There was a beautiful iced cake waiting, with seven candles on it. Caroline sat bemused, clinging onto her new friend for dear life.

For Phoebe, the day was ruined. She felt like a child with her nose up against the window, looking through the glass into something to which she was no longer party. She took a deep breath and sat down: time to play the hostess, time to pin on a smile.

'Isn't this wonderful, all of us together? What a wonderful end to the day . . .'

3

Callie couldn't wait for the summer holidays to begin even though it was a turning out to be a time of sad farewells. The Laird family was moving to a bigger farm in the Borders, and Marthe was going to visit her family in Belgium for the summer. Callie was to spend the whole time with Aunt Phee, travelling down to the south of France with her friends. They would cross the Channel to Boulogne to tour Paris, then take a train right down to a place called Nice on the Mediterranean. Mrs Ibell was busy sewing cotton dresses and sunhats, putting liver salts in her trunk in case the foreign food didn't suit her. Marthe was escorting her on the train to London to meet Aunt Phee, then taking a steamer across to Ostend. In preparation, they had studied their journeys on the map on the Nursery wall. Marthe spoke good French and made Callie practise some of the phrases from her language book.

Marthe was packing her own suitcase and not saying much at all. A letter had come from Aunt Phee with all their instructions, but when she read it, Marthe had started to cry and stared out the window, holding the new skirt she had made herself in the shorter style that showed off her slim legs. Her hair was bobbed and Callie thought she looked very pretty.

'Are you sick?' Callie rushed to hug her.

'No . . . just sad.'

'Why?'

'Sometimes things have to end . . . But I'm being silly. Come on, let's find some of your books to put in the trunk.'

Callie wondered if Marthe had found a boyfriend who might carry her off somewhere far away from Dalradnor.

It was up to Tam and Nan to see that Cullein got his walks because they couldn't take him across the sea. Callie knew she'd miss him badly. Perhaps Sir Lionel might call in on his annual holiday and check she was looking after Cullein well. He never brought his wife or daughter, which always upset Mrs Ibell. 'It's a gey queer state of affairs is that . . . they stay not five miles from here with the Balfours, and have never called in here all the years I waited on them until now . . .'

Callie liked the old gentleman. He brought her comics to read and sweeties in a pokey hat cone with half a crown hidden at the bottom for her to save or spend as she liked. He always looked sad when he said goodbye. With the twins leaving, who would she play with when she got home? She was always falling in and out with girls who teased her for being Orphan Annie. It wasn't her fault she had no brothers or sister or parents. There were lots of girls in the school who had lost their fathers in the Great War. Aunt Phee lost her fiancé. She kept a picture of him in a silver frame in her bedroom. He had a uniform on, and he was Sir Lionel's son, too, with his name on the war memorial. Aunt Phee was always very sad when she looked at his picture.

At last, the day came for the train journey down to London. It was a hot and dusty drive to Glasgow Central Station but she loved the bustle of the porters with their luggage, the crowds on the platform waving off the travellers, the big paper stall where they bought a *Girl's Own* and a Fry's Five Boys for the journey. There was so much to see out of the window as the train rattled its way south. Marthe brought out sandwiches and a Thermos at Carlisle, and they played hangman and noughts and crosses. Then at Lancaster Marthe got out her knitting and made Callie read her book and try to nap. At every station, Callie asked if they were nearly there and Marthe laughed and said, 'Be patient.' Then they talked in Flemish just for the fun of it, but soon Marthe grew serious.

'Never forget it, make it your secret language. No one else will understand you. That could be fun one day.'

Callie smiled and nodded. She was quite good at understanding Marthe, even when she spoke quickly.

Suddenly the green fields turned to brick houses and factories, chimneys and tunnels, and they drew into Euston Station at long last. At the end of the platform, Aunt Phee was waiting, waving. She looked quite different from the last time Callie had seen her, with a permanent wave in her short hair and a little beret clinging onto the side. She wore a short cotton shift dress that came just to her knee, with silk stockings and heeled shoes with straps across her foot.

'Look at you, like a boiled lobster in that kilt. Couldn't you have put something thinner on the girl?' she snapped at Marthe.

'It was cool when we left, and better to save her new clothes for her holiday,' Marthe said, looking cross.

'I suppose so. Come along, we'll get a taxi.' Phee turned to Marthe. 'What time's your boat train? Might as well say goodbye here; I'll take over now. You might want to freshen yourself up.'

Callie felt she was a parcel being passed across. 'Can't Marthe come with us?' she asked, but Phee ignored her.

'Better to split up now. I've got tons to do before we leave tomorrow. Well, Marthe, have a lovely holiday . . . and a safe journey. Oh, Kitty says to send her best regards to all your family and hopes everyone is settled back home now,' she added.

Marthe bent to kiss Callie. 'Be a good girl and have a wonderful time. I shall miss you.' Her voice was trembling.

'We'll call for you on the way home, won't we?' Callie turned to Phee, seeing Marthe looking upset.

'Of course, if there's time. I'm sure we'll pay a visit.'

'I wish you were coming with us.' Callie clung to her tightly. Marthe was the most important person in her life, the one true fixture both night and day. 'I don't want you to go,' she said in Flemish, and Marthe whispered in her ear, 'Don't worry . . . I will always be there for you.'

'Don't make a fuss,' Phee interrupted them. 'Marthe has her own life to lead. She doesn't want you making a scene in public. You'll see her again . . .'

Callie waved and waved as Phoebe drew her away until Marthe was lost to her in the crowds. Suddenly they were out in the bright sunlight among crawling traffic, honking horns, drays, buses, cars. It was like Glasgow but three times as busy, with people rushing up and down the pavements. Where did they all come from? Sitting in the taxi as if they were in a bubble, Callie gazed out at the buildings towering above her, and people staring out of bus windows. She felt very small amongst all this rush and bustle.

Aunt Phee, however, sat back, looking relaxed. 'Are you excited?' she smiled.

'A bit,' Callie replied, feeling shy. 'Where are we staying?'

'In my apartment off Marylebone High Street. You'll love it. I've made up your bedroom in the latest style. Tomorrow we've got an early start for Dover to catch the ferry. Sailing to France, just like I did when I went to war with the concert party.'

'But my French isn't very good,' Callie said.

'You'll know more than me, and everyone speaks English. I want to show you all the wonderful places. We're going to have such a wonderful holiday together. A special holiday to remember.'

Callie said nothing, wishing she was safe back by the loch, chasing sticks with Cullein. She ought to feel excited but she didn't. Instead she had a sick feeling in the pit of her tummy that nothing would ever be the same again.

4

Phoebe couldn't sleep. The responsibility of making sure Caroline had a good holiday lay heavy on her chest. It was hot and noisy outside. She felt ashamed of pointing out how the little girl looked in that shabby kilt and blouse, like a country mouse come up to town. That would have to change now Marthe was out of the way. They'd have time to get to know each other much better in the next four weeks.

Everything was planned: suitable clothes for the beach and sun, walks and swimming parties with Maisie's friends. Even Billy was going to call in with his latest protégé, and he was good with children. Caroline would blossom in the sunshine, lose that pale face. Her time would be filled with visits to châteaux and cathedrals, vineyards and gardens. Plans for her education were already in hand.

Miss Cameron's Academy had been fine for her early years but now the child needed a more formal structure to her day in a good boarding school, one where she'd meet the right type of girl, get a decent grounding in the basics before being finished abroad. She must have every opportunity to take her proper place in Society, eventually making a suitable marriage, unhampered by the shame of her birth. There was no reason yet to break the secrecy of her true identity.

Lionel Seton-Ross was keeping his end of the bargain. His financial advisers continued to ensure Arthur's fiancée and his daughter were financially secure. Phoebe never touched a penny of any future inheritance coming from Arthur's estate; the house in Scotland was the only gift she'd accepted. Everything must come to Caroline. She kept herself in London through her work in the theatre.

Times had changed for the former Gaiety Girl. She was still young but there were prettier girls on display now in the new fashion style, and she was too curvy to model. Her heyday was over, but she found a niche playing character parts: northern maids and matrons with broad accents. She got laughs for her Yorkshire plain speaking, and there were some film parts coming. She now had an agent who kept her name to the fore. It was not what Phoebe Faye might have dreamed of, but the musical comedy theatre was long gone. Her new acting roles paid the rent and bills, and kept her in smart outfits and work when so many were jobless and hungry. It was all a far cry from her humble beginnings in Leeds. Her looks, voice and stage personality had shone from an early age, bringing her to the attention of the great impresario George Edwardes. She'd lost her broad accent by the time she'd arrived at King's Cross Station, but now she was using it to secure film parts.

If she found herself 'resting' she helped Maisie Gibbons with acting and singing classes in the stage school, mostly stage expression and lyrical interpretation. She was glad Caroline had not shown one iota of interest in the theatre. It was all dogs, ponies, scuffed knees and country pursuits. Caroline was destined for better things, and giving her this taste of continental cuisine and customs was the first step in her further education.

Phoebe smiled, thinking how at eleven she'd been living in a back-to-back house in Hunslet, carrying her dancing pump bag and music to auditions, earning shillings for each performance, unaware of the privileged world her own daughter was now growing up in.

Let no one say she wasn't giving her the best of everything in life. 'Deeds not words,' she sighed, thinking of Emily Davison flinging herself at the King's horse in front of her, and Arthur in his grey topper, chewing game pie on Derby day. At least his daughter would never face hunger and hardship in a world war that blighted so many lives. There were no spare men left for Kitty or Maisie and their friends to marry once the war was over. 'Oh, Arthur,' she sighed, unable to sleep in the heat of the night. Why must all the decisions be left to me? Why did you have to leave me? She lay back, and for the first time in years let herself relive every moment of that precious weekend together in 1916.

1916

Phoebe was finding it a strain waiting in the wings for her entrance, knowing Arthur was watching the show. Once the curtain calls had been taken and the applause had died down, she made a dash for the dressing room to change into her prettiest outfit and her rose velvet cloak with the swan's-down trimmings. She must look perfect: not too theatrical, not recognizable as one of the Gaiety postcard girls, just a girl out on the town with her soldier boy.

He was waiting at the stage door in uniform.

'Let's walk, get some fresh air,' she suggested. It was starlit frosty night and her breath was like smoke. They strolled to Trafalgar Square and down Piccadilly towards St James's, and then he guided her down into Jermyn Street where he'd booked a late supper in the Cavendish Hotel.

Phoebe had been here before as a guest of the proprietor, Miss Rosa Lewis, who was once a confidante of the old king and famed for her delicious cuisine. Mr Edwardes, the Guvnor, introduced the girls from his theatre and some of them were given supper and a chance to cheer up officers on leave. Nothing inappropriate, of course, but they did lend sparkle and glamour to the dining room.

'I've got a billet here. My father's a friend of Miss Lewis and she always looks after us when we're in town.' Arthur smiled. 'It's much more private here than in the other restaurants. I want us not to feel we have to join another crowd.'

They were guided to a quiet table behind a screen of jardinières in the long panelled dining room. It was busy but there was no one in she knew. Phoebe felt herself relaxing and suddenly ravenous.

'The food is exquisite here. Miss Rosa supervises everything herself. Upstairs are about a hundred rooms, and some have permanent guests. She's so kind to chaps who are hard up and on leave. I heard she finds ways for the rich old men to pay extra on their bills so she doesn't have to charge serving soldiers a bean . . . I always feel at home here. But enough about me.' He grasped her hand. 'I thought you were magnificent tonight. It's a really good revue and that Leslie Henson is a hoot . . . How are you? You look tons better than when I last saw you in France. You'd lost so much weight.'

'We seem to dash from one hospital show to another, from one camp to the next. You know what it's like, too tired sometimes to eat. When we met in Calais I thought you looked as if you've come from hellfire corner.' She didn't mean to bring up the war but he still looked strained.

'I'm afraid a week with my parents is never restful. Mama can be very demanding. Wouldn't let me out of sight, kept pressing these silly girls to sit next to me at the dining table.'

'She means well, wanting you to have pretty company,' was the best Phoebe could offer, feeling sick at the thought of this matchmaking. 'And your sister . . .?'

'Verity came up for a day, grilled me for information, kept talking about poor chaps from Eton who've gone west . . . Poor girl, there aren't going to be many of her sort left if this goes on much longer. It's a slaughterhouse out there, and now there's the gas attacks . . .' He paused, then visibly rallied. 'No more war talk – I just want to look in your face and forget all that stuff. I can't believe how fate brought us together again. I never did understand why we stopped seeing each other.'

Phoebe sipped her wine. 'It seemed the right thing to do when your mother—'

'Mother spoke to you? When?' He leaned forward, clasping her hand even tighter.

'On Derby Day, when we met them for lunch. She said if we got serious, you'd have to resign from the Guards.'

Arthur banged down his glass. 'How dare she interfere? Why didn't you tell me then?'

'I couldn't, and then there was that terrible accident with Miss Davison and the racehorse. I couldn't think of anything else after that.'

'I'm sorry. All the time we've wasted, all the letters I might have had from you . . . It would have been better if I had resigned and joined another regiment. There are hardly any Guards officers left after Mons and the Marne.' Arthur shook his head. 'My mother lives in another world and it's one that will never return. This bloody war is stripping all the old hierarchy away. We've lost so many heirs and titles and school chums, good soldiers in all ranks. You've seen where they end up: in some moribund tent coughing their guts up or in a surgical ward praying for a quick release from pain. Phoebe, I've missed you so much. I've tried to find other girls to fill your place but it was always you at the back of my mind when we were . . .'

Phoebe found herself crying. She didn't want to make a scene. 'I think I'm going to faint,' she whispered. 'It's very warm in here.'

'Don't worry, we can go to my suite and dine there, if you don't mind.'

She nodded and he guided her up the stairs and along a creaking corridor to his room on the second floor. There was a brief point of hesitation when she knew it would be wiser to decline and ask for a taxi, but she waved away caution. What would be would be. They needed time alone together. There was an urgency to this night that must not be denied.

He opened the door into a pretty sitting room lined with sporting prints and chintzy curtains. There was a dining alcove and a bedroom, where Phoebe put her cloak. The bedroom was strewn with Arthur's clothes and it smelled of pipe tobacco and Penhaligon's Hamman Bouquet, a favourite scent of the stage door johnnies. Arthur had taken as much care in his toilette as she had done.

They sat together as supper was set out for them. Phoebe sipped her champagne, not tasting anything but the bubbles up her nostrils, aware of a tension growing between them so that when the door was shut, she just fell into his arms and sobbed. 'I'm sorry, I thought it was the best for you to let you go.'

He touched her lips with his little finger and she felt the cool gold of his signet ring on her cheek. 'You are here now and that's all that matters. This is the best moment of my leave. You've no idea how I've longed for this. I used to walk past the theatre hoping I'd see you. I wrote but you never replied. Let's not waste time over what could've been. We have now and we have this time alone.'

She kissed him slowly, tentatively at first, and then the flood-gates of longing just overwhelmed them both. It was as if a rushing wave engulfed them with an urgency to get closer, to feel through the layers to raw skin, to act out for real all those false clinches that Phoebe knew so well onstage. The supper lay cold on their plates as they clung together, tearing off shirts and dress layers, loosening stays, so they lay almost naked on the bed, exploring each other, smiling into the huge gold mirror adorning the wall so every movement was heightened by the sight of each other's responses. There was a tenderness and then a roar of passion that could have only one ending. She clasped him as he entered her, wincing at first, but riding his powerful thrusts with excitement as the feelings inside her body erupted into a burst of sensations.

They lay sated with lovemaking, tired but satisfied in the strangest of physical ways. Phoebe looked at her lover in the lamplight. This was what it was all about, this coming together, this physical loving, and it was the most natural thing in the world to be doing with him. Why had she denied herself all this pleasure? Why had she denied what she had sensed from their very first encounter at Miss Lily Elsie's wedding all those years ago? But no matter. Now they were one. This beautiful man would be in her life from now on. She'd not be parted from him again. He was sleeping and she covered him with the fallen counterpane, crept in beside him and curled into his shape. No going back now.

Later, they lay together in the bath, soaking and soaping each other, laughing as if they had all the time in the world to enjoy discovering new ways to please their bodies. When breakfast came, she noted there was enough for two people. Wrapped in his dressing gown, she sat brazenly in the open, waiting to be served: eggs, ham, toast, fruit and freshly baked rolls, coffee in a tall silver jug, a feast for hungry lovers.

'So what are we going to do today?' Arthur smiled. 'I think we'll go and buy a ring, don't you?'

'Perhaps I ought to go to rehearsal and change out of my evening clothes first?'

'You will come back later? It's my last day.'

'I know, I know, I'll do my best.' She was thinking on her feet. What could she skip to be with him? If she went back to the flat in Little Portland Street there'd be questions and more questions. Perhaps she could purchase a few items and find a special chemist she'd heard about, who sold douches and such stuff. She mustn't take any chances.

It was a different woman who walked out of the Cavendish than had walked in. They were a couple now. No one could change that. She knew she wasn't going to spoil his last day. She was going to do something she'd never done before: she'd call in sick and miss a performance – surely they owed her this one break – yet it went against all her principles.

As they strolled along the street she realized that Arthur now came before her career. If she did marry him, he'd be in the foreground of her life, not the backdrop. It was a strange and sudden turnaround in her thinking. Perhaps it was seeing the scar on his shoulder where a bullet had grazed him. He'd been saved by his leather jerkin, he said. She could've been visiting him in hospital, or worse. He'd been lucky. The man beside him had got a bullet in his eye, piercing his brain.

Phoebe made the phone call from a public telephone, crying off with a stomach upset that might hazard her performance. She sent one of her postcards to her flat, telling the girls she was going to visit Arthur's family at last. They walked through St James's Park, seeing much of it was made into allotments or used as training ground. Feeling the chilly air on their faces, they made for Bond Street and Fenwick, where he bought her a warm coat with matching fur Cossack-style hat and muff. They strolled around the shops and turned towards the Burlington Arcade, where they lingered at the windows of the jewellers' shops. Arthur found the exact shop he was seeking and marched in.

'We want an engagement ring,' he announced.

'Arthur!' Phoebe held back. 'You haven't asked me yet,' she said blushing.

'But you will, won't you?' he pleaded.

The startled assistant hovered over the table, waiting for her reply.

'Please wait.' Phoebe tried to get her thoughts in order. 'You have to do this properly . . . your parents, my family . . . I don't want you to rush into anything you may later regret . . . Please.'

'I can't wait. Come on, sit down and choose something pretty.'

Phoebe didn't know where to put herself. 'Can we please discuss this in private?' she asked, making for the door.

'Are you refusing me?'

'No, of course not.' She smiled. 'But a surprise would be nice. It must be your choice.'

'Right then, you go outside like a good girl and I'll find something I think you'll like. By rights you ought have something from the family, but we haven't time for that.'

Phoebe edged backwards out of the door, feeling foolish, wondering how this had all come about. Within minutes he was out carrying a package. 'If it's the wrong size, that's your fault. So let's find a place to celebrate. The Ritz . . . on this occasion.'

So, by luncheon, Phoebe found herself sitting in the ornate gold dining room with its icing sugar plastered ceiling, surrounded by other diners as Arthur brought out his choice and handed it to her.

'There, your surprise.'

She opened the blue leather box lined with ice-blue velvet on which sat a beautiful hoop of large diamonds and sapphires set in gold.

'Blue to match your eyes, and diamonds for our love to last forever. You like it?'

'I love it. Thank you . . .' But try as she might to get it on, the ring was too small. Tears of disappointment filled her eyes. 'It's so sparkly, so lovely, but my knuckles are swollen . . .' she cried.

'We can get it stretched. You're my girl now, Phoebe Faye.'

'Phoebe Boardman's my real name. Phoebe Annie Boardman. Nothing's real in the theatre.'

'You are real to me whatever your given name. Now I can go back knowing you'll be waiting for me.'

'You didn't need to buy a ring for me to do that. You mustn't tell anyone yet. I can't do the concerts at the Front if they think I have a personal connection to anyone there. I have to do my bit. I just want to be useful.' She drank in his drawn cheeks and his tired eyes.

'Of course you do. We'll keep it a secret between the two of us and then next leave we'll get married. Look, I've got to get the train from Waterloo at six. You will see me off?'

They returned to his room at the Cavendish and locked the door. How quickly those precious hours sped by until it was time to dress and make their way to the crowded station, full of troops and anxious women amongst the bustle of steam, smoke, commuting office workers and uniforms of all hues.

Phoebe clung onto his arm, wishing the ring now on her pinkie finger was on her left hand for all to admire. She'd been foolish not to have her finger measured but that didn't matter now.

'Don't stay too long on the platform. I want to remember you smiling. Write soon and often; I don't know how long it'll be before my next leave . . .'Arthur looked down at her. 'It's been everything I dreamed of and more. Don't let's ever quarrel again, my dearest Phoebe.'

'Please stay safe for me . . . Don't take any risks . . . I couldn't bear to lose you now,' she cried as they clung to each other until the whistle blew and he had to jump into an open carriage. She followed him, waving, right to the end of the platform where she stood until the last puff of steam had vanished. It was dark and the moon shone bright in a starry sky. She lingered, unable to tear herself away from that sacred spot.

'Come on, miss, time to go,' said a platform porter. 'He'll be back before long.'

Phoebe shivered, reluctantly picking her frozen feet off the cold stone and making her way back through crowds of weeping women to the station entrance. She paused outside, suddenly feeling that utter loneliness of being alone in a crowd. I must keep busy, she thought, turning to see the time on the Waterloo Clock. If she took a cab she might still make the show . . .

*   *   *

How different the capital looks when you are in love, Phoebe thought the next morning. Everything around her seemed brighter and cheerier, much less drab. Every uniform she saw in the street reminded her of Arthur. She wanted to shout her happiness from the rooftops, but she just hugged it around herself like a fur coat. This is my precious secret, she told herself, as she hid the blue leather box with her ring inside at the back of her underwear drawer. She would tell everyone the good news, but not just yet. Just for the moment this secret was hers alone.

She woke from her reverie with tears streaming down her face. They had never met face to face again and after Arthur's death she never looked at another man. It was as if he'd been her one chance of happiness until Fate tore him from her. She'd no desire ever to be hurt like that again. Theirs was a generous, passionate love, enough to last a lifetime. Now, all her ambition and yearnings must be channelled into Caroline's future, no matter what.

Meeting Marthe on the station had been awkward and for a moment she thought the nursemaid might give the game away she looked so upset. Once the letter giving her notice was sent, there was no turning back. Besides, it was time Marthe led her own life. She was far too attached to Caroline, and the girl was too old for a nursemaid. Marthe's life was back in Belgium and Phoebe had paid her handsomely in lieu of notice. With superb references she'd soon find a good position in another family. Thankfully she'd not made a fuss, and as a reward they would call in on their way home. Then it would be term time and Caroline would be sent to one of the best boarding schools in the north, recommended by Kitty's friends.

The house at Dalradnor would still be there for holidays, though Caroline must come to London for her long vacations. It would be the best way to shape her into a young lady instead of an overgrown tomboy. In time she would learn to accept the changes without any fuss.

Dear Mrs Ibell, Tam and Cullein

I crossed the sea and wasn't sick. We went to Paris and looked at a lot of pictures and we went up the Eiffel Tower. We have hot chocolate for breakfast and no porridge and flaky cressents with jam. I have been to fairy castles like in picture books but now we are near Nice. It is very hot and sunny and the sea is blue like the picture. My favourite ice cream is green with sprinkles of chocolate on the top. I hope Cullein is missing me.

Love Callie

5

The sea was sparkling, the scenery beautiful, with palm trees waving and bending like fans. On the hillsides, looking across the bay, were perched villas all the colours in a sugared almond jar: pink, turquoise, gold and apricot, with red-tiled sloping roofs. Their villa had a garden with a swing and a dipping pool. Aunty Maisie brought friends to stay and took Callie for walks and ice creams by the plage. They all took a car to the lavender fields above Grasse where the perfume was so strong it made Callie sneeze. They trawled through the open markets in Cannes, fingering strange fruits, vegetables and bunches of herbs all the colours of the rainbow. Callie bought a lace hanky for Marthe and tubes of chocolate-dusted walnuts for Mrs Ibell.

Sometimes she felt horribly homesick for Dalradnor but she swallowed back the longing, knowing she'd return soon with such stories to tell them all. Everything was different in France: the street smells, the houses, the food, the chatter. Girls paraded with parasols to shade their faces, children wore such pretty dresses and matching hats. She swam in the sea in a new cotton bathing costume with polka dots on it, not the knitted navy-blue one she'd brought from home, which stretched and sagged when it got wet. Aunt Phee bought her a lace-edged fan and a straw hat, and made her nap in the afternoons when she wanted to play out. There was a party dress with a beautiful dropped waist and sash that she had to put on when they dined in a restaurant with waiters who treated her like a grown-up and brought her water in her own wine glass.

Uncle Billy Demaine called in with his friend Lyall, who was an actor in films, and Callie got his autograph. She rode on donkeys, and in coaches drawn by tired ponies along the Corniche. It was all fun but she was glad when it was time to pack up and head north. She sent postcards to the twins and to Marthe in Bruges. They would be collecting her on the way back and she hoped she'd had a good holiday too.

The train north took an age and they changed at Paris to visit a place called Albert. Nowhere could have been more different from Nice or Paris. There, emerging from the station Callie was surprised to see, all around, broken buildings and trees, and ditches down the sides of the roads. Across the fields there were fences inside which were lined up row upon row of little white crosses, hundreds of them. These were the graves of soldiers who fell in the Great War, Aunt Phee explained, and she felt sad that they were stuck out there so far from home, but at least not alone.

Then, when Aunt Phee had looked awhile, they took a taxi to a tiny village where in the square Aunt Phee produced a photograph of a monument and passed it around the old men gathered there, asking in a mixture of English and broken French if they knew the place. The old men sucked on their pipes and shook their heads, not understanding her words, so Callie helped out as best she could. Someone pointed to the priest's house, and luckily the priest spoke enough English to show them where to find the monument, close to a place called Ginchy, so they set out again down the country roads.

'Stop!' cried Aunt Phee to the taxi driver when they had gone a short distance. 'Look over there . . . *Arretez ici!*' She and Callie jumped from the car to find the path, but there wasn't one. Undaunted, Aunt Phee marched her through a prickly stubble field in her best shoes, over the churned-up ground, to a tall stone pillar fenced around with a chain. She stood in silence for a few minutes, looking stricken, and then paced round it. 'This is Arthur's place, where he fell in battle. Sir Lionel bought this bit of land so he would always have a grave.'

'Is he down there?' Callie asked, curious.

'No,' her aunt sighed. 'They buried him here but . . . there were guns and explosions. He was lost, but his friends told the family the exact spot. I wanted you to see this for yourself.'

Callie stood not knowing what to do. Should she bow her head and say a prayer? But what if he wasn't there? She read out his name: 'Major Arthur B. Seton-Ross, MC 14 September 1916.'

'He died a few days before our wedding day,' said Aunt Phee, staring down at the ground. 'If only he knew . . .'

'Knew what?'

'Nothing you would understand.' Sometimes Aunt Phee went silent and shut herself off so Callie never knew quite how to be with her. She'd learned over the holiday just to turn away and get on with something else. This was one of those times when she wasn't wanted.

Phoebe stared up at the stone obelisk in dismay. She'd so wanted to take this detour to see the place for herself but it wasn't what she was expecting. The monument stood alone, a symbol of his parents' grief, a costly, futile gesture, as if there was nothing left in the world to commemorate him. Yet here she was standing with his child, who was the very image of her father in so many ways. This was the time to say, 'Here is your father, who won a medal for his bravery,' but she couldn't break the silence she'd kept all these years, and even had she found the courage, this dreary, muddy ploughed field was not the place.

Why did peacetime take so much more courage to live out than those heady danger-filled days of war? She thought about those concerts under bombardment, the match-lit walks in the dark under the stars when the troops lined the path with flickering lucifers to guide the artistes into their cars after a show.

Those were the best days of her life. They lived in danger and she was loved by a brave man. This ugly stone was cold, empty, reminding her that the dead were long gone and never coming back. Arthur belonged to another, forgotten time. No one wanted reminding of it now. All that was left was the memory of their time together.

His bones might be crushed somewhere in this farmer's field. He was nowhere, but his child lived, and with this came the sudden sickening thought that she'd give anything to have him back in Caroline's place. She shuddered and turned away from the rage she was feeling. *How could* you *think such a terrible thing? But you have.*

'Come along, we've seen enough crosses for one day.'

Callie followed behind her aunt as they ploughed their way back to the waiting car. If there was nothing here why had Sir Lionel put up a stone? She understood why Aunt Phee needed to come and see it – they had delayed their journey just to do this and she could see it had made her sad – but the place didn't look like a battlefield, just a churned-up field with stumps of trees poking up and the lonely monument pointing to the sky.

Callie was impatient to move on. It was time to go to collect Marthe. She knew so much about her brothers, Jan and Piet, and her sister, Marie. Now she would be meeting them.

As they left the village, Aunt Phee went quiet. They drove down long lanes, straight and boring, with ruined buildings, and children stood by the road staring as if they'd never seen a motor car before. They stopped overnight in Lille. Then they took the train east towards the coast and arrived in Bruges. It was just as she'd seen on Marthe's postcards, with tall buildings with stepped roofs just like Dalradnor. She knew the address was somewhere in Predikherenstraat but she couldn't think of the number, she was so excited. They sat in the Markt square sipping hot chocolate, looking up, waiting for the clock to chime on the tall tower.

'We must buy lace and chocolates to take home with us,' Aunt Phee smiled as they watched shoppers going past. 'Then we can take a horse cab and tour round the canal and pretty brick streets.'

'Can we fetch Marthe first? She'll know the best places and show us round.'

'She'll be at work.'

Callie was puzzled. How could she be at work when she was coming home? It was better not to say anything because Aunt Phee had been very snappy since that visit to the monument and was always in a hurry.

They found the long street full of shops and tall houses. They asked in a little florist's for the van Hooges and the woman pointed up the street. They knocked at the door but got no answer so they wandered round the city admiring the cathedral and the Burg square, the quaint shops full of intricate lace tablecloths and collars, then stood on the canal bridges watching the barges shunting down the water. They chose gifts and found a clean hotel. It was time to find somewhere to eat and Callie was tired.

'Can't we go back again?'

'Now don't go getting upset if Marthe isn't there. It's late. We'll call on them in the morning before we leave.'

Callie was puzzled again. Hadn't she sent the van Hooges a postcard telling them when they would arrive?

In the morning after breakfast, they called again and a woman opened the door. She was not smiling. 'So you've come. I heard there were strangers at my door. Marthe is at work. She stays at the doctor's house. The references you gave her were excellent.' There was a coolness in her voice when she spoke to Aunt Phee, but she saw Callie looking crestfallen. 'You'd better come in.' Her English was good. Callie was confused. References were what maids got when they left a house. Why did Marthe need references?

'Can I go and see her?' she asked in Flemish. Mrs van Hooge looked surprised.

'No, dear, not when she is working, but she gave me a letter just in case you called. You speak very well, Callie.' She smiled, handing her a note in an envelope.

Callie stared at her aunt. 'Is she not coming back with us?'

There was a moment when no one spoke. The two women looked at each other and then at Callie. 'She does not know?' said Mrs van Hooge, folding her arms across her bosom in disapproval.

'No, I didn't want to spoil her holiday. I will explain later. She got so attached . . .'

'I can offer you some tea,' Marthe's mother said very politely but her eyes were angry. She turned to Callie and smiled. 'You will always be welcome here, Callie. Marthe is very sorry not to say goodbye. She misses you very much.' She spoke in Flemish, knowing Aunt Phee would not understand.

'I think we'd better be off. Thank you for seeing us. I think you will agree it was time for Marthe to come home to her family.'

'That was for her to decide in her own good time, Miss Faye. Timing is important.'

The atmosphere was uncomfortable as Aunt Phee hustled Callie out of the door. Her cheeks flushed as Callie began to cry. 'Now don't make a fuss out in the street.'

Callie was too shocked to do anything but walk down the street in a daze, swallowing back tears. Marthe had left her, gone to another position, and she never got to say a proper goodbye. Her heart was bursting with panic. Who would look after her now?

'Don't be sad. We'll go and have ice cream.'

'I don't want ice cream. I feel sick,' Callie whimpered. She knew it wasn't polite to howl in the street but she could hardly contain her disappointment.

Later, they sat in the train chugging along the coast back to France. Callie looked out over the flat fields and dykes, seeing the great expanse of blue sky, lost in her confusion. Why had

Phee bothered to take her to Bruges when she knew Marthe was not coming back? What was worse was that Marthe had known this too. They had kept it all a big secret from her and it made her feel small and stupid. She didn't understand grown-ups at all. She turned her body away from Aunt Phee in anger. She could tell her aunt was uncomfortable, trying to smile and offer her sweets.

'You have to understand, you're too old for a nursemaid now. Marthe wanted to return to her family . . .'

'She never said that to me . . .'

'Grown-ups don't have to tell children all their plans. Besides, you'll have a new school to look forward to where you can stay and play with lots of new friends.'

That was how she found out she was enrolled in St Margaret's Girls' School on the Scottish east coast. She would not be living at Dalradnor any more except for in the holidays. This second blow left her momentarily speechless.

'But what about Cullein and Hector, my pony?' she asked eventually, her voice trembling.

'They'll be well looked after. Mrs Ibell will keep an eye on things and Tam will take the dog.'

So it had all been planned behind her back. Everyone had known but her and now she'd have to stay in London and she felt sick. 'I want to go home now to see Cullein. He'll think I don't want him any more.' She felt tears running down her cheeks

'You're a big girl now. You'll love your new school. It's one of the best in Scotland with lots of games and things.' Aunt Phee tried to chivvy her up but she didn't want to listen to another word. She sat in the saloon in the ferry as the ship rolled one way and another making Aunt Phee go green. Callie smiled at her discomfort, glad she was out of the way and she pulled out Marthe's letter. This was not being shared by anyone. It was written in Flemish.

My dearest Callie,

I am sorry I could not say farewell to you as I would have wished. I have loved every minute of watching you grown up. Now you are ready for big adventures and Miss Faye would like you to go away to school. She asked me not to speak to you before we all left. I was sad about all of this hiding away. I will miss you but I am always your friend and if you wish to write to me I will write back. This is not what I choose but Miss Faye said it was time to go our separate ways.

Your loving friend,

Marthe van Hooge

So it was all Aunt Phee's doing. Marthe was made to leave. Why, why, why? For the first time in her life she didn't trust her aunt. In fact she hated her and would never speak to her again. Callie sank into the chair, trying not to cry. It wasn't fair that Aunt Phee was the only relative she had left in the world who would look after her. She knew deep down that she'd have to do what her aunt wanted, but the thought of living for months with a bunch of girls she hadn't yet met, and away from her beloved pets, filled her with horror.

Phoebe retched in the lavatories, feeling like death warmed up. Her daughter was sitting in the saloon in a sulk of gloom and sullen silence. She will thank me for it one day, Phoebe tried to reason with herself. Going to Bruges had been a mistake and perhaps she should have prepared the girl earlier for the changes to come, but what was done was done, and after all she had no experience of young girls of this age. The sooner Caroline learned that life sprang surprises on you, the better. It was not as if she was sending her to Dotheboys Hall. St Margaret's was a prestigious, progressive and expensive school. She would get a first-class education in fresh air and beautiful surroundings.

The school was alma mater to some pioneering doctors and

teachers. Caroline was lucky to be accepted but Kitty and her friend Chrystal Macmillan had put in a word. Sir Lionel himself wrote that he couldn't have chosen better for such a bright child. But as they journeyed north, Phee realized that the holiday had ended on a sour note and that it was all her fault. Mrs van Hooge was right. Timing was everything.

They arrived at Dalradnor tired and jaded. Caroline shot off to see her pets without a thank you or a backward glance. If she felt any unease at the decisions, Phoebe did not want to show it to the staff but busied herself making sure the child had everything on the long list of uniform and equipment. Kitting her out in thick winter coat, a regulation tweed suit for Sunday church, underwear and sports clothes all took time; then everything had to be tagged with her name by Mrs Ibell, who tutted now and then but said nothing until the trunk was packed full and sent on by rail.

Phoebe never saw Caroline from morning to dusk for those last few balmy days of late summer, when the walled garden was filled with the hum of bees in the flowerbeds, the smell of ripe apples and bramble bushes. There was a golden light on the stone house and the water rippled on the loch like diamonds. She had first seen it in this light as she carried the new-born baby into the peace of the garden, mourning that Arthur would never see it. Now the baby was a strapping girl, all legs and energy. How could she not think of this as home?

Then, on the day of their departure, Caroline stood pale-faced in her new navy-blue uniform like a victim about to be sent to the gallows.

'It won't be long to mid-term. You can always come back here and bring a friend,' said Mrs Ibell, trying to comfort her.

'I'll have to go to London with *her*,' Caroline snapped, staring at Phoebe.

'Now that's no way to be talking about your betters, young

lady. Let's no' be having bad words afore ye go. You'll have a grand time at yon school and grow six inches.'

Callie rushed to hug the housekeeper, trying not to cry. 'I'll write to you.'

To Phoebe she was politeness itself on the car journey all the way to Arbroath. They left Tam with the car at the gate, and as they walked up the drive, approaching the tall greystone buildings of the school, built like a castle, Callie was impressed by the beautiful grounds. There were parents, motor cars, chauffeurs, girls with violin cases and hordes of friends greeting each other with excitement. The new arrivals were ticked off on a list by prefects in gowns with perfect manners.

'Say your goodbyes here, girls,' said a teacher, also in a gown and mortarboard.

Phoebe stopped, hoping she would get a hug, a sign that she had been forgiven for being cruel to be kind.

Caroline turned sharply. 'You can go now. I'll be fine. Goodbye, and thank you for coming with me.' For once those Arthur-blue eyes were as cool as ice, her jaw firm and composed and lips closed in dismissal.

So that's all the thanks I get, Phoebe sighed as she walked slowly back to the gate. What else did you expect? She could hear Kitty's accusing tone in her ear. *You take away everything she's ever known, even her little dog, and you expect her to be grateful? Just give her time.* Will she ever thank me for it, she wondered. Her stomach tightened and her legs were heavy. She felt so uneasy. Lingering at the entrance, she wanted to turn and rush back up the drive to pull her daughter out of the line of new arrivals, but when she retraced her steps they'd all gone inside out of view. What have I done? she cried into the wind. Suddenly she felt breathless with panic, as if she'd just thrown something precious away, not knowing if she might ever find it again . . .

6

Phoebe travelled north and stayed overnight in a hotel. For the long summer holidays, Caroline was to stay at Dalradnor to give her a chance to catch up with her dog and pony, Hector. No doubt Sir Lionel would engineer a secret visit as he continued to take an interest in his granddaughter.

Phoebe had just finished filming a silent thriller starring Ivor Novello and directed by Fred Hitchcock. After the success of *The Lodger*, he was doing another creepy one. It was only a walk-on part but she was in good company. The news was all about talking-picture technology, and that would make a huge difference to her career prospects. Some of the silent actors had terrible voices. She'd take Callie down to the studios as a treat, and she was sure the McAllisters would ask to her to stay with her school friend Primrose. The two girls made an odd couple but Caroline liked going to their home in Yorkshire.

Harrogate was only a few miles from Leeds but so different in character and tone. It was where the wealthy lived, with elegant shops, a famous spa, and it had countryside beyond. Phoebe had never talked about Leeds or her connections there, or elaborated on the myth about Joe and Beryl. Callie had stopped asking about her parents years ago. Sometimes Phoebe wondered about Ted, the only family she had left, if indeed he was still alive. It was possible they wouldn't even recognize each other now.

Phoebe liked visiting St Margaret's. The huge stone school filled her with awe, with its neat trimmed borders, the sea crashing onto the shingle just beyond the grounds. It was a perfect place for a boarding school. Arthur would be proud that his daughter was being educated here. As her car approached, she could see the bandstand ready for the school orchestra, the sports arena cordoned off. She found her way to the sixth form and met an enthusiastic group of young ladies all asking intelligent searching questions, and she enjoyed being as honest as she could about her film and theatre experiences. Luncheon was served in a marquee for special guests and parents, with girls in their smart gingham summer dresses darting around trying to be helpful.

The end-of-year pageant took place on the lawn. It was a depiction of the march of the suffrage movement from Victorians in crinolines through to the Pankhurst militants chaining themselves to railings and being arrested. It wasn't a bad show: lots of overacting, melodrama, girls dressed as prisoners in sackcloth aprons and bonnets, girls marching in the colours, carrying silver arrows to denote being in prison and singing the suffragette anthem 'Shoulder to Shoulder'.

Phoebe kept searching out Caroline and her friend in the hordes of girls but it was mainly fifth and sixth formers taking part. They'd meet up for tea.

The pageant reached its climax and everyone was clapping when suddenly there was a loud and unexpected peal of bells from the old bell tower. People looked up to see movement on the roof. Two girls were climbing up with something wrapped round them. In the sunshine no one could miss that one of them had bright red hair and the other was edging her way up to where the weather vane swung with the wind. There were gasps from the audience of parents. Phoebe went cold with terror. It was Emily Davison all over again. There was nothing she could do but pray, *Not my child, please, God, not my child* . . .

'Are you all right? You don't have to come any further,' yelled Callie, seeing the look in her friend Primmy's eyes as they scrabbled on the roof, edging round the narrow balustrade.

'I said I'd do it and I will.' Primmy began to unwrap the banner they'd made from their pillowcases. 'Here, you grab this end.'

Callie sensed Prim had gone far enough. This was her plan and she must execute it. 'Go back down now . . . I can do the rest. There's not enough room for two of us,' she ordered, but Primmy clung on. 'It needs two of us and you know it.'

'I can do it and that's an order,' Callie shouted, seeing all the faces far below looking up at them. Suddenly it didn't seem such a good idea to raise their banner in public. It should have been done at dead of night, but they were here now and she'd see it through. Primmy must leave, though, and get to safety. It was higher than she'd thought. Getting into the old bell tower had been easy enough, but they'd dislodged stones climbing up outside and both girls were unnerved at the ease with which they skittered away beneath their feet. 'Go back, Primmy, please,' Callie yelled, and waited, clinging on tight to her position, for Primrose to back down and out of sight.

If Callie stretched hard, the weather vane was in reach. They'd made a loop to go round it but it was a much longer stretch than they had anticipated. Straining every muscle in her arm, she reached as high as she dared and on the second attempt she got the banner round. The words inked out on the cloth were 'VICTORY FOR THE TRAILBLAZERS', and she then slung her own blazer, with its distinctive navy-blue material with red and gold piping, round the weather vane for good measure. It had seemed a huge joke at the planning stage but now it didn't seem so funny, and even from the bell tower roof it was clear to Callie that no one was laughing down there.

For a second of terror she clung, feeling her feet slipping, but with the sense of real danger came a strange exhilaration too. *You did it!* If she got up here she would make it down, but retracing her footholds wasn't easy. She could see the janitor running with his tall ladder, and men with heavy blankets acting like firemen in case she fell. That was when she froze, her limbs stiff with fear at the thought that Aunt Phee was seeing all this, waiting and worrying. It was supposed to be a day of triumph, not tragedy. *Hell's bells . . . what do I do now?* was racing through her mind. *Stay calm, one foot at a time, back down inch by inch and don't look down. The stones will hold your weight.* She felt the sweat trickling on her forehead and her palms were slippery. Slowly, she edged back to the balustrade and knew she was safe, but with this came the sinking feeling that her trouble would be only just beginning when she touched solid ground.

'I'd like to know what you thought you'd achieved by that demonstration of stupidity, Caroline?' Miss Corcoran had the two girls standing in front of her desk with their parents behind. 'Making an exhibition in public and putting your lives in danger, embarrassing your parents and aunt, Primrose?'

Phoebe watched her daughter bow her head. No one watching had seen anything but danger, and she still could hardly breathe at the thought of what might have been.

'I thought it was a good idea to remind everyone of your motto, miss.'

'My what?' Miss Corcoran bellowed. Phoebe dug her nails into her palms, wishing she was anywhere but here.

'You asked us to be trailblazers so we took my blazer on a trail.'

'I see. So this was some joke at the school's expense?'

'No, Miss Corcoran. We have our trailblazers club, Callie and me. We wanted to do something daring like the suffragettes.'

'But you could've been killed climbing that tower. It's centuries old and out of bounds, as you well know. How on earth did you get in there?'

'We used our initiative, like you always say we should,' Primrose replied, looking at her parents, who could hardly contain their smiles at this riposte.

Miss Corcoran didn't see anything amusing at all.

'That was a foolhardy needless prank that could have ended in tragedy and brought our school into disrepute. We pride ourselves on instilling discipline and common sense here.'

Primrose's mother stepped forward. 'We sent Primmy here because we knew you prime girls to think for themselves and take risks. These two did something risky and daring, as they saw it, where we, as parents, could see only danger. I think they are still a little young to recognize the difference, but I also think they've learned their lesson.' She turned to Phoebe. 'What do you think, Miss Faye, since it was your niece leading the way?'

'No, Mummy, Callie made me leave. She looked after me. We both planned it together.' Primrose was in tears. 'It's not all her fault.'

'I think you have an answer there, Miss Corcoran.' Phoebe felt bold to reply. 'Two silly girls trying to do something daring and then finding that danger has its own price, I suspect. I don't know what else to say in their favour.'

'We can't let this go unpunished. It sets a bad example, however well-meaning and immature. I shall have to think of something suitable as a correction. Thank you, that is all for now. Girls, you will have the whole vacation to dwell of how this foolishness can be amended . . .'

With that they were all dismissed. Phoebe was just relieved Caroline wasn't expelled on the spot. 'What on earth were you thinking of?' she whispered, wanting to shake the girl.

Primrose and Caroline, white-faced, stood huddled together looking up at their banner. 'It's still up there. We did it. Who'll take it down?'

'That's enough from you two toe-rags,' Betty McAllister smiled. 'I wouldn't like to be in your shoes next term.'

'If there is a next term,' Phoebe said heavily.

'Oh, don't worry, I know Dorothy. She'll be secretly impressed with their escapade. Here are two of her charges who won't ever flinch when danger comes calling. Trailblazers, indeed . . . I bet she doesn't use that word again in a hurry. Come on, let's see if there's any tea left.'

Phoebe watched Primrose's parents stroll down the path arm in arm. It's all right for you, she thought. There are two of you to keep a check on your wild child. I have to do it all alone. Yet the panic she felt at the thought she might have lost her daughter was something she would never forget. As for the blazer, it was just an expensive piece of cloth, easily replaced, nothing like the loss of her child.

As they walked down towards the tea marquee in silence, she put her arms round Caroline. 'Don't you ever scare me like that again, young lady!'

July 1933

Dear Marthe

Thank you for the invitation to your wedding. I can't come as I am going camping with the Guides in the Cairngorms. Primmy and me are Patrol Leaders and going for our senior badges. I hope you and André will be very happy. Aunt Phee is sending you a present from us. It has been a horrible summer. Cullein ate something bad and had to be put to sleep. He is buried in the walled garden. I'll miss him very much. Me and Primmy are staying in London until the holiday.

Love Callie

7

August

'If there's a war, I'd want to be doing something important, wouldn't you?' said Callie, staring down at a picture of her aunt in a uniform. 'Not prancing around in make-up, pretending to be someone else.'

Callie was so glad she had Primmy's company that summer. From their very first terrifying day at St Maggie's she'd found a friend in Primrose, who'd stood in the new girls' queue looking as scared as she was. They'd stuck together like limpets, listening and saying little. They were allotted the same dorm.

Primrose was such a funny name for a girl with the brightest orange hair Callie had ever seen. It stuck out in a frizz in the damp sea air, coiling into the tightest curls and impossible to plait, so she was given permission to have it bobbed short into a halo round her head. She had the greenest eyes and freckles, was hopeless at games but a wizard in maths and all the sciences, with an effortless ability to remember stuff. She soaked up knowledge like a sponge, whereas Callie had to listen and take notes and swot up, and still came near the bottom in everything but French and German.

Now Primmy wasn't listening, engrossed in Aunt Phee's special scrapbook, a big red leather album with pages full of theatre programmes, stage photos and postcards going right back to her Gaiety Girl days. 'Wasn't she pretty?' Primmy smiled. 'I mean, she's not old or anything, but she looks like a film star in these postcards, and those picture hats . . .'

'I think they're hideous, especially the cartwheel ones. Can you imagine walking down the street in one of those now? They're so fussy.' Callie loved the sleek straight skirts and cloche hats she saw on the London streets, but she still preferred her kilt and jumper to any of her other clothes.

'I like the ones of her in uniform too.' Primmy turned the page to point to one photo taken in a hospital ward. 'She served in France.'

'Only in some concert party, not like your mother in field hospital,' Callie replied. Betty McAllister had been much braver, going across the Greek mountains to help the Serbian army.

'Mummy says cheering people up is as important as making them better,' Primmy answered back, always wanting to put a good slant on things. She carried on turning the pages in her own time. She was determined in that way, not letting Callie bully her into saying things she didn't mean. At the back of the album there was a pile of loose bits that spilled out onto the table: postcards and letters. Primmy lifted one up. 'Who's Mr Harry Boardman? She never sent this postcard; it's still got a clean stamp on it . . .'

'I think that's her father . . . my grandfather,' Callie replied. She peered at it more closely, having not bothered with the scrapbook for ages.

'I didn't know he lived in Leeds. Does he still live there?'

'He died, like my mother and father. I never knew him.' The Boardmans never featured in her life: no Christmas cards or presents or letters. She'd forgotten that he was Phee's own father. 'Do you know Leeds?' She was curious now.

'A little bit. Hunslet is south, I think. We pass it on the train. Do you have other relatives there?'

'I think there's an uncle there.'

'We could go and find him. It's not that far from Harrogate.'

'I'm not sure. I think my aunt fell out with her family. She's never talked about him,' Callie said.

'But if he's your real uncle there might be cousins there.'

Callie glanced at the address. 'I suppose it would do no harm to see.'

Primmy pulled out the postcard from the rest. 'This could be an adventure, finding your long-lost relatives. Then you can surprise your aunt with our findings like in the *Anne of Green Gables* stories.' Prim really liked those stories because of Anne Shirley suffering for her red hair.

'I'll see,' Callie replied cautiously, but she did pocket some of Aunt Phee's old postcards just so she could look at them in private.

Two days later they took a train north together, their rucksacks and suitcases in tow. Callie loved staying with the McAllisters. There was always a bustle of brothers and dogs, and telephones ringing in the hall. Prim's brother Hamish was a keen Boy Scout but he was going to college to be a doctor, almost grown up but still fun. Dr Betty ran some welfare clinic for mothers and babies, and Dr Jim had consulting rooms at the side of their house. The girls were left to amuse themselves but everyone met up for evening supper in the dining room where Callie found the chatter deafening and raucous after the quiet of Phee's apartments.

It was Prim's big idea that they could go on the train to Leeds in search of the uncle, who Callie recalled was named Ted.

'You did bring the card with the address on?' Prim began.

'No.' Callie saw Prim's look of dismay. 'But it was Peel Street.'

'What number?'

'Can't remember.'

'Honestly, you'll never make a detective.' Prim was reading Dorothy L. Sayers' detective story *Strong Poison*, and she raved about Harriet Vane.

It didn't take long to get into the city and take a bus down the Hunslet Road. It was an area full of dark sooty cobbled streets. The houses were back to back with no gardens. This must be where Aunt Phee was brought up, and it came as a shock to Callie. Primmy wasn't bothered by the poor streets. She seemed to understand that not every family lived like they did. Callie knew only about Kensington, St Maggie's and Dalradnor. She felt uneasy. 'Are you sure we're in the right place?' she asked Prim, who was marching ahead, staring at the street names.

'This is where people live, close to the mills and mines and jobs. We're lucky to have green spaces around us. Surely you've seen the tenements in Glasgow, or do you sleep on your way into town?'

'I don't think we should go any further. I've seen enough.'

'Don't be such a snob. If your parents lived round here, you should know where. We could find their graveyard.'

'No!' Callie replied, not wanting to think about that. She'd imagined them buried in some country churchyard, not this grimy city.

'I never took you for a coward. Let's knock on a door,' Primmy challenged. She rapped on the first door at the end of Peel Street and when it opened she smiled.

'Excuse me, we're looking for a Mr Boardman, Ted Boardman.'

'Oh, aye, why's that then?' The woman, who had a shawl on her head, looked at them with suspicion. 'The Boardmans flitted years ago but I think one of them lives near Gladstone Street, the little one, dunno his name.' She shut the door firmly in their faces.

'See, we have a lead now. Gladstone Street; can't be far.' Primmy was pleased.

Callie hesitated. 'No, let's go back now into Leeds. He'll be at work.'

'He may do shift work. Isn't this a ripping wheeze?' The trouble with Prim was she had no fear. She marched straight to the nearest corner shop, bought a quarter of midget gems to share and came out smiling. 'Gladstone Street is just round the corner.'

Callie felt uncomfortable and conspicuous in her kilt when men standing smoking on the corner were clearly eyeing them up as strangers.

The streets were all identical: rows of black houses, two windows up and one down, with a basement sunk into the ground. The doorsteps were chalky white and the net valances on the windows twitched as they passed.

'You can do it this time,' Prim ordered as she rapped the knocker of the first house to ask where Mr Boardman lived.

An old lady pointed up the street with a toothless smile. There was no going back now. Callie dragged her feet to the appointed house, hoping no one was inside, but as soon as she knocked it opened straight into a living room where a woman in a faded apron with wisps of dark hair stared at them both with surprise.

'I don't buy from the doorstep.'

'No, is this Mr Boardman's . . . Ted Boardman's house?'

'Who's asking?' The woman eyed them both cautiously.

'I'm Caroline, Joe's daughter,' Callie announced.

'You'd better come inside . . . Ted, you've got a visitor,' she shouted.

A man was lying on a makeshift bed close to the range. The room smelled of Lysol and cough linctus, but it was spotless and tidy. The man lifted his head in surprise.

'So who's this then, Hilda?'

'She says she's Joe's daughter. You'd better sit down and shout, miss. He's very deaf.'

'Who told her that, then?' The man stared at her. He had hollow cheeks, sunken eyes and a pallor that suggested he was an invalid.

'I'm Caroline Boardman. This is my friend Primrose. We thought we'd look you up as I'm Joe and Beryl's daughter, you see, and I don't know much about my family.' Callie paused, hoping he'd heard her.

'So who told you that cock-and-bull story?'

'Ted, now none of that . . .'

'My aunt Phoebe told me, your sister.' Disconcerted, Callie held out a postcard of Phee in her Gaiety days. He took one look and burst out laughing.

'Is that what she told you? Our Phoebe was allus a romancer. By heck, she's pulled a right stunt here.' He stared closely at Callie. 'I'll say this, you take after her, right enough.'

'My mother, Beryl Poole?'

'Never . . . Beryl married Ernie Mathers, no kiddies either, and our Joe was knocked off his bike on the Wakefield Road in a blackout. He wasn't married neither. This is our Phoebe, all right – went to London and never looked back. Not as I blame her. She saw her dad right but never turned up at his funeral. He were good enough to give her a start on the stage – I'll forgive her for that – but telling you a pack of lies . . . Sorry, young lady, whoever you are, if you're a relation o' mine it's the first time I heard of it and I'm wondering why. I think you should be asking our Phoebe some hard questions. It's not for me to say owt more on the matter. Glad to make your acquaintance. You never know what the wind'll blow in these days.'

'Pack it in, Ted. The poor kid's had a shock.' Hilda turned to Callie and said kindly, 'Sorry we can't be more helpful.'

Callie didn't know what to say to Ted Boardman's revelation but Primmy stepped in to fill the silence.

'Thank you for your help. I can see there's been a misunderstanding. We're sorry to have troubled you on your day off.'

'Day off?' Ted sneered. 'My days are all off since they shut up shop. No work for anyone in this street, or didn't you notice them hanging around on the pavements?. Hilda does some charring to tide us over. I don't suppose Phoebe is out of work.'

'She's in motion picture films and she teaches singing.'

'Aye, she allus did have a grand pair of lungs and big dreams. Never married, then?' It was Ted's turn to fish for answers.

'Her fiancé was killed on the Somme. We went to his grave in France once.'

'Aye, there were a lot o' lads round here as never made it home. Sorry to have squashed your little story but I'll not speak ill of the dead. Joe fathered no babby. He was no womanizer – just Beryl. You go back to my sister and tell her to get her facts right afore she sends youngsters to my door.'

'I didn't mean to offend,' Callie croaked, swallowing back her tears.

'Hey, I'm not blaming you. It's not your fault, but someone's not being straight with you.'

'Thank you, Mr Boardman.' Primrose backed towards the door. 'Come on, Callie, time to go.'

'Stay and have a cuppa,' said Hilda. 'Kettle's on the hob. It's nice to have a bit of company.'

'Thank you, but we have to be on our way. I think Callie's got a lot to think about.'

'She's not the only one,' said Ted. 'I'll say this, the apple don't fall far from the tree. Let us know when you find the true story,' he added more kindly. 'You're always welcome here, whoever you are. Nice to see pretty faces brightening up the place.'

The girls walked down the street in silence. 'This is all my fault. I pushed you into it . . . Sorry,' said Primrose, trying to grab Callie's hand but Callie shook her off.

'Just leave me alone.' She fell silent but her friend stayed close and, eventually, Callie turned to her, distress on her face. 'Oh, Primmy, who am I? What did he mean about apples not falling far from the trees?'

'I don't know, but I think you'd better ask your aunt Phee just what she meant by telling you lies.'

The knowledge sat heavy on Callie's heart all holiday. At first it spoiled everything at the Guide camp. She kept wandering off on her own to recall what the man Ted had said to them. She kept seeing that look on his face, his laughter at her tale and his denial of any knowledge of her. Why had she been told all this? There had to be an explanation and only one fitted the bill.

She must be a waif and stray adopted in secret so Aunt Phee could have a child to bring up, a child of her own. She was one of those poor orphan babies given away and this story was spun to protect her from the shameful truth of her birth. It explained why there were no pictures in the house of her parents, no little mementoes left for her to inherit, and why Aunt Phee didn't talk about her own background and her upbringing in the back-streets of Leeds, which was so different from the privileged education she had provided for Callie.

Primmy was quiet, too, and upset for forcing her to go on the wild-goose chase. She kept fussing round, wanting to make it right, but no one could ever make this right for Callie now. She really was an Orphan Annie after all.

It was hard for her not to wallow in self-pity about her plight, but eventually the mountains did work some magic, the river walks soothed her spirit and camping under the stars, with fires and late-night singing, was fun. 'Will you be all right? Have you written to your aunt?' Prim asked, as they folded up the tents and prepared to go home.

'I'm fine and I'm saying nothing, not yet. It's not really important,' Callie lied.

'Are you sure? You ought to know the truth.'

'When I need your advice, I'll ask for it,' she snapped, then was immediately contrite. 'Sorry . . . just leave me alone.'

She knew Prim was upset, but this was her burden to bear and to deal with in her own time. There was one other person who might know something and that was Marthe. Callie vowed to write to her as soon as she got home. Marthe wouldn't lie to her or let her down . . . but then she remembered Marthe was married and busy with her new life, and she sank into hopelessness again.

Why couldn't you just rub out stuff you didn't want to know about once you knew it, like rubbing out mistakes with an eraser, she wondered.

There was, however, one place that wouldn't change just because she was feeling strange and lost. Dalradnor was her home and she couldn't wait to get back to the safety of its walls. There, all her troubles would fade. That was the only place where she truly belonged now.

8

Phoebe noticed the change in Caroline the minute she saw her in Dalradnor. It was if as she had curled up inside and closed the door on everyone, going for long walks and rides alone, picking at the meals Nan Ibell so lovingly prepared, choosing to sit on the window seat in the stairwell, head in a book.

'I thought the Highland camp would put colour in her cheeks,' Phoebe whispered to the housekeeper.

'May be it is the time of the month . . . She's quite the young lady now and I know she misses the wee dog. Dinna fasch yerself . . . she's at that awkward age, neither fish nor fowl.' Nan was whisking up a chocolate cake. 'This'll cheer her up.'

'Has she fallen out with her friend?'

'No, I just think she's a bitty lost off with hersel'. It'll soon be term time. How long will she stay up in the school?'

'Nothing is settled. I thought Switzerland might be a good place to finish her off but now I'm not sure.'

'That'll cost a pretty penny,' sniffed the housekeeper. 'Aren't there places closer to home, in London?' Was there a hint of rebuke in that question?

'She's good with languages and she'll improve her French. There'd be skiing a chance to make new friends, all that sort of thing.'

'Aye, a change of scene may do her good. She's just no'

herself. I'm wondering if something is worrying her. Girls of
that age get awful stirred up . . . A young man, perhaps?'

'Surely not, she's only sixteen.' In Phoebe's eyes she was still
a harum-scarum in black stockings and gymslip. 'Time enough
for all that when she's out.'

Phoebe still clung to the hope that she could find someone to
help the girl have a proper Season but they had no real aristo-
cratic connections willing to oblige. Sir Lionel's wife would
have nothing to do with the two of them now. It was Miss
Corcoran who had suggested a language school or secretarial
training. 'She's not university material, I'm afraid. A good all-
rounder but not dedicated to key subjects, I find.'

Phoebe was glad she'd made time to come north for the
remainder of the school holidays but they hadn't spent much
time together so far. She was planning trips to Edinburgh and
Stirling Castle, and the art gallery in Glasgow, and perhaps to
take in a show at the Alhambra Theatre.

Times were hard in the city, the shipyards idle and men on
street corners with that pinched look of poverty, but the motion
pictures she was making seemed to get packed houses. She had
a part in a Jessie Matthews musical and one with Jack Buchanan.
The talkies had opened up a whole new world of sound for
audiences and Phoebe's voice was superior to those of many
stars. There was plenty of work for her, and like the wartime
concerts of old, the talkies cheered folk in these grim times.

Something, however, was definitely bothering Caroline. She
wasn't one of those 'I want' sort of girls; in fact buying clothes
for her was a waste of time. She wore her kilt or jodhpurs and
carried a book to read. She had no idea how pretty she could
look in a dress and jacket. Phoebe sighed, catching a glimpse of
herself in the mirror as she left Nan to her baking and returned
to the drawing room. Lines were appearing with flecks of grey,
her waist was thicker and she had to watch how much she ate
or the camera would double her backside. Her forties meant a

slow fading as her daughter bloomed, but that was part of the rhythm of life. You couldn't hold back time, she sighed. Thanks goodness she had made the leap into character acting. Her post-card days were long gone, but with a bit of slap, clever lighting and a tint in her hair she was ageing well enough.

She wandered through the old house, searching out the girl, and finally discovered Caroline hunched over a book on the bench close to Cullein's grave in the walled garden.

'What are you reading?' she asked out of genuinely inter-ested. She was not a book reader herself.

Caroline closed her book swiftly and turned away slumped. 'Nothing.'

'Oh, come on, what's up? You look like a wet wakes week in Huddersfield.' The joke fell flat.

'I'm fine.' The girl didn't look up so Phoebe took her cour-age and sat down.

'Nan says you're off your food. You know how she hates waste, and with so many of her family unemployed, it's a shame not to empty your plate.'

'I'm not hungry and she gives me too much.'

'But you were always starving. Are you ill? Is it your monthly time?' That was one thing she'd made sure Caroline knew about and was prepared for, although she knew the school gave the girls a serious lecture about the facts of life when they turned fourteen.

'Stop fussing.' The 'go away' was left unspoken.

'But I worry about you. You look so miserable. Tell your aunt Phoebe.' She moved in closer but Caroline backed away.

'Are you my real aunt or is that another of your tales?' Out came the grenade, and she knew she'd hit the mark as she felt the impact.

'What do you mean? I've been here all your life.'

'But are you really my aunt?'

'What is all this about? Of course, I'm a Boardman.'

'Well, don't give me that shit about my mother and father. I've seen Uncle Ted and he says it's all lies.'

Fear seeped into Phoebe's limbs and her heart was suddenly racing. She took a deep breath, cleared her throat. 'When was that?' she said carefully, trying to stay composed.

'Primmy found a letter you never sent in your scrapbook with an address on it. She dared me to go and see if there was family there. We went to Peel Street and then to Gladstone Street where I met Ted and Hilda Boardman.'

'I see. And what did he tell you?' Phoebe swallowed her panic and tried to sound matter-of-fact.

'I showed him one of your postcards. He laughed at it and said I must ask you what you were playing at, passing his dead brother off as a married man. Beryl is married with no children, so why did you lie to me about them?'

'Look, dear, I just wanted to spare you the truth. It seemed the easiest way to protect you.'

'Why should I need protecting? So you adopted me and brought me up as your own – what orphanage did you buy me from, and then pretended to be my aunt? What's so wrong in being adopted?'

Phoebe felt faint. Caroline had got everything so wrong – how could she explain without hurting her further? Kitty had warned her that this day would come and now there was no hiding from what she'd chosen to do all those years ago. She wished she were here to advise her. Nothing for it, however, but to battle on alone.

'First, you were never adopted. Secondly, you are not an orphan but a child born from the love of two young people in wartime, a child who could never have a father because he died serving his country. Your mother wanted to protect you because they were unable to marry before you were born.' Phoebe found she was trembling. 'Do you understand what I am saying?'

'Of course, I'm illegitimate, a bastard born to an unmarried mother,' Caroline replied, her voice icy, her eyes flashing like flints.

'No . . . well, yes . . . in the eyes of Society and the law, perhaps, but you were a loved child. It was an unfortunate act of fate that robbed you of both parents.'

'So where is this mother of mine?' Callie demanded furiously. 'Did she die too or give me to you as a souvenir?'

'Can't you see, Caroline? Do I have to spell it out to you?' Phoebe pleaded, reaching for her hand.

'Oh, no, it's not you? Surely not you . . .?' Caroline jumped up, horror on her face. 'How could you . . . how could you let me think all these years you were my aunt when you were really my own mother? I don't believe this. Ted said you'd pulled a stunt but I never thought even you could be so cruel as to deny your own baby!'

'Oh, do listen please . . .' Phoebe pleaded. 'I had to protect us both. When Arthur knew about you, he made sure we'd have a home, and Sir Lionel has always—'

'So he knew the truth all along? I'm his granddaughter, and you let me think all these lies. You ought to be ashamed of yourself . . . Get away from me,' she screamed in rage, running towards the house.

Phoebe collapsed on her knees on the gravel path. 'How could you think I didn't want you?' she yelled after her. Yet even as she cried out she knew that part of her was play-acting a scene out of a melodrama. *Get up, stop this. Everything has a price and now you're paying yours. Leave the girl to come to and she'll understand.* Thus spoke her heart to her mind as she flopped on the bench, staring at a bee buzzing into late blush rose where Cullein lay buried. *You have stripped her bare of all certainties, why shouldn't she hate your guts? But you are her mother – her only mother – and you must make amends and rebuild the broken bridge between you. It has to come right. It* must *come right.*

9

Callie raced from the garden to the stable block where Hector was peering out to greet her. 'Come on, boy, you and I are going for a ride.' She flung his saddle over him and walked him out of the yard, across the field to join the old bridle path she knew so well. She wanted to get as far away from Dalradnor as she could. The revelation was burning into her brain. Phee was her mother, her own mother, and all this time she'd acted like a distant aunt. It was disgusting, mean and utterly despicable. How she hated her now for lying to her.

Callie felt the wind in her face, the rhythm of the ride calming her down. She mustn't take out her fury on old Hector. He was all she had left in the world. They rested under a tree and she walked him to spare him her weight. She sort of knew where she was heading. If she carried on down the bridleway, and crossed the little packhorse bridge over the river, she would come to the Balfours' estate, with its grey stone house with castellated roof and turrets. There was just a chance Sir Lionel would be in residence.

Thoughts were buzzing like a swarm of bees in her head. No wonder Sir Lionel knew when her birthday was and brought gifts. It all made sense now, as did the visit to his son's monument all those years ago. Sir Lionel's son was her father and she never knew it.

She jumped off Hector, tethered him by a stream to graze, and walked across the wide lawn and up the steps to the front door. Banging hard, she waited until a servant, in a black jacket, opened the door.

'Miss Boardman to see Sir Lionel Seton-Ross.'

'He's away with the shoot, miss,' came the reply.

'Who is it, Fraser?' A sharp-faced woman in tweeds came to the door. 'Oh, it's you. You'd better come in.'

Callie had never seen the woman before. 'I'm sorry to interrupt you. I'm Caroline Boardman from Dalradnor House.'

'I know who you are. I wondered when you'd come calling.' There was a sneer in the woman's voice as she marched her through the marble hall and into the drawing room.

Callie had enough composure to remember her manners. 'Excuse me, and who might you be then?'

'Verity Seton-Ross.' She plonked herself down on a sofa, motioned Callie to sit opposite and pulled a cigarette case out of her cardigan pocket. 'What do you want?' she snapped.

'I came to see Sir Lionel. There are things I need to know, but I can wait.' She stood, too nervous to sit.

'Hmm, let's have a look at you.' Verity beckoned her to a chair by the fireside. 'So you know, then?'

'If you mean that I am Sir Lionel's granddaughter, yes, I've just heard . . .'

'Arthur was my brother, but if you think that makes me your aunt, you can forget any familiarity. Your mother was never welcome in this family. I don't know what she's told you but she set her cap at my brother from the day they first met. You have no claim on our estate. Arthur gave her every penny you'll ever get from us. If that is what you are here for?'

Callie shot up, drawing herself up to her full height. 'I rode here to see if what Aunt Phee has told me could possibly be true. I want nothing from any of you − or her.' She paused. 'And I've had enough of aunts to last a lifetime. No one has given me the courtesy of the truth until today. Can you imagine what it feels like to be an uninvited bastard? I thought I might find an ounce of sympathy here – instead you accuse me of wanting money. I don't think I can take any more of this. Good day, Miss Seton-Ross.'

She raced out of the door into the hall with its pillars and echoing walls. Verity Seton-Ross was chasing after her. 'Come back here, young lady!'

'No I won't. You can all go to hell!'

Callie fled past the startled servant, flinging wide the front door herself, then out and down the steps towards Hector. 'I want Marthe, I want Marthe . . .' she sobbed, but there was no one but the old pony to comfort her as she rode away, crying into his shaggy mane.

'What'll I do now, boy? Where do we go now?'

It was getting dark and Phoebe was worried. Caroline had been away for hours with only a thin shirt and jodhpurs on. She paced the drawing room, continually looking out of the window.

Mrs Ibell was told only that there'd been a row and the girl had run off. 'Better to call the bobby,' she advised. 'That *wee besom* knows how to pull your bells, staying out in the dark so late.'

'We'll give her a few more minutes. She'll shelter in a byre somewhere. She wouldn't want Hector to catch a chill,' Phoebe reasoned.

The sound of a car on the gravel had her dashing to the door. Out climbed Sir Lionel, still in his gun tweeds, and then his daughter. Phoebe was relieved to see Sir Lionel; he would know what to do.

'I've just heard. Where is she?' said the old man, leaning on his stick.

'Not a sign of her yet. How did you know she's missing? Ah . . . so she called on you?'

It was Verity who stepped forward. 'Papa was out so it was I who saw her, gave her piece of my mind, didn't realize the state she was in. I suppose I didn't help things one iota.' It was the nearest to Verity making an apology that Phoebe had ever heard.

'If anything happens to that girl . . .' Sir Lionel turned to Phoebe. 'So you told her the truth at long last.'

'What was I to do? She called on my family, heard half the story, then she got it into her head she was adopted. Do sit down. I think it's time to call in extra forces. Since she lost Cullein, the pony's been her only consolation.'

'I'll find her another Cairn, if it will help.' Lionel sat down, wiping the rain from his forehead.

'I don't think that will help now, with respect. I did what I thought was right at the time for all of us. I promised not to bring your name into disrepute and I needed to protect my own reputation. Now, I've run out of ideas. She trusts you but I don't think she'll ever listen to me again. I'm so out of my depth.' Phoebe looked up her visitors in despair. 'What a mess I've made of this.'

'She's at that awkward age,' Verity offered. 'A change of scenery might help. Is she still at St Maggie's?'

'I had thought of sending her abroad for a while, to a finishing school, but now I'm not sure,' Phoebe sighed, knowing their next encounters would be frosty and awkward if she didn't get this right.

'If I can give you one word of advice, Miss Faye . . .? This poor girl has been left out of all the major decisions in her life. I think she is old enough now to be asked just what she wants rather than to be told, don't you think?. Co-operation gets better results in my experience,' Sir Lionel offered.

'I don't think she's going to listen to anything I say,' Phoebe replied, tears threatening.

'But she might well listen to me. Verity, what do you think?'

'She's quite a wilful young filly, headstrong, plain-speaking, and not afraid to stand up for herself. She didn't deserve my outburst, but she took in on the chin. There's a lot of potential there. She's no shrinking violet, and so like Arthur in looks, it choked me at first to see her standing there. If Miss Faye thinks Caroline's going abroad might help, then it's worth a try. She'll survive all this, you'll see.'

'Let's just pray she doesn't do anything silly . . .'

The door opened and Nan Ibell put her head round the door with a smile. 'Just to let you know there's a drowned rat come to my kitchen door. I've given her hot soup and rolls, and I'll pack her off to bed with a hot-water bottle. I think the girl's had enough lectures for one day. Better she sleeps it off. Shall I bring you a wee dram, Sir Lionel?'

'Make it three, please, Mrs Ibell,' ordered Phoebe, sinking back in relief. 'Thank God she's safe.'

Tomorrow perhaps she'd take Lionel's advice and listen instead of lecturing. There was no escaping her responsibilities. The two of them had to make a fresh start together if they were to salvage anything from the wreckage of the past few hours, though it wasn't going to be easy. She recalled Kitty's warnings all those years ago, the warnings she'd ignored. How on earth was she going to bridge the gulf between herself and her daughter now?

10

Callie's reward for all the upheaval and upset of her discovery was to leave school and spend her time at Dalradnor and in London, having an extended holiday. Then at Easter, she was to go to a finishing school, close to Marthe and André, in a château in West Flanders. It had been to her nursemaid that she poured out her heart when she found out the truth. Marthe wrote back with kind words:

> Knowing is better than guessing, and you must understand why Miss Faye would want to hide this unfortunate situation from Society. Don't forget now you will know your grandfather better, and Miss Verity sounds a sensible type. Remember she lost her only brother in the war. Sir Lionel is no longer a myste-rious stranger, and he will guide you to prepare you for a useful life. Learning languages is never wasted. If my parents had not fled to England in 1914, I would never have experienced life in another country or spoken English or had the privilege of being your dear friend. Don't be afraid to take risks in life.

Marthe always made things sound better, just like Primmy.

Aunt Phee did her best to smooth over the tensions between them, but at first she tried too hard, always checking on her.

When she had a film part, it was much more relaxed as she had no time to fuss, Then there was Aunt Maisie's dancing school, where she spent the rest of her time.

Château Grooten lay north-west of Brussels, not far from Bruges, set in gracious parkland with a lake behind it. It was a spectacular fairy-tale French castle in pink stone. It had towers and turrets, and wonderful dormer windows jutting out of the rooftops in what Callie knew now was Gothic style. There were graduated steps leading up to the entrance and a carved portico in white stone, which glinted in the sunlight. It was a palace in miniature. Marthe, however, was not impressed. She had met her at the station and taken over from her escort. Callie stayed just for two nights in their terraced house in Brussels and delighted in playing peep-o with little Mathilde, singing her the lullabies she could still recall from her own childhood days.

'Isn't this enormous? Callie exclaimed as they walked up the path from the bus stop.

'It could all do with a fresh coat of paint, and the windows need vinegar,' Marthe observed critically. 'There are weeds on the gravel path. Are you sure this is the right place?'

'It belongs to the Countess van Grooten – yes, this is the house.'

'If there's a problem you must write to me and come back to us. I shall come in with you, just in case.'

Dear Marthe, she always made her feel so safe and so at ease. If only she felt like that with Phee, Callie thought.

They rang the bell and a petite woman of about fifty with an elegant chignon at the nape of her neck and a long string of heavy pearls opened the door.

'Ah, l'Anglaise . . . entrez . . . et vous?' She stared up at Marthe. 'Your maid?' she asked in English.

'Mais non, je suis Madame Kortrik. A friend of the family,' Marthe added in English.

'Belgique . . .?'

'*Exactement . . .*'

The countess dismissed poor Marthe with a sniff and she made to leave, but not before she whispered in Callie's ear in Flemish, 'Beware of this dragon.'

Callie stood with her suitcase in the elaborately tiled hall, eyeing the silver armour and swords on the walls.

'The other girls have all arrived. You are late. It is not polite to keep your hostess waiting. Go and unpack and we will meet in the dining room at five. I shall read the rules.'

Callie had no time to do anything but struggle upstairs and find where the chattering she could hear was coming from. She found a huge bedroom with six iron bedsteads on bare floor-boards, and windows draped with silk curtains topped by an elaborate pelmet with frayed fringing dangling down. The room was faded and bare. The five girls, sitting on their beds, stared at her. They'd left the bed nearest the draughts of the huge window for her.

'I hope you've brought some warm clothes. It's life in the Frigidaire here,' said a pretty American girl with black hair. 'It's a dump. Wait till Papa finds out we're stuck in the eighteenth century. I'm Sophie.'

'Oh, I don't know, it's better than my boarding school dorm in Scotland. We'll survive. It should be summer soon. It's rather a beautiful house . . .' Callie tried to sound cheery.

'It's a wreck; it needs a decorator,' said another American girl, almost in tears. 'I'm Vanessa.'

'Darling, you should see some of the stately homes I've slept in . . . This is a palace. I'm Clementine but Madame insists I'm called Clemence,' said a willowy English girl, holding out her hand.

Another, plumper, girl stepped forward. 'I think she's fallen on hard times. She's a widow from the war and I heard there were three sons to educate. She only takes us in to pay the bills, but she's good. My sister came two years ago. I'm

Pamela, by the way, and what name has she given you?' She
smiled at Callie.

'I'm Caroline, but I only answer to Callie. I think that's
French enough.' Suddenly a gong rang downstairs, and Callie
threw her case on the bed, pulled her stockings straight and
shoved her hair behind her ears, hoping she would pass
muster.

Her disarray did not go unnoticed as Madame glared at her
with contempt as she addressed the new intake. 'You are an
investment – your parents have invested their assets in your
welfare, an education fitting for society girls and those unfor-
tunates among you who must earn a living. Now I will impart
the finishing touches so that should one of you be so fortunate
as to marry the Prince of Wales, no one will say you don't have
the grooming and graces of a princess-in-waiting. You understand me?'

She eyed them one by one with a piercing glare. 'I am looking for snake hips and fine bones, but alas,' she sighed, 'nothing
do I see but slumped shoulders and puppy fat. You must look
like racehorses, not cart horses. I am looking for pearls and
simple elegance, Vanessa, not glittery trinkets. We French are
the masters of making the most of what we have. You see I am
petite, but if I lift my figure, my hair, my neck, I grow inches,
and with heels I can be a gazelle.'

Callie was trying to keep a straight face at the thought of
anyone round this table as a gazelle.

'Three things I teach: how to walk, how to dress, how to
conduct yourself with grace and charm. I allow no smoking in
my salon – it spoils the skin; no Belgian chocolates or pastries –
they thicken what should be slender. I demand correct standing,
fresh air and, above all, a curious mind. We plan many visits so
that you can lace your conversations with interesting anecdotes.
Your parents will get value for their investment in you here,'
she smiled. 'Now you may talk.'

Everyone was too shocked to say a word, but pulled themselves out of their chairs and tried to walk elegantly to the door
before collapsing in giggles. The grooming marathon had begun.

There were visits to every museum in Bruges, which
Madame said was the Venice of the North. They watched the
lace makers at work; admired all the Dutch and Flemish paint-
ers. Mornings were crammed with activity, but in the afternoons
the countess disappeared to her room, leaving her pupils to
read on the lawn, go riding or swimming. The food was delicious but Spartan. Callie had never eaten so many eggs and
vegetables. The two American girls complained bitterly about
the portion sizes until they noticed their waistbands were
slacker, feeling bones rather than flesh. Soon the girls began to
relax and share their experiences.

'I was supposed to go to Miss Porter's Academy, the best
finishing school in the States,' said Vanessa. 'That was until they
couldn't take me . . .' she confided. 'I had the wrong surname.
There are no Greenbergs or Cohens allowed into the school so
my pa decided Europe would be better. I love it here, well, not
quite here . . .'

Everyone laughed, knowing this was an endurance test of
sticking together and seeing it through.

'Do you think we'll get a diploma?' Vanessa asked.

The other girls seemed to look to Callie as the fount of all
knowledge, as if she was some sort of mothering prefect, especially when they got stuck in language classes. It was like St
Maggie's all over again.

'We'll have to pass the gazelle test first,' she suggested. They
all fell about laughing.

A few weeks later, the faded grandeur of the countess's
château took on another dimension with the unexpected arrival
of one of her sons. He turned up at the dining table in a dinner
jacket and wowed all the girls with his Gallic charm. He had
dark curly hair, enormous grey eyes, and an electric smile that

crackled the air as six pair of eyes examined this Adonis with a collective sigh.

'*Mes enfants*, this is my son, Louis-Ferrand, who I thought was in the Ardennes but is now on vacation. He is at the university.' He smiled at each of them and Callie tried not to blush. 'Vanessa, Adele, Sophie, Clemence, Pamela and Caroline . . .' the countess continued, bowing to each in turn.

'*Enchanté*,' he said in a deep voice.

When they returned to their drawing room Vanessa pretended to swoon. 'Oh, what a hunk of manhood!'

'I think she did that on purpose to sharpen us up. Nothing like a handsome male to cause a flutter in the hencoop. Look at you all, batting your eyelashes, blushing. He's only a student,' Callie said.

'So?' Pamela replied. 'What's wrong in practising our charm on him?'

'Bags I get first pick,' whispered Clemmie.

'We can take it in turns and see who scores a bull's-eye,' Vanessa added.

Callie felt sorry for Ferrand. He'd come home on vacation to face a roomful of love-starved girls all waiting to be noticed. 'I vote we leave the poor boy alone. He looks as if he wants peace and quiet, not pestering. Count me out.'

'Don't be so stuffy, Callie . . . Miss Goody Two-shoes. Still, one less for the competition,' Vanessa laughed. 'Go and read your book.'

Callie didn't mind being the odd one out. The girls were hungry for attention and Ferrand was going to be the sole object of their interest now. She felt protective of him. Madame had pictures of her sons in gilt silver frames everywhere. Anyone could see she'd not be letting foreign girls interfere with her time with her precious boy.

Two afternoons later, Callie saddled up one of the school's horses and rode out into the copse and along the path towards the other side of the lake at the back of the estate. It was getting warm so she tethered Alphonse, and stripped off her shoes and socks to cool off in the water, splashing about as she used to do at Dalradnor. A movement under a tree suddenly startled her. Had someone been following her? For a second she froze, but then Ferrand stepped out of the shade, holding something in his hand.

'*Pardon, mademoiselle . . . je vous en pris . . .* I think this belongs to Alphonse.' He was holding a horseshoe. He strolled to the horse, waiting in the shade. '*Bien sûr.* He has lost it on the path.'

'I better walk him back then, sorry.' Callie felt flustered at being caught playing in the water like a child. 'I hope it's not done any damage.'

'He's fine.' Ferrand flashed a smile. 'Are you enjoying your visit? Maman can be very . . . how you say . . . demanding?'

'Don't worry, I have an escape plan,' she laughed, thinking how close by the van Hooge family were. She told him about Marthe and how Marthe had been her nursemaid. 'My father died in the war at Lesboeufs.' It was the first time she'd ever talked openly about Arthur Seton-Ross, especially to a stranger, but somehow it felt natural.

Ferrand spoke excellent English and she shocked him by practising some Flemish. 'Don't let Maman hear you speaking this, Caroline. She is so proud of being French. My father was Flemish. I prefer just to be Belgian.' In addition to his studies at university, he was training as a cavalry officer. 'Not that we use horses as they once did, and I prefer to study rather than carry on the family tradition.'

'My mother was in the theatre and now is in films but I'm not going to follow her into that. I can't sing a note in tune.' She walked in the direction of the bridle path while he followed on horseback, showing her the way to the blacksmith's forge where they left Alphonse to be re-shod.

'I'm going to be so late,' she sighed, 'and the countess hates us to keep her waiting.'

'Then up you come. Acteon can hold two of us for a kilometre or two.'

And so it was that Callie arrived back holding onto Ferrand, facing a posse of open-mouthed, envious students. She dismounted and thanked her rescuer, feeling her cheeks burning, but not with the sun.

'So, the dark horse wins the race. My pa always says you limeys are a tricky race to beat.'

'Oh, please, it was nothing like that. Poor Alphonse lost a shoe.'

'And Sir Galahad came to the rescue, smart girl,' laughed Pamela.

'For the want of a nail the shoe was lost, for the want of the shoe, the horse was lost and for the want of a horse . . . the battle was won,' Clemmie teased, pushing Callie up the stairs. 'I wonder what our countess will say to this.'

How could she say anything when there was nothing to talk about? But when Ferrand left suddenly for Brussels, Callie felt as if the sun had gone out a little.

Then, two weeks later, a letter arrived in strange handwriting. It was from Ferrand, saying how much he had enjoyed their ride. He would be coming home for another weekend and wondered if she would like to accompany him for a picnic.

Callie hid the letter from prying eyes, secretly thrilled that she would be seeing him again. She'd never bothered much with boys, or friends' brothers, and she'd always shied away from all the silly talk about Valentino and film star heroes, but now she was discovering a whole new side to herself, a yearning, daydreamy secret self, waiting for when Ferrand appeared again. There was a fluttering excitement in her whole body. She couldn't wait to be alone with him and when the momentous weekend arrived and he passed a note into her hand arranging the rendezvous, she was shaking with a strange fever.

They rode out separately from the woods to end of the estate wall as Callie wasn't allowed out of the château grounds without permission. She trusted no one had noticed anything unusual in her disappearing as she often took solitary rides. They dismounted under the shade of large oak tree. Ferrand produced a knapsack and pulled from it baguettes, cream cheese, a little fruit tart and a bottle of chilled white wine. He'd even brought napkins and wine glasses. This was a proper picnic. They sat munching, silent, each aware of the other gazing out.

'Have you visited England?' Callie asked.

'*Mais oui*, several times with Maman.'

'Your mother is very proud of you, I think.'

'She has plans. For Karel it will be the seminary, and for Jean-Luc, my eldest brother, the estate. It leaves me free to continue my studies in Ancient Civilizations, but we must all do some military training in case there is another war. It is hard for her without her husband . . . For your mother, too?'

Callie didn't want to spoil the moment thinking about Aunt Phee. She smiled and shrugged, lying back, feeling the sun on her face. 'There can't be another war,' she said.

'Who knows? They say Germany is building new roads and its army in secret. They will avenge their defeat . . .'

'But they are not allowed to arm . . . It won't happen again, not in our lifetime, surely?'

'Don't worry, the Belgian army will be there to protect you,' he laughed. Suddenly he bent over her and kissed her cheek gently. Callie felt her whole body explode with excitement. 'You don't mind that I kiss you?' he whispered, and she could smell the wine on his breath.

'No one has ever kissed me before,' she smiled. 'I don't mind.'

'Why ever not? You are lovely. The others girls are pretty but like children. How old are you?'

'Nearly eighteen.'

'Then I will kiss you as a woman.' His lips crushed hers with more intensity as they clung together, until Callie began to be afraid at the passion his kiss evoked.

She sat up, shocked and pushed him away.

'It's different to kiss like this,' Ferrand said. 'But I must not take advantage of you. It is not fair . . . you are our guest and . . .' He turned away as he spoke.

'Why not fair?' Now Callie didn't want their kissing to end. 'Come, let's head back. We don't want to spoil our secret.'

They rode back in silence together, separating just before they came in full view of the château. 'Tomorrow, we will kiss some more?' he smiled, waving as he left her to see to her mount. She felt she was floating on a cloud of warm air, reliving in her head the passionate kiss, her first kiss, and how she wanted to go on kissing him forever.

'You are late again, Miss Boardman. Where have you been?' snapped the countess, when Callie returned, but it was Ferrand, entering through the front door just behind her, who came to her rescue.

'She's been out riding with me.'

'Is that so? Go and change for dinner,' Madame ordered, then turned to her son. 'I want a word with you . . .'

Callie raced up the stairs. Tonight she would dress with the utmost care, nothing too flashy or skimpy, but as a lady who had just been kissed by a handsome man. The others were busy primping themselves and for once the bathroom was empty. She hoped there was enough lukewarm water to have a quick soak in the tub and borrow some of the attar of rose oil that was sitting on the basin ledge.

Lying in the bath was a luxury, and Callie soaked in the anticipation of seeing Ferrand again. He had changed her world from girlish dreams to womanly desires. If he kissed her again in the moonlight, how would she resist the passion with his hands all over her body?

There was a brief tap on the door and in marched the countess with a face like thunder.

'Get dressed, Caroline. I will talk with you, now.'

Callie jumped out from the tub and grabbed a bath towel, aware that the woman was staring at her naked body. Wrapped only in the towel, she followed her down the corridor to her study.

'Now, young lady, this has to stop, this silliness!'

The countess pointed to a chair behind her desk. 'You are young, you are both still children, too young for this nonsense. I will not have you making eyes at my son, leading him on to make promises he cannot keep.'

Caroline sat, not understanding the torrent of rapid French. 'Pardon?' she offered.

'I forget you speak French like a Belgian peasant. My sons are not for the likes of you. You are English and a Protestant. We are Catholic. He is highborn; you, I gather, are an actress's daughter with no father or family of note. *C'est incroyable!* There is to be an end to this at once. He is promised to my cousin's child, Albertine d'Orlange. He knows his duty to the family. Do not think this is the first time his eyes have led him astray. I do not bring young girls into this house to have them try to seduce my sons. I bring you into my home because I have a roof to repair and bills to pay, not because I want to be subject to all your noise and troublesome behaviour. Do you understand what I am saying?' she cried, waving her hands in the air.

Callie nodded in shock, unable to utter a word to defend herself or deny the allegations thrown at her with such venom. So this was a game he played with every batch of students. Was she no more than a toy to be picked out to play with? How could he betray his fiancée, if this was the case? Callie felt sick at his cruelty.

'Go and get dressed,' the countess snapped.

'Perhaps it would be better if I do not dine,' Callie offered.

'You will dine and show the stiff lip of a true English girl. Say nothing and do not make scenes you will later regret.'

Callie fled back to the bedroom. All the girls were gone, leaving her to fix her dress alone with shaking hands, and unravel her plaits so her hair fell down onto her shoulders in soft coils of sun-bleached gold. She swallowed her tears, not quite believing what had just happened in the study. Now she must go down those stairs with her head held high and not give Ferrand the satisfaction of knowing she knew his little game. She gathered herself, drew back her shoulders and left the room.

Everyone looked up at her entrance. The countess sat at the head of the table as usual, all charm itself.

'*Alors, chérie*. I see the sun has caught your face.'

Callie noticed an empty chair by her side. Ferrand was late too. The woman missed nothing and pointed to the empty chair. 'Alas, my son had to return to his studies at the last moment. He sends his apologies . . . *Il est très désolé,* but of course, duty comes first, *n'est-ce pas?*' She was looking directly at Callie.

Callie ate the dinner in a daze of confusion and embarrassment. His *maman* had ticked him off and he'd departed promptly at her bidding without an apology or explanation. What a wimp!

So she was nothing to him but a pleasant afternoon's diversion. She felt so disappointed. It was then she understood what Ted Boardman had meant when he'd told her that the apple doesn't fall far from the tree. Perhaps she was more like her mother than she'd thought, recognizing the actress within herself too. It took every ounce of courage to smile and chat to the other girls, giving not one hint of how much she was hurting inside. Let this be a lesson to you, she thought. Keep away from silly young men still tied to their mother's apron strings. You can do better than that.

11

When Caroline stepped off the boat train at Waterloo Station, Phoebe couldn't believe the change in her. She was stretched out somehow, with sun-bleached hair, standing tall and striding towards her with a new-found confidence. The gawky girl had been replaced by a stylish young lady in a smart linen two-piece, a jaunty trilby perched on her head.

'At last,' Phoebe cried, holding out her arms. 'I was beginning to think you were never coming home.' They pecked each other on the cheek.

'There was so much to do with Marthe and her new baby. She's an absolute darling and I am her godmother.'

Phoebe felt a pang of jealousy, knowing Marthe always came first with Callie, but she smiled and said, 'You must tell me all about them when we get home.'

'I thought we were going north?'

'You need to unpack and draw breath after your travels. There's been a change of plan, but come along.' Phoebe didn't want to go into things on the platform. 'You'll have time to see your new friends.'

'I don't have new friends.'

'Surely you made some friends at that school?'

'No one special. Let's find a taxi. I need a bath; it was so hot and sticky on the train.' Caroline sighed, marching out of the station.

It was just like when Callie had returned from St Margaret's, Phoebe thought. The schoolgirl dumped her case, jumped into the bath, then lounged on her bed with a book. But she was eighteen now, and her whole future must be planned.

Once back at the flat, out poured laundry and presents, and on went the wireless. Phoebe's sitting room was soon filled with dance music and cigarette smoke.

'You're not starting that filthy habit, are you?' she asked.

'Everyone smokes. I've bought an ivory holder. It's the chic way to puff.' Caroline shrugged off her disapproval.

'Is that all you learned abroad?'

'I can mix a Gin Sling, cook a mean omelette, choose the best pearls and play poker.' She saw the dismay on her mother's face. 'Only joking, but we had two American girls who were wizards at card games. We used to play for make-up.' She paused. 'Aren't you busy with another film?'

'We're all helping Maisie with the dance school. I've hit a bit of a slump. My agent's always on the prowl but there's nothing suitable just now. We're giving tea dances for beginners in the afternoons at the school, so I wondered if you could help us out.'

'You know I have two left feet,' Caroline dismissed her suggestion, picking up a magazine.

'No . . . just in the office, telephone duty. It's all a bit of a mess in there . . .'

'But I've not done any secretarial work,' Caroline replied, not interested in her mother's news after all this time.

'You'll soon pick it up, just for a few weeks until it's quiet. Everyone wants to learn new dances for the Season's parties.'

'But what about Dalradnor? Primmy's supposed to be staying.'

'Caroline, you've just been abroad for six months. Haven't you had enough holidays?' Phoebe didn't mean to be sharp but the girl must learn there was a time to play and a time to help out. It wasn't good to loll about doing nothing.

'Oh, I see, now I have to pay my dues.' Caroline got up and walked to the kitchen. 'Not back five minutes and it's out with the shovel and spade.' Already they were sniping at each other.

'You can go up there for a week, if you must, but it really would help Maisie out if you could give her some of your time. She's not been well and Kitty's quite worried,' Phoebe explained.

Caroline turned round. 'Why didn't you say that in the first place? What's wrong?'

'Women's troubles, a bit of a growth. They've taken everything away but it's left her exhausted. Billy does what he can to cover for her but Kitty is afraid she might need other treatments.'

'I'm sorry, poor Maisie. Why didn't you tell me? Honestly, I'm always the last to know. Of course I'll help, but don't expect me to do any dancing.'

Phoebe was relieved there'd be another person on board to help. Maisie had cancer, a bad one that no one wanted to address except Kitty. 'As far as the other staff go, it's just a bowel complaint. Maisie must rest and not move around too much,' Kitty had confided in Phoebe. 'She'll sit on a chair to conduct her classes. But I'm sure it's spread. Her face is liverish and her skin in sallow. We're going to have to cover for her where we can.'

Phoebe couldn't bear the thought of losing Maisie. Billy Demaine was doing his best to stand in and she was almost full time too. It would be good if Caroline was part of the business; there was always the chance she might take it over one day. The annual visit to Dalradnor was a luxury they could ill afford this year. The old place would be safe in the hands of Nan Ibell and her daughter, Mima Johnstone. It could wait. Caroline had had a year of fun and games; now it was time she went to work.

The Gibbons School of Dance was just off Kensington High Street, in a large town house that had seen better days, but which still had a ballroom on the first floor up a gracious staircase. This was used as a studio, the walls covered with large gilt-framed mirrors. It had a sprung oak floor, which smelled of wood stain, and there were barres on two sides so professional dancers could hire the room for morning classes. The anteroom was a changing area and the former library was an office and staff room.

Phee wasn't joking when she said things were in a mess. There were bills and letters stuffed into the desk drawers, bills clipped together and pinned to the wall, unopened mail, piles of the *Stage* gathering dust, coffee cups gathering mould, a rickety typewriter and a telephone on a large leather-topped desk ringed with ancient tea stains. A kettle and a tin of broken biscuits made up the sum of office equipment. Callie was expected to work miracles. It was about as far away from the Château Grooten's elegance and her lazy summer by the lake as it was possible to get. Callie smiled, thinking of her fury at Ferrand's dalliance until she'd got his abject letter of apology. She'd nearly thrown it unopened in the bin but she was curious to see how he would wangle his way out his desertion.

I am sorry to leave without a word but I could not listen to Maman a minute longer. I knew she would lash you with her tongue. She cannot accept I have a life of my own to live with friends who I choose, not her. I am not engaged to anyone, nor do I intend to marry for years, but always she wants to impress her will on us. My brother Karel has at least escaped her now he's entered the seminary, and she has driven Jean-Luc into the army. As for me. I hope to study abroad, so Maman will have to make plans for herself from now on.

Please forgive me for leaving you to face her disappointment, but it was better that I walk away. One day she must learn that a parent cannot force her child to live the life she wants. I did enjoy those two lovely days with you. I hope we meet again.

Louis-Ferrand van Grooten

There was no address to reply to, nor was one necessary. It was just a little romance in the summer sun, and now it was over. It was a relief to know he'd not been playing with her affections, that her first impressions were true. He was just a young student flexing his wings, wanting to fly free. She almost felt sorry for the countess, whom she realized lived in a world of fantasy and was in danger of losing all her children.

As she stared round the office, there was no doubting she was back to earth with a bump.

Callie was stuck with the daunting task of running the office out of duty for a few weeks, but once she saw how diminished Maisie was by her illness she knew she must not let her down.

Callie noticed how Phee's long-time friends all stuck together in a crisis. They'd been through a war, suffered losses and disappointments, but still found time to laugh and smile. How could you not admire their generation? She felt the draught of friendships in her own life. Primrose was up at Oxford now, and Callie went to spend two days with her as a guest in college. It was like a glorified boarding school with golden stone lecture rooms. She tried hard not to be envious of Primmy making new friends while she was stuck with the oldies. They wrote to each other regularly, but their paths were already separating.

One afternoon, a group of new clients burst into the studio for ballroom lessons. Callie was busy collecting names and telephone details in case of cancellations when a familiar voice from the château rang out behind her.

'Good Lord, it's our dark horse,' snorted Pamela Carluke. 'Callie Boardman, what are you doing here?'

'This is where I help out with my aunts,' Callie flushed. How smart Pam and Clemmie looked in their winter coats and pretty hats. 'I'm surprised you're allowed out on your own,' she teased, knowing debs never went anywhere unescorted.

'Safety in numbers, dear girl and we're building up a head of steam for the coming-out parties. Must cut the mustard on the dance floor, if we're to catch the best toffs . . . And you? Did you ever see that gorgeous student boy again?'

'What do you think?' Callie winked, seeing Phee hovering. 'Dragon mother had other plans.'

Pamela turned to her friends. 'The countess was a Gorgon but clever with it. Callie and I will tell all later.'

Jem, employed to teach ballroom, soon barked orders to start the class, getting the girls to pair up and practise the steps while Callie watched with envy at their swift progress. He knew what he was doing and took no cheek from them.

When it was over Pam dashed into the office. 'We're going for tea. Come and join us if you can.'

'Go on, dear, you've earned a break,' Phee was quick to respond 'Nice to see you did make friends after all.'

Callie grabbed her hat and coat and followed the debs down the stairs, feeling nervous. She didn't really know Clemmie and Pam well, or their set at all, but they had asked her and it was such a relief to be out in the fresh air and in the company of girls, not old ladies. Suddenly, London wasn't such a lonely place after all.

The after-class tea parties became regular events on Thursdays, and Callie started to join in the tango class. The music was just too inviting. Clemmie was a natural dancer, arching her back in the poses that Jem demonstrated. Those months at the château had slimmed the girls down, so after an exhausting hour of dancing they allowed themselves to scoff French patisseries in a wonderful tearoom close to Harrods.

'You must come with us and try out the dancing at the 400 Club. They have the best bands in town. Do say you'll come,' Pam begged. 'You'll meet all the crowd. Tell your aunt it's quite safe. All our brothers and cousins are quite safe in taxis,' she added with a wink.

'What should one wear?' Callie asked, knowing the debs would have loads of wonderful evening wear at their disposal.

'Not too much – a bit steamy in there. You must show off ze snake 'ips, *mais non*? Do the dragon lady proud. It'll be a hoot,' said Clemmie.

Callie's first outing with them took much preparation. She'd been given one of Maisie's slinky blue slub satin evening dresses, cut on the bias, and altered by Phee so it fitted like a glove. She had her hair waved and pinned in the latest salon style and borrowed Kitty's old fur cape, which stank of camphor mothballs.

'I wore that the night I met your father,' said Phee, her mouth full of pins. 'You are going to look so good in this.' They were trying so hard to get along together but it was difficult. Callie knew Phee wanted her to ask about their romance but she wasn't playing ball on that one. She had no interest in how her mother and father met.

Callie was put in a taxi armed with her fare home, lipstick and spare stockings, comb and extra pins. Her anxiety mounted as she neared her destination. *What if nobody will dance with me? What if the girls don't show up?* She wished she hadn't agreed to come.

They were meeting in the basement bar of the Ritz and there was a horde of new faces all staring in her direction: boys called Jock and Biff, Nigel, Pongo and Paddy, gangling young men in tails, escorting their sisters and friends called Hermione, Cecilia or Annabelle. Pam brought her sister, Poppy, and Clemmie, her cousin, Belinda.

Pam looked her up and down with a smile. 'Golly, Callie, you look the bee's knees. Midnight blue suits you.'

Everyone was knocking back gins and fizz. Somehow she found a glass in her hand and soon she felt a warm glow inside. It was late when they headed out to Leicester Square. The club was close to the Alhambra Theatre, in a basement that was a subterranean world of soft lights and smoke where you could dance all night.

The walls were covered in red silk and velvet curtains. There were plush banquettes at the sides, and gilded standard lamps and single candles on the dining tables. It was packed. Callie was expecting a ballroom with chandeliers but this was much more exciting and glamorous. The band was playing from a stage while couples circled round the floor. Young, old, everyone seemed to know each other. Perhaps the boys were at school together and the girls had shared nannies and walks in the park.

'Gosh, I hope Daddy's not here with his girlfriend,' whispered Belinda. 'I don't want Mummy to know. He's supposed to be working late in the Commons.'

Once seated, they started to pair off, dancing to the swing music that the coloured musicians did so well. 'You can trip round the floor with me, if you like,' said Nigel, offering Callie his hand. 'But I must warn you, I'm not much good at this stuff.'

Never was a truer word spoken, thought Callie, as she limped back to the seats with bruised toes. Perhaps it was better to sit the next one out, but it turned out to be a tango.

'Come on, Callie, let's show them what we've learned,' yelled Pam above the noise. 'You be the man, you're the tallest.' They tried to recall Jem's instructions but, without his discipline, made a pig's ear of it. Then a couple took to the floor who really knew their steps. He looked dashing in tails, while she was in a slinky red dress with a slit up the side, showing her perfect thighs.

'Are these exhibition dancers?' Callie asked.

'No, that's Toby just showing off. Quite the mover. The Welsh wizard, we call him. Now he is definitely N.S.I.T.,' Pam smirked. 'Just look where his hand is, heading south . . .'

Callie couldn't take her eyes off the couple as they took centre stage. They were electric with their haughty, smouldering eyes and their dramatic poses. 'How come he dances so well?'

'Toby comes and goes; lives abroad. Look at his tanned face and those shoulders . . . bit of a mystery man. Do you want to meet him?'

'Oh, no!' He scared Callie, with that magnetic look in his eyes as he swirled his partner round, seemingly oblivious to everyone else. The girls stepped back to join the others, but then the tango finished and suddenly Pamela headed out to the beautiful couple and brought them across.

'My friend wants to meet you,' she smiled, all innocence. 'Mr Toby Lloyd-Jones . . . Miss Caroline Boardman.'

Callie was furious, remembering her own humiliatingly bad dancing. 'We were just admiring your technique,' she stammered. 'We're trying to learn, but if I had a hundred classes I'd never dance like you two.' She turned for support but the girls had melted away.

'I haven't seen you here before,' Toby replied, eyeing her with interest.

'I met Clemmie and Pam at school in Belgium. This's quite a place and the music is terrific.' Callie was trying to sound casual but it wasn't working. He looked at home in the dark recesses of the club while she felt like an ingénue. He was older than her crowd – at least thirty, judging by the creases in his face.

'This is Pearl, who's attached to the band.' The girl with coffee-coloured skin and big black eyes smiled at Callie. 'Better be off now. I'll be singing soon,' she excused herself. 'Bye, Toby, darling.' She kissed him on the lips.

Callie tried to back away but Toby blocked her path. 'Like to dance with me? Looks like you've been deserted by your partner.' Without waiting for a reply he swept her into a quickstep that had her shoes polishing the floor. He led her with ease and she relaxed, realizing he knew what he was about.

'So you're not used to the fleshpots of London, then?' he asked.

'I prefer Scotland; we have a house up there. But my aunt's ill – she has a dance studio – so I'm helping in the office for a while.' She knew she was gabbling, trying not to stumble. He smelled of aftershave, tobacco and something rich and exciting she couldn't put a name to.

'The music here is the best in town and it's a great place to meet up. Pity is I can't get here too often.'

'Pamela says you work abroad,' Callie offered.

'Did she now? I come and go, helping people invest in developing projects. In fact, I'm pushing a development in Cairo, along the Nile river. We're hoping to expand. I must have a word with her brothers . . .'

'Egypt – how wonderful. I've read a lot about Tutankhamun and the tombs of the Pharaohs.' She tried to impress him with her slender knowledge.

'You have to take a camel ride to see the pyramids at sunrise over the desert to get the real scale of the tombs,' he replied, looking down at her.

'Really, I'd love to see that. I've seen Mont Blanc and the Eiffel Tower, but nothing like that. You are lucky.' She was enjoying every second of dancing in his strong arms. It was a shame that the music had to end.

'Let's find a seat and I'll get drinks,' he offered.

'I really ought to go back to the others,' she said, knowing it was only polite to stay with her crowd, though the pull of his attention was tempting. She felt flattered that he wanted to talk to her. 'OK, just one drink then. Thank you.'

He found a quiet corner and an empty banquette, then went to the bar for a bottle of champagne. Clemmie took this opportunity to dash across.

'There you go again, snatching the best catch in the room tonight. How do you do it?'

'Do what?' Callie whispered. 'We're only having a drink. He's a bit old for me.'

'Nonsense. It's good to have someone who knows what's what. Not seen him here for ages. You've struck lucky. Here today, gone tomorrow is Toby, so enjoy him while you can . . . and tell us all on Thursday.'

Callie didn't know what was going on. She'd only come to dance, not to pick up the first man who danced with her, but Clemmie was right, Toby did have the knack of making her feel special. She thought of her little holiday romance. This man would not have a mother breathing down his neck, but he might be married. There was something too good to be true about Lloyd-Jones and she meant to dig it out. When he returned with the champagne and glasses she began her inter-rogation with a smile. 'Do you have family in London?'

'In Wales. My parents retired to their country house for the quiet life. I'm their only child,' he said, tapping his cigarette on his gold case.

'So no family of your own then?'

'Good Lord, married, me . . . not yet. Got to find the right girl. They keep escaping me.' He gave a rich throaty laugh, looking straight into her eyes so she had to turn away, feeling silly and obvious.

'I didn't mean . . .'

'You're right to check.' He looked around. 'Who knows what sordid little secrets are hidden in this crowd tonight? Now you might have some young buck chasing after you, too.'

'Gosh, no, not me,' she replied a little too quickly. 'Plenty of time for all that ball-and-chain stuff. I'm only eighteen.'

'There we go then, both of us fancy-free and looking for fun.' This time he caught her gaze and held it a little too long. 'You do know you are a very attractive young lady and I think you know what you want – and how to get it.'

Callie felt herself going hot and a *frisson* of tension shot through her body as he reached out to touch her arm. 'I must see you again. Not here, but for supper. There's a place I know where we can dine in peace without everyone watching every move.'

'I'd have to ask Aunt Phee. I live with her in Marylebone,' she replied.

'Then I'll come and meet her. She can check my credentials and my bank balance, if it worries her.'

Now he was flustering her. 'I'm sure she'll be fine and I'd like to have supper with you.'

'That's settled then. We'll meet up and perhaps go shopping. You can help me choose some stuff for my new apartment. It's not ready yet so I'm renting a room. Not sure when I'll be heading back to the heat and dust of Cairo. It depends . . . got a few more appointments. Come on, let's dance the night away . . .'

Later, he put her in a taxi with a promise to meet her on Wednesday in Burlington Arcade. 'Good night, and be good,' he smiled, pecking her on the cheek. 'Just a little on account . . . I'm so glad you came tonight.'

Callie returned home in a dream. She'd never met anyone like Toby before: sophisticated, wealthy, worldly but charming. He'd not pushed himself on her in any way. He'd made her feel special and desired, and she couldn't wait to see him again.

12

Phoebe could see the change in Callie after that first night with her friends in the 400 Club. It had put a blossom in her cheeks and she was taking such care with her appearance, becoming quite the fashion plate. Gone was the girl in kilt and gumboots. She'd gone into town and came back with an exquisite silk scarf in muted pastel shades, so tasteful and expensive. She'd been out for dinner with her crowd and dancing at the Embassy, the Florida, nightclubs Phee knew of but had never ventured into. Her companions were good types from county families, just the sort she'd wanted for her daughter, knowing she could hold her own with any of them in looks and accomplishments. The investment in Callie's education had paid off, which was cheering when everything at the Gibbons School of Dance was going downhill. Maisie was confined to bed now and needed constant nursing. The noise from the ballroom had to be muted so as not to disturb her. Phoebe's heart was full of dread.

Callie worked wonders in the office, bringing order out of chaos. What would happen when Maisie died no one knew. Phee hoped they could carry on the lease, as the classes were full, yet she dreaded the loss of her old friend and the ending of an era. At least Caroline wasn't moping around. She was hardly at home and there was something about her that made Phoebe suspect she might be in love.

'Who are you out with tonight? I didn't catch his name,' she ventured, making light-hearted banter.

'I didn't say it was a he, did I?' Caroline flushed.

'Don't be so shocked. I don't mind if there's a special boy. I was young once. At your age I met Arthur, and I'm not in my dotage yet,' Phoebe laughed, but Caroline tensed up.

'He's not a boy. His name is Toby and he's from Wales, but he's going abroad soon . . . to Egypt.'

'Is he a soldier . . . an officer?'

'No, he's in business, an investor in a development company.'

'That sounds important. Why don't you bring him for tea one day?' Phoebe was still trying to sound casual but she was aware that this was a step forward for Caroline.

'I'm not sure. He's very busy. He's nice, good-looking, you'll like him.'

'I can see you're quite smitten. How old is he, then?'

Caroline shifted her gaze. 'Older than me, of course, but age doesn't matter, does it?'

'It depends.' Phoebe felt a flicker of unease. Caroline was being cagey about his age. She was young and inexperienced, and Phoebe hoped she'd not be let down by a man far more worldly than she.

A week later, late in the evening, Caroline bounced into Phoebe's bedroom with a grin on her face. 'Toby's invited us to the Ritz for luncheon. I told him you were anxious to meet him so he suggested this. He's very generous, but please don't wear that fussy hat with the netting. It's ghastly and doesn't match your two-piece.'

Phoebe had always loved that hat. This was an important meeting so she must look the part, curious to meet the man who was making her daughter critical and fussy about appearance.

'And don't go on about me being hopeless at school,' Callie added.

'I'd never say that, and you weren't hopeless, just not academic like Primrose. I don't suppose you want me to tell him I was born in the backstreets of Leeds either?' She couldn't help the jibe.

'And don't spoil it with all your questions.'

Phoebe froze for a second. 'Do you want me to come or not? From where I'm sitting, I can see you have a bad case of the jitters. He must take me as I am or not. It's not me he's interested it. I'm only the mother . . .'

'Actually, he thinks you're my aunt. I didn't want all that stuff coming out yet . . .' There was an awkward silence.

'I thought we'd got over all that.' Phoebe said quietly. She was trying to stay calm but she felt hurt that Caroline was hiding their relationship. 'Why didn't you tell him I am a war widow? It is better to be straight with people, darling.'

'Listen who's talking.' Caroline backed away, shutting the door.

Clearly this was no jolly boyfriend but someone who really mattered to Callie. That twinge of fear stabbed Phoebe again, twisting her gut into knots. *How do I play this one, then?*

Toby Lloyd-Jones was waiting for them at the bar: a stocky, youngish man in a smart handmade suit. His features were even, with strong chin and piercing eyes, and he had that dark curling hair she'd seen on many Welsh actors. His striking face was coarsened by the sun.

He held out his hand smiling. 'Miss Faye, I've heard all about you. One of the gorgeous Gaiety Girls much admired by my papa. I am so glad you could come today.'

He was not what she was expecting; much older than she'd wish.

They ate a splendid lunch: smoked salmon mousse, *poulet rôti* and good wine in a glittering dining room. Caroline was nervous, looking lovely in her powder-blue dress and jacket with a hat that framed her features to perfection. Someone had helped her choose this outfit and Phoebe could guess who.

'When are you leaving for Egypt? Caroline tells me you are based there.'

'Not exactly sure yet. I represent one of the Delta development companies. We are investing in infrastructure, properties and estates along the Nile. There's such a potential in this growing area. I have been busy making contacts. Cairo is such an amazing site for development. The Suez Canal has made journeys from Europe to the Far East much shorter. Now we have government support.' Toby Lloyd-Jones talked at length about his success, a little too fervently for Phoebe's liking, like a preacher trying to convince you about his new-found faith.

'Do you intend to live out there?'

'For a while, to see things through, of course, I wouldn't want to inflict that sort of climate on my family when the time comes,' he offered, looking at Caroline, who blushed.

So that was the set-up. He looked at her daughter as if he could eat her and she was looking up at him with a bold adoring gaze that filled Phoebe with alarm. What's going on here? What had she missed all these past weeks?

'You're quite right,' she nodded. 'It would be a mistake to burden a wife with such a change in culture and uncertainty, especially in these worrying times. The unrest in northern Spain some say was only a rehearsal for a bigger show to come.'

Caroline glared at her, ignoring her reference to the trouble in Europe. 'When people are in love, it doesn't matter where they live as long as they are together.' She clutched her napkin to her lips. 'Egypt sounds so romantic.'

'I'm sure it is — for a while — but what do the women do while men are at work, sit around in shade and play cards?'

'There's a marvellous Country Club on an island outside Cairo with a swimming pool, tennis courts, dining rooms, amazing parties under the stars,' Toby replied. 'It's really very civilized.'

'But it's a long way from home, weeks on a ship,' Phoebe suggested.

'Ah, now there's talk of a regular air flight with Imperial Airways. The world is shrinking, Miss Faye. That's why these investments are such good value.'

'Are you trying to sell me some, young man?' She forced a laugh.

'Phee!' Caroline whispered under her breath.

'Of course not, Miss Faye. I wouldn't dream of using this occasion. It's just my enthusiasm that carries me away.'

He smiled but she recognized impatience, a flicker of frustration in his half-smile. His eyes were hooded and as he blinked she thought of the falcons she'd seen tethered at Dalradnor Show, and her stomach churned. Caroline was besotted by his charm, but Phoebe felt uneasy. He was direct, polite, but she sensed a steel claw in the leather glove. She'd seen enough of Mr Lloyd-Jones for one afternoon.

'Unfortunately I have to give classes at four. That was a superb luncheon and I'm so pleased to meet you at last. You have given me much to think about, Mr Lloyd-Jones.'

'Toby, please,' he said, rising as she did.'

'All in good time . . . I'm old-fashioned enough not to be on first-name terms so soon. We hardly know each other.' She made a graceful exit off stage left towards the powder room, but Caroline came racing after her.

'How could you be so rude?'

'I wasn't rude, just correct. That man was trying to sell me shares in some tin-pot scheme in the desert.'

'He was not. He just wanted you to know what he's about.'

'And what are you about with him?' she snapped.

'I love him and I want to marry him,' Caroline replied.

'Has he asked you?

'No, but he will soon.'

'Oh, Caroline, you're too young for such a commitment. You don't know anything about him.'

'I know enough to know I can't live without him, and I won't . . .'

'Let's discuss this later. Now's not the time. If he loves you he'll wait until you're of age. You need to broaden your experience of men.'

'You didn't.'

'That was different. There was a war. Everything speeds up in wartime. Do be sensible. I don't want to spoil your first experience, but be careful or it'll end in tears.'

'You're just jealous because I've got what you'll never have. Toby and I love each other and I don't want anyone else.' Caroline spat back at her.

'So I see, but wait, darling, please. People change. There's just something about him . . . I'm not sure about.' She was doing her best but it wasn't working.

'I'm not listening to any more of this.' Caroline marched out of the cloakroom, slamming the door, leaving Phoebe feeling sick. *Why do things always go so wrong between us? How am I ever going to put this right now?*

'Everything fine? You look worried,' said Toby, jumping up. 'Your aunt is quite a woman. I hope I didn't over do things . . .' He paused, searching for her reaction.

'No, she's fine. Let's not talk about her. Did you mean all that about Egypt and the clubs and a wife?'

'Why, are you volunteering?' he smiled.

'If there's a vacancy,' she smiled back, eyeing him as their feet touched under the table and a slow hand lingered around her thigh.

'I'd like to try the applicant out to see if she's up to the mark.'

'Let's go then and I'll give you a demonstration.' Part of her wondered how she could be saying such things, but with Toby there was no holding back. She'd not be going back to face Phee in the studio, all po-faced and stiff-lipped. She didn't want to waste any of their precious time together, not when she had a fail-safe rubber cap ready for any action. What would her mother say if she knew she'd been fitted up in Harley Street by a doctor? They weren't going to take any risks. Toby was careful like that, waiting patiently until she was protected. He'd been so attentive, buying her beautiful lingerie to wear for his eyes only, gorgeous silks, which she kept in his mirrored room at the Cavendish Hotel, making no moves on her until she'd begun to think there was something wrong.

All that biology was useful in school, but could never prepare her for the shock of having such a strong man's body caressing hers and entering her with such finesse and skill that she scarcely felt the loss of her virginity. She couldn't wait to go back to his little room to experiment even more. The thought of being his wife was wonderful. How dare Phee say she didn't trust him? He'd lavished her with gifts, clothes, wined and dined her until she was drunk with desire for his body on hers. Sometimes he came back from work with a bottle of champagne. 'Scored a hit!' he'd laugh. Other times he came back with only a worried frown on his brow. 'Waste of time, couldn't shift the bugger.' That was when he took her roughly, like an animal, in a passionate coupling that left her bruised and exhausted.

He was changing her in ways others noticed. Pamela had remarked that she looked tired. 'Is he working you too hard?' she sniggered. 'We know all about your big romance and we know you've done it with him. It's written all over your face, you naughty girl.' She didn't go out with the girls now, except for their Thursday teas when they caught up on gossip. 'The Welsh Wizard's had his wicked way . . . so watch out. Hardly see you these days. Where's this cave he carries you to?'

Callie was sure they were all jealous but she didn't want to spoil the spell by sharing any details. Now she would have a new exciting life abroad. Ought she to tell him the truth about Phee when he asked about her family? Why should she? He said very little about his. She'd mentioned Sir Lionel a few times, and that they owned a house in the Trossachs and that she had a small allowance until she was twenty-one.

'I'd never ask you for a penny,' he said. 'But some names of friends who might be interested in investments would be useful.' Callie couldn't think of any he didn't already know from the 400 Club. He never asked again.

They left the Ritz and strolled down Jermyn Street to his room at the Cavendish Hotel. At the door he hesitated for a moment. 'You know I'll be off soon – any chance of you coming along for the ride?' He paused. 'We'd have such fun driving through France to Marseilles, and then a ship across the Med, or will you be stuck making tea for your aunts?'

'I'm not sure. I ought to give them notice. One of my aunts is ill.' For all she was angry with Phee, she couldn't just run out on them – or could she?

'Can't hang around long, darling . . . things to do. We'd pick up a car once we're across the Channel. Let's elope so there's none of all that wedding fuss. Come with me next week or we'll have to wait months.'

'It's very tempting,' she smiled, but suddenly she was feeling unsure. It all seemed such a rush.

'Then come inside and let me tempt you. Time for some active persuasion . . . I may have a little trick or two that'll have you gasping for more.' He grabbed her arm firmly and marched her to his room. She couldn't wait to sample the delicious delights he had in store.

Caroline didn't come home that night, or the next. Phoebe was furious, worried sick. Callie had never done such a thing before, and she hadn't even told her mother where she was. Phoebe almost called the police. What if this man was an abductor, or worse? She just knew Toby Lloyd-Jones was a chancer, turning her daughter's silly head. He was taking advantage of a naïve young girl and he'd drop her once he was bored. She'd seen this happen in the theatre when dashing stage-door johnnies courted the chorus girls, promised them the earth and then left them high and dry. If only she could find out more about him and his family, but what with the studio classes and another call to a film casting, she'd no time for investigations just now. Then Caroline came home, defiant, sullen, and Phoebe told her just how worried she'd been. They snapped at each other until Phoebe could stand it no longer.

'Don't you realize you're just his latest plaything? There's only one thing he's after—'

'He wants to marry me,' Caroline interrupted calmly, as if she'd been waiting for just such a moment to pounce.

'Is that what he said to get you into his bed?'

'He didn't need to. I was in it already. Why do you dislike him?'

'There's something phoney about him. I can't just put my finger on it, but I will.'

'Oh, do what you like. You just don't want me to be happy. How can you understand how I feel about him?'

'I think I've got the score. He's just using you, you silly girl. There's more to marriage than sex.'

'How would you know?' Caroline did her usual stomping act into her room. 'I'm going out.'

'I haven't time to argue with you now. If you go out make sure you lock up, and make sure you call in and see Maisie.' There was no reply.

When Phoebe called in at the school later to relieve Kitty's watch at Maisie's bedside, she found everyone gathered there, looking at the doctor with concern.

'It won't be long now. She's weakening by the hour. Her legs are cold. I've given her another draught. You'll want to say your farewells,' he advised.

They took it in turns to sit by Maisie's bed, chatting as if she could hear them. Billy was in tears and Jem had obviously been crying, too. Kitty was being her usual professional self, but her face was white and strained with emotion.

Phoebe recalled how kind Maisie had been when she went into labour in their flat, the day after she heard Arthur had been killed. How her friends had seen her through the darkest of times, holding the baby with her, protecting her secret. Kitty and Maisie were like sisters, the sisters she had never had.

'Did Caroline call in today?' she asked.

'If she did, she didn't come up. Perhaps she'll call in later,' Kitty offered. 'She's always been very fond of Maisie.'

It wasn't like Caroline to neglect her duty, but Caroline wasn't herself any more, Phoebe thought. Still, she'd be sorry not to say goodbye.

Maisie slipped away in the small hours of the night without any fuss, just one lingering breath and then nothing. Kitty did what was necessary, laying her out with loving care as only nurses knew how. They sat in the staff room drinking tea and reminiscing. Billy and Jem drove Phoebe home and she let herself in, not wanting to wake her ungrateful daughter, falling into her own bed fully clothed, sleeping through the morning rush hour noise. It was only when she pulled up the blind that she saw the envelope on her dressing table. Inside was one of her own publicity postcard shots.

Toby and I have decided to marry abroad with or without your consent. I have taken what I need so don't come looking for us. This is best all round. Don't worry I'll send you a postcard from the pyramids.
Callie

Phoebe drifted in shock to Caroline's room. The bed was made, the wardrobe half open, revealing empty hangers. Her leather suitcase was gone, drawers clearly emptied in a hurry, and her passport was missing from the mother-of-pearl-inlay deed box. So this was a defiant elopement, meant to cause maximum hurt. What mother wants to be denied preparations for her own daughter's wedding? Caroline could not have made herself any clearer in disowning her. Perhaps if she'd had more tact and time it could all have been prevented. Now it was too late. Phoebe wondered if the price of her keeping her daughter's birth secret would ever be paid in full. This is what came of not having a father to protect and advise her. She'd made such a mess of parenting alone.

Phoebe sank down weeping on Caroline's cold bed, fingering the silk quilted counterpane with longing. 'Oh, you silly, silly girl,' she cried. 'You'll find yourself lying on a bed of nails before too long. Who will help you then?'

13

The *Marie-Solange* docked in Alexandria, heaving to port as Callie hung over the rail drinking in all the strange sights: the bustle of men in what looked to her like nightshirts, scurrying with ropes; others with baskets, holding out their wares, ready to mob the passengers.

'Here at last,' she cried as Toby put his arm on her shoulder.

'Welcome to the wonders of the Orient, Mrs Lloyd-Jones.'

Callie couldn't believe all that had happened in the past weeks. It was like some exotic dream, fleeing in the dead of night on the overnight ferry to Boulogne, a morning train to Paris and then onwards to Marseilles. There was no leisurely car journey down to the south because poor Toby in his haste had mislaid his driving licence. She hadn't minded their rough sleeping arrangements. Everything was all new and exciting, with Toby charging through France like a bull on the loose. They took cheap rooms by the port until they found a ship and a captain who agreed to marry them for a fee. They bought a gold wedding band and Toby promised to find her a beautiful ring when they got to Cairo.

The ceremony was brief – just a few words in the presence of some staff – and they filled in forms with their full names. Callie was amused to see that her new husband signed as Tobias Obediah Lloyd-Jones. Toby was not amused. 'No kid should be burdened with such handles. Don't ever tell a soul.'

The Med was choppy and she felt sick for half the crossing, lying in their little cabin, holding her stomach. It was not the most glamorous honeymoon but luxury didn't matter when you were in love, she thought, admiring her wedding band. It had given them time together just to make love, to wander the decks looking out towards their new destination.

Now, seeing the harbour alive with porters and ships, carts and passengers, she sighed with pleasure. This was for real and not some dream. There was another long train journey to Cairo ahead. Already she could feel the morning heat searing her face and she went to find her hat with a brim. They had little luggage. What was there to take but clothes and documents?

Soon they were mobbed by street sellers pushing their goods, by porters, by drink sellers. Callie felt a panic at the crush. Scents assaulting her nostrils, flies bombed her face and sweat was trickling down between her breasts. They were guided onto the Cairo train, which was steaming up to depart. The sight of the big black engine was familiar and calming. She could see there was some civilization here: a mixture of old and new, tramways and caravans of camels alongside street cars and donkey carts. Women, head to toe in black coverings, sauntered in the shade, and European girls like herself in short dresses and picture hats walked with parasols.

Toby swatted off the *guli guli* men. 'If you give to beggars and street fakirs, you'll be flooded with them. They don't take no for an answer.'

They sat in a compartment, staring out over a sea of scrub and sand until they reached a greener delta of shrubs and palms, and the beginnings of the road into the city.

'See how the villas are taking over the desert. The garden suburbs are full of potential for development.' He pointed to the sprawl of bungalows shimmering in the desert heat.

'Is this where we'll be living?' Callie asked, assuming Toby had a home waiting to receive her.

''Fraid not . . . just a hotel for the moment, but we'll start house hunting and you can make it just as you wish,' he replied.

Callie smiled, trying to hide her disappointment. They'd been living out of a suitcase for three weeks and all her clothes were filthy and crumpled. This was not how she imagined arriving, but there was plenty of time now to begin a new life here and it was too hot to rush about. A hotel would have a bath and laundry service, and ready dinners. It would give her time to adjust to the heat and city. Living with Toby was not quite what she had expected. He was a restless soul, pacing on deck, writing letters of introduction, chain smoking. He never picked up a book or paper except for the business pages, looking at currency rates and market news. The rest of the headlines he ignored. He was so dedicated to his work, she thought with pride.

They were living off her savings. She drew out every penny she could find from her bank accounts without arousing suspicion. She'd even had to buy the wedding ring as they'd spent too much on expensive meals and rent in Marseilles. Toby promised he would make it up to her when he got back to his office.

'I'm looking forward to meeting your colleagues,' she said.

'I've always worked alone, but I have useful contacts in the city and clubs.'

'So what exactly will you be doing here?' Callie realized she knew very little about his professional life.

'I help people find good investments in properties and land.'

She was puzzled. 'I thought you were in investments like a broker?'

'Oh, I am. I invest in people's dreams to get rich by investing in land abroad with the promise of good returns. I do some buying and selling for other people who don't want others to know how wealthy and interested they are. I get commission for introducing clients to clients, that sort of thing.'

'Is that why you wanted names of my friends?' she asked with not a little concern.

'Sort of. Contacts among the rich and famous are always useful, and if you don't ask you don't get,' he dismissed her question. 'Your crowd was full of good connections.'

'They're not my crowd. I hardly knew most of them,' she said.

'But you were all school chums.'

'Not really. I only met Pam and Clemmie at finishing school. I went to a girls' boarding school near Arbroath. It seems ages and ages ago, another world. I wonder what they think of us running off in the night.'

'I'm sure they think us very romantic. You young girls are all for romance,' he laughed. 'Anyway, who cares what they think? You'll be fine here, a prime asset to me with your looks and charm. I'm sure you'll make lots of girlfriends and get me lots of introductions.' Toby smiled, showing his line of straight teeth. 'Who can resist those pale English rose looks when most of the girls here have skin like leather? People will love you and make me the luckiest man in town.'

Callie thought this a strangely worded compliment. She was more than a business asset, she was his new wife. Sometimes she found his flattering words just a tiny bit false. She shrugged and turned away to stare out of the window, exhausted with the heat and the travelling.

Toby hired a smart gharry, a horse-drawn carriage, so they could drive slowly through Cairo and take in the sights. 'They call it the Paris of the Nile,' he said, pointing out gracious stone buildings with château-like flourishes: banks, theatres, apartment blocks. Callie saw only jams of donkey carts mixed with saloon cars, men running in and out trying to sell them fly swatters and cups of water. There was a pungent sickly smell of toilets, dung and rotten fruit. She felt increasingly frightened at the strangeness of it all. How would she ever make her way in this exotic city?

As if to make up for their unglamorous journey they booked into the smart Continental Hotel and dined most nights either in the roof-top garden or in Shepheard's Hotel. It had a tiled Moorish hall dining room, and here she caught her first glimpse of the wealthy Cairenes, a cosmopolitan group of French, army officers and well-dressed British women and men with loud voices and haughty manners.

'Welcome to your new home, darling. Take a look round. No one here can hold a candle to you. You look so fresh and untarnished.' Toby raised his glass to her and her spirits lifted with the wine and delicious dishes. 'It's going to be a wonderful experience. We'll tour the pyramids on camels' backs, sail down the Nile in a felucca, dance each night at the Gezira Club. I'll take you to the Khan el-Khalili souk. We'll watch the Sufi whirling dervishes. I'm promising you the time of your life.'

All this was ahead of them – their whole lives together – and she smiled, relieved that Toby did love her for herself and not her connections. He wanted her to be happy, knowing that she had fled from everyone she knew to be with him. What must Kitty and Marthe, dear Maisie think of all this? Phee would be furious and embarrassed by their elopement. Prim, Pam and Clemmie would be so jealous. She would send postcards to all of them in due course, but tonight she was just going to relax and soak in the magic that was Egypt.

The house they found to rent was a modern European-style bungalow with a veranda on the sides out of the sun. It had three bedrooms, each with a hook in the ceiling for the mosquito nets that must cover them every night. It was furnished with green bamboo cane furniture and cushions. Hassan came with the property. He would clean and cook, and a man tended all the gardens on the estate. The garden was shady with palms, a fig tree, and lots of dusty green plants Callie couldn't name. Cicadas screeched in the heat and she saw ants on their trail to a corner she must avoid. Hassan warned of snakes coiled in the shrubbery, but there was a hammock where she could lie safely and admire the pale coffee stucco walls and cream paintwork of the wooden shutters. This was her very first home and she was so proud choosing kelim rugs for the tiled floors, soft drapes for their bedroom from Cicurel, the renowned department store, where she also bought cotton lawn to be made up into thin shirts and day dresses. The only disappointment was that Toby never got round to taking her to all the places whose names he'd wafted before her when they first arrived. She didn't venture far on her own. Her French came to good use but she felt unnerved by the vibrant bustle of the streets. The European women she saw in shops and restaurants made her think of London and the Thursday tearoom gossips with a pang of yearning.

She did go to matins in the cathedral, hoping for introductions, but Toby wouldn't step over the door. 'I hate those places,' he said with such venom that she didn't ask why.

One day, returning from a trip into the city, Callie found a letter waiting for her. The handwriting was familiar, and she opened it in trepidation, thinking it would be a reprimand from Phee, but the news it contained took the feet from under her and she ran to the privacy of her bedroom to try to make sense of it all. That evening, Toby found her in tears, lying on their bed.

'Aunt Maisie died on the very night we left and I never went to say goodbye,' she sobbed. 'It was so mean of me.'

Toby picked up the letter in surprise. 'I told you not to send our address to anyone just yet, not until you're more settled. Letters from home only upset you.'

'You'd better read the rest of it,' Callie snapped. 'What does she mean about the Cavendish Hotel?'

'How did your aunt know about that?' he replied.

'Well, she went and met the manager, Miss Lewis. Why didn't you tell me you never paid your bill?'

'How dare she interfere, the nosy old bat . . .?'

'Toby, she's my—' Callie stopped, seeing how angry he was. 'What happened? I'm your wife – you can tell me.'

'It was all just a mistake. I wrote a cheque. I suppose it bounced. I didn't want you to find out.'

'Is that why we had to leave in such a rush? Why didn't you tell me? I could've helped.'

'That's not the way it works, darling. My credit was a bit stretched, not enough commission came through. It's not important now.'

'But it means people know you're in trouble. People talk. We must pay that bill.'

'Oh, don't go on. It was only a temporary blip. I'm fine now, and we've got a house and are all set up to entertain. I've got guests tomorrow night, can you put on a show?'

'Of course,' Callie said, wiping her eyes. 'I'll rustle up something I learned in Belgium.'

'Not mussels and chips, I hope,' he laughed.

'Toby! I mean real French cuisine, but I'll need Hassan to wait on table, and I must have a decent dress. There's nothing in my wardrobe but day dresses.'

'You get what you need. If this goes well we'll be set up. Dress to impress, my darling.'

Next morning, Callie tried to push Phee's letter to the back of her mind. There would be time enough to reply when things were on a sounder footing, and she would insist that the bill be paid from her allowance somehow.

Hassan was sent to the open market for fresh vegetables and spices. Callie took a gharry to Lappas grocery store for the rest of her ingredients and treated herself to fresh flowers. Then she trailed round looking for a suitable frock, but found a silk two-piece pant and loose oriental kaftan top, which she thought daring and very modern. There would be time for a bath and to restyle her hair in a loose chignon with a flower behind her ear while the *poulet aux fines herbes* was simmering. She also bought a delicate *tarte aux pruneaux* from Groppi, the famous patisserie. Countess van Grooten herself would be proud of the dining-table arrangements. It was such fun being a hostess that Callie almost forgot about Toby's cheating on his bill. Phee's letter had 'I told you so' written between the lines.

Her mother wouldn't understand the vagaries of business, the expensive dinners necessary to garner clients. At least now she knew she would keep a good eye on their spending. Tonight was the exception and she looked forward to meeting new couples, making friends and supporting Toby in everything he did to make their life out here a success.

Now everything was ready, the house sparkled, Hassan was wearing a smart new tunic and Callie poured herself the first drink of the evening to steady her nerves. Would they like what she had cooked? She mustn't let her husband down.

She had drunk her gin, and no one had yet arrived. She waited and waited as the clock ticked long past the appointed hour, but still no one came. Her nerves had now been replaced by worry, and she paced the room, wondering what she should do.

Toby was late, very late, and she feared the worst. Eventually, with a rush of relief, she heard his car door slam. There were noises in the hall and in he fell with two very drunk young men, who leered up at her with interest.

'You sly devil, where've you been hiding her away?' said one, eyeing her with interest.

'Darling, sorry we're a bit late . . . took a detour onto a houseboat club . . . just for a snifter. Time just flew by . . . it all smells delicious.'

Callie tried to stay calm; the perfect hostess never shows her fury. 'The casserole is almost dry. Hassan will serve it now before it's ruined.' She pointed to the dining room, trying not to shake. 'Toby, where are the wives?' she whispered. 'I've set for eight . . .'

'Sorry, darling, no wives this time, Ollie and Pinky haven't caught any yet, but I've rich pickings here,' he whispered back. 'Be nice to them, old girl.' His speech was slurred and, when they passed her, Ollie managed to slide his hand down her thigh. Pinky saw the hors d'oeuvres, turned green and dashed for the bathroom to be sick. After that, he sat slumped, unable to eat anything but managed to knock her new china plates onto the tiled floor.

No one ate much nor had any conversation. They sat drinking whisky, then fell asleep on the sofa. Callie couldn't wait to see the back of them as they staggered into a gharry to be taken home in the small hours.

'You told me they were important clients,' Callie said. 'I went to so much trouble and expense. I might as well have just put two whisky bottles in their hands.'

'They've had a good night. I paid for everything and now they've met you they know we are a kosher couple.'

'What were they expecting, a harem?' she snapped, tired and desperately disappointed. 'Even I know about those houseboats on the river front.'

'Look, it's all part of the game. You set the scene, charm the snake out of the basket . . . they're looking for a warehouse site for their import-export business. I know one coming up cheap. It's slowly, slowly, catchee monkey in this game. I'll have their signatures on paper by the end of the week and we'll be quids in, just you see. It'll all have been worth it.'

Only they didn't sign and Toby stormed round the bungalow in a foul mood, slamming doors, sulking like a spoiled child, while Callie worried how she would make her budget stretch to see them through the week. Everything was complicated in the grown-up world of finance. Married women were expected to spend hours alone, which challenged her own endurance to its limit. She must find something to do or she'd go mad in this tiny place in this heat. Toby still hadn't taken her to any British clubs and she wondered if there was a problem. Had he not paid his fees there? She berated herself for the disloyal thought but she felt let down.

Where was all the romance she'd been promised? All she saw were streets full of flies and rubbish, dirt and poverty, barefoot children astride the shoulders of their veiled mothers, beggars, tired donkeys, smelly camels and horses worn out with overwork. How could she keep sending cheery postcards about a pretend life she wasn't living?

Nothing was as she dreamed it would be and, worst of all, the more she lived with Toby, the less she found she really knew about him. What was truth and what were exaggerations? Did he lie to her too? That was what frightened her most of all. She wondered just who she had married.

Just as she began to despair, Toby redeemed his thoughtlessness with an act of contrition. He arrived home with a corsage of orchids and told her to put on her new outfit. 'We're going to the Gezira Club for dinner. Don't say I don't keep my promises. Hassan can have the night off, we'll drive over the Lion bridge and park ourselves in the Country Club, and just in case you'd thought I'd forgotten, here . . .' he smiled, pushing a box into her hand.

Inside was another box, leather, containing a beautiful antique gold ring with large blue stones. 'They're only zircons but they match your eyes, and I know it will fit you.'

Callie gasped with surprise. 'It's so unusual. I can wear it tonight, Oh, thank you.' She kissed him on the lips. 'Can we afford it?'

'Got some commission today . . . Can't have you turning up there with no jewellery, so go and make yourself beautiful. I intend to show you off tonight and I'm feeling lucky . . .'

The Gezira was everything she imagined, set in a park alongside a racecourse and gardens with a golf course and tennis courts, a turquoise-tiled swimming pool and a veranda terrace where ex-pats clinked their glasses by candlelight. The women looked so elegant in their shimmering evening dresses, diamonds at their necks and wrists. There were others in shorter frocks and cocktail hats, and army officers in dress uniform. Waiters weaved their way silently, carrying trays of sparkling crystal glasses.

Callie could not help but be overawed by such a smart ensemble of compatriots. Toby worked the room with slick confidence. 'You must meet my new wife, Caroline, straight off the ship and knowing no one yet.' The women eyed her up and down with interest, smiled and then went back to their conversations, leaving her stranded.

'Don't worry, plenty more to go at. They can be a bit cliquey. You have to understand there's a pecking order in the British community, according to rank, wealth and connections. We have to work our way up, get noticed, play a good hand at bridge or do the church flowers. Everyone knows their place but there are, thank God, a few rebels who don't mind welcoming strangers into their midst. We'll find them by the bar.'

Callie stayed out on the balcony to breathe the night air, admiring the manicured gardens, walls covered with white jasmine and pink oleander, banks of huge orange lilies and blue plumbago flowers dripping from the walls, shimming in the late sun. Some of the groups outside wore funny tubes of gauze on their arms and legs. So that was how they stopped the insects incessantly feasting on their limbs. And this was the famous Club – she sighed – a cloistered cocoon of elegance and comfort, an oasis for the rich and important from the dirty cluttered city. Here foreigners could forget what they passed each day in their taxis. Once through the guarded gates they entered a more familiar world, with safety in numbers.

'You OK?' A very English voice startled her from this reverie. Callie turned to see a striking woman much older than herself, smiling at her. She was wearing a peacock-blue silk dress, which fitted round her full figure, and a gauzy silk stole over her shoulders. Around her neck hung a geometric chunk of gold necklace glinting in the candlelight. 'You look like I did when I first arrived. I'm Monica . . . Monica Battersby.' She held out her hand.

'Caroline, Callie Lloyd-Jones, Toby's wife.'

'Ah, dear Toby, he tries very hard to fit in. How on earth did he persuade you to leave England's green and pleasant land to jump into this pool of piranhas?'

'You don't like the Club?'

'It's fine if you want to ride, or swim, but the women here can be prize bitches. You have to be invited into their circle. Take my advice, keep clear of their coven. It's pathetic seeing them all sucking up to the Ambassador's wife like fifth formers to their Head Girl.'

Callie laughed. 'I don't know anyone yet. It's all a bit daunting.' She sensed Monica was the sort of women who was used to confidences.

'You poor thing. I expect Toby's out all day and night building his empire . . . Kenneth is just as bad. I shall have to take you under my wing. Do you paint?'

Callie shook her head. 'I don't seem to do much – it's too hot – but I love riding.'

'You'll get used to it. You do need to build your own life and interests here or you'll go mad. It's a wonderful world out here, full of life and colour. Perhaps I might help and show you some places? I'm keen on photography and the light here is amazing. Let's meet up again. Have you sampled the delights of Groppi's tearoom yet?'

A tall man was hovering behind her new-found friend. 'Darling, I want you to meet the Padmores . . . Good evening.' He smiled at Callie.

'This is Caroline and she needs some assistance. I'll ring you . . .'

Callie quickly wrote their number down on Monica's calling card before her husband whisked her away.

'Who was that?' Toby arrived late on the scene, staring at the departing couple.

'Monica Battersby, wife of Kenneth Battersby.'

'Not wife, darling, Ken Bromwell's bit on the side, so I've heard. He's got a cheek, but being chief executive of an oil company . . . a useful chap to know. She's quite a looker for her age. You can see the attraction. She must have the hide of a rhinoceros to turn up in this lot.'

'Where's Mrs Bromwell?'

'I forget, you're an innocent about these arrangements. She's in London with the children. It's what happens here if the wives go home . . . only natural.' Toby lit them each a cigarette and smiled. The evening was going well.

'But if a wife goes astray, what then?' Callie was curious.

'That's another matter. There are rules, unwritten, of course. Discretion is one of them. What happens in a marriage is always private. Any peculiar out-of-hours arrangements are never discussed, and unless you are very rich and powerful, you hide your little sidelines out of the public eye.'

A gong rang and they were called into the ballroom for a formal dinner, finding themselves sitting almost out the door with an odd couple in shabby dinner jacket and crumpled dress, who were either very deaf or rude because they ignored them all evening. Callie smiled as Monica waved to her from a discreet corner table. Hers was the only friendly face in the room. How many years did it take to make top table? How many thousand voluntary acts and ingratiations did the acolytes have to submit to before they were honoured with an invitation? I don't care, she thought, feeling smug. I'm young and I have Toby, and that's all that matters. But Monica was right, it was time to take up something for herself. It would fill the empty hours when there was nothing but a bottle of gin for company.

Monica was true to her word and rang her, inviting her to lunch at the Mena House Hotel, horrified that she'd not yet seen the pyramids. 'Pick you up and we'll have a shufti round the tombs. Bring your swimming costume, there's a good pool at the hotel.

They drove out of the city suburbs towards the desert, to the hotel, which sat opposite the world-famous site. It was a strange mixture of Moorish and English architecture but their lunch was super. Monica made Callie pose on the back of a camel to have her photo taken before choosing the best horses to ride over the paths and out into the desert. Callie was struck by the magnificence of the golden slabs pointing to the dusty pink sky, but at her feet all she could see was rubble, rubbish, dung and litter. They bought postcards of the majestic sphinx lying in its pit, its carved features softened by the desert winds.

They swam in the hotel pool then lay on loungers and ate apricot ice creams. The heat was making Callie sleepy. Monica lay in a beautiful multicoloured sarong, her body shaded from the sun. 'Never put your face in the sun or you'll end up with crocodile hide,' she cautioned.

'How long have you been here?' Callie asked.

'Do you mean how did I end up unmarried and someone's mistress? Long enough to fall in love with this mysterious place and become bored. Long enough to find a decent chap. We have an understanding.' She looked up, pulling down her sunglasses to study Callie's reaction. 'You're not shocked?'

'Why should I be? I eloped with Tony after only a few months. We married on board ship.'

'British or foreign?'

'Does it matter? French, I think,' Callie replied, smiling.

'It does if you want it to be legal. Still, I see you've got spark. Is it working out?'

'What do you mean?' Callie went on the defensive.

'Love's young dream in a bungalow in the garden suburbs. How are you coping?'

'We're fine,' Callie said, wafting away the flies, her cheeks flushing. How dare she suggest there might be problems?

'It's just that you don't strike me as the average company wife. Tell me about yourself. How old are you . . .?' Somehow Monica elicited everything without giving much away about herself. 'And you speak Flemish and Belgian French. Good for you. Are you serious about finding something to do? What about the patter of tiny feet?'

'Toby's not keen . . . not yet. Plenty of time. Do you have children?'

'Too late for me now. Ken has a family, almost grown up. My fiancé was killed in the war. I was nursing and found myself out here. When it ended, I couldn't settle. I took a post as a nanny here. That's when I met Ken. It was awkward, of course, but we have an amicable arrangement that works, I hope.'

They swam and then changed for dinner. For once Toby came on time to join them, but Ken was delayed so they drove back to the bungalow for a snifter instead, and Monica promised to return the compliment in her apartment on the island of Zamelek.

'She's a strange one, very bright but a bit closed. Couldn't get anything much out of her,' Toby said.

'I like Monica. She's from Manchester. She's confident in herself and a bit lonely too.'

'Well, what do you expect when the nanny steals the master?' Toby shouted from the bathroom. 'Come to bed, darling.'

'In a minute,' she called, wanting to stretch out her limbs in the cool night air. Monica was kind and interesting, but there was a shell around her that was hard to penetrate, a reserve that protected her from all the social rejection she must receive here. Here was a single woman, a mistress, independent, brittle but not shallow. There was something enigmatic about Monica Battersby that Callie couldn't help admiring. It was so good to have found a friend.

*   *   *

Phoebe looked forward to the postcards from Cairo. She had quite a collection now: the pyramids of Giza, Memphis, sail boats on the Nile, the Tombs of the Caliphs, and the beaches of Alexandria where Caroline decamped in the hot summers with her friend Monica, who, judging by the photo snaps, was not much younger than Phoebe herself.

They were cheery updates, saying little but giving her a picture of her daughter having a gay old time with her husband. Primrose sent a Christmas card saying she received Callie's letters, and so did Marthe in Brussels. Kitty received a lovely letter of condolence about Maisie apologizing for her absence and trying to explain how an elopement saved all the fuss of a wedding.

The incident at the Cavendish Hotel had shocked Phoebe when she found out in a roundabout way through the dance studio. It was Pamela Carluke who'd hinted that Toby had defaulted on his bill. Phoebe felt she must return to the place where she'd known only happiness with Arthur to pay Toby's dues. How could she forget that wonderful little room with the wall mirrors where they had dined after the show and where her own child was conceived? How could she forget the joy of being in Arthur's arms, thinking they had a whole future ahead of them? How strange that it was the very place where Caroline had . . . But she mustn't dwell on such a coincidence. Toby's deceptions had soiled this sacred place for her and she went to meet Rosa Lewis to make amends.

'Let me reimburse you.'

Rose waved her offer away. 'There's no point now, but he'll never cross my door again. Some you win and some you lose. I think his poor wife will find out one of these days. He who is faithful in little is faithful in much, I once read, and I don't think that is this rogue's philosophy, do you? Tell her to watch her bank balance with that chancer.'

These words chilled Phoebe to the core. How could she warn Caroline? Any criticism of her inamorato would be seen a sour grapes. Better to wait and watch but worry in private. Thank goodness she was busy at Elstree and Pinewood Studios, where they were churning out motion pictures. She was in demand for character work; housekeepers, country ladies in tweeds, land-ladies were her speciality roles. She mustn't grumble, but when the door closed each night she felt as if part of her was missing.

London was changing and there were rumours of war. First Italy had invaded Ethiopia, now Spain was at war with itself, and there was worrying news from Germany for her Jewish friends in the theatre, whose families were under threat of persecution. Where would it all end? Hadn't they fought the war to end all wars? All those brave young men sacrificed, and now it might happen all over again if the doom-mongers were to be believed. At least Caroline was safe in Egypt, living the life of Riley. Perhaps there'd be news of a baby, though she'd never see it unless she took a long trip out. However, not once had she been invited.

That first fury with her daughter hadn't lasted long once the shock had faded. She was just sad that Caroline was so naïve as to choose the first dashing man who showed an interest in her, one whom she'd heard had a poor reputation with girls. Did she realize she was marrying an unreliable cheat? It was so hard to sit and watch someone you love fall into a trap of her own making. She worried that all this was her fault for being reticent about her past. Callie had seen Ted more recently than Phoebe had herself, and look what misunderstanding had come of being secretive then. If only she had held up Arthur as an example of bravery and sacrifice, a man of gentlemanly virtues, then perhaps Caroline would have had a better example to follow. Her own silence was to blame for this.

Now the poor girl would have to learn the hard way, would be hurt and disillusioned. It was path everyone took at some time in their life. It was the nails along that pathway that made us stronger in the end, so they said. Phoebe was not sure. She must trust to Providence to guide her daughter from harm.

14

Callie sat out on the veranda of the beach cabin, admiring the long curved golden beach of Sidi Bishr, and eyeing the box of pastries from Bandriot's café with lust. She was spending her vacation with Monica and Ken while Toby was travelling to Palestine to meet clients. It was high summer and Alexandria was the coolest place on the coast. She loved Ken's summer villa, with its shady palms and lush gardens, a far cry from her own modest bungalow.

Alexandria looked so different here from the port where they first arrived two years ago. It was teeming with holidaymakers of all nationalities, always a cosmopolitan crowd on the promenade: Greeks, Lebanese, Maltese, French, as well the British families who rented beach huts for the summer, their children digging sandcastles with their nursemaids. The scene reminded her of Dalradnor summers with Marthe, except there they were without the flies. 'Not true,' she thought, remembering the Scottish pests called midges.

Monica was bringing back friends for drinks while Callie was lazing with the latest novel from England, which Primrose had said she must read, though she was finding it heavy-going. This was two weeks away from the office, but it was too hot to do anything but drink sherbet and take siestas.

She'd found a temporary position filling in for a girl who had returned to England for a family bereavement. Jarrolds was a small company providing candidates for other clerical positions in the city. Applications arrived from all over Europe and Callie's language skills came in useful. There was nothing taxing about sifting through applications and arranging interviews, but it was useful to be picking up typing skills and getting to know the business quarter of the city, too. It was something to get her up in the morning, especially when Toby was away, and it gave her a little salary to augment their dwindling funds. She could never understand how their money disappeared. Toby's income seemed to be either famine or feast, and when it was feast it all vanished to pay for the famine debts.

Money was something they argued over constantly. He never wanted to pay bills on time while she insisted they did, reminding him of the Cavendish Hotel debt, which made him sulk and slam the door. Then he'd refuse to sleep with her, saying he was too hot, and he'd sleep out on the veranda. The passion of that first year had cooled into a worrying indifference in the second, an avoidance of closeness that hurt her more than she wanted to admit. It was as if she was now part of the furniture, invisible unless needed, and once or twice she suspected that when he'd stayed out all night he had not been alone. It was as if they no longer had much to share.

Coming away with Monica was a lifeline, just the tonic Callie needed. Her friend had filled so many gaps in her life. They went shopping in the souks to buys silks, cottons and linens, and finished off with tea somewhere. Monica helped her find a good hairdresser, who chopped off her hair and pressed it close to her head in the latest fashion. They also found a good tailor who made up her office suits in cool linens, and Monica led their days out exploring the Nile delta. Monica encouraged her to keep up her French, to read more demanding books and poetry, and to listen to serious music. If she sensed Callie's unhappiness she said nothing.

Now Monica was walking down the beach with the group she'd gathered up. 'Caroline, I want you to meet my good friends Sebastien and his wife, Yvette, and little Elise.'

Callie looked up to see a smart young couple in shorts and sunhats, with a darling baby in a white lawn sundress and bonnet, who was pointing at the sea. 'And they've brought along their friend and colleague, Ferrand . . .'

Callie turned to him with surprise. She would recognize that strong face anywhere.

'Ferrand?' she gasped

'*Caroline, c'est incroyable!* This is amazing.' He turned to the others. 'It is a small world, *n'est-ce pas?*'

'I can't believe this. What are you doing here?' she laughed. He looked so different from how he'd been in her château days, with his nut-brown arms in a silk shirt and linen shorts. '*Incroyable!*'

'I'm on the run . . . just a poor school teacher,' he replied, his eyes sparkling.

Sebastien shook his head to intervene. 'Don't listen to him, he's far too modest. He's at the university writing a study of Rubens and Van Dyck, and teaching Renaissance art.'

Between them they demolished the cakes, and then the family went to play by the shore with their baby and returned later with delicious pistachio ice creams, before they all made for the villa, sun-kissed and ready for a siesta. En route they discussed the new Germany and news of pogroms against the Jewish communities.

'It's not looking good in Europe now. My parents are in commerce in Paris. I don't like to hear such things,' said Yvette, clutching Elise to her.

'It won't come to that, surely, not after the last war. My brother Jean-Luc and his army are well trained,' said Ferrand, who kept staring at Callie.

'It's not the training. It's about equipment and armaments,' Monica answered. 'None of us is prepared in the way that

Germany is. They are developing sophisticated weapons, Ken tells me, and they'll want oil, and that means Libya and the Persian oilfields, so we'd better watch out here, too. No one will be safe if they go up in flames.'

That evening they talked late into the night, clinking glasses by soft lamplight. Callie couldn't take her eyes off Ferrand's face. It was alive with interest, animated when he argued his point, his hands waving in the air. How he had changed in the past years. His features were fuller, more mature, but he had that same unruly dark hair worn long onto his shirt collar. When he turned to watch her she sensed his eyes piercing into her, as if he thought her opinion mattered. How different he was from Toby.

The others drifted back into the villa while Callie and Ferrand sat on the steps, smoking, watching the moths fluttering to the lights as music came floating through the door, a familiar ballad from the 400 Club era that filled Callie with nostalgia, 'Begin the Beguine'.

She found herself swaying to the rhythm.

'Like to dance?' he said. 'It's too good a tune to waste.'

Callie stood up slowly and walked down onto the terrace, knowing she should refuse but knowing she would not . . . They melted into each other's curves, dancing as the melody lent its own magic to the night under the stars.

He was taller than she recalled, but his effect on her was just the same when he smiled down on her with such intense serious eyes.

'This is how it happens in books, isn't it?' he whispered. 'Just one look, a spark . . . Do you think it's written in the stars that we should meet again like this, or am I too drunk to know what I am saying to you? Please forgive me, Caroline . . .'

'Callie, Callie to my friends.' What was happening? He was right, it must be the music and the wine and the heat. She turned her face up to his and their lips met. It was so simple, one look, one dance and their love affair was about to begin all over again.

* * *

'I saw what happened between you two the moment your eyes met it recognition,' laughed Monica as they sipped their morning coffee.

'I can't believe I did that,' Callie confessed. 'It was like a spell.'

'It's called a *coup de foudre* . . . the lightning flash, a bolt out of the blue, a dangerous exhilarating moment of recognition. Here is the one, the one I've been waiting for, the love of my life.'

'Don't be silly. I'm married. I don't believe in such things. We first met when I was a kid. I must be tired, and Toby and I are just a bit humdrum together. Perhaps I'm bored. Time to go home and be a proper wife.' She didn't want to think about returning home but she knew she must.

'It won't make any difference. It's happened and there's no pretending you weren't both smitten by the sight of each other. Your passion ignited, lit up in neon lights for all of us to see.' Monica said. 'It's the night, the stars and the siren song of the desert . . .' She was mocking her.

'No, no, it's just too much sun and wine, just a summer flirtation for a bored housewife, far too indulgent to contemplate.'

'Plenty people out here have flings, indulge their passions . . . It can happen.' Monica smiled wistfully.

'Oh, Monica, I didn't mean you and Ken. I'm sorry.'

'Callie, we're older, had our moments and seen it all before. We're comfortable with our arrangement; that yearning stage is long past. Those early months of lust don't last; nothing lasts, it just evolves into something softer and more permanent, if you are lucky.'

'I won't betray my husband with another man. Anyway, it won't come to that. I must leave tomorrow; my holiday is over.'

'Running away solves nothing. What will be, will be. If you were truly satisfied in your marriage you might notice Ferrand but look away and forget him,' Monica smiled, giving her some Northern home truth she didn't want to hear.

'It was that music. The beguine is so seductive – the words, everything, conspired against us. Is he married?'

'Didn't you even ask?' Monica roared with laughter. 'There you go, both of you drunk with desire. Sebastien and Yvette were very amused.'

'Did you all plan this?' Callie accused.

'Of course not, he just tagged along with them. I couldn't tell him to go away, now, could I?

'Oh, Monica, what am I going to do?' Callie cried, feeling out of her depth by the strength of these emotions and arguments.

'You do nothing, you wait and see what the Fates have in store. You are now in their power, I'm afraid, in the lap of the Gods.'

'Don't say that, it sounds like some Greek tragedy. I'm going for a walk along the beach to clear my head.' She jumped up, wanting to get as far away as she could from this conversation.

'Dear Callie, calm down. Let it be . . . What's coming for you will not pass you by, so you might as well enjoy it while it lasts.'

On the way back to Cairo, Callie sat bolt upright in the carriage, desperate for things to be normal. To be safe home and yet dreading the moment she'd open the door to the sameness of it all. She didn't feel normal, not with this fire inside. How could she face Toby again and he not recognize her treachery? The holiday in Alexandria had turned her skin golden, her hair was bleached with the sun and her body toned with swimming and riding. Now she must return to Jarrolds' office and keep busy, and not allow herself to think of Ferrand working somewhere in the university close by. After all, there had been only one brief kiss, and it was fortunate that he'd arrived at the very end of her holiday, not at the beginning.

Perhaps Monica was right. Perhaps it was only a little flirtation on a starry night with an old lover, she excused herself. How could you fall in love again at one glance? Perhaps she was trying to recapture that first kiss of all those years ago. It was madness, and hadn't Toby swept her off her feet the first time they met too? She'd seen too many romantic movies. The problem was that she and Toby were stuck in a constant stalemate of coming and going, never really spending time together, never sharing or entertaining mutual friends. He had his business cronies and she had Monica and letters from home.

How pathetic she was being, imagining this was some grand passion. It was just a sign that there wasn't enough in her life to occupy her racing mind. She needed a challenge, a new venture, and she knew what just might fill the yawning gap between them.

When Callie arrived back home, Toby was sitting on the veranda smiling, and she flung her arms round him in relief. 'I've missed you . . . oh, how I've missed us,' she cried.

He almost fell back in surprise. 'What's this, what's this . . . it's only been two weeks. What are you after? Dinner in the Continental or a new dress? I've loads to tell you.'

'Did your trip go well? You never wrote or rang,' she scolded.

'Too busy now I'm going to open an office in Haifa.'

'This is news! Do we have to move, then?' she replied with a surge of relief. Perhaps this was the solution to everything.

'No, nothing like that, but I'll be on the road. I've bought a new car. Come and look. Wait till you see its open-top roof, perfect for those long desert roads.'

Callie went cold. 'Does that mean you'll be staying out there?'

'Don't worry, I'll come back when I can. Got to get things up and going. Arabs can be such slackers if there's no one cracking the whip.'

'So you're taking on staff? I could help, too,' she offered. If they worked together she might understand his business better.

'You stay here by the telephone, my eyes and ears in Cairo . . . come and see my new baby.'

Callie was dragged round to the back of the house to admire a sleek American roadster painted olive green, with a canvas roof. 'This looks expensive.' She sighed.

'Only the best. Got to look the part. It gives customers confidence when I turn up with this little honey.'

'It's very nice,' she lied, feeling sick at how much he must have spent on the purchase.

'Nice! Is that all you can say?' Toby snapped. They walked back indoors in silence.

'I'm going to miss you . . . and talking of babies . . .' She paused to gather herself to seize the moment. 'Don't you think it's time we had one of our own? It would be company for me if you're going to be away so much.'

'All in good time. You know how I feel about other folk's brats . . . not sure I could cope with one of my own.'

'But I'd be the one looking after it,' she continued, knowing it was now or never to have this discussion.

'And I'd have to fund the nurses and school fees and all that stuff.'

'Are you saying you don't want children ever?' She felt suddenly cold, not wanting to hear his reply.

'Now don't start going all broody on me. How can we make babies if I'm away?' he laughed, completely failing to read her desperation.

'I could come to Haifa with you, make trips for two instead of one,' she smiled, knowing they would then have to sleep together.

'Wouldn't work. I work alone, always have. Anyway, you knew my feelings on the matter from the start.' Toby poured himself a drink. 'Want one?'

Callie shook her head, suddenly flattened. 'I thought you'd change your mind. I thought children were a natural part of a marriage,' she offered.

'Not in my book. Smelly nappies, puking, sour milk stains, screaming in the night – not my ideas of fun.'

It was the reply she dreaded, but she was too shocked to protest further. A stone weight landed heavy on her heart as she realized Toby meant what he said. He was a spoiled selfish brat who did what he wanted without consulting her. And he liked life as it was. Why had she been so blind to his self-centred world? As he sat there, slouched on the sofa, she saw him through a clear lens for the first time. To save this marriage the choices were grim. She must accept his decision and either live with it or walk way. Persuading him to see her point of view was not going to happen. She sat paralysed with disappointment.

'Now don't go all quiet on me, darling. I'll take you out tonight to celebrate your return.'

'No, thank you. Let's just stay in for a change and make the most of our time together while we can.' She smiled, but it was a bitter smile filled with shock and uncertainty. It was as if they were now waving at each other from opposite banks of a river, which had suddenly risen up to divide them. There was no bridge in sight.

Dear Marthe

I hardly know how to write this, but you of all people will look on my words with forgiveness. I came to Cairo with such hopes of happiness with Toby, but now I have fallen in love with a wonderful man who is everything my husband is not: cultured, gentle and very clever. He is Belgian, would you believe, the very young man I first met all those years ago, and now I feel as if I've known him all my life.

My husband works away. He is always busy making and losing money. He doesn't want us to have children. He hates them. I have tried to change his mind but he is adamant and I feel so cheated, so lonely and so desperate. My new love fills the empty space in my heart. We met again by chance. I didn't intend to betray my vows, such as they were – made not before God in a church but on board ship – but I cannot live a lie.

Ferrand lectures in the university and I have work in the city. He sought me out through friends to renew our friendship and we have found a rendezvous in a quiet tearoom where we can lunch in private. Then we go back to his apartment for siesta time. I have such peace when I am with him. My French is improving by the hour.

I know you will be disappointed in me. For you there is no ending to a marriage, and it is for the procreation of children. Toby has always insisted we take precautions to prevent this natural process so our loving times have gradually faded away to nothing. I fear he finds comfort elsewhere.

I came to the city with such expectations. After three years, I do not feel that anything much has been achieved by my being here. Believe me, I have tried to make it work but our house is not a home, just a joyless residence. I feel so ashamed to have failed, but it takes two to make a marriage work and I fear Toby has been tired of the bonds of wedlock for some time. He acts like the bachelor he's always been.

I don't understand why this is so but I suspect it is something to do with his upbringing in Wales. In all the time we have been here, he's not had so much as a Christmas card from his family, and when I ask him about them, the only answer I get is: 'The past is my business and it's passed.' What I to do? I feel so torn. Do I abandon my new chance of happiness and stay in a loveless marriage, or do I burn my anchored boat and sail off to be with Ferrand? Divorce is such an ugly word.

Please write and tell me what to do. I can't ask my mother. She did warn me I was making a big mistake and now I know how right she was. Perhaps it's better that I walk away and return home for a while to think things through but I no longer know where home is.

Your loving desperate friend,
Callie

15

The lovers were lying in bed in Ferrand's apartment on the Isle of Zamalek. His room had high ceilings with a fan whirring the air, tall bookshelves filled with art books, interesting ornaments, copper bowls and ancient artefacts. The shutters were closed against the world as Ferrand rested his arm on the pillow, gazing down at Callie.

'I'll never get used to this. Each time is so special, so very natural. I wish you wouldn't get dressed and go back. What is there to go back to but an empty house?'

'Because I must, just in case Toby returns unexpectedly.'

'It's weeks since you last saw him. He doesn't deserve you.'

'He's my husband and I owe him some loyalty.'

'You owe him nothing, not now. You were too young when you married him; people grow apart. It happens.' He kissed her lips as if to make the point, but Callie was not convinced.

'I feel as old as Methuselah sometimes, weary of all this hiding away, but Toby told me discretion is everything. I owe him that at least.'

'So why does he live in Haifa and not invite you to join him? I want us to be together. My contract here ends soon and I'm not sure I want to renew it. Maman has not been well. Jean-Luc is busy and Karel is a priest. Things are hotting up back home, I fear. It's time to go back and I want you to come with me, Callie.'

'That's impossible. Your mother would never accept me. A divorced English Protestant for her son? Never!'

'You are not marrying my mother. She will learn to love you as I do. I'll not rush you, but perhaps our time in Cairo has come to its natural end. It has served its purpose in bringing us here to find each other again. I still can't believe what luck that was.' Ferrand smiled his mischievous warm smile, which melted Callie's resolve and left her wanting more of him every day.

'I must do this correctly,' she said. She must discuss everything with Toby in private when he was sober and then see a lawyer about a permanent separation. People kept up appearances here; discretion was everything. 'I hope only Monica knows about us.'

'If you believe that . . .' he sighed. 'This is a small village, *ma chérie*. Everyone knows everything. Servants talk, gossip fuels more gossip . . . but that shouldn't concern us. We have to be together. Life is too short to live apart. Who knows what is round the corner if Germany starts marching west?' He kissed her again, pushing her back down, but Callie rolled away.

'I have to go. I love you so much. I thought I loved Toby but that was just a rehearsal for this wondrous thing.' She dressed hurriedly and made for the door. 'I don't think I could've survived this past year without being with you every afternoon. There has to be a way out with dignity and mutual consent. Can't think how . . . but I'm going to try.'

That was the trouble. Toby was seldom there to discuss anything, and when he was he was tiddly, restless, wanting them to go out in his sports car to the Gezira. It was the last place she felt comfortable. Monica and Ken were camping out in the desert, taking photographs of Nomadic tribes. They did so much together. The only time Callie arranged for her and Toby to sail up the Nile on a cruise, Toby got a bout of sandfly fever and was in hospital for two weeks, furious with her for messing up his schedules.

*   *   *

When Callie returned to the bungalow, Hassan was waiting on the veranda, wringing his hands. 'Madam, you have visitors. They are police, I think.'

She rushed into the drawing room where two men in linen suits stood up. 'Mrs Lloyd-Jones? Sorry to trouble you. We're from the British Legation.'

'What's wrong? Is it Toby . . . an accident?' She felt weak and sat down.

'Nothing like that, just an enquiry. When will Mr Tobias Jones return from work?'

'I'm not sure. He's in Haifa. He never lets me know till the last minute,' she said, puzzled by the formal use of his name. 'Can I help you? Do sit down. Hassan will bring some tea.' She summoned the servant and gave him orders, trying not to shake.

'There are certain legal matters we need to discuss with your husband, matters outstanding.'

'Has he not being paying his taxes . . .? He is very forgetful,' she said apologetically.

'No, it's a question of the legality of certain documents. Our clients have made complaints. They handed over sums for the purchase of shares in the Delta Property Development Company and nothing has been forthcoming. They've rung the offices to no avail, and now we find those offices have been vacated with no forwarding address.'

'I don't understand. Toby said he was opening a second office in Haifa and you say he's closed the Cairo one? I don't understand.' Callie's hands were shaking as she tried to pour the tea.

'There is a suspicion that he has taken money from clients and so far they have received no confirmation of the purchase of shares. Furthermore, the land said to be developed has, according to our inquiries, no permissions for any development.'

'You mean that he's defrauded them?'

'I'm afraid so, Mrs Jones. You do have your husband's contact address in Haifa?'

'No. He told me he was working from hotels until he found somewhere permanent. He usually rings me from hotels.' Suddenly, Callie felt their eyes were sharply fixed on her, staring at her with suspicion. 'I know it sound irregular but he's always been on the move and I've had no reason not to trust him.' Her heart was hammering now. Did they think she was involved? They must be wondering how a wife could not know where her husband worked.

'You do realize there is no registered office for his company? Mr Jones has a lot of explaining to do. Are you part of his business enterprise too?'

Callie shook her head. She must think clearly. 'He's never involved me in anything. I'm as mystified as you are. He's never allowed me to help in his paper work. I had a part-time post with Jarrolds recruitment offices until recently.'

'Did you ever wonder where all your husband's moneys came from?'

'Well, none of it came here, as you can see.' She gestured with annoyance. 'This is a rented furnished property; the other furnishings I bought myself. I've always kept to a tight budget. There is no money. Though he did buy a big car . . . behind my back, as it happens.'

'Do you have moneys of your own, Mrs Jones?'

'Only in England: a trust from my late father . . .'

'And you've never signed anything over to Mr Jones?'

'No . . .' She paused as a terrible sinking realization struck her. 'There was a form recently he asked me to sign. I never really read through it. He said it was just a tax form. You don't think—'

'How long have you been married?'

'Over three years,' she croaked, her throat tight with the tension mounting.

'And you have family here to vouch for you?'

'We have no children. My family is in London. You might as well know I eloped with Toby against their wishes. I've never met one relation of his. They have an estate somewhere in mid-Wales, I think.'

'Is that what he told you? Interesting . . . From our records we find that his father is the Reverend Obediah Jones, a Baptist preacher in Cardiff. His family disowned him after he stole his mother's jewellery and ran away from his boarding school with the under matron.'

Callie sat back in shock. 'It's all lies then?' she cried. 'Everything he's told me is lies?'

'I'm afraid so. We have reason to believe that your husband got wind of the complaints and has headed from Palestine, maybe to Istanbul on a false passport. I'm sorry to bring this to your attention. We had to check just how you stood in all this. I would advise you to find someone to represent you, should clients make a claim on your estate. These are serious allegations: obtaining money by deception, forging signatures, issuing false documents – clever stuff but criminal offences.'

'I don't know what to say. I've not heard from Toby for two weeks but that's not unusual. Our marriage has not been working for some time. I was going to ask for a separation but this . . . Will he be caught? How could he do these things and leave me to carry . . .? Forgive me.' Callie began to shake with shock.

'Is there anyone who can stay with you?'

Callie nodded. 'I have friends. What must I do now?'

'Do nothing. We will keep you informed. There will be statements to make to the police, and further investigations. I don't suppose you have any of your husband's bank statements?'

She shook her head, knowing Toby always kept those in a locked portfolio case separate from their own account. 'I can give you ours,' she offered, 'but there's nothing much in there. I can't believe he'd do this to me. I trusted him implicitly with everything to do with our moneys.' A cold fear clutched her. 'Do you think he forged my signature too? He wouldn't steal from his own wife, would he?'

'You must check immediately with your lawyers in London. I'm afraid men with no consciences do very strange things when cornered, Mrs Jones.'

When they left she collapsed on her bed, exhausted. It all made sense now. He'd milked cash cows in London, had brought her to Cairo as a screen and had now moved on to Palestine. He wanted no ties or a wife who was no longer useful to him. Had he stolen her father's funds and left her penniless? Angry clients would demand justice for their losses. The marriage she'd thought was crumbling now lay in total ruins before her. Toby was a confidence trickster preying on the gullible and those who wanted to get rich quick with his tempting schemes. Now he'd vanished, leaving her under suspicion too.

She phoned Monica, who came to comfort her, plying her with gin and putting her to bed. 'Sleep it off. This will pass. You are free now to be with Ferrand.'

'You jest,' Callie cried. 'How can I be free with all this round my neck? Someone has to make amends.'

'You are as much a victim as they are. Ferrand will come for you. You can put all this behind you. Toby's done you a favour, set you free.' Monica patted her hand. 'It will all look better in the morning. Go to sleep . . .'

It felt even worse in the morning. If only the solution was as simple as disappearing with her lover into the sunset, leaving behind all the chaos and disgrace. It may not mean much but she was still Toby's wife and she had her pride. She would not go to another man to be rescued. She'd see this through, no matter what it cost. Only when she'd made amends and taken responsibility for her own laziness and stupidity would she be free to join Ferrand. This was the time to stand on her own feet for once and face what must be faced. Only then would she deserve some happiness of her own.

*   *   *

Three weeks later, Callie stood waving from the deck of SS *Otranto*, watching until her friends were just specks on the shore. In the whirlwind of the past days she'd faced angry interviews with irate businessmen, convinced she must have known about Toby's activities. Monica's partner, Ken, guided her through the maelstrom of accusations, alongside a good lawyer, who proved Callie's innocence and suggested she left for Britain on the next ship and put it all down to experience. They even helped her buy a ticket.

Ferrand's contract was up and he wanted to go with her, but she was adamant she wanted to return alone. They would meet up as a soon as she felt she could face him again, she promised.

Of Toby there was not a word. He'd vanished into the Levant, along with his assets, under a new name. By now she was glad he'd forced the issue, removing himself from her life so she owed him nothing. All that was left was the humiliation and the exhaustion of this emotional nightmare. She hoped the sea voyage would give her time to compose herself, to regain her appetite and find some strength to face Phee's disappointment when she turned up on her doorstep.

In those terrible days of questions and accusations, seeing the rage on victims' faces, she had stared down at the Nile wondering if she should end it all in the water's inviting murkiness. She could wade in with her pockets full of pebbles and just sink into oblivion. *What have I done with my life but mess it up?* she asked herself. But in those moments of despair she could feel the warmth of Ferrand's love, holding her together, preserving her sanity.

Her friends wouldn't understand. Primrose had got a first-class degree at Oxford. She was set for success. Even Pamela was modelling for a couturier. But Callie had nothing to show them but a failed marriage and an empty purse. There were a few treasures she'd packed away. It was hard to recall how they had arrived in Cairo with just a suitcase between them, love's young dream, full of hopes, and now she was leaving with a trunk full of broken dreams. She'd sold Toby's ring. She wanted no part in his ill–gotten gains.

Ferrand had been wonderful, trying to tempt her out into the city for a farewell supper under the cool night sky, but she hadn't felt able to face public scrutiny.

'You've nothing to be ashamed of,' he'd soothed her.

'Haven't I? I've let myself and others down. Why didn't I question him more, be suspicious and take more interest in our affairs?'

'Stop beating yourself round the head. You trusted him and he wasn't worthy of your trust. Come here, let me put a smile back on your face.' He'd opened his arms to her. 'Mistakes are the great turning points in our lives; like pearls, they're to be cherished. They're what make us stronger if we learn from them. We all have to make them. Let's not waste your last night with sad talk. We'll look to the future together. You can still change your ticket and stay with me here,' he'd offered.

Dear kind Ferrand, Monica and Ken, what good friends they had been, supporting her in her distress. She must prove herself worthy of their trust.

Callie had clung to her lover on that last night, making love until dawn, pressing herself into his body as if to make an imprint of it on herself for the lonely nights ahead.

Now, as the sea breeze chilled her cheeks, she faced her return journey with resignation and not a little fear and defiance. You made the bed, she sighed, and you must lie thereon.

She dined each night alone, not wishing to join in the jollities on board. There was a couple she recognized from the Gezira Club, who kept staring at her with interest, so she kept to her cabin after that, composing what she would say to Phee.

The sea was choppy in the Bay of Biscay and her stomach heaved as the ship rolled. The air suddenly felt damp and chilly, and the change of climate made her shiver. How eagerly she'd fled British soil and now she needed it for refuge. It was not the homecoming she ever imagined, and yet . . .

As the ship glided into Southampton water, there was a glimmer of change within her, a sneaking suspicion that perhaps she might not be returning alone, an awareness of an absence, strange sensations in her body, a queasiness even though she generally had good sea legs. She searched her diary for confirmation. Could it possibly be true that hope lay within? Could a new life be growing amidst all the chaos of the past months? Could it be in her darkest hour there was dawning promise of hope? If so, then she must make a decision for them both. There was a telegram to send to prepare Phee and break the silence between them.

'ARRIVING SOUTHAMPTON TOMORROW. BED FOR THE NIGHT PLEASE. HEADING FOR DALRADNOR. CAROLINE. PS. YOU WERE RIGHT.'

16

Phoebe packed as soon as the telegram arrived saying Caroline's
baby was on its way. She cancelled her appointments and made
for the first train north. She'd begged her to stay in London for
the confinement, close by in case of complications. Kitty told
her to stop fussing, that her daughter was the epitome of rude
health, and the fresh air of Dalradnor was much better for baby
than the city smoke.

'But what if anything goes wrong?'

'Scottish hospitals and doctors are some of the finest in the
world. Just go and don't interfere, woman!' Kitty shooed her on
her way.

All through the long journey Phoebe couldn't concentrate
on her novel. I have got to get it right this time, she reminded
herself, praying poor Caroline would not suffer too much. Her
own birth had been quick and straightforward. Perhaps it was
something mothers passed on. If she couldn't bear Callie's pain
herself, she would at least be there to encourage her in labour.

It was the longest journey of her life. At each stop or delay she
paced the corridor. She hoped her daughter had booked a decent
midwife in the nursing home she'd chosen on the outskirts of
Glasgow. Ever since her unexpected return, Phoebe had sensed
a deep sadness in her eyes and manner. There was only half a

story forthcoming from her so far: how Toby had absconded with other people's funds, leaving her to face the music and prove her innocence in his affairs, and leaving her pregnant to boot. Now, Callie had only one wish: to find somewhere to pick up the pieces of her broken life. Phoebe admired the dignity with which she went about her affairs, returning to Benson and Harlow, her solicitors, to assess Toby's damage to their finances. It was better than they'd expected, mainly because Arthur's trust were still untouched and must include Phoebe's agreement in any draw on his estate. Now she was of age, it was time to make sure Caroline was provided for. Dalradnor would one day be hers. It was key that she had a base in these uncertain times. Anyone who picked up a paper sensed it was only a matter of time before Herr Hitler would want to push westwards, and Britain and her allies would have to respond. Preparations for war, halted after the Munich crisis last year, were now back in evidence. They were building air-raid shelters in every street so perhaps London was not the best place for a baby.

After twenty years of a sort of peace, would she be asked to start up concert parties all over again, Phoebe wondered. Of course she'd do her bit, but not at the cost of her family's needs. If Caroline asked for her help, she must be there, and do it properly this time.

As they drew closer to Glasgow, her heart lifted. This could be a fresh start for both of them. She'd tried hard not to ask too many questions or to say, 'I told you so.' One look at Caroline's thin body and tired eyes and she sensed she'd suffered enough. It was a pity that Toby's child would always be there to remind her of the mistake, but how can you put blame on a baby for its father's failings and bad nature? He or she would be Phoebe's first grandchild and carry some of Arthur within too.

Sir Lionel was pleased to hear the news. He was resting in a nursing home, confined to a wheelchair after a stroke, but proving himself a friend to Caroline as always. There was

Primrose, too, a reliable presence somewhere in the background with her placid common sense. There were good friends in Egypt, judging by the letters waiting for Callie's arrival home: Monica Battersby, and a nice-sounding professor called Ferrand whose letters put a smile on her face and a blush to her cheeks. He had invited her to stay near Brussels but she wouldn't budge from Dalradnor once she was settled back among the hills. She'd made good allies just as Phoebe had done with Kitty, Maisie and Billy over the years. Even Verity Seton-Ross was no longer hostile after that incident in Scotland. It was a sign of a good heart and warmth to keep friendships in good order. Perhaps that was something she herself could take a little credit for . . .

By the time she arrived at the house, Mima Johnstone, Nan's daughter, had supper ready.

'No news yet, Miss Faye, but I don't think it will be long. The Home promised to ring us as soon as it's born. She'll do fine, so no worries . . .'

It was an endless sleepless night, pacing the floor, begging the phone to ring. Phoebe relived each stage of her own labour and her heart raced with panic: what if . . . what if . . .?

It was dawn when the phone rang and she raced down the stairs barefoot, her hands shaking as she lifted the earpiece.

'Dr Maclean. Just to let you know, all's well that ends well. Wee bitty struggle but the baby's out and fine . . . A boy, "a wee scoot", as the midwives call the boys. Eight pounds five ounces, looking like a fine rugby prop in the making.'

'And Caroline?'

'Tired but smiling. It wasn't the easiest of births so she'll need to rest here for a couple of weeks.'

'When can I see them?' Phoebe wanted to jump round the hall in excitement.

'Perhaps tomorrow evening. I've knocked her out now to give her some rest.'

'Oh, thank you,' Phoebe replied, replacing the receiver. Then she sank down on the step, crying with relief.

I have a grandson, she smiled, and began to make lists of suitable names, only half listening to the morning wireless broadcast, which mentioned something about German troops marching into the Sudetenland in Czechoslovakia.

Caroline kept looking to the crib with astonishment and wonder. How could that pink chubby-faced new person have come out of her body so perfectly formed? 'You are my son, my gorgeous boy,' she whispered, wanting to nuzzle him, smell the newness of him, but Nurse Hislop was having none of this spoiling.

'Time for baby to sleep off his long journey. He took his time and you've got the stitches to prove it. He'll wake when you have enough milk to satisfy him. Nature knows best.'

Why did they have to be separated, she sighed. If he were her foal, she'd be licking him and suckling by now. It was relief to have it all over and done with. If only Ferrand could see the result of their loving. But that couldn't be, not for a long time . . .

As far as everyone was concerned this was Toby's son, born in wedlock. Thank God she had a wedding band on her finger. What Phee didn't know wouldn't upset her. It was no one's business but her own. Not even Ferrand was party to this secret. Time enough for revelations when they were free to be together. She lived for his letters but she'd made no hint of a pregnancy. It would just complicate things and she needed time to recuperate from The Cairo Disaster – TCD for short – as she called Toby now. There was no further word of his whereabouts but she guessed he'd be lying low in some Turkish bar, planning his next schemes.

Once she'd returned from Egypt to the beloved arms of Dalradnor Lodge, life with Toby in Cairo had quickly begun to feel like a distant nightmare. She'd built up her strength with long walks and gentle rides. Baby was an unexpected reward for any disappointments and anxiety, a bonus gift that belonged to her and Dalradnor.

Now there were two weeks lying-in to recover from the hard birthing, time to think about their future and choose names for her little prince. No one would guess his provenance, and that was how it was going to stay.

'Why Desmond?' Phoebe was holding her grandson, rocking him, searching for Arthur's eyes, for any resemblance. 'Are you sure about this?' she nearly said, but bit her tongue just in time.

'I just like the sound of it. Desmond Louis Lionel Lloyd-Jones. I know it's a bit of a long handle but it trips off my tongue.'

Phoebe smiled. Old Sir Lionel would be pleased, but why the Louis?

'I'm not giving him anything to do with Tobias Obediah Jones, but there are so many Joneses so I'm keeping the Lloyd part.'

'I thought you might have something Scottish,' Phoebe offered.

'No, this is his name and he's registered now so that's another thing off my list. Did you bring the thank you chocolates for the nurses?'

Caroline was being so efficient with her orders and lists, sitting in bed at the nursing home like a Queen Bee, writing postcards, receiving cards and gifts: romper suits, knitted jackets and bootees. Kitty sent a beautiful quilted pram set for the old pram they had found in the attic. Mima disinfected it with Jeyes Fluid and made new sheets and pillow slips. Now it was waiting in the hall for his lordship to arrive home that afternoon.

Phoebe had to admit Desmond was a fine-looking specimen, long-limbed, with a fuzz of dark hair and blue eyes. Caroline was cooing over his matinée jacket and his flannelette nightgown as if he were a doll. She'd put mittens on his hands to stop him scratching his face. Then he was swaddled in a fine wool shawl that Nan Ibell had knitted, even with her failing eyesight. Finally he wore a tammy bonnet in blue check to round off his going-home outfit. No prince of the realm could be dressed any better than he was, Phoebe smiled as they made their way to the waiting car and Burrell, their gardener, who was driving them home.

In those months before the birth, Caroline had learned to drive and bought herself a smart Morris estate car suitable for country roads. She tried to plan everything. Cairo had definitely changed her from a dizzy girl to a determined young woman who would now bring up her child alone. Phoebe looked on her with awe these days.

How could she not recall her own quiet arrival at Dalradnor all those years ago, with Marthe and baby, carrying the burden of her shameful secret under cloak of darkness, but finding only warmth and acceptance here? How could she not be grateful that, on hearing of her pregnancy, Arthur had made sure his family were provided for, no matter what happened. She recalled that frosty meeting with the lawyers when Verity and Lionel's wife had thrown fits on hearing of Arthur's child and the change to his will. Now another fatherless bairn was arriving, but this time to a fanfare of joy. He would not be blamed for the criminal acts of his father and must never be sullied by Toby's reputation. Caroline would protect him from what was not his fault, as she'd tried to protect Caroline from her origins. At least her daughter would make a better job of it than she'd done. Here in Dalradnor, no matter what happened in the world outside, little Desmond would be safe from harm.

17

Ma chère Callie

We have been apart too long so I am coming to collect you
and take you back with me. Where have you been hiding?
Have you forgotten me? Why such long silences? I have taken
a post in Lille, at the university, in September so I want you to
be with me always. Come to London and we can make
arrangements.

Louis-Ferrand

Callie knew this invitation must come but she wasn't ready
to take Desmond back to Château Grooten for family scrutiny.
It was better for her and Ferrand to stay in London and have a
private time together, and only after that would she introduce
the baby to his father back in Scotland.

Dear Ferrand

I will come to meet you in London. There's so much I want
to share with you. Then we could come back here to Dalradnor
where so many people want to meet you.

I can't wait to be with you again. I have missed you so much,
but there are important things to discuss in private. Tell me
when you will arrive and I will be there to meet you.

Your loving
Callie

'Would you mind staying on a little longer?' she asked Phee, knowing she would oblige. 'Ferrand is coming to London and I'd like to see him again.' She added, 'I'd prefer to see him alone for a few days . . .' Her voice trailed off as she felt herself blushing.

'Of course. I saw your face when that letter arrived. You mustn't let *that* woman interfere.'

It was sweet how Phee felt that the countess was some bullying dragon who needed to be banished.

'Don't worry, Ferrand has the measure of his mother. I do want to see him again. If it wasn't for him in Cairo . . .' she paused. 'I have to see how it will be between us. Cairo is one sultry place; back north, in the chill and rain, perhaps there'll be nothing between us.'

'How sensible you are,' Phee smiled. 'A break from baby will do you no harm. He won't realize you've gone and I can see to his routine. Mima is his slave. I'm so glad you feel you can trust me with him. It's such a long time since I had anything to do with little ones.' She stopped to gauge Callie's response. 'It was different then, in the war.'

'I know, Phee.' Her mother was trying to compensate for all those absences. She'd stayed on, settling back into the old house for the summer, enjoying its peace and garden. She paced the floor with Desmond when he screamed with colic, singing old music-hall songs to him. She'd escaped back to London just for a few weeks, leaving Callie to enjoy the summer shows and events, pushing baby round the village, showing him off to the shopkeepers, putting him in a makeshift sling and walking him round the lochside in the dappled shade, singing to him '*Slaap, kindje, slaap . . .*' Marthe's old Flemish lullaby. But it was 'The Skye Boat Song' that he loved best, opening his eyes as she rocked him.

During these few months of isolation Callie felt as if she was building up her strength for the next part of her life. In the wings was the promise of a life with Ferrand in France. How would he react to the news he had a son who bore part of his name? How could he not adore his boy, knowing he'd cemented their loving under the Cairo sun? She didn't want the countess demanding answers, finding out she was not even divorced but suspended in mid-air by Toby's disappearance. If Toby had gone for good it would be seven long years before she was free to marry again.

If Ferrand did not accept this, then she would bring up her child alone, as Phee had done, and he would have no part in his upbringing. Every moment she was with Desmond she was more and more enchanted by his smile and his waiting arms. It would be hard to leave him even for a week, but this was too important a reunion to let slip.

Callie began her preparations for London with a long over-due visit to a famous Kelvinside hair salon for a restyle. They refused to give her a permanent wave, instead cutting her thick hair into a pretty bob and hand-waving it. She had nothing new in her wardrobe and her figure had filled out into curves so she treated herself to a new dress and shoes in Daly's of Sauchiehall Street. After, she had afternoon tea at the cinema, watching *The Wizard of Oz*. It felt strange not to be rushing back to feed Desmond, but she wanted to make sure she also had a little trousseau of silk underwear. She felt so excited to think she'd be in Ferrand's arms again soon.

On 26 August, she took the train south to stay in Phee's flat off Marylebone High Street, from where she'd take the train to Dover to meet Ferrand's ferry from Ostend. For once there was no bag of nappies and bottles, blankets and baby toys to carry. She sensed even at Glasgow Central Station an atmosphere of excitement tinged with unease. People were on the move, and when she arrived in London she was amazed to see sandbags outside buildings and air-raid precaution signs. The newspapers she had read on the train were full of accounts of the German army gathering on the border with Poland only a few days ago.

Could this mean Britain would be going to war with Germany and Russia?

When Kitty called in to welcome her, Callie was full of questions. 'What's going on?'

'Have you not been listening to the wireless?' Kitty scolded. 'We're arranging the evacuation of patients to hospitals outside the capital in case of . . .' she paused. 'Look, don't even think of leaving the country. The balloon could go up at any moment.'

'But surely it can't affect us? Ferrand's on his way from France.'

'Chamberlain said only in March that if Poland was attacked, we could not stand by and let them be overrun. There's thousands of city children being evacuated to the country. "Surplus mouths to feed," is what they call it. Sorry to be a Job's comforter but you should go home in case there's an air raid,' Kitty ordered.

Callie's heart sank. She'd just thought it was all bluff, and after Munich there would be peace again, but Aunt Kitty didn't exaggerate. It wasn't her style. When she'd gone Callie put on the wireless and listened to every bulletin. There was talk of queues at the Channel ports, both sides. Holidaymakers were returning from the Continent with stories of fleeing refugees and panic. Even so, Callie decided she was going to Dover to wait for her lover, no matter how long it took for them to be reunited.

The train was packed with foreigners heading home. She listened to the chatter of French families, hanging out of the window at each delay in a siding, waiting for troop trains to pass them. The ferry port under the great cliffs was teaming with passengers queuing for tickets, lugging cases and tired children. There were cars snaking down the hill, waiting to board the ferries. Callie watched incoming ships offloading a cargo of humanity, hundreds of people pouring down the gang plank. 'It's chaos the other end,' shouted one man to those waiting in the queue to board. 'We've left our car behind. They're filling the hold with passengers.'

This can't be happening, Callie cried as she waited by the dock gates, trying not to miss any passenger returning. The ferry from Ostend came and went and there was still no sign of Ferrand.

Perhaps she'd missed him and he'd already headed for the waiting trains and was making his way to the flat. He had the address so it would be better to wait for him there, after all, she decided. Callie returned to London, weary and sick with disappointment, hoping against hope that Ferrand would arrive at any moment in a taxi. She was hot and sticky and needed a bath. The flat seemed chilly and too quiet. Already she was missing her son. What if Ferrand had changed his mind? What if his mother had found out she was married and had brought her influence to bear? But there were a hundred more valid reasons why he might have been delayed.

Then the phone rang, shrill in the lonely silence, but it was only Phee, checking she'd arrived safely and giving her a bulletin on baby.

'I'm so glad I've caught you,' Phee went on, sounding relieved. 'Don't leave the country, not now. It looks like war is about to start. The papers say British travellers are advised to leave the Continent as soon as possible. Did you meet your friend?'

'Not yet. He's been delayed. The ferries are packed but he'll be here soon,' Callie said, more for her own benefit than Phee's.

She waited three days, wondering why he didn't ring or send a telegram, and just as she'd given up hope there was a letter, a hasty scribbled note.

Darling,

  I can't come. I am recalled back early to Lille for the emergency. It looks as if I am needed. I will be enlisting, should Belgian neutrality be compromised. Jean-Luc advised me to

return to the château and make preparations for Maman, who
fears it may be requisitioned, as it was before. I am so desperately sorry to let you down but you are always in my thoughts
at this sad time. I will write when I know more. Take care, my
darling. Go home to 'Bonnie Scotland'.

    Your ever loving Louis-Ferrand

She felt such anger she couldn't sleep. Why was war spoiling
everything? What had it to do with them? Why hadn't she gone
to join Ferrand earlier: blown caution to the wind and arrived
with Desmond? You silly woman, she berated herself, what
does it matter what others think about his paternity? But it did
matter. She knew only too well what secrets were hidden
around herself, and now she'd done the very same thing with
her own baby. She felt such panic now at the thought of being
separated from Ferrand by war. She must write and tell him
about their son before it was too late.

She paced the flat all night until she was exhausted, watching
all the preparations from the windows, hearing the headlines
called by newspaper vendors, hearing the grind of air-raid sirens
practising and people scurrying, looking for the shelter. There
was nothing for it but to return home, but even that was easier
said than done.

Callie had never seen so many trains heading out of the capital. She followed lines of children in crocodile queues, some in
school uniforms and carrying suitcases; others in coats with
sagging hems and plimsolls, carrying brown-paper parcels;
women pushing go-chairs with babies plugged into rubber
dummies. She watched mothers trying to hide their tears as they
waved their children off. Babies wailed as their mothers wept
and Callie felt guilty to be going back to her own baby.

The train companies were overstretched, the tracks were
overcrowded, and delays in sidings became the order of the day.
The compartments were packed with soldiers and sailors

heading north to their barracks. Everyone had a false jokey sense of excitement. For once, the English reserve was shattered by the news that the whole world was going up in flames before long. Many had to stand from Euston to Glasgow, or crouch down in the corridors, and as the steamer rattle over the Douglas Moors, all the lights went out. It was a ghastly endless journey. The toilets blocked and the smell of human bodies grew ripe in the heat. At least they would be safe in Stirlingshire, but Phee's flat was another matter. Callie had brought with her all the documents and jewellery she could find in case of an air raid.

It was the middle of the night when she arrived back exhausted. On Sunday, 3 September, Phee woke her to listen to the Prime Minister's address to the nation. Mima, and Mr Burrell, the gardener, stood with them, listening to his solemn words, not daring to speak until it was over.

'Lord help all those soldiers. I'm awful glad my faither's no' here to see us go through all that stuff again. What did they all die for last time?' Mima cried.

Callie was too heart-sick to do anything but sigh as she looked to Desmond in his play pen, rolling round, completely oblivious to what was happening. Here, he was safe from bombs, but if there was an invasion, what then?

'I shall go back to London and put my flat in good order,' said Phee. 'Stock up on a few bits and pieces. Desmond will need things as he grows.'

'He'll manage. We'll all manage fine,' Callie replied.

'I think we should clear the bottom lawn for a pig pen. We're fine for eggs, but a bit of pork will come in handy for Christmas,' Colin Burrell suggested. 'We can turn over the flowerbeds and increase the winter root crops too. There's talk of ration cards and petrol coupons so I can put the Morris in the stable.'

'Oh, not yet, please,' Callie cried. She loved the car she had nicknamed 'Boris'. 'Let's wait and see. I suppose we ought to offer accommodation for evacuees.'

'Don't be too hasty, Miss Caroline. With such a wee bairn in the house, you never know what germs strangers might bring with them,' Mima was quick to jump in.

'Everyone will have to do their bit, Mima. An untidy noisy house is a small sacrifice to make.' She was feeling guilty to be living so far away from any threat of danger when Ferrand and his family, across the Channel, feared the worst after what had happened to their country twenty years before. He was right to want to protect them as she must protect hers.

That evening she sat down and wrote a letter, pouring her heart out to him.

My darling,

I am so sorry you couldn't come to London. I wanted to take you to Scotland to see our son, yes, our son, Desmond Louis. Born a few months ago in March. I so wanted you to meet him and for us to be together, but it looks as if this must be delayed. How cruel of fate to give us such promise of happiness, only to whisk it away from us. I am sorry to withhold this wonderful news but the heart has its reasons. It is a long story. I wanted to be sure my son has a name of his own in his own country before . . . I was wrong and now we are all paying the price.

He is a beautiful little boy and I enclose a snapshot for you. Please forgive me for not telling you sooner. Now I fear it will be many months before you will see him for yourself.

Callie couldn't carry on. Tears were streaming down her face, falling and smudging the paper. It was too stark, too brutal a confession. How could he forgive her for holding out on him like this? What would it do to him, knowing he was trapped on one side of the Channel and she on the other? Perhaps it was better to write when the situation was clearer, safer. This was not the right time to be revealing her secret. She would wait a little longer, though she wondered how their love would survive such separation. That was the risk she must take.

She knew they would be no different from thousands of other wives and soldiers facing the same dilemma. Now it was enough to know she alone must secure the fabric and gardens of Dalradnor for the future.

She found herself walking over the house, patting its walls with affection. This was their fortress and safe haven, a firm buttress against hardships to come. This was home, and here she must stay.

18

Phoebe returned south to a very different atmosphere in the city. The streets were full of uniforms, blackout blinds and unlit streetlights plunging the roads in utter darkness, and window panes were crisscrossed with tape.

Film work was patchy with so many actors and technicians being called up, but her agent found her a small part in a new film that told the story of what might happen if a village was invaded by paratroopers. It was a harrowing tale, and so close to everyone's secret fears, but with a strong cast and beautiful setting it would be very plausible.

The new Charlie Chaplin film, *The Great Dictator*, which took the rise out of Hitler, promised to be a rousing success, but the big hit was, of course, *Gone with the Wind*, with the stellar cast of Clark Gable, Leslie Howard and Vivien Leigh. This epic tale of the deep American South, filmed in Technicolor, packed out the once-empty cinemas for three showings a day. Phoebe saw it three times, carried away by its story, its characters and the romance of its location. She knew that, with its success, there'd be more work in costume dramas and thrillers. She wasn't in the full flush of youth but she could still play decent roles.

The peace of Dalradnor felt miles away and she missed the baby. The flat felt empty and quiet. Kitty was working long shifts and Billy was waiting for the theatres to re-open. London felt tense, waiting for the war to really begin, marking time, girding its loins in defensive preparations. Phoebe didn't hesitate to return north for Christmas and Hogmanay, cadging a lift with some of the crew from the film studios, who were going to be making public information films and therefore had a petrol allowance.

Little Desmond was plumper, grabbing at his toys, delighted to see his granny. Primrose made a brief but welcome visit. She was working as a clerk in the Foreign Office, she told them. Her hair was bobbed and rolled into the latest style and Caroline was cheered to see her old friend and show off her baby. She'd hit the doldrums over all her Belgium friends. Their letters were irregular and at Christmas there was only a card from Marthe and nothing from Ferrand.

Caroline had hired a farmer's daughter, Jessie Dixon, to be a nursemaid to Desmond. She was proving a hard-working motherly type and gave Callie freedom to get on with local war work. The poor boy would be surrounded by devoted woman at his beck and call, if they weren't careful, Phoebe thought.

The Women's Voluntary Service took up some of Callie's time. So far no one had been billeted on them, but it could be only a matter of time. There were welfare clinics, distributions of ration cards and gas masks, all the paraphernalia of war. Caroline refused to put her baby anywhere near the horrific bell-tent gas mask intended for infants. 'It'll give him nightmares, trapped in this,' she defended her decision. 'Boris the Morris' was now in service as a temporary ambulance and delivery vehicle, with a small allowance of petrol, and Callie's ability to drive was proving invaluable.

Desmond's first birthday seemed to come round so quickly. Phoebe managed to have Caroline's old rocking horse repaired as his present. Caroline had loved it literally to bits. It was a large dapple grey, too big for him just yet, but it sat in the Nursery window, ready for use.

The sight of the beautiful rocking horse took Phoebe back to her own childhood, with far more modest toys. This led once more to thoughts of her brother, Ted, and she knew it was time she rebuilt the bridge between them. She had put it to the back of her mind for years, but with the war making everyone's life uncertain it was silly to delay any longer. She found his address and, giving him no warning to reject her, turned up on his doorstep, having disregarded government advice not to travel.

She was shocked to see how old he looked, and worn. It pained her to think of him and his wife stuck in the backstreets while she lived in such luxury.

He had greeted her with contempt rather than surprise. 'So here comes the Queen of the May, slumming it.' He eyed her, shaking his head. 'I hope you're proud of what you did, sending that young kiddie to my door, making me do yer own dirty work. Joe's daughter, indeed. You allus were one for tall tales but that takes the biscuit.'

'Now, Ted, don't get excited, it's bad for your chest,' his wife warned. 'Do come in and sit yersel' down. She's yer own flesh and blood so behave! Pleased to meet you. I'm Hilda.'

'Yes, I know. Caroline said you were kind to them. I'm sorry I've stayed away so long.'

'Sorry! You don't know the meaning of the word, blackening Joe's name when he can't defend hissel',' Ted spluttered. 'You were not brought up to deceive. Our mam and dad, God rest their souls, had good hearts, but all that prancing on the stage's turned your head, swelled it so it were too big to grace our door. You're nothing but a trumped-up chorus girl as got hersel' in trouble with a soldier, or am I mistaken? Don't you go putting on airs and graces wi' me. I want nowt to do wi' you.' He turned his face to the fire.

Phoebe bowed her head. 'I'm sorry, but I just want to make amends. I had to do what was best for the child and me. It was done with a good heart but secrets have a way of coming out all wrong.'

'You can say that again. Has she dumped you, gone off and left in a huff?'

'No, she's fine, with a bonny little boy . . . I know I haven't been the best of sisters but now I'm in a position to help you both.'

'I want nothing from you,' Ted snapped.

'You haven't heard what I'm suggesting. There's some nice cottages up Far Headingley and I could rent one of them for you, somewhere less damp and smoky in north of the city.'

'It's a bit late for all that now. We can manage fine where we are,' Ted replied.

'So you're too proud now to give your wife and you a chance of a better life? You're just as bad as I am, Ted Boardman, you and your pride.'

'Shut up bickering, the both of you,' said Hilda. 'Thank you for such a kind offer. I'd like that very much, and if you won't go, I will.' She winked at Phoebe. 'My washing will dry whiter up there. Now let's just have a cup of tea and a drop scone and stop all this argy-bargy. It's making my head ache. I want to hear all your news about your grandson.'

With the help of Primrose's parents in Harrogate they found just the right cottage in Far Headingley, close to a butcher's and a grocery shop, with a cinema in walking distance and a good bus service into town. If only she'd done this sooner, Phoebe thought, but at least they were now on speaking terms.

Being at war brought home how fragile life might be and how uncertain were all of their futures. Phoebe was fortunate in having the funds available to give her brother choices he otherwise could never make. She was so anxious that this belated gesture would heal the past wounds of neglect. The answer came in the form of a newsy letter from Hilda, thanking Caroline for the photos of Desmond she had sent them, and praising their new accommodation.

In the spring of 1940, everything changed, with news of the blitzkrieg invasions of Holland and Belgium. Then the retreat from Dunkirk catapulted the country into a bleak summer prospect of invasion. Yet London continued about its business throughout the summer, and people took comfort in dance halls and the picture houses until the bombs came raining down on them each night.

Phoebe, back at her flat and working on a film, got used to droning aircraft overhead, sirens wailing, the ack-ack guns blasting from the parks and the searchlights arched over the night sky, but the lack of sleep was another matter. She found it impossible to doze off in those crowded brick shelters. The earth shuddered with bomb blasts and the screaming whines of approaching planes dropping incendiaries, and trying to be British and not panic took all of her fortitude. When she heard the all clear she staggered out into the night to the stench of cordite, leaking gas pipes, the ring of ambulance bells and fire engines, and her heart went out to all those trapped in the blazing infernos that lit up the sky with a sickly orange glow.

After each raid there were terrible sights along the streets, and the foggy September mornings were thick with smoke and the sickly smell of death. Phoebe was lucky as her flat escaped damage but one afternoon, Billy came to the door in tears, bringing the awful news that Kitty's hospital had taken a direct hit as she was ushering patients to safety. There wouldn't even be a body left to mourn.

Phoebe went cold with shock, unable to cry or feel anything at first. Her two best friends were gone. Something died within her that afternoon.

Kitty had always been there to support her, strong when she'd been weak. Her good judgement had saved Phoebe on many occasions. Who could she turn to now to give her guidance? When Billy had gone home, still crying, she sat on in her silent room, utterly stunned by the loss. What was the purpose in living amongst all this destruction? Hadn't she seen enough? Was this what being human was all about – the death of people she loved? The anger flared up, burning inside her at such helplessness. She suddenly felt old and utterly alone.

A week after the funeral service for Kitty and her nurses, the raids began again. The bombs dropped even closer to Oxford Street and the surrounding areas. In the air-raid shelter, no one could sleep, and Phoebe sat clutching her handbag and rug, listening to ear-splitting explosions while an elderly neighbour played on his harmonica the old war tunes she'd sung so many times.

When at last the all clear sounded and they walked out in first light, the whole landscape had changed and she knew it was bad news. Her mansion block had taken a direct hit. Where the four-storeys of apartments rose up, there was just a yawning gap of burning metal, charred furniture, smoking rubble and all the bits of people's homes mangled into strange sculptures.

'Back, back! Gas!' yelled the wardens as the street was cordoned off.

There was nothing worth salvaging. Thank God Caroline had insisted she take her photo albums, scrapbooks and the precious document box containing Arthur's letters up to Scotland, just in case. Now she was homeless, with only the clothes on her back and her handbag full of papers. She couldn't cry; it was only stuff. She'd lost a friend far more precious in this terrible month.

'Come along, dearie, to the hall for a cuppa,' said a woman in uniform. 'That's it, you've had a shock.' She wrapped a blanket round Phoebe's shoulders and shoved a cup of sweet tea into her hand. Phoebe moved in a daze from queue to queue, registering herself.

'Anywhere to stay, love?' an official asked. She shook her head at first. Then she remembered.

'I'll go to my daughter's,' she announced.

'Where's that then? We need a forwarding address for your papers.'

'Dalradnor Lodge in Stirlingshire. There'll be a bed for me there.'

'Not tonight, there won't,' came the reply. 'We could find you a hotel.'

'The Cavendish, Jermyn Street . . . I'll go there, if it's still standing.' She sighed: that was where she'd once been so happy. Arthur would be waiting there.

19

The evacuee family arrived at Dalradnor one afternoon in July 1940. They'd been billeted in a Glasgow church hall for a week after arriving by ship from Guernsey, welcomed into the city and promised homes for the duration. Callie had bedrooms to spare and didn't mind being first on the list, having learned that this poor family had been on the move since 21 June. She was given a mother and three children. Madame Laplanche was a native of Brittany, married to a resident Guernsey farmer who had shoved his family onto the waiting ships while he remained to tend their market garden on the island, now under occupation. There were two girls, Bettine and Louise, and a boy called Jacques, all of them of school age. Louise looked as if she was recovering from something infectious.

'Mercy me, look at the poor wee souls,' said Mima as she hurried off to boil the kettle. 'They'll need a bath, by the smell of them.'

'*Merci, madame*, thank you . . .' said Madame Laplanche. 'We are most grateful.'

There was little luggage, just a battered suitcase full of clean underwear and rosaries and photos of their market garden. The clothes had been donated by the refugee reception committee, but very few fitted them. It was a warm summer and the children could play outside and be kitted out later with uniforms for the start of school at the end of August.

Callie knew it was her duty to give a home to refugees. She kept thinking about how Marthe and her family had fled to Britain and been taken in by Aunt Kitty's parents in 1914. She knew they were now living under occupation too. Ferrand wrote briefly saying he'd joined Jean-Luc in the army, but his letters stopped coming once the country was overrun. It was too late now to send the letter she'd attempted so many times and shoved in a drawer. No doubt the château would be in foreign hands by now, and she felt sorry for the countess.

They were getting to be a houseful: Jessie and Desmond in the Nursery, Madame shared a large bedroom with her girls, and Jacques slept in the dressing room next to it. Phee's room was filling up with clutter. Then one day in September she suddenly appeared on the doorstep without warning, clutching all she had left from her London life and needing a permanent roof over her head.

She looked stricken as Callie hugged her and led her to a chair, and Mima plied her with tea with a spoonful of the precious sugar ration. Only when she told them all the sad news of Kitty's death did she collapse on the sofa and cry over her loss. It was awful to see her so shell-shocked, and Callie wept with her over the sad news.

With so many mouths to feed at the Lodge Callie thanked goodness for the hens and the pig and the rows of vegetables in the kitchen garden and the borders. Madame was happiest helping in the kitchen, and Mima enjoyed her company. She could make meals out of nothing and added new ideas to Mima's old dishes to make them taste richer. She was an excellent seamstress, sewing shirts out of thin sheets, turning collars, altering donated skirts into little outfits for the girls, and making Desmond a winter coat and bonnet out of a man's old tweed jacket. She even found favour with Mr Burrell for showing him how her husband tended his crops.

It was quiet enough while the children were in school, but when they rampaged around the house on wet afternoons they gave Phoebe a headache.

Callie felt the strain of keeping the peace and giving her mother time to recover. She took her for long walks to let her talk out all the things she'd seen in London. Phee was in no hurry to return there, but she knew that if her agent rang she must leave.

'I feel like a spare part here,' she sighed one morning as Callie prepared to go to her WVS meeting. 'You're all so busy, what should I do?'

'Do what you do best, Mother,' Callie said, pausing to realize what she'd just said. 'Get back on the stage and cheer us all up. There must be concert parties in need of your direction.'

'I'm too old for prancing about,' Phee sighed, looking at her crow's feet in the mirror.

'No, you're not; just ring round. I'm sure the hospitals are always on the lookout for entertainers with your experience. Listen to me telling my grandmother to suck eggs.' They both laughed and Callie was relieved to see a spark of life back in Phee's eyes.

But what am I doing for the war effort? she pondered in the night when sleep was elusive. Bringing up a child, helping evacuees and WVS work – is it enough? Anyone can do those things efficiently, given all the help and space in the house.

She'd been impressed by Primrose in her smart suit arriving on her doorstep one weekend. She was now working for the Ministry of Economic Warfare but was vague about her duties as if they were hush-hush in some way. Callie felt a surge of envy at her freedom and the stories of the famous parties she'd been to in London. But Primmy was single and fancy-free – why shouldn't she make the most of all the fun going on down there?

'Have you ever met any Belgian soldiers, officers who might know the van Grooten brothers?' Callie asked. It was a long shot to expect them to have come over with the Dunkirk evacuation. Ferrand would have telephoned her.

'There's plenty of Free Frenchies and Poles. They make broadcasts to the Continent, I think. Come to London and I'll take you to some hidey-holes where they might know. It's about time you hit the town.'

'I can't, not with all this lot to sort out.'

'Rubbish. There's enough adults here to allow you a weekend pass. Little Des has got his jolly Jessie at his beck and call until she's called up.'

'Oh, please, not yet. She's such a bouncy girl, and practical too, but Phee's not herself. The bombing's unnerved her, and Aunt Kitty going like that, but she'll buck up once she treads the boards again. How's your lot?'

'Daddy's in the Medical Corps, Mummy's taking on all the welfare clinics and Hamish's joined up. Haven't a clue what he's up to now.'

'Who knows where any of us will be by the end of the war,' Callie said.

'Goose-stepping to Hitler's tunes perhaps?' Primmy smiled. 'I think not . . . May take some time, but we'll get there in the end.'

'I just wish I could do more.'

'You're bringing up the next generation, keeping the home fires burning and all that. Surely that's enough?'

'I'm sure you're doing something far more important, making a real difference. I ought to join up too,' In the face of all Primrose's news, Callie suddenly felt guilty about her situation.

'You can't, you're needed here. It won't come to that.' Primmy was trying to reassure her but it wasn't working.

'Remember what Corky used to say at St Maggie's? "Miss McAllister . . . be useful and be a trailblazer!"'

'And look where that got us, stuck up a gumtree with no ladder!' Primmy roared. 'What you need is a break from all this domesticity. You are coming up to town and that's an order.'

Primrose returned to London leaving Callie to chew the cud on all these frustrations during a sleepless night. They'd not even had one air raid here. She couldn't just sit out the war in comfort and safety. It wasn't right.

As if in answer to a prayer, the very next morning a letter arrived that was to change everything.

'What's it all about? It looks official,' asked Phee, watching her picking the letter up and then putting it down all through breakfast.

'You know we sent all those photographs of Ostend and all the countryside round the château, the ones they asked us for on the news? I think it's to do with that. I've been asked to go to London to discuss things further.' Callie couldn't quite believe in the coincidence of such an unexpected request.

'That's a long way to go just for some holiday snaps. It's not a ruse to do with Toby, is it? Perhaps they're testing you,' Phee replied, looking concerned and rereading the letter for clues.

'I haven't heard from him in years, and probably never will until we divorce. Perhaps they want more details of the area. I did get to know it quite well. Primmy offered to put me up if I need a break. She's been on at me to visit her.'

'London isn't safe. Don't put yourself at risk, not with a baby.' Trust Phee to be sensible.

'I'll be careful. I'm curious, and the Ministry do offer a travel permit. Desmond will be fine surrounded by his devoted fans while I'm away.' There was something about the letter that intrigued her, something vague yet official in its letterhead. She'd never heard of the Ministry of Economic Warfare – or had she? Didn't Primmy work there? Perhaps she'd put them up to this?

Callie dressed with care for the interview, trying not to look as if she'd been awake all night, stuck in a railway siding during an air raid, listening to bombs blasting in the distance. Primmy had left the key to her bedsit under a brick in the wall. She worked out of town during the week so Callie let herself into the chaos of her room. It was a shock to see the ruins and bomb sites, never shown on the Pathé News. How could people carry on working with buses strewn across the pavements, shops shuttered, broken glass and rubble everywhere? But London was taking it and she felt proud that nothing was hindering the war effort.

The address was a hotel close to Westminster Abbey. She had to give her name to the doorkeeper and wait until summoned. It was not much of a place, shabby and down at heel; the sort of place you'd walk past and never notice. But travellers needed beds and they must be in short supply, she thought as she sat at the top of the stairs, waiting for the door to open. This was not what she had been expecting.

A man came out to greet her – tall, distinguished-looking – but he didn't give her his name and she found herself in room with a desk and two old chairs, bare and chilly. He addressed her in French, much to her surprise, expecting her to reply at speed, which she did. On the desk was a picture postcard curled at the edges as if it had been rolled up.

'I think this belongs to you.' He shoved it across the desk for her to examine. 'How do you come to know the person who's sent it?'

She saw the handwriting and stared at it in surprise. 'It's from Louis-Ferrand van Grooten. We met in Cairo.'

'I gather then he was your lover there.'

Callie stiffened at his bluntness. She shrugged and said nothing.

'Come now, Mrs Lloyd-Jones, or is it just Mrs Toby Jones?' He then reeled off all her history with added details of Toby's fraudulent activities, how he was now living off an assumed name, and how she'd met Ferrand in Alexandria and begun a relationship with him there.

'Do you know where van Grooten lives now?'

Callie swallowed the shock of all his revelations and smiled. 'I thought I was here to discuss some photographs . . .'

'You lived in Belgium for some months. Your accent is a little tainted but Countess van Grooten took you in at her school. That is correct?' It was his turn to pause, watching her very carefully.

'I was with a group of other girls there, yes, and we went on trips.'

'You also had a Belgian nursemaid, a Flemish refugee?'

'Marthe . . . is she safe?'

'And you understand Flemish?'

'A little.' Where was all this leading? 'What is this about?'

'We're looking for suitable translators and others to do various duties. Your background interests us. That is all, Mrs Jones.'

'So why do you have Ferrand's postcard?' she asked.

'It was given to us by, shall we say, unusual methods to bypass the ruling powers.'

Then he changed the subject. 'What are your feelings about the occupation of Belgium? Have you maintained any contact with your friends there?'

She sensed he was fishing for the strength of her political opinions and she shook her head. 'There's so little to read in our papers. I am worried, of course, about all my friends there. If there's anything I can do to help them . . . What is happening?' The discussion in French was difficult at first, but she relaxed into familiar idioms. Why all this concern with Belgium, though?

The man then stood up. 'Thank you for your co-operation. Needless to say this interview is extremely confidential and, should we need to interview you further, I require an address.'

She gave them Primrose's address and her own in Scotland.

'Ah, a beautiful spot, good fishing, too. I see you have evacuees billeted and a young son. I presume he is van Grooten's boy?' His homework was so thorough it was unnerving. No one had ever presumed this out loud before.

'He's my son. Who his father is, is my business,' she snapped.

'Very discreet of you, Mrs Jones, like the fact that you were never actually married to your husband.'

'We were married,' she protested. 'Off the coast of Marseilles in 1935 on board the *Marie Solange*, by the captain.' How dare he pry into her personal life like this?

'It was not a British vessel, then, and no notification was ever made to the General Register Office at St Catherine's House? In which case it means nothing,' he added.

'I didn't know that was necessary,' Callie replied with surprise. 'Does it matter?'

'Only if you ever wished to divorce. If there's no evidence of a legal union you are a free agent, as is Mr Jones, free to marry who you please, and it looks as if there's a man in Belgium waiting to do the honour. Good day, Mrs Jones, or is it, in fact, Miss Boardman?'

Callie stumbled out of the door and down the steps in shock. Had she just dreamed this up? Who was this rude man? The cheek of him, prying into her private life, knowing such intimate details. And why was he saying all this to her? She clutched Ferrand's postcard with relief. He was alive and still thinking about her. Could she really be free to be with him? Perhaps Toby had always known their marriage was void. Why would that not surprise her?

She found the nearest café and pored over the postcard in disbelief. It looked as if it had once been rolled tight into the size of a cigarette, and the tinted photograph was cracked.

My darling,

I hope this finds you safe. It is difficult here. My brother was killed and Maman is distraught. She can no longer live where she would choose. I am back at my post and do what I can to help people to safety. I long for you to be here. How chilly it is far from the warmer climes we both knew when you were in my arms night and day. I will wait until we are together again.

There was no signature, nor was one needed. There was nothing mentioned to incriminate anyone else, no names or places, just her name and address. Who had brought this out of the country? What did he mean by helping people to safety? Every sentence was full of hidden meaning and she scoured it again with tears misting the words.

Oh, why have I not told you about Desmond? What danger are you in, helping escapees to safety and a chance of freedom?

So much was left unsaid. Because of this simple postcard she was part of some secret world. The man at that desk hinted that her language, tainted as it was, might be useful. What would this mean if they called for her again? Did she want to get involved? She could walk away right now and catch the first train home and no one would judge her or think the worst of her if she did. But her feet were rooted to the spot. Maybe at last she could be useful in this clandestine shadowy world that lay beyond the brown-stained door. She sensed danger and she sensed challenge, but the decision to act was not in her hands yet. Had she failed at the first hurdle? Would she even get a second chance? Only when she knew the outcome of this strange meeting could she decide which path to take.

20

Phoebe was enjoying her new role in ENSA, the entertainment wing of the Forces. It was like the old days in Boulogne all over again, when she sang in Lena Ashwell's concert party for the YMCA. Yet despite the initial derision of her theatrical friends that ENSA stood for Every Night Something Awful, she was back in uniform and doing war work. It was good to smell the greasepaint again, even if they were as often as not bumping up some remote track in a charabanc, rolling over stones and cowpats to some far-flung outpost to give the frozen soldiers a bit of cheer.

The Stardrop Troupe were a motley crew: a tenor with a suspicious toupee, a pretty concert pianist with corkscrew curls and an amazing embonpoint, three giggling chorus girls whose high kicks with their tree-trunk legs would send the poor conscripts into raptures, and a sad-eyed Jewish violinist who got them weeping in their tea. Phoebe was the classy bit, reading poetry and stirring speeches, with the odd comedy sketch to lighten the mood. It was all a bit makeshift, especially when the piano was in the last stages of consumption, the stage was only a pile of pallets covered with old carpet and the theatre a freezing barn with flickering footlights, but they always finished with a rousing singsong; and she was the mother hen, making sure all the girls got back to their billets with their virtue intact.

There was usually a potato-pie supper with suet pastry as thick as a doormat, followed by slabs of army fruitcake, and drinks in the officers' mess if they were lucky. If they were honoured by some bigwig musical star arriving at the last minute they had to give him or her the curtained-off bit of room, press the star's costumes or find some orderly to do so, and see them to the nearest good hotel.

Phoebe loved visiting hospitals best, seeing the eager faces of convalescing soldiers and sailors as the troupe sang through their repertoire of old songs. It brought back such memories of being in Miss Lena's concert party and that first encounter with Arthur in the officers' mess after a show. He looked like a demi-god, home from the battle, mud-stained, but so handsome and weary. How could she have nearly not gone and missed the love of her life . . .? She'd never forget those wondrous days when she was young and full of hope, lying in his arms in the Cavendish Hotel, shopping for a ring in Burlington Arcade. If only Arthur had lived . . . but would he now be in danger a second time? She was so weary of war and the misery it brought.

It was good to be heading back to Dalradnor for a few days' respite; a bath and a hearty meal and she was revived. The routine of the house ran like clockwork. Mima and Madame Laplanche saw to the children while Jessie Dixon kept Desmond amused. Caroline kept disappearing in her brand-new uniform of the First Aid Nursing Yeomanry, an outfit that seemed to have her traipsing here and there on courses. She was vague about her duties, something to do with translating messages in a clerking office. What a change in her when she'd returned from London, excited to be offered this role, though Phoebe had been horrified.

'How can you think of joining up with a baby?' she'd said.

'I've not joined up . . . I've got a job being useful. I can't just sit here for the duration when there's a houseful of women quite capable of keeping the home fires burning. You should know that after your experience.' She'd given her mother an accusing look. Why did it always come back to this? Phoebe asked herself. How could she disapprove when she'd done exactly the same in leaving Caroline with Marthe in this very place all those years ago?

Jessie had the measure of her charge but Phoebe didn't want her daughter to miss out on her child, who was growing fast, three years old now and full of curiosity. Desmond was an intelligent little chap, tall for his age, independent, and he didn't look a bit like Toby, thank goodness. Jacques was his playmate and together the four children romped around the gardens, getting in Burrell's hair, collecting eggs, making dens in the wood. Anyone could see he was a happy boy. When Caroline came back from London she brought everyone treats and the children precious sweets. She devoted all her leave to her son.

There'd been rumours of terrible raids in Glasgow but no one knew much as some areas were cordoned off. The Clyde docks were regular targets and housing was destroyed close by. At Dalradnor, they only heard the drone of planes at night and were spared, being deep in the countryside.

Phoebe reasoned with herself that Caroline should be allowed to play her part in the war effort as she thought fit, but why was she never in the same place twice? Once, she came back bruised, with her fingernails torn and her palms blistered. She said she'd fallen badly in the blackout but she couldn't look Phoebe in the eye. Phoebe sensed not to pry but something kept niggling her about this new job. She wondered just how safe it was, and quite what Caroline was hiding from her now.

21

Callie stared at her reflection in the mirror. She'd lost weight with all those early morning crosscountry runs, night marches and lectures in the country house outside London. She still couldn't believe they'd chosen her for training for overseas service. When the interviewer explained the dangerous work being done behind enemy lines, she swallowed hard for a second and then didn't hesitate to ask to be considered for duty. He explained she'd have to risk her life, be at the mercy of strangers, ignore people who might recognize her and live undercover.

'Let me make something clear. Where you go there'll be no Free zones. Failure will mean only one thing. I have to be honest with you. This is no place for a woman with a young son, but your accent and your knowledge of the district might be useful in helping us keep the escape routes open into France and beyond. It is vital work. Many brave couriers have been betrayed and shot. You don't have to make your decision now, but sleep on it.'

That night she'd lain on Primmy's camp bed, eyes wide open, wishing she could share it all with her friend, but to talk would mean she couldn't keep a secret. How could she even think of leaving little Desmond motherless and fatherless if the worst came to the worst? How could she live a life of lies, deceiving all who loved her?

She'd prayed for guidance but nothing had come but this overwhelming desire to be useful to her country. She'd had a privileged education, with all the comforts of country living; now it was time to give something back. Out there somewhere Ferrand was also fighting for his country and in danger. Perhaps if they survived there would be a future for them together with their boy. It was strange, but she could feel his love for her burning as strongly as hers for him. She must prove herself worthy of that future happiness, not by sitting idly by in her Scottish retreat but by facing danger head-on. She'd made it through all the initial interviews and tests, unlike many others, so the following day she signed the Official Secrets Act and only then did she learn what really lay behind these secret missions.

Now her muscles ached but were honed and tougher. She had little aptitude for wireless skills but was learning how to code and decode messages, handle weapons, blend into a crowd and lose her follower when they practised in the street. She studied maps, trying to memorize all the places she'd visited before the war. To be invisible and not draw any attention to oneself was crucial to survival as a courier, but to observe the slightest changes around you was a skill that might make the difference between survival or arrest.

A woman alone going about her business was less likely to be questioned than a young man of military age. This was what had decided the authorities reluctantly to allow women into this dangerous work. In her training group were native French speakers of all types and ages. At every stage they were marked and assessed. She was getting used to feeling observed for any tiny infringement that might give her away, even down to how she left an empty plate, French or English fashion. Not to look right, left and right again when crossing the road, but the opposite, for cars being driven on the other side. She must become her new persona: a nursemaid between jobs, travelling to find her next assignment in Brussels.

There was so much to learn and so little time to perfect every detail of dress and hair. Her dental fillings were removed and replaced with continental ones; the clothes she would wear had to be of the right cloth and labels. Even the seams must be genuine. The couriers' underwear was brought back from abroad or given by Belgian refugees. Nothing was left to chance.

She was responsible for the safe conduct of important code messages and information. If weapons or instructions were found on her, that meant instant death if she was lucky, or a trip to prison and the torture cells. She would have to become as good, if not better, an actress than her own mother had been. One slip, one failure to absorb all the new instructions, evasion tactics and initiative tests and she'd be back in Dalradnor, or sent to the Outer Hebrides to sit out the war sworn to secrecy. It was as if she were living in two worlds now.

Much as she adored her son and her home, they had to come second to this call to duty. They were what she was fighting for. Desmond must grow up in freedom and peace, and if she could help hasten that day then all the sacrifice would be worthwhile. I'm going to see this through, no matter what, she thought. She hoped Miss Corcoran and the school would be proud of her trailblazing one day.

The worst course was at Arisaig in the north-west of Scotland. Here, they went through survival training, scrambling up rock faces, living rough, killing anything that would grace the pot, evading a hunt with dogs on their track. Many were called but few were chosen. All this was designed to give them a fighting chance of survival if the worst happened. Callie learned how to stun a man, shoot to kill, to fight and knife an opponent if sprung on. Phee had spotted her bruised fingers and hands after the course, giving her a suspicious look, but to her credit she asked nothing.

If only she could tell her mother a little of this mission, but she feared to let slip anything. There would come a moment when she might have to write a will and prepare a pile of cheery postcards to be sent on her behalf. She had wrapped presents for Desmond and the others for Christmas, just in case she wasn't there to give them. That was the worst bit, and she tried not to choke at the thought of missing his face on Christmas morning. It was a hard decision to stay the course, but there was no turning back when she thought of Ferrand in danger.

She'd scraped through so far, but her cover story was not embedded deep enough yet and the clock was ticking. She had to *become* Marthe, recall how she went about things, those little phrases she came out with. One day, they would come for her and she'd have to leave silently. This was making every second of her visits to Dalradnor so precious. She tried to prise Desmond away from Jessie for a picnic and buggy ride but he wanted his playmates to come and had a tantrum. She read him bedtime stories and wrapped him in a towel after bath time, hugging him to her chest, singing 'The Skye Boat Song': 'Speed, bonnie boat, like a bird on the wing . . . over the sea to Skye.'

She would soon be a bird on the wing flying high and then plunging to earth in an alien land, fleeing from the wrath of the enemy as Bonnie Prince Charlie had. Then Desmond looked up at her and smiled. 'Sing it again, Mummy.' How could she ever think of letting him go? It was agony to cut off this natural urge to stay put and forget the whole bally business of secret warfare, but she must. She was committed to serving her country as best she could.

On the journey back to camp, her training always kicked in. Dalradnor life faded away as she rehearsed in her head how she would approach the parachute course the following week. The very thought of jumping out of the sky and trusting herself to a piece of silk churned her guts to liquid, but she was not going to let the team down at this late stage. Failure was what she feared most.

*　　*　　*

There was a light shining into her eyes, rousing her from sleep. 'On your feet! What is your name? Speak.' An arm dragged her out of the bed. 'Who are you? What are you doing here?' First in German and then in French.

Where am I? What is happening? Callie staggered along, her sleepy eyes trying to focus on the rough handling. This was some nightmare. Men in Gestapo uniform with those armbands were dragging her off her feet, pushing her down steps and, when she slipped on the cold stone, kicking her up, pushing her through a prison door in the darkness. All she could see was a blinding light in her face and shadowy figures standing behind watching, too many to escape. 'Up there on the chair . . . Who are you?'

'Charlotte Blanken, sir,' she found herself whispering.

'Speak up. These papers are false. You are a British spy.'

'No, sir, I am a nursemaid. My papers are correct. What is this about?' She felt a slap across her cheek and her eyes watered.

'We ask the questions. We know who you are. British whore. Here to make trouble for our men. Strip her . . .'

They tore off the top of her pyjamas and her vest, leaving her breasts exposed, humiliating her in front of the staring faces. What on earth was going on? Had she landed in Belgium? Her memory blanked for a second. Had she landed badly concussed? How had she got here? Was this real?

'I assure you, I am Charlotte Blanken. I was going to the staffing agency in Brussels. They have work for me in an orphanage, in the kindergarten—'

'Enough of these lies. Do you think we believe your story? You are a courier sent to find enemies across the borders into France. Who sent you? Give us the name of your contacts. Stand up. Look, she's had a baby; her nipples are dark. She lies. This is no mademoiselle.' Someone tore at her pyjamas. 'See, stretch marks on her stomach. You lie, you whore. The British send us their whores to seduce our men.'

'I had a baby but he died. I am disgraced from my family. My mother is dead. My father made me leave.' Why was she saying all this, trying to get their sympathy, trying to cover for her obvious misnomer? They made her stand for hours until she was hoarse with protesting her innocence.

'You tell us lies to save your skin. There are better ways to stop these questions. Tell us what we already know. You are a British agent. You flew in from RAF Tempsford and before that you took your instructions from the Palace House at Beaulieu Abbey. We know everything . . .'

'I don't understand. This is nonsense. I am a Belgian citizen. My mother was French my father is Flemish. How can you say I am English?'

They pulled her down into a chair and tied her arms behind her back.

'Tell us the truth and we'll spare you the *baignoire*.' Her accuser pointed to a bath full of dirty water and covered in bloodstains. She didn't want to look at it but she did, and then shot them a look of pure contempt. It took every ounce of strength not to break into English. *Stick to your story, refuse to be cowed*. Who had betrayed her and taken her prisoner? She couldn't remember and their shouting befuddled her. It must be some dream she had to break through.

The questioning went on, her ears stinging from blows, her hands aching with the twisting of the rope. She couldn't contain her bladder and wet herself. They laughed but she clung to her story. 'I am Charlotte Blanken. I am a nurse and I sing "*Slaap, kindje ,slaap*" . . .' She found herself singing. 'I am not listening to you. I want to go home,' she wept. 'You have no right to keep me here.'

Suddenly the flashlight went out as someone pulled back a screen and daylight flooded in. She saw the soldiers removing their caps and smiling at each other, familiar faces she'd seen from training. A blanket was thrown over her but she couldn't stop shivering. 'You bastards!' she yelled as she was escorted out into the corridor. Someone shoved a drink into her hand but she was too weak to hold it and it crashed on the stone floor. This was the test all agents must pass before they were allowed any further. It was too real for comfort, too embarrassing. How had she stood up to it? Too weary now to care, she was told to go and sleep it off and return for debriefing later.

What if it had been true? There'd be no bed rest, just a foul prison cell and more of the same day after day until her spirit was broken. Callie sank on her pillow, trying to blot out the fear, the pain and the humiliation. No one warned her how bad this would feel. How could she survive it for real?

The last weeks in Beaulieu Abbey on the Hampshire coast were intense, living in little cottages within the beautiful grounds, sharing with her fellow agents, none of whom used their real names or gave any indication where they were heading. Here they were drilled in how to recognize enemy army uniforms and rank, to distinguish between Abwehr and Gestapo ranks and uniforms. All contacts must be with intermediaries with signals and passwords, and there were danger signs to learn to read on windows and doors. Callie's role as a courier was made plain to her: to decode messages and send them to the WT operator; to spot a good landing field. She had to learn how to move safely at night, avoiding the curfew. After months of hard training she knew the real war raged outside these walls but theirs was a special sort of campaign.

The victory at El Alamein was a signpost to future successes. She was relieved that Cairo was safe. How faraway that life seemed now. She wondered if Monica and Ken were still living there. These thoughts brought back memories of those afternoon siestas with Ferrand, before the world went crazy. If only she had gone to him when he asked they could be sharing danger together.

Only the knowledge that Desmond would be busy with his little friends and Jessie consoled her. Soldiers across the world would also be sacrificing their babies' childhoods, too, but her separation from her little boy hurt just the same. Phoebe would think her selfish to be putting her needs before his. If only she could whisper to her what she was doing, but the trainees were sworn to tell no one and her oath was sacred. Only when permission was granted to share this secret would she ever tell anyone the truth. They might guess but she would never break the burden of her silence.

The debriefing was thorough but she'd not done too badly. Just one or two glaring hesitations, and she must think only in French. The Flemish lullaby and the weeping, breaking into a simpering whine had been convincing, as if her mind could not take in their accusations.

'The answer to the stretch marks was good. Showed you could think on your feet. Your cover has to be flexible and heartfelt. Impressive, but don't expect any sympathy from your interrogators. You saw the bath and what we threaten. To survive the water torture you have to stay calm. They won't drown you if you've told them nothing.'

Callie was glad of the tranquillity of the Abbey gardens to recover from her ordeal. It reminded her of Dalradnor and the rose garden, a quiet oasis of calm in a troubled world. If she passed she'd be sent to a waiting place to finalize all the necessary arrangements and await the call. If she didn't pass she'd be sent somewhere out of the way to sit out the war where she could tell no one of her failure. This test was only a rehearsal but perhaps the experience might help save her life if she was unlucky.

The scent of the roses and herbs mixed together brought back memories of those first months nursing Desmond and singing to him. Would she ever see her son again? How would they explain her absence to him? She prayed that what she was doing was for the best; to help hasten the end of the war so that all children could live in peace.

22

'Would you mind if I took my day off tomorrow?' Jessie asked Phoebe one morning after breakfast. 'Only my young man has a pass and I'd like to bring him home to meet my family,' she smiled.

Jessie had met a young airman at a dance in Stirling and his name was always on her lips. Bob Kane was Australian, by all accounts, but of Scottish parentage, and he was making a big impression on the farmer's daughter. As it happened, Phoebe had no engagements that week and Madame and Mima were always on hand to take over. It was a pity Caroline hadn't made the effort to get to her son's birthday party, but she'd ordered a second-hand tricycle painted in bright red with a little bell on the handlebars, which was his pride and joy. He careered round the paths full of excitement and it was time they started thinking about his education.

It really was annoying, her being so unreliable. She'd written to say her unit was going abroad but she'd let them know where as soon as she could. They'd gone down to London for a week, staying in a hotel. Caroline had taken Desmond to the park and used her coupons to kit him out in new clothes. They'd watched a musical together with Primrose, and she'd given Phoebe a parcel of presents to wrap, should she not be back for Christmas. Primrose was looking shifty but said nothing, so when Phoebe got her alone she pounced.

'What's going on? Where's she off to now?'

'I don't know and I won't ask. That's not how it works. Careless talk and all that . . .'

'I do think she's being so thoughtless,' Phoebe added.

'Oh, don't say that. I think she's very brave. She doesn't want to leave you all but she has to do her duty.' Primrose looked so shocked at this criticism that it suddenly dawned on Phoebe that Caroline might be doing dangerous work, and she felt a stab of fear.

'Please tell me what she's up to.'

'I can't. I don't know, and if I did I wouldn't be allowed to tell you. All I do know is there are ways to win this war other than a line of tanks in the desert.'

'All this cloak-and-dagger stuff.' Phoebe sighed. 'I hope she knows what she's getting herself into.'

'I'm sure she's only too well aware . . . I'll certainly miss her company.'

'But she has a son – who'll look after him if the ship goes down?' Phoebe asked, thinking of how dangerous the waters around Britain were.

'She'll take every care to come back to him.' Primrose did not sound too convincing.

Phoebe tossed and turned in her hotel bed, trying to work out what Caroline was doing that was so hush-hush. It could be something to do with speaking French so well, perhaps. Would she be left holding the baby for the duration? Thank goodness Jessie Dixon was still in post, but for how long? Unmarried girls were needed for the war effort.

Now, in the fourth year of war, the weariness was hitting everyone one way or another: shortages, homelessness, rationing, same old rules and restrictions, no seaside trips, no unnecessary travel, no new clothes or provisions. She was sick of it all and the lack of real news. She had the worry of Caroline at the back of her mind as well. Every few months, postcards dropped on the doormat that said nothing much, and Desmond hardly bothered to look at them. Mummy was just a photograph in a silver frame, which they kissed every night.

Phoebe had to smile, knowing he was more worried about getting a fresh egg for his breakfast or some sweeties from the stores in the village, or whether Jacques was still his friend. It was this overwhelming sense of responsibility for a precious grandchild that worried her. She was not getting any younger and he could be a handful at times. She hoped Jessie wouldn't leave them to join up. Then what would she do . . . send him to boarding school? Always at the back of her mind was Caroline. Where was she? What was she doing that was so important it couldn't be shared?

23

The call came at the beginning of March, when a black car with rear windows curtained off from view arrived at the secret house near Huntingdon where Callie was resting up. It was dusk when she was driven to an airbase somewhere off the Great North Road. She peered out, trying to catch a glimpse of the country-side in the fading light. A long drive led to a mansion where she met Mrs Cameron, the Belgian Section Liaison officer who had mentored and shadowed her throughout her training. Mrs Cameron was a quiet intense woman with piercing dark eyes and she missed nothing of Callie's mission outfit as she stepped out of the car. This specially concocted going-away suit was entirely accurate for an out-of-work nursemaid going about her business on the streets of Brussels. It had a worn baggy skirt – useful for a quick getaway on a bicycle.

'The shoes are wrong,' Mrs Cameron said, pointing to them. 'Who will have leather shoes there by now? We'll have to find something more synthetic or sole them with tyre rubber.'

Callie was made to turn out her pockets in case anything had been overlooked: a bus ticket, an English cigarette stub, matches or lipstick. She had done this many times since she'd be made to wear these clothes and get a feel for them. Only then was she given a shabby handbag containing her identity card, ration book, a travel permit and a few cheap cosmetics, a crushed photo of an old couple. Her brief was to make her way from the

DZ – the drop zone – take a train to Brussels and wait around a café off the Grand Place until someone would approach her. She was warned to be careful. There was some uncertainty about how safe some of the resistance groups were now. Her role was to find safe printing houses and distribute leaflets and propaganda around the streets. She had a bulging wallet of passes and a wad of Belgian francs to pass over.

Later, she was transported to the hangar of the aerodrome where overalls were put on top of her clothes and she was strapped into her jumpsuit and helmet and all the paraphernalia she knew well by now. Mrs Cameron waited with her as she smoked her last cigarette on English soil, shook her hand and wished her luck, but not before she offered her pills: knockouts to thwart anyone suspicious, some concoction to keep her awake, and a cynanide lethal pill. This last one she refused, knowing now there would be no way out from torture, but she would not consider the possibility of death. She had too much to live for. It was the moment when the enormity of what she was about to do thumped into her chest. She walked across the tarmac trying not to shake and wondering if she would ever return.

There was the routine to follow, the checking of her harness, the hooking- up. As the engines throbbed and taxied away, she couldn't believe she'd let herself in for this mission. She just hoped she'd have a decent jump and that the reception party had got the right message over the air waves. She really didn't want to have to hide her parachute and make her way alone in a part of Belgium she barely knew.

The training kicked in and she lined up her feet dangling out of the opening, waiting for the green light when she must slide out into the abyss. There was no time to panic as she shot out into the night. The terror of the yawning space eased when she felt the jerk of the harness as the parachute unfurled above her head. Below she could see the faint flickering lights of the reception party. So far so good. For a few seconds, all she could feel was the euphoria of floating like a balloon in the air, relieved to be alive. It was a perfect landing, the best she'd ever done out of her five jumps. Then she saw the faces of her allies before they turned their flickering torches onto her face.

'Come,' said a rough voice. 'The flags are flying high.' He'd given her the right password and she responded with her own phrase.

'You have the codes for us?' The man's face was half hidden.

'Give me a chance to catch my breath,' she whispered, taking off her helmet to reveal her tousled blond hair.

'A woman?' she heard them mutter in surprise. 'What next. They must be desperate.' The men laughed.

'Our leader won't like this,' said a middle-aged man with a moustache.

'Tough. I can do my job as well as any man. Who notices a woman on a street?' She was boasting, annoyed that they were not taking her seriously. They muttered amongst themselves out of earshot. Trust her to land among a rough-looking lot of bigoted men. She had orders to stay put with them for twenty-four hours before breaking away to make her rendezvous.

'Where are you heading?' said the man with the moustache.

'That's my business,' she replied. No one should ask such a question.

'We can't pass you on unless we have the address and pass-word. Those were our instructions from London,' he said, pointing her to an old farmhouse. 'Come and get warm. We have to check that you are going to a safe place. There've been many arrests. Brussels is a dangerous place. Let me check it out first. The name?'

'A café close to the Grand Place. It is supposed to be safe.' It was good they were taking these precautions for her, she thought.

'And the name of your contact? I can check if he is still free,' the man insisted.

'The less you know the better for you. That's what I was told,' Callie snapped, suddenly feeling tired, hungry and dying for a pee. No one was offering her even a glass of acorn coffee.

'Let's see what's in your bag. I need to see your identity papers. I hope they're better than the first lot they sent.' He examined them with a sneer. 'This print is poor and the stamp too faint. You won't get far with these. We'll have to get you better ones. You'll stay here until it is safe to travel but you mustn't be seen. The farmer's wife might be jealous.'

Callie was too tired to protest. It was raining and the men pointed to a barn door. One of them pushed a blanket over her head to keep her dry. 'Don't want that fine raincoat soaked. Go ahead. It'll be safe to cross the yard.'

She walked ahead, grateful for the warmth of the covering until she felt someone shove her. 'Hurry up.' Her hand out went instinctively and she felt someone twisting it behind her back and grabbing the other. 'Stop fooling around!' she snapped. 'Just because I'm female . . . What the hell . . .! It's been a long night, boys.' It was then that she saw a figure step out of the shadows, and she froze. It was a soldier in German uniform.

'Don't worry about him; he's a tame one in borrowed uniform.' They opened the barn door, not letting go of Callie's hands. Now she felt sick with fear. This wasn't right. None of it felt right. Waiting for her inside the barn was a man in a leather coat and trilby. The sight of him brought a terrible realization that she had fallen straight into a trap, dropped into enemy hands like a gift from on high. At least she'd not given them her contact's name or the codes rolled in her cigarette lighter. But they already knew her destination and she felt sick that she'd betrayed it so trustingly.

They tied her hands behind her back, snatching her handbag containing her cash and her lighter and her compact. They bundled her into a van and drove through the night. No one said a word to her. She wanted to spit at them for being traitors to their country but she must now protect herself and her cover. All those months of training down the pan because somewhere someone was feeding false information to HQ, deceiving the wireless operators. How many other agents had fallen for the same tricks? All she felt was a burning rage. What they wanted now from her was the next contact, but they'd not get that. She didn't know him or her, thank God. You can't tell what you don't know, but how long would it take them to find this out for themselves?

They kept her awake for four nights and days in a room as awful as the one in Beaulieu where she'd practised for her mission. Questions merged into more questions and threats. They knew about Special Ops training houses, how the networks linked and where the wireless operators worked. They knew her codename, Meerkat, but that was all.

'I have no names to give you. If you know our methods then you will know I don't know them. I have nothing else to say. I can give you nothing more.' She tried to stand firm but also remembered to look helpless and uncertain hoping, despite what she had been told, perhaps to play on her interrogator's sympathies.

'Who persuaded you into this foolish enterprise? How can the British stoop so low as to use their women for such missions?' The interrogator, who wore an Abwehr uniform, searched her face.

'My boyfriend was killed in the war. I fight for his country and my own.'

'You will have to do better than that, Charlotte. Your cover is convincing, your papers are adequate. Where is your radio set?'

She managed to smile: so they didn't know her mission. 'I have no wireless. I have poor fingers. You can see. I know nothing about such a set.' She held out her bruised hands.

'We have sent a message to London to tell them you have arrived safely. Your future is in our hands. You can work with us or against us. It is your choice. Take us to your rendezvous and then you will be spared. Co-operate and you'll not be sent away to a place no decent woman of rank would ever survive. We want the codes.'

'What codes?'

'The ones you said you had on landing.'

'I have no codes. Your men made me feel small so I boasted. They said women were no good.' She was thinking fast, trying to remember what she had actually said to them.

'You will take us to your contact.' His voice was hardening.

'I told you, I have no contact. I was told to wait further instructions. You have my codename. That is all I have.' She feared the worst now.

'Take her away and let her rot for a few weeks. She might be more amenable when she's sat alone in a cell.' The man waved her away. She hoped at least she'd convinced him she was a novice courier and not very competent, just a minnow in the pond and not a wireless operator who they could add to their collection of stooges or shoot on sight.

That night, she sat in the dark damp fusty cell working through everything she'd said and withheld. The networks were ruined and there was nothing she could do to warn HQ. She had achieved nothing but a few weeks' respite before they started on her again.

Next time, they stripped her, took away her good clothes and left her half naked, but she'd given them some half-truths, stayed true to her training. By a stroke of luck, they'd given her back her bag, emptied of cash and the compact, but the cheap cigarette lighter in which her paper was hidden remained inside unexamined. She would ditch it as soon as she found a safe opportunity.

Callie wondered how long they would feed her and keep her here, and if she gave them nothing more, what next? Would London realize she'd been betrayed and arrested? She knew she must keep fit and exercise even on the cell's stone floor, doing a routine of stretches the instructor had taught her. How long did she have before they sent her to a place where she'd never see daylight and freedom again?

The postcards kept coming but there was something not quite right about them, Phoebe decided. They weren't real, just a few lines of, 'I am well and missing you all. Kisses from Mummy.' Every time she wrote to Primrose to ask her if she'd heard from Caroline there was never a satisfactory answer. 'She's doing splendid work with her team.' It didn't take a genius to work out she was somewhere in France now that D–Day had dawned and Jerry was on the run. Once France was liberated she'd come home at long last.

Caroline had not seen her son for over a year and he no longer asked about her at bedtimes or kissed her photo with any enthusiasm. I might not have been the world's best mother myself, Phoebe thought, but this absence is ridiculous. She was watching Desmond playing snap with Jessie. They'd managed to keep her at Dalradnor even though she was now engaged to Bob Kane and planning a life in Australia. Bob called in when he could and played football with Desmond and Jacques. 'This boy needs a man about the house,' he laughed ruffling the little boy's mop of dark curls. 'He's turning into a Sheila with all you women at his beck and call.'

Desmond was enrolled at the village school and got plenty of stern teaching from Miss Armour-Brown, but the more pliable females of his home were soon to be reduced in number. A long overdue Red Cross postcard arrived for Madame from her husband: not the usual twenty-five words this time, but real news. There were plans for their repatriation back to Guernsey as soon as it was safe. This sent the Laplanche family into a flurry of sewing and buying presents to take back.

That left only Jessie and the boy living in with Phoebe, and if Jessie upped sticks, just the two of them. Sometimes in the silence of the night, Phoebe wondered if Caroline was ever coming back to them. It was time she made more enquiries at the address she had been given in London. It was time for some honest answers.

Her ENSA engagements continued, but she found them tiring. Sometimes she fell asleep between acts and there was no spring in her step on stage. Her agent kept trying for new character parts at the film studios but there was always some crisis in Dalradnor to attend to: the coke boiler breaking down, the cart needing attention. The strain of keeping everyone clothed, fed and warm through a devilishly cold winter was taking its toll on her. Old Dr McClusky said her blood pressure was too high and she must rest more. Sir Lionel had died and Verity moved south, leaving Phoebe feeling more isolated. They had little in common except the link to Arthur and Caroline, but they exchanged cards at Christmas, this, Phoebe's only link with Arthur's family now.

It was hard going back to London to face all the ruins. The mansion apartments were still as she'd left them, but picked over by looters and now with weeds growing through the rubble. There was no one who really mattered to her in town. Billy had found somewhere near Brighton to live.

Phoebe wrote to the Ministry demanding more information, but all she got in return were assurances that Caroline was doing important work and would contact her as soon as she was free to do so. She felt she was being fobbed off yet again, and the uneasy feeling that Caroline was not as safe as they made out wouldn't leave her. When will we ever see you again? she cried, but there was no one to answer her.

24

St-Gilles Prison stood like a fortress on the outskirts of Brussels, a grey forbidding place. Few sounds from outside penetrated its thick walls: the occasional muffled hum of night bombers and the horns of prison traffic through the gates. Callie felt the gloom of incarceration closing round her, the endless monotony of routine with day following dragging day as she watched the summer shaft of strong light beam through the high window on the cell wall gradually turning into the thin glimmer of winter as the days shortened.

She marked off the days of the week with scratches on the stone floor. Nine months she'd been left to rot, and after those first intense bursts of questioning when she'd stuck rigidly to her story and given nothing more away, they'd shut her up in solitary confinement. There had been a brief interlude of company when they had introduced a pretty prisoner with a sympathetic ear, imprisoned for black marketeering – or so she said. All smiles and sympathy, she was trying to ferret out information – a set-up if ever there was one – and when Callie refused to discuss anything with her the prisoner disappeared as quickly as she had arrived. A change of company had its comforts – another voice, another story – but now she was left to moulder over her coming fate.

Every sound became familiar: the changing of the guard, the morning slop-out, the spy hole in the door opening as a torch beamed in on her face as the shadows fell. The food was basic: hard bread, thin soup, slops, and never enough to drink to slake her constant thirst. She felt her body weakening.

If only she had a photograph of someone she cared for to stare at, instead of bare walls. She invented stories about the old couple standing under an apple tree in her cover photo.

Surely, if the Gestapo were going to dispose of her, they would have done so already. Were they playing a cat-and-mouse game? She had no useful information to give them now. She tried tapping messages in Morse code on the heating pipe that ran around the wall, but so far had had no response. There were whispers that the Allies were on the march and it wouldn't be long to Liberation, but she didn't believe them. Hope was dangerous. She must prepare for the worst. In the exercise yard she gleaned what she could about other political prisoners as they paced feet behind each other, watched by guards if they drew too close. All she heard was that many men had been sent to the Tir National to be shot. She thought of Edith Cavell, a heroine every schoolgirl knew. Her last days were spent in this very prison and Callie took courage from the story of her bravery in her final moments.

Getting from one day to the next without falling into that ever gaping pit of despair was what mattered most. It was hard to live with fear and hunger gnawing in her gut. She heard sobs and screams in the night but so far no one had tortured her, though the threat hung over her like a silent menace, as did the fear of going insane in this isolation.

There were some redeeming acts of kindness. A Flemish wardress brought her a Bible, blunt scissors to cut her toenails, and some tattered books. She looked into her face as if Callie was a human being worthy of respect. Sometimes her soup had extra meat floating in it, enough to chew and feel the nourishment. To survive, she must find a sanctuary in this dark place. Survival of the spirit was its own form of resistance. Her training had briefly touched on how to survive in prison. She kept on tapping her Morse code but no one answered. Was she alone on this upper floor? She had a pencil to make notes in her Bible margins. She even asked for a priest, but none turned up. Every night she did battle with the bugs that would feed on her if not caught. There was a whole army of them in her straw mattress that she would never overcome.

Each day, she retreated into a form of mental exercise, taking one bit of her life, stripping it into minute detail and recalling every pleasant part she could. How the loch shimmered in the sunlight at Dalradnor and the snow on the hills glistened in the sun. She visited every room of the house, the stables, the gardens where the roses were in full bloom. She rode Hector again and relived her childhood sitting in a tree with the twins from the farm, Niven and Nairn. She took the train from Milngavie into Glasgow and visited all the famous department stores, pausing to admire the Argyll Arcade full of jewellery shops. She smelled the chalk and ink in Miss Cameron's classroom. In this way she could leave the four walls and roam at will into the Scottish countryside.

This treat had to be earned by an hour of stretches and poses to flex her slack muscles and calm her breathing. How she'd cursed the PT trainer for increasing repetitions and making her sweat, but now the exercise was a lifesaver. She pressed her arms against the wall to strengthen her upper body, ran on the spot, but with so little decent food she knew not to exhaust herself. There were occasional showers when she relished the icy chill to cleanse her body and got rid of her lice-ridden clothes. Her periods had ceased, which was a blessing, but she was wasting away in this place.

There were good days, but also bad days with too much time to dwell on all that she was missing. What had she achieved? Only failure and betrayal, and there was always the terror that she'd never see her son again. At night, it took all her willpower and bloody-mindedness not to go mad with these dark thoughts. There had to be hope that the Allies would arrive one day.

Bombing raids were more frequent. It was after one such night raid that the door opened and the wardress shouted at her to get dressed: '*Schnell. Alles einpacken!*'

What a joke; all she had was a ragged pillowcase with a change of underwear, a Bible, and a stump of a toothbrush. Did this mean the end? She hardly dared to hope after all this time.

'Am I free?'

The wardress laughed. 'Agents like you will never be free. Special orders from Berlin, you are to be sent to somewhere safer in Germany. Your escort is waiting.' For once, the woman did not look her in the face but whispered as she left, 'You will need more than good luck where you're going.'

Callie was amongst a group of women bundled into a truck with no windows, escorted by guards onto a train and sealed in a darkened compartment with more guards. They travelled east through the darkness for days and nights. Eventually, exhausted, starving, aching, they were pushed off the train in a siding with their luggage and marched for many miles under female guards before being shoved through the large iron gates of a labour camp north of Berlin at a place called Ravensbrück. Little did Callie know that she was entering *L'enfer des Femmes*, the Women's Hell.

25

Desmond blew out the six candles on his birthday cake. Mima had made a sponge rolled into an engine shape, covered in real chocolate powder and dotted with dolly mixtures. Jessie had given him magic colouring books and knitted him a new jumper made from unravelling the wool from one of Mummy's old ones, kept in her trunk for when she came home again. Granny Phee gave him a pound note to spend on anything he liked, and some sweetie coupons too. He'd invited three boys from school for tea and they played football and tag in the garden until the gong rang.

He liked being six but he wished Jacques and the girls were still here to play with him. They were now back in Guernsey, and the house wasn't the same. Jessie was going to leave him too as he was too old for a nursemaid now. When Mummy came back, he'd be sent away to school, Granny said, but he liked the little school in the village and he was now in Mr Pearson's class. He could read all the posters in the shop and on the church notice board. He didn't want to go away.

When he grew up he wanted to be in the Royal Air Force like Sergeant Kane, Jessie's special friend. He was tall and wore a scratchy uniform with stripes on his arm. He brought him bits of a Jerry plane, which he swapped for marbles in the playground. The sergeant teased him about his curls and threatened to cut them off. He told him he looked like a 'Sheila', but Sheila Prentiss in his class didn't look a bit like him.

Jessie would be going to Australia after she was married and he would be a page boy at the wedding. Bob Kane said boys shouldn't dress up, but Jessie said he was going to wear his kilt and jacket, and that kilts were worn only by the bravest of soldiers. She said that she'd not marry him if Desmond couldn't wear his kilt and carry the ring.

Granny Phee came home from the theatre for the Easter wedding in the parish church. It was exciting seeing all the other airmen, their uniforms making an arch up the path and the villagers standing by the gate to watch the bride going in. She did look pretty in a pink frock and carrying a bouquet of flowers, and on her head she wore a pink hat covered with net. All her sisters wore dresses and carried posies. The church was so full of flowers it made him sneeze. He wore heather on his jacket for good luck.

They had a special tent in the garden for the guests to have tea and photographs. How could Jessie ever leave him and go so far away? He couldn't remember a time when she wasn't there at night to tuck him in or comfort him if he had a bad dream. Granny Phee said when the war was over Jessie would go on a big ship across the world to make her home with Sergeant Kane and meet his family, who had a farm just like Jessie's family had, but he didn't want to think about that now.

'Why can't I go with her?' he asked.

Granny looked shocked. 'You don't belong to her. When your mummy comes home, she'll be looking after you,' she replied, pointing to the photo in the silver frame.

He didn't know who that lady was and he didn't want her to come back. He wanted to go with Jessie on the big ship and be a pirate on the sea and live with Jessie for ever. It was bad enough after the wedding when she went on holiday with her husband to Edinburgh for a few days in a hotel. It was such a relief to see her back in the house again, and she brought him some Edinburgh rock and a tie to match the tartan of his kilt.

He had run to meet her, clinging to her. Granny had been kind and kept showing him pictures from her stage book and school pictures of his mummy with pigtails and school uniform. Sometimes they had lived in London, but that house was bombed and now Granny had to live here when she wasn't with the Stardrop Troupe, but she didn't run around or play games outside like Jessie. She liked quiet games and listening to the wireless while he played ludo and snakes and ladders with Jessie before bedtime. Granny was always making trunk calls about Mummy to people he didn't know.

There'd been trouble at school when someone said his dad must be a conchie. That meant he didn't fight in the war. He told them to shut up and he hadn't got a father – he didn't need one – and the older boys laughed at him and called him 'a right wee Jessie'. 'You can't have a baby without a dad!' He didn't understand what they meant so he kicked out at them and it turned into a fight. Mr Pearson came into the playground and called them into line. They all got six from the tawse on the palm of their hands for fighting.

Although it hurt, Desmond didn't cry until he got home. There was no one to tell what had happened. Jessie had gone to see her husband off on the train to the docks and came back all teary-eyed, so he couldn't tell her. Everyone was sad. Granny Phee was sad because there had been no more postcards from Mummy for months. Everyone was whispering in corners, behind doors.

One day, Granny came into his bedroom and said Mummy wouldn't be coming home for a long time so he must be brave and not cry. They were trying to find out where she was, but he didn't mind her being lost. All he could think about was if Jessie left him behind when she went on the ship. Then suddenly there was a holiday from school and the bells were ringing everywhere to tell them war was over and won. They flew flags from the top of the school hall and had a tea party in the village street with buns and sandwiches, jelly and pop, even though it was raining. Then they went into the parish room for dancing while Jimmy Baird played his accordion. Miss Armour sat at the piano and they had a sing-song, and everyone was laughing even though there was still fighting far away.

Jessie said Sergeant Bob was going to have to carry on over there until it ended but once it was finished she'd be on a list of sailing brides to be with him, and Desmond started to cry.

'I want to come too. Don't leave me here. I want to stay with you.'

She cuddled him. 'I know, hen, but it wouldn't be right. You belong to Miss Caroline. She'll come back soon to be your mammy.'

He shook his head. That was no comfort at all.

26

In the half-light of dawn the women were corralled through the gates by snarling dogs and armed guards. All Callie could see was row upon row of barrack huts. The women were pushed into one hut for processing, stripped and deloused with powder, all their body hair shaved in front of men eyeing their nakedness. Callie was given a faded uniform of blue shirt and a skirt that might once have been red, a headscarf to cover her bald head. There was no protesting at this humiliation. They were all too stunned and weary by the long journey. All her belongings from the outside world were taken from her, but she managed to hold onto her boots. She was registered as Charlotte Blanken, a Belgian political prisoner, this status indicated by the red triangle badge on her sleeve along with a number. They were marched out into the cold and taken to more wooden huts, told to find a space for themselves by female warders with black armbands, who walked up and down with whips to keep order.

The hut had a central aisle and three-tier bunks jam-packed with human beings, crammed like animals in cages. The smell made her want to vomit – a rank odour of urine, sick, sweat and fear – but she was too shocked to do anything. Her one thought was: how do I survive this?

After almost a year of solitary confinement, to see this teeming mass of humanity overwhelmed her: stick-thin females dressed in rags, staring at her with hopeless eyes, hollow cheeks and white skin. She had heard rumours of such camps, but to find herself forced into such a place made her shake with horror. Panic rose as she searched for a single face that looked alive with a little hope left. No one said anything, showed much interest in her arrival. She was just one more body to squeeze work out of until she gave up or was disposed of.

Months of honing an instinct to survive made her hide her true identity. Here, as in St-Gilles Prison, she was Lotte Blanken, Belgian nursemaid and French speaker. This was no place for Caroline, the true bit of herself, a mother with a son who lived in Dalradnor, and who has trained with the SOE. Those precious facts were like hoarded gems, her currency for survival. They might starve her body but her true self must be hidden from view. They mustn't touch this bit of her soul for if they did she'd be lost for ever.

She heard someone speaking French and then others replying. Was this a barracks of foreigners? She sought out the voices and stood before them, introducing herself. '*Lotte, et vous?*'

She was in luck. They were recent arrivals, eager for any news of the outside world. She told them what she knew about the liberation of France. An older woman with white hair grasped her hand. 'It won't be long then; Holy Mary, hear my prayer.' She crossed herself. 'I am Celine. I was arrested for helping soldiers to escape forced labour. My husband was shot. This is Madeleine, and this Marie. 'Why are you here?'

Callie told them her cover story. She was a nursemaid to a fine house near Bruges who had travelled with the family abroad and spoke English. She'd helped airmen escape down a secret line and for that she was betrayed. They accepted her story without question. She only wished it were true. The truth was far more mundane. She had done nothing to help the Resistance but survive, but she was now a witness to all of this.

'We've heard that the new internees are being sent off to work in other camps – farm work, indoor work or road building – but you have to look young and strong. They work you to the bone and then it is the crematorium,' said Madeleine, holding out her hand to Callie. She was short, with dark eyes and a stubble of black hair. 'You might as well know how things are in this hell on earth. Thousands of women live here, packed like sardines in a tin. There's a place they call the Youth Camp, where you'll be sent if you are sick. No one ever returns from there.'

Callie listened with a sinking heart. 'One more thing,' the girl added in a whisper. 'Watch the warders, especially the one with the whip and the thick plaits. She will smile and help you at first, give you extra bread, but she wants a fee. She takes her favourites to a place where you must satisfy her desires and when she tires of you, watch out. Even more . . . there are some who'll set their dogs on you if you look at them, just for the fun of it. I'm sorry, but you have to know these things. To them, we are all animals, just numbers, but in here we have names and lives we once lived.'

Celine smiled. 'Don't worry. Keep your hands clean and watch your food; turn your back and it will be stolen. Stick with us, Lotte. It can't be long until the Russians come. The guards are afraid of them and yet they treat the Russian women worst of all, especially after the defeat at Stalingrad. News comes through the gates even in this godforsaken place. You hear terrible things in the work sorties.'

Nothing they told her could prepare her mind for the sights she was forced to witness each day or the pain she must bear on the work parties. Bodies hung from scaffolds after public executions. Long lines of frozen girls and children lined up for *Appel* before dawn, line upon frozen line not daring to move as the guards counted them and picked some at random to beat them down to the ground and set the dogs on to finish them off.

'You must stand still, not look, not draw attention to your fear and disgust, try to look defeated not angry and hold onto your dignity. Don't give them the satisfaction of making you less than you are,' said Celine. 'Together we will survive. Look over the wire to the trees, to the birds flying. One day we'll be free like them.'

Callie clung onto her sanity as her body adjusted to the cold and the thin clothes, the screams and the pathos. The smell of the latrines overwhelmed her. It was only a matter of time before she fell sick. She fought off the night creepers who tried to steal her bowl and hidden crusts. She kept to the shadows when the female dominatrix was on the prowl. The four of them squeezed onto the top bunk for warmth and protection. The December snows of 1944 covered the camp, disguising its horrors and ugliness. To stand on that frozen square for hours made inmates faint with chill, but you mustn't move or waver. To her relief Callie joined the French women's works gang sent to a place outside the walls, where the food and living quarters were a little better. They were made to dig vegetables out of the frozen ground. Then they were sent to another camp further afield to hack stones and shift hard core to make new roads. Callie's fingers and feet were numb with chill. She had so little protection from the cold with the overalls they were given, but she still kept boots on her feet and tied them to her body each night.

'We have to escape.' Madeleine was always full of plans, searching out gates and ways to bribe the other workers.

'Not in this weather,' Celine argued, coughing harder each time they went out. She was finding it hard to keep up with them. They tried to cover for her, making sure the guard didn't see. It took twelve of them to pull the heavy roller across the hard core, pulling until the sweat poured and their arms were numb, but they mustn't stop. One woman fainted and lay on the frozen rubble, unable to get up. The guard stood over her and whipped her with his baton until she curled up to protect herself.

'Get on with your work!' he ordered the others, as he dragged the woman to the side and shot her.

'Do nothing,' muttered Celine, seeing Callie's face. 'His time is coming.'

'How can you be sure?' Callie whispered.

'I know, in my heart, it will be only a matter of time and we will be saved. Do not dwell on these things or they will destroy you.'

They returned to the camp, aching, angry and starving. The body of the woman lay where she fell, frozen into the ground. Soon Callie saw so much death, she hardly glanced, though her heart was stricken by such cruelty. In this terrible place there was no mercy, no allowances. Every one of them was nothing more than a disposable workhorse, the choice only to work or die. There were plenty more where they came from, but the rage inside Callie burned into her bones. I will survive and tell how it was, she vowed. The others said nothing. All that mattered was fuel and food and surviving until the morning *Appel*.

'There is only one certain way out of here,' sighed Marie, the youngest of Callie's friends, 'and that is through the fiery furnace of the crematorium. They think we have no souls here, that we are the walking dead, but we will get out of here another way.'

'Let's not think on these things,' said Celine. 'I have a game we can play. Lie on the bunk and each one tell us your favourite menu. Pretend we're in a brasserie and you can order what you like.'

'It'll only make me hungry,' groaned Madeleine. 'But I would like *pot au feu*, with thick dark sauce, a green salad with vinaigrette, some Vignotte cheese and Maman's special dessert, *tarte aux pommes*.'

'How would you set your table, what colour of cloth and what flowers in the vase?' Celine encouraged her to spin out her story.

They took it in turns to describe the dishes and Callie found she could picture them in her head and taste the garlic and herbs. She chose Mima's shepherd's pie with a buttery crust, followed by strawberries and Capaldi's best ice cream. Her mouth watered from just the picture of it in her mind. For a few minutes they had lifted themselves out of this living hell to another place. She thanked God that she'd found such good friends. They had saved her sanity and her life for a few days more.

Another time, they decided it would be everyone's birthday and each must prepare to give the others surprise gifts, easier said than done. On the sortie in the sub camp, there were banks of spring flowers pushing their way through the grass, enough for Callie to make a daisy chain of tiny flower heads, which she threaded together into a necklace for Celine. Celine was growing thinner and more breathless every day, and by the end of the twelve-hour shift she struggled to get up and they had to hold her on the way home, but she wore the necklace with such pleasure.

A week later came the medical inspection they all dreaded. They were lined up before the guards and warders and told to lift their skirts high above their waists so that their hipbones protruded. They were made to run in front of the SS guards and camp doctor, who was looking for swollen feet and knees. Callie was so busy proving her fitness she didn't notice Celine struggling at first until she was pulled out. 'Run!' the guard shouted at her. Celine did her best but she couldn't keep up. She was too weak and her knees were swollen. She fell on the floor, coughing with exhaustion. 'To the recovery bay,' said the doctor. The guards threw her onto a waiting cart. Once it was full of broken women, it left for the Youth Camp. The others stood stunned at her sudden departure, not able even to say goodbye. Then they were dismissed. No one spoke. What was there to say? Each knew they'd never see their friend again. Just one more cruel humiliation to bear.

'We have to get away now. Celine would want us to survive,' whispered Marie. That night they said prayers and wept.

Callie had no feelings left to pray. She felt so numb, she couldn't even summon up any rage to fuel her resolve. For the first time in months, she wanted to curl up and die. She couldn't bear to think what was happening to her friend, alone and in pain. There were no priests in sight to give her comfort. Her heart cried, Why? While her friends prayed, she curled up on the bunk, all hope gone.

'You mustn't give up or you're dead,' Marie tried to encourage her. 'Celine will soon be free but she will never see her children again. Who is waiting for you to come home? You must hold on to your hope, Lotte! Fight them all the way, hold on to your will to live.'

Those were darkest hours, when she felt her mind was slipping away. She could no longer recognize herself as Caroline nor could she see Desmond in her mind's eye. Lotte Blanken was who she was now; this bony starved body covered in sores, a creature who'd seen too many horrors. Maddy recognized how she was sinking into self-pity.

'Remember, one day at a time, we work on and stay angry,' she said, shaking Callie back to life with plots to escape. 'Stick together and we might live. Alone you are dead. We mustn't get sent back to Ravensbrück. This place is better than that death camp. Slacken off and you will be sent for punishment there. Don't give the sadists the satisfaction of beating you to death.'

A few days later, they were sent forward to yet another camp at Markkleeberg, working on roads in atrocious spring weather with only overalls and shawls that Maddy had sewn for them from Celine's blanket. Hauling the dreaded roller drained every ounce of their strength. They were all beginning to weaken, but news trickled through that the Allies were at last fighting their way east through Germany and this buoyed up their frozen limbs.

Then, a month later, without warning, they were pulled out into the yard one night and told to gather their belongings for a march west. It was late and snow still lay hard on the ground. They put on their overalls and shawls to add a little warmth and hoped their broken boots, patched and leaking, would protect their feet. Maddy had also sewn them over-socks from scraps of clothing no longer needed, squirrelled away and worked at in secret whenever she could. They'd brought Celine's hidden stores, only a pathetic little bundle, but Marie hugged them into her chest as if they were bringing Celine herself with them.

They marched all night, mile after frozen mile in a silent column. The guards beamed their torches along the lines at regular intervals but never counted them.

'This is our chance,' whispered Maddy, seeing the road curving through a dark forest of tall trees. 'Peel off one by one and hide.'

There was no time to think as Callie watched Maddy dart behind a tree. No one noticed and none of the prisoners dared look in her direction. Then Marie bent down to fiddle with her boot and vanished, and Callie knew it was now or never as she scarpered into the darkness. Fear put wings on her feet. No shots rang out, no dogs barked, just the silence of the snow and the crackle of twigs. She waited hardly daring to breathe until the column marched away. How many others had taken this chance of freedom?

There was a strange eeriness in the forest, a great void of light, and the piercing chill froze her breath. Encircled, defence-less, frightened that she was now alone in an unknown wilderness of snow, Callie crept deeper into the forest. If she stood still she might never move from the spot but be left frozen in death as she had seen so many poor victims in the camp. Keep moving, keep living, she urged her will.

Now, at last, there was hope. As dawn broke she pushed further into the forest, hoping against hope that she would find her friends. With no food or shelter she hadn't a clue where they were heading. They must be found, and soon.

'Over here, over here . . .' a welcome voice whispered. They were hiding behind tree trunks, waiting for her. She hugged them with a delirium of gratitude.

'We did it! We're free!' Marie was dancing in the snow. 'But what do we do next, Maddy?'

Now it was Callie's turn to take the lead. 'We'll find food and shelter and make a fire.'

Maddy looked at her with surprise. 'And just how do we do that without being caught?'

'I'll show you,' Callie heard herself say. There were still bits she could bring to mind about those survival trials in Arisaig. She had the scars to prove it. 'We need dry sticks and tinder; something for trapping.' Suddenly she felt alert, alive. They were in terrible danger with no papers or money, but for the moment she knew how to keep them all safe just as they had saved her in the camp. Now she would repay their trust by fixing a fire, catching something to roast and finding water. Only then could they make plans.

27

Phoebe waited daily for news of Caroline, writing letters to the Ministry requesting information. Nothing was forthcoming, so she contacted her local MP. He was busy preparing for the coming General Election but he promised to look into matters. For Phoebe, sleep was more and more elusive and she was stung with headaches. Desmond was being a handful, wanting to play out with local boys in the village, who were friends with him one minute and enemies the next. His school work was suffering and Jessie warned that he was getting into the wrong company. Sometimes Jessie took Desmond to the family farm just to get him out of Phoebe's hair.

Bob Kane was in a service in the Far East and Jessie was anxious for him. The war might be over here, but rations were getting tighter than ever. How she looked forward to being reunited with him, in a new life, in a bright and warm place.

It was time for Phoebe to find new accommodation down south and pick up her career, what was left of it. She decided to start looking for a preparatory school somewhere close to London so she could have Desmond in the holidays. The burden of the child's education and welfare weighed on her mind. I'm too old to be his parent, she sighed. What else could she do until Caroline came home? It wasn't fair to have to make important decisions without her.

One afternoon in July, an army staff car rolled up the drive and a woman emerged in WAAF uniform. She introduced herself as Mrs Cameron, who liaised between various official departments including the FANY. Phoebe was tired and harassed, hoping she'd learn something about Caroline, but also hoping the woman wouldn't stay long. Desmond had been naughty again in school and Jessie had removed him out of her way.

Phoebe took the woman into the drawing room and Mima produced afternoon tea on a tray with fresh soda scones and rhubarb jam. Let no one say that standards had slipped at Dalradnor.

'What a fine house this is,' said Mrs Cameron, looking round at the landscape oil paintings on the walls and the view down to the loch from the windows. 'Miss Faye, I'm sure you must be anxious to know how we are progressing with Mrs Lloyd-Jones's whereabouts. I'm sorry you've had to wait so long but we are still making enquiries. Since the war ended the continent is full of soldiers, refugees and prisoners trying to get home.'

'Where is my daughter?' Phoebe no longer wanted any pretence about their relationship, any misunderstanding about her concern.

'That's the problem. We can't be sure what happened to her.'

'What do you mean? She was in the services. There must be records. Yes, I did guess she'd gone abroad.' Phoebe looked at the lady, who smiled as she sipped her tea.

'I'm afraid it's not that simple. Caroline was doing specialized work.'

'What sort of work?' Phoebe interrupted.

'I'm not at liberty to say but work of national importance . . .' She looked up to see if Phoebe was picking up on what was not being said.

'Where?' This hedging about was not good enough.

'In Belgium . . . during the occupation.'

Phoebe shook her head. 'I knew she was holding out on me . . . that figures. She had a Belgian nurse and a boyfriend. Is she with him?'

'Any addresses you have might be helpful at this stage. She disappeared from our radar . . . Don't be alarmed. It's only a matter of time before she'll turn up safe and sound.'

'Has she been held captive?'

'We think so. Records are being checked and in due course—'

'In due course! How long will it take? The war's been over for months . . .' Phoebe felt her anger flaring up. This was ridiculous.

'It depends on many other factors,' Mrs Cameron sat back. 'You have to understand—'

'Is she still alive?' Phoebe blurted out, her heart beating fast.

'Unfortunately, I can't give you a straight answer. We just don't know. I'm sorry. As soon as we hear anything . . . We know she was in St-Gilles in Brussels. Someone saw her there in 1944.'

'But that's a year ago . . . Where can she be now? So all those postcards we received . . was it you who . . .?' Phoebe wanted to shake the woman as she sat there admiring the wallpaper.

'That is normal procedure for all our service personnel.'

She was being cagey again and very cautious, giving nothing away, but Phoebe wanted more than platitudes. 'You've been feeding me false hope all this time? Are you also saying we must prepare ourselves for the worst of outcomes?'

'Not necessarily, but only time will give us the full facts. I'm sorry to burden you with uncertainty. It's only fair to be honest at this early stage.'

'But surely, you can tell me what on earth she was doing in Belgium?'

Mrs Cameron chewed on her scone and didn't answer.

'Dammit all, she has a young son! What am I going to tell him?' Phoebe pounced into the silence.

'Nothing at the moment but there's always hope in these cases . . .'

'So there are other women like Caroline? How many have returned?'

'Some have returned safe and sound from labour camps in Germany,' Mrs Cameron replied, smiling.

'And the others?'

'I'm not at liberty to say. I have no access to other departments.'

'I see,' Phoebe said curtly. 'My own child disappears into the mist on important duties and I will be the last to know what she was doing and why?'

'I'm sorry to be so circumspect, Miss Faye, but there are rules about how much information we can release. You have been told as much as we know. We will keep you informed, I promise you. It would be what Caroline would have wished.'

'You talk as if she were dead.'

'I didn't mean to . . . I do apologize. It's been a long drive here. I did want to explain to you in person. There's always hope,' Mrs Cameron said, rising up. 'I wish I could have brought more definite news.'

'No news is good news in this household.' Phoebe sighed, feeling faint as she stood up quickly.

'Let's hope so. I'll ring as soon as we have more news. I am so glad to have met you. You must be so proud of your daughter. She is a brave determined young lady.' With that accolade she departed promptly, leaving Phoebe standing at the door unable to move for the shock of her words and shaking with fear.

She staggered back into the drawing room and flopped into the armchair, her eyes shutting with despair. *Oh, Caroline, where are you? What made you do such a foolhardy thing?* She lay back, her head throbbing as if hammers were chipping into her brain.

When Mima came in to clear away the tray, she found Phoebe sitting staring through the window, her face twisted, her tongue hanging loose, her body lopsided, unable to lift her arms. 'Madam!' Mima cried. 'Jessie, come down quickly . . . I'll ring for the doctor. Don't move.'

Phoebe couldn't speak, smile or move, frozen by this sudden weakness down her side, imprisoned in the chair. What on earth was happening now, she thought as the room faded from view.

28

Callie struggled to make the spark and light the dry tinder from the forest floor. They hugged the tiny blaze, warming stones to ease their frozen fingers but always fearful the smoke would give them away. They found a few pine cones with seeds inside and roasted them, melting snow in their cans for the warmth of hot water, chewing on the last of their black crusts, making each mouthful last, not knowing when they would eat again.

'We can't stay here,' Maddy warned. 'If we head west we might meet the Allies. We just keep walking.'

'But we don't know where they are. Perhaps we should head back to town and get more news,' Marie suggested.

'Are you mad? We'd be recognized in these things,' Maddy argued.

'Not if we travel by night. I have an idea,' Callie added. 'If we can get rid of the camp stripes, we have the dark overalls, but if we could find some things to cover up . . .'

'But how?' Maddy was not convinced. 'We have no papers; we'll be caught and sent back. I'd rather die than go back there.'

'It won't come to that, I promise,' Callie tried to reassure her friend. 'Trust me.'

They spent the second night sleeping in a bombed-out house on the edges of Markkleeberg. Callie did a quick recce, seeing what looked like a farmhouse in the distance. They daren't risk asking for help there but she saw crops in the field. The morning was breezy and fair, and there was washing strung along the hedge, fluttering in the breeze. How she longed for clean linen on her skin.

'Stay under cover,' she ordered.

'Where're you going?'

'Over there,' she smiled, pointing to the farmhouse.

'Are you off your head?' Marie grabbed her arm.

'We have to get rid of these shirts. It's important. I'll grab what I can.'

'And have the dogs on you?' Maddy cried.

'There are ways . . .'

Her old training was kicking in. She crawled along the ground downwind of the dogs, if there were any, creeping along the hedge, covered in mud. She pulled a man's shirt and a sheet from the hedge, then a vest with sleeves, some socks. There was a tempting blouse on the line but she saw a dog suddenly rouse itself to investigate and she crept back, crushing her booty underneath her body.

The girls rushed out to pull her back undercover, delighted with her haul. They carried the clothing deep into the forest. Between them they were able to cover their camp uniforms sufficiently. It was too cold to think of removing them completely and losing their warmth. They tore the thin sheet into squares of headscarves to cover their stubbly heads and the rest they draped into neckerchiefs to hide their uniforms.

The effort to scavenge had cost Callie nervous energy and she found she was weakening faster than the others. They knew they must keep walking, hungry and blistered, always on the fringes of daylight, but progress was slow and they drank where they could, even dirty rainwater. By the time they'd not eaten for three days, all of them had stomachs cramps and Callie began to vomit and retch. She had taken in too much foul liquid and fever was beginning to make her shiver. She didn't want to hold them back but she was finding it hard to walk. When they

reached the outskirts of Leipzig she knew she could go no
further.

'Leave me here,' she pleaded, but the others ignored her.

They were just moving on again when they saw in the distance
a posse of SS soldiers walking towards them. Callie's heart sank.
They had no identity papers or permits and it was nearly dark.

'Say nothing, either of you. Leave this to me and look very
sick,' Maddy whispered as they clung to each other.

'Papers,' shouted one of the soldiers, eyeing them with suspicion. Maddy stood tall and spoke in almost perfect German.
'We have no papers, they are back at the camp.' She pointed
vaguely into the distance. 'We're French field workers in the
forest. Look, we're covered in pine needles. This one is very
sick and we got separated. We've got permission to take her for
treatment. You can see she has a fever. Don't stand too
close . . . It may be TB.'

The soldier stepped back at her words, eyeing Callie with
interest, seeing the sweat rolling down her brow. It stood to
reason she needed two girls to help her walk. 'Carry on,' he
ordered, and they staggered into the twilight, shaking with
relief. Maddy had saved them once again. 'You have to stand
firm, look them in the eye and lie through your teeth in good
German. That's one of the benefits of having lived on the border
in Alsace,' she said with pride in her eyes.

As they got ever closer to the city, they met men and families
trundling along with hand carts piled with mattresses and children and chickens. They were heading west, fleeing the city
already defeated by bombs and hunger.

'The Russians are coming!' they warned them. 'Go back!'

'We have to find shelter,' Marie insisted eventually, turning
round to survey the increasingly deserted city street. 'We can't
go on any more.' She spotted a church tower. 'Let's ask for
sanctuary over there.' She pointed. 'They'll not turn us out of
God's house. It's our only hope.'

It was an effort for Callie even to walk up the steps. Marie opened the great wooden door but inside was chilly and the darkness lit only by flickering candles. Callie sank to the floor exhausted, looking up at the painted ceiling as it swirled above her head. It was clearly Catholic, not Lutheran, with all those golden statues peering down at her with pity.

Out of the shadows a priest emerged from behind the confessional. 'Can I help you?'

Marie kneeled before him. 'Help us, please . . . We place ourselves on your mercy, Father. Our friend is very sick. We are French labourers. We need your help. We've not eaten for over three days. We've walked so long, we can go no further,' she pleaded.

'You are escapees?' he said, examining each of them in turn.

'From the labour camp at Markkleeberg. We were made to march. If we go back we will be hanged. Please help us,' Maddy added in German. 'We have nowhere else to go. Lotte is very sick from bad water . . .'

The priest locked the church door and beckoned to them. 'Come with me. Can you all climb the stairs?' He guided them up the twisting belfry tower step by step to a platform around the bells. Callie had to crawl each agonizing step on her hands and knees. 'You must wait here. I will bring food.'

When he had gone, Maddy and Marie wondered aloud if he would betray them to the local police. Were they truly safe? Only time would tell. Callie was past worrying. The angels on the ceiling were spinning round her as she floated in and out of consciousness. She lay in a stupor of sweat and pain, not caring if she lived or died.

Callie was woken by a bell. Staring at a tiled room, unable to focus at first, she saw vague figures gliding around her. There was a basin and jug. She was lying in clean sheets in a bed and there was an arched window looking out to a tree in full leaf, letting in the warm glow of sunshine on her face. She tried to sit up but flopped back, weak and faint. Then she saw a pink face in a headdress staring at her. 'You are back with us,' the woman said in halting French. 'Our mystery lady returns.'

'*Merci, Madame, mais oui,*' Callie replied instinctively. 'Where am I, back in Brussels?' Had she been dreaming such a nightmare?

'In the Convent Hospital of St Elisabeth . . . Don't worry, the war is over. You are no longer the enemy or we, yours. Father Bernhardt brought you to us. He found you collapsed in his church.'

'Is this the prison hospital?' She could remember a kind warder somewhere but the rest was a blur. Who was Father Bernhardt?

'Just rest, you've have been very ill. Don't try to move yet. It is enough that you're awake after such a terrible time. Your body shut down but now it is ready to live again.'

'Where am I?' Callie couldn't take all this change in. Her head was all fuzzy and mixed up. She dreamed she'd been in a forest and running from soldiers, and there were dogs and guns and people hanging from trees, skeletons on the floor in the snow. Her mind had lost its power like an engine run out of steam so the wheels wouldn't turn in the cogs. Why couldn't she remember anything? What was she doing in a convent? She lay back, exhausted by the effort of trying to think. Who was she? She started to panic, realizing she couldn't even think of her name. Later that day, a doctor in a white coat and spectacles came to examine her. He tapped her chest and tested her muscles, looked in her mouth but not into her eyes.

'Who am I?' she asked, speaking like a helpless child.

'This form says you are a French labourer brought in by a priest in need of attention,' he replied, still not looking at her. His French was slow and halting. 'You had enteric fever complicated by malnutrition and infected sores.'

'Please help me to remember,' she asked.

He didn't look up from his writing. 'Be patient, young lady. It takes time to recover from serious illness. You will remember when you are ready to remember. There are usually good reasons why people choose to forget. The nurses say you called out in your fever and sang some nursery rhyme in Dutch. That may help you remember.' He gave her a strange look. 'Your clothes were burned. They were regulation items from a labour camp. That fact may help you too, and at some time in your life you had a child. Your body tells me that. These pieces of the jigsaw might amount to something or nothing.' He left her, briskly moving on to another room. His words made no sense and she had no will to worry what they meant. It was enough to be dry and warm and clean. If this was heaven then she was well satisfied.

Phoebe found the exercises frustrating. It was hopeless trying to lift her useless arm. It curled like a hook, flopping on her chest. She had no patience, no strength, no mobility down one side, her speech, when it came back, was a garbled mumble of sounds. She couldn't hold a decent conversation. The hospital in Glasgow had done a good job and now she was convalescing in a nursing home overlooking the Clyde, but her progress was too slow. They told her that she'd probably had a series of little strokes but the damage was done in the big one in the summer. They told her she'd make more progress if she practised her exercises a bit more, got on her feet and learned to accept the disability. There would be sticks to help her walk and a wheelchair when she was tired. It was up to herself how much more strength she gained. The speech therapist promised good results if she kept attending sessions, and as an actress and singer she knew how to develop her breathing and produce sounds, but half the time she couldn't be bothered. The doctor told her being depressed was a normal part of recovery. 'You've had shock to your system and such an independent woman like yourself will take it hard at first.'

He didn't understand how it felt to be grounded, unable to converse and walk in a straight line. She'd hardly had a day's illness in her life. The worst bit was it seemed hard to concentrate on much except wireless programmes, but then she found herself falling asleep at odd times and missing the gist of the discussion or the play.

Thank goodness for Mima and Jessie holding the fort at Dalradnor, but for how much longer? What on earth was she going to do with Desmond? And still there was no news of Caroline. *Oh, Caroline, where are you? Are you still alive?* She must be dead and they were delaying telling her until she was strong enough to bear bad news. There was no other explanation for her disappearance.

It looked as if her grandson was her sole responsibility. How could she cope now with a lively six-year-old boy? He needed someone younger in his life, like Jessie, but she was planning her exit as soon as her permits came through with her ticket to sail. There was nothing for it: he'd have to go to a good boarding school, but closer to home than she'd been planning, but what to do with him in the long holidays . . .?

She lay trying to sort out his future. It gave her something to think about other than her own aches and pains. Perhaps it was time to find his father and make him take on his paternal duties, or at least find his family in Wales. They might take Desmond off her hands while she convalesced. But Caroline had never had anything to do with them, and with his father's criminal history it was probably better not stir up that hornets' nest.

Worrying about all of this was not helping her get back on her feet. If she could just find Desmond a placement for a few months – a year at most, she reckoned – it might give her a chance to recover enough to pick up her career. This stroke had ruined all her plans for the future. Nothing had gone smoothly in her life, so why be surprised at another knock-back? What must be borne must be borne. There must be a way forward, Phoebe knew, but at this very moment whatever might lie ahead was covered by mist and darkness.

As she grew in strength, Callie found peace and comfort in the convent routine, a quiet refuge for her confused thoughts. The chapel was a sanctuary where she could smell the incense soothing her troubled mind, take time to listen to the music and voices and calm her fevered brain. It was here she had that first glimmer of recollection, seeing the decorated ceiling and the angels looking down on her, recalling crawling up those tortuous steps to the belfry like an act of penance.

When the old priest, the one they called Father Bernhardt, came to check on her progress, he told her everything he knew about the two girls who had saved her life.

'You are a Belgian prisoner from the camps. May God in His mercy forgive all those who perpetrated such inhumanity on helpless women and children. At least they made the villagers walk through the camp to see the horrors that now the world knows we are capable of when a mad man . . .' He broke off to wipe the tears from his eyes. 'But that is our shame, not yours. They called you Lotte and said you were arrested in Brussels.'

'Thank you for saving us. My friends – are they still here?' Callie asked, beginning to picture them in her mind. Madeleine and Marie – their names suddenly popped into her head and she smiled.

Father Bernhardt shook his head. 'When the American troops took over the city, they were shipped back with many other prisoners and labourers. It was those girls who saved you, and someone they called Celine.'

Celine – the name pierced her like sunlight burning through mist and suddenly she saw that poor woman in that last dance of death before the guards. She saw the dogs and heard them snarl, she smelled the fear and shame as it all came flooding back, and she shielded her eyes to block out the images. 'Celine, we couldn't save,' Callie whispered. She told him everything she could recall and he wept with her in silence.

'You are remembering now.'

'Yes, I remember, but I wish I didn't. How do I live with such horror in my heart?' she cried.

'God will give you the strength to find your way back into the past. It looks like the journey is beginning now you are stronger. He makes the back for the burden, they say, but where was He in those terrible places?' The old man rose from his chair with a heavy sigh. 'We will have to live with our shameful part for the rest of history, I fear. I wish you well, pilgrim, Lotte, whoever you are . . . May God be with you, child.'

In the weeks that followed, she recalled more and more of the pain, but when she tried to recall just why she was in the camp, it was as if a great iron door shut in her face. It loomed and towered over her like a giant's face, padlocked, with no key. She kept searching for the key but there was nothing. In her dreams came strange pictures she couldn't quite reach: a house with a pitched roof, water shimmering on a lake, an old horse in a field. There were faces darting into her sight and disappearing before she could recognize them. She woke trying to clasp onto the fading dreams, chasing those fleeting images that were calling out to her until they made her head ache with longing.

At least she could now make herself useful, helping other patients, fetching and carrying, saving the legs of the older nuns. She liked mending anything in the linen baskets, hems and sheets, learning the intricate embroidery stitches the sisters did so well. She sat with the lace makers, fascinated as they twisted their bobbins, making little items to sell. Soon she sensed her time with the nuns was coming to an end. They couldn't support her for ever. She was not a Roman Catholic, she had no instinct for their worship, no knowledge of their rituals or of the Mass, although she found solace sitting at the back, letting the sounds of the services soothe her wounded spirit.

Her dreams grew more persistent, more vivid, and that prison door barrier began to shrink into a wooden gate and then a stone wall with a stile so she could climb over into a landscape full of hills and lakes. One dawn, late in November, somewhere between waking and sleeping, she saw a child running towards her, racing a brown dog over green grass, a boy with a mop of dark curls. 'Sing it again, Mummy,' he called out to her, and Callie sat bolt upright. 'Desmond? Is that you?' She was calling out in English. 'Desmond, come back, Desmond,' she screamed, bringing a nun running to see what the noise was.

'Lotte, what is it? Another bad dream?'

'Look!' Callie pointed to the bare wall. 'I have a son . . . see. Desmond. He was here just now. I have to go home to him.' She reached out to hold him but he had vanished. 'Desmond!' she kept calling. 'Wait for me.'

A nun brought camomile tea to calm her anxiety as the sisters gathered round, hearing her speak her native tongue for the first time. She lay back exhausted but smiling with relief. The locked door had opened, the gate was ajar and she was free to follow the path home. 'I must write a letter. I need a postcard and a stamp. I have to tell them I am coming home, please,' she begged as she smiled. 'Please help me find my way back to England.'

Sister Berenice was too astonished not to comply. 'This is a miracle,' she whispered to the other nuns.

'Not a miracle, Sister,' another nurse replied, smiling down at Callie. 'Just a mother's instinct. She must find her son.'

They found an old postcard of the city, one of the cathedral, and she scribbled down a note in shaky handwriting: 'Darling boy, Mummy is safe and coming home to you soon.'. She addressed it in full to Dalradnor Lodge in Scotland. One of the novices took it to the post office.

In that strange post-war winter of 1945, when Europe was still in turmoil with opposing forces fighting for the control of the country, armed disaffected ex-soldiers and refugees roamed through the country, searching out cash and valuables, bonds, anything to steal and pawn for food and weapons. In one of these desperate robberies and raids, the Leipzig mail sacks were ransacked and letters were scattered to the four winds. Callie's postcard lay rotting along the trackside, sodden and unread.

29

'Now this is to be our wee secret, Desmond.' Jessie pressed her finger to her lips as she sat him on her knee. 'You have to promise not to tell a soul what we're doing. Do you understand me, hen?'

'Can I come with you then?' Desmond curled into her body.

'Yes, I know you want to, but I'm not sure if your granny wants you to go so far away. It's a very long way and we'll never get back again. I won't be able to buy more tickets.'

Desmond nodded. Jessie had her serious face on and he was listening very hard. If he was a good boy and didn't get into trouble at school, she would take him to see Uncle Bob in Australia for a holiday on a big ship far away. He would live with them and be their little boy and he wouldn't see Granny Phee any more. It was a very big secret. Poor Granny hobbled with a stick and her left arm didn't work, and he sometimes couldn't understand what she said to him. She didn't like noise in the house and had to sleep a lot. She would be pleased to be quiet when they were gone.

Jessie was busy packing her clothes and wedding presents: the china tea set with roses all over it, a silver candlestick and leather photo albums of the farm and all her sisters, along with her wedding portrait in a frame. All this stuff was going in the big trunk for the journey and she had a new suitcase for the rest of their clothes. She kept slipping in his shirts and trousers, pyjamas and socks. 'It'll be summer when we get there and it gets very hot.'

She had a book she kept reading to him, *The English Brides' Guide to Australia*. It told her what to expect and how to get used to the climate, what insects to look out for. Uncle Bob was no longer in uniform , not since he fell off his motor bike and injured himself. He had been in hospital and his mother wrote saying Jessie must come and help him get back to normal again. She had got permission to be on one of the first ships making the crossing.

Granny Phee was not happy about her leaving so soon before Christmas and suggested Desmond would have to go to Grove Park Preparatory School after the holidays. They'd had a row about that. 'You can't put a wee boy in a place like that,' Jessie argued, while he sat listening at the top of the stairs.

'What else can I do?'

'Let me take him with me,' Jessie said. 'He'll love the outdoor life and all that sunshine. They have oranges there all year round. It's a new country for young people.'

'That wouldn't be suitable, not with his mother . . . until there's word . . .' Granny always stopped when her name was mentioned.

'Miss Faye, we both know she's never coming back now. Better to face facts and make plans.' Desmond had never heard Jessie talk back to his granny before.

'We can't be certain. If I was sure, it might be a different matter. You can't just take a boy to the other side of the world. He is my grandson. He has a father somewhere.'

'And a fat lot of good that's done him. I look on him as my own. I know he wants to come with me. It's worth considera-tion.'

Desmond slid down the steps one by one to hear what Granny said next. 'I want to go with Jessie,' he yelled, just so she knew what he thought.

'Don't be silly, young man. She's only your nursemaid, not your mother. I won't have it. You must stay with your own kind,' she shouted back in an angry voice.

He hated school. He hated Dalradnor since Granny Phee came back from hospital. It smelled of bedpans and school dinners, not like it used to do. He didn't want to live with an old lady any more.

As the time grew closer for Jessie to leave for Southampton, no one was speaking, and it was then that Jessie told him their big secret. 'You will have to be my nephew. We'll not use your first name on your papers but your second name, Louis, and I will call you Lou. You have to remember this when the gentlemen ask why you are travelling with me. I'm your aunt Jessie and you must never tell anyone anything else or they'll send you back and I'll be in trouble.'

Desmond nodded and hugged all this to himself. If only the rough boys who plagued him in the playground realized just what a wonderful time he was going to have on a real warship called HMS *Stirling Castle*, but no one must ever know.

There was a farewell supper for Jessie. Mima made steak pie and tatties with a special trifle to follow, and ice cream. All Jessie's friends came to wish her well and give her presents. Granny gave her precious clothing coupons to buy something pretty for her to meet Uncle Bob. Mima and Mr Burrell gave her an album of postcards of the district. Desmond made a card and wrote '*Bon Voyage*', which Granny made him spell out on the back. It meant 'safe journey', she told him. For one second he felt sad never to see her again, but he knew she was tired of having him around all the time.

The next day Jessie woke him at dawn. It was pitch-black and she helped him dress quietly, slipping down the stairs with her suitcase out through the back door. They walked to the station to catch the milk train into Glasgow Central and were in Southampton in time to go through customs and board the ship.

'How will Granny know where I am?' he asked, aware that the porter had seen them boarding the local train.

'I left her a letter explaining everything. She never wakes until lunchtime. She won't stop us, I just know it. So don't worry, she'll be much better off now we're gone.'

Phoebe kept reading Jessie's note over and over again in disbelief; the sheer cheek of her to take this decision out of her hands. By the time she was *compos mentis* and found the letter on the drawing-room mantelpiece, it had been far too late to catch up with them. She knew she ought to call the police but something held her back. Perhaps at last she'd have some peace and quiet and time to herself, time to do those exercises and contact her agent. There might be something she could do to revive her career. She might write her memoirs, as other Gaiety Girls were doing. Life wasn't over yet. She'd had a lucky escape, a warning to take things easier. Perhaps Jessie had done her a favour – only time would tell – and she could always take the long sea voyage trip and fetch Desmond back home. She sat back, letting Mima wait on her.

Her housekeeper was tight-lipped and shocked at Jessie's betrayal, but not surprised. 'She was awful close to the wee boy. I can see how she got to thinking he was her own.' She sighed. 'She must have been planning this for months. I didna think she was such a sleekit sort of lassie . . . Oh, there's the phone . . . maybe she's changed her mind.' Mima rushed to the hall to answer the bell, returning to say, 'It's a trunk call from London for you, Miss Faye, from yon Ministry in London.'

Phoebe struggled up to the telephone and took the receiver. The voice on the other was speaking too quickly. 'Mrs Cameron, I'm not hearing you, the lines crackling . . . yes, I'll sit down.' Phoebe lowered herself slowly onto the hall chair, waiting for the bad news coming.

'I see . . . yes, yes . . . when . . . where? I don't believe it . . . after all these months. I see . . . When? It is wonderful news.

Wait until I tell Desmond . . .' Phoebe flopped back as the phone dropped out of her hand onto the tiled floor with a crash.

Mima came rushing in and took one look at her stricken face. 'Oh, dearie me, it's come at last. I'm so sorry. It's always a shock . . .' she made to comfort her.

'No, Mima, no . . . It's good news . . .' Phoebe was crying. 'Caroline's coming back to us . . . she's alive!' She buried her face in her hand to hold in all the emotion – relief, shock and confusion – as it overwhelmed her. This is what she'd prayed for. It was the very best of news, but now the realization of what it would mean was dawning. 'My daughter's coming home to her family. How can I look her in the face, Mima? How am I going to tell her about Desmond and Jessie? How can I explain . . .? Whatever am I going to do now?'

30

Callie stared up the driveway of Château Grooten in horror and disbelief at the devastation before her. It was as if some giant bulldozer had flattened the building, leaving nothing but crushed masonry and charred timbers. The house must have taken a direct hit. She sighed, thinking of the fairy-tale mansion it once had been, with its turrets and Gothic windows, all those gracious rooms now stripped of all dignity, humbled into this mess of rubble. She'd come to pay her respects, more in hope than expectation, and now her worst fears were realized. The van Grooten family was gone and she knew deep in her heart that Ferrand was not among the survivors. She had felt his absence increasingly since her recovery.

Once her memory returned, and with it all the images of their past loving, her body yearned for physical comfort, but there was none as she limped back to life.

Instead, she was processed by an efficient bureaucracy. She was passed over to American authorities for security checks. She knew she must cling to her British military identity, as was the rule. She gave them her cover name and code identity, to be checked in London. HQ confirmed her details as agent Charlotte Blanken, and she was released into British care and flown to Brussels by military plane for an overnight stop on her way to London. Time was short and she knew what she must do before she returned home.

A driver took her to find Marthe van Hooge but the house now belonged to someone else and there was no forwarding address. She persuaded the young officer to drive her out to the Château Grooten on the off chance that Ferrand might be waiting for her there, as he did in her dreams. It was a silly fantasy she'd clutched all the way from Leipzig but she could not discard her hopes, however unlikely.

As Callie neared the ruin she saw that there was a man in black – tall, dark hair – stooping over the rubble, picking things up and placing them carefully into a wheelbarrow. She stopped, staring. Surely it could not be . . . and yet . . . She felt a sudden rush of joy to her heart. Her lover was restored to her, just as she'd dreamed! She ran up the gravel path, dodging the stones and masonry, hardly daring to breathe with excitement, until the man looked up and she was plummeted back to reality. It was not Ferrand. She feared he was just a looter, picking over the bones like a vulture.

'Can I help you?' he asked. He seemed entirely self-possessed in his task; his was not the furtive demeanour of a thief.

'I was looking for the Countess van Grooten . . . I was here before the war,' she said, wondering who the man in black might be.

'Ah, Maman's school for young ladies . . . Those were the days, and now this.' He stood up, holding out his hand. 'I'm Karel, her son. I'm afraid the news is not good. And you are . . .?'

'Caroline, a friend of Louis-Ferrand, your brother.' She paused, realizing she was about to learn the truth, not wanting to see the look on his face. 'He spoke often of his brother the priest, and of Jean-Luc . . . How are they both?' She had to ask. She had to know.

He bowed his head. 'You are Ferrand's English lady.' There was something old-fashioned about the way he skirted over their relationship. 'He wouldn't wish to see this ruin. He had such plans, but I suppose we all had plans. Now only the land remains,' he said with a Gallic shrug of the shoulders.

She knew what was coming from the way he was hesitating to answer her question.

'He's dead?' she asked, wanting to shield him from having to say the words.

'I'm afraid so, like so many brave patriots.' He looked at her sideways as if to gauge her reaction. 'I'm sorry.'

'How?' she asked. Better to know in one fell swoop what she'd long suspected, although she felt herself reeling from the news.

'This is no place to talk over such precious matters. There's still the cottage by the stables. I'll find you a drink,' Karel said kindly, obviously seeing her distress. 'You came alone?'

'I have a driver but I'm sure he'll wait by the gate.'

They walked in silence. Callie was trying to absorb his words but there was an empty hole, a numb sickening lurch in her gut as a wave of sadness seeped through her limbs.

The single room was cluttered with pictures and candelabra, pans and broken treasures, a cushion singed with smoke and books burned around the edges. It smelled of smoke and despair.

'We saved what we could from the embers. German officers commandeered the house but it was fought over in the liberation. My mother lived here until she died. Then one night the entire house was destroyed.'

How could the proud Countess have borne such an invasion and be reduced to one room?

'And Ferrand?' She wanted to know his story. Karel shoved a glass of brandy into her hand and pointed to a wooden chair.

'After the defeat of the army and the beginning of the occupation, they tried to persuade us that things would go unchanged, but it did not last. He took a post as a professor in the university and resisted as best he could the takeover of our language and the curriculum. Everything had to be in German. All the teachers were watched. He got involved with a resistance movement, distributing leaflets and antipropaganda. They took over a newspaper and put it on the streets. It made fun of the conquerors, but it was only a matter of time before they were betrayed, arrested and executed. There was nothing I could do. I wasn't even allowed to visit him in St-Gilles Prison. I tried.' He was in tears as he spoke.

Callie gasped, shaking her head. Ferrand had been in the very same place as she. Had they been close to each other, separated only by stone walls and stairs? If only . . . But after Ravensbrück, how could anything shock her any more? She felt emptied of hope now.

'The news of his death killed my mother. We lost Jean-Luc at Dunkirk. He was trying to cross to Britain. He drowned . . . Now there's nothing left of our family, no future, no heirs. I am a priest . . . or I was. I fear I'm no longer sure of my vocation. We have a saying: "Waste, error and war all go together and, of course, truth soon disappears too."'

Callie reached out and took his hand.

'It was a priest in Germany who saved my life and nuns who healed me. I am so sorry. Ferrand was the love of my life. We had such a short time together. He would have made a wonderful father,' she said.

'Alas, there are no more sons . . .'

Callie smiled through her tears. 'That's where you are wrong. I have a son, Desmond Louis. He's Ferrand's boy, waiting in Scotland.'

Karel covered his face with emotion. 'And he never knew this?'

'I was going to tell him when he came to visit us, but then war came and we never met again. I'm going home to be with him now. I just hoped for a miracle . . .'

Karel shook his head. 'This is the miracle, Caroline, a hope for the future in this dark world. I thought everything was gone, and now this?' He gulped down his drink as if to steady himself.

'If only my brother had known, it might have kept him from taking risks.' He opened another bottle. His hands were shaking with excitement and emotion as Callie began to describe Desmond, his black curls and blue eyes.

'I haven't seen him for three years. He's nearly seven. I thought I was doing my duty but I didn't really think of the cost or that I'd be away so long. I am one of the few lucky ones to survive. Let's hope there'll be a better future for him and all the other children separated by war.' Karel nodded and passed over the brandy to her. She swallowed it in one gulp as they sat in silence, thinking about what they had learned.

After several minutes, Karel got up, went over to a large wooden dresser by the wall, opened a drawer and pulled out a box. 'Your son must have this then, from his father. It's all I can give him. We've not even a photograph of any of us.'

'Don't worry, I have a few of Ferrand from Cairo.' Callie fumbled with the clasp of the box. Inside was a medal, a *Croix de Guerre* with a red-and-green-striped ribbon attached.

'It's for bravery, the country's highest honour . . . You must tell your son all about Louis-Ferrand.'

'Thank you, I will, I promise. He will treasure this all his life. But what will you do now?'

'I have my church and house. The land will be farmed, but this house . . . there is no point. I have no use for it. What use are things without the people who give them meaning?' he sighed. 'Come now and see where our relatives lie in peace.'

He walked her round to the little church and cemetery, leaving her alone to walk down the rows of van Grootens, reading the names. She saw the countess, her picture in a stone frame, and one of Jean-Luc in uniform.

'Ferrand's not here. Maman demanded his body but it was not given back.'

Callie searched for something to say to comfort him. There were so many souls whose ashes were blown to the four winds, she thought, so much death and destruction. Her mind went blank at the image of the crematorium chimney in the camp and the sickly smell of burned flesh that hung over the whole place. Karel saw her stumble and reached out to hold her arm.

'You go home to your family and cherish them. Tell them what you can, tell them what you've seen. It's the only way to make sure it never happens again. I can live easier knowing there is a little bit of my brother out there in the world. All wasn't destroyed as I thought. Thank you for coming. I'm glad to have met you. Please keep in touch. I would like to see my nephew one day.'

'And I should like him to meet you,' Callie replied, shaking his hand firmly. 'Tomorrow, I fly to London. Remember us in your prayers. It's not going to be easy to go home after all this time away.'

Part Two

DESMOND

1945–7

Speed, bonnie boat, like a bird on the wing.
Onward! the sailors cry;
Carry the lad that's born to be king
Over the sea to Skye.

'The Skye Boat Song', lyrics by Sir Harold Boulton, 1884

31

Desmond looked up at the great grey bulk of metal that was the *Stirling Castle*. How did such a big ship manage to float on water when it was so heavy? It rose up above him into the sky, so he held Jessie's hand very tightly as they climbed on board.

'Now remember to call me Aunt Jessie and I'll be calling you Lou. You haven't forgotten, have you? It's very important.'

Desmond nodded, more interested in exploring the deck and watching the soldiers lined up on the dockside, with their Boy Scout hats with a turned-up side. They were waiting to come on board, going home from the wars, Jessie said. Scotland seemed very far away now and he wondered if Granny Phee would miss them.

They had to share a big cabin with a lady and her little baby who was called Dulcie. Jessie took him round the decks and he stopped by the railings, watching the ship being loaded with boxes and cars, sailors rushing around shouting orders to the cranes. There were lots of ladies crying and waving to their families. Dulcie's mother was sobbing into a hanky. He'd never seen a grown-up cry before and Jessie was doing her best to calm her down.

Mrs Jackson was on her way to join her husband, like Jessie. 'I'll never see me mum again,' she yelled. 'Let me off the ship. I can't go.'

Jessie kept patting her hand like she did with him when he fell and hurt himself. 'Look, Elsie, you are taking your baby to see her pa and begin a new life where there'll be sunshine and oranges, wonderful beaches for her to play on and everyone is happy there. You can write and telephone home. Your husband'll be counting the weeks till you arrive. Think how you'd feel if he was waiting and you never came and he never saw his little girl again? Think about all those poor souls whose husbands are never coming back to play with their little ones?'

That did the trick, and with a final sniff on Jessie's hanky she went for a cup of tea in the big dining room.

'Are you going to cry, Aunt Jessie?' he asked, staring at her carefully.

'Why should I cry? I can't wait to get out of this drab grey miserable winter. Bob's promised me a wonderful life down under – and you, too, of course. He'll be pleased you came along, too.'

There was a map of the world on the wall of the big play-room set aside for young kiddies. Desmond thought it wasn't too far from Southampton across and down to Australia. He could almost stretch it with his hand – it wouldn't take too long – but as the days turned into weeks it was as if they were living in a floating palace in a world of its own, only the Sunday services marking the start to another week.

Every day there was something exciting to explore: life boat drill to muster stations, just in case . . . games to play like table tennis, and drill, which the soldier's teacher did with the mothers and older children. They raced with bean bags and did jumping jacks and bends. They had relays and sports days. Jessie was good at deck tennis and Elsie joined in, while Desmond wheeled Dulcie up and down to help her sleep in her go-chair.

There was a cinema for children, and adults later. He saw Donald Duck and Charlie Chaplin, Pluto, Mickey Mouse and the film *Snow White and the Seven Dwarfs*. Nurses helped mind the babies to give their mothers a rest, but Desmond was too old for that and did some lessons at a table. He tagged along with Jessie to the tea dancing. Sometimes when the music started the ladies had to dance with each other but then the PT instructor, Mr Boyd, and some of the soldiers were allowed to dance too. Desmond liked doing the Gay Gordons, singing 'The Hokey Cokey', and skimming along the wooden floor, until he got a splinter in his knee.

The best thing of all was the food. Jessie said she'd never seen so much food in her life. For breakfast there was porridge and cereals and toast and bacon. For lunches there was cold beef and salad and pies, and then in the evening they started all over again with soup and hot dinners and ice creams and pop to drink.

'I shall get so fat, Bob won't recognize me,' Jessie complained, patting her stomach and laughing.

'You're not fat, you're cuddly,' said Mr Boyd, and she blushed. Jessie was very pretty with her red hair all coiled up so when she jumped her curls bobbed up and down.

'You've so many waves in your hair, it's making me seasick,' Mr Boyd said. He was a soldier's policeman and on his way back to somewhere called a girl's name, Adelaide. He looked like a big brown bear with arms like Popeye. 'Tough on the outside and soft as butter inside,' whispered Jessie to Mrs Jackson when they left the dancing. There was always a clutch of soldiers waiting to have a dance with them and walk them back to the cabin, but Jessie was having none of them.

'I'm a respectable married woman,' she said, waving goodbye to them all. 'Louis, here, is my young man. He can see me safely home.'

Desmond was proud that she chose him but he liked Big Jim Boyd, who sat with them at mealtimes and always found an extra bun for him while Jessie's back was turned.

'Where are you off to, sonny, when you land?' he asked, but Desmond didn't know. 'So what's yer uncle Bob like?' he added, and seemed very interested in Jessie's family.

Desmond told him about her being his nursemaid.

'So she's not your real aunty then?'

Desmond blushed, knowing he'd given the game away. 'Oh, yes, she's always been with me, and I was a pageboy at her wedding,' he added proudly. Telling fibs wasn't as easy as grown-ups thought.

Soon the winter chill gave way to warm sunshine, and grey clouds to bright blue skies.

They were spending more and more time with Big Jim. He told them about his beautiful city and how his family built houses. Now he'd travelled the world he wanted to go back to see his family and settle down. 'With someone just like your aunty Jessie,' he winked. 'Has she got a twin sister somewhere, Louis?'

Desmond looked serious. 'I don't think so, have you?'

Jessie turned quite pink in the face. 'Away with such nonsense. I'm sure there'll be plenty of Aussie lassies waiting by the docks to snap you up off the ship. He's just teasing, Louis, don't encourage him.'

He didn't understand grown-ups. They said one thing and did another. Aunt Jessie dressed up in her new dancing frock, tied up her hair in a bunch of curls and joined in the ballroom dances. Desmond wondered if Sergeant Bob would mind this, but he couldn't remember what he looked like now. Big Jim was good-looking and he never ruffled his curls and called him girly. He took time to show him round the ship and talked to him about the kangaroos and wallabies and koala bears in his picture book.

'Now you remember to cover up your arms and shoulders and put sun cream on your face or your skin'll peel like bark. Our sun makes you ill if you stay in it too long and we have forest fires in the summer.' He seemed worried that they might be going somewhere rough. 'It's not all oranges and sunshine. Outback life is tough, with little water and poor tracks. There are no schools in some places.' Desmond thought that sounded brilliant, but said nothing. 'Do you know where you're heading, Jess?' he'd kept asking, but she didn't know either.

'Bob's family have a farmstead somewhere in South Australia. I hoped it would be like Scotland,' she sighed. 'But I guess not. To be honest, we never talked much about it.'

'Our country is huge, yours is tiny. I wish you the best of luck in your new life,' he said one night. 'I just wish . . .'

Jessie smiled and patted his hand. 'That's kind of you to worry about us, but we're going to be fine, aren't we, Louie?'

On the last night, Desmond watched them dancing the waltz and he knew Big Jim and Jessie were dancing like sweethearts and wanted to be alone so he wandered off out of sight while they said their goodbyes. If they did kissy stuff, he didn't want to see. It would only make him worry what Bob would think if he knew she was kissing another soldier.

Elsie Jackson was in the cabin, trying to settle Dulcie. 'The little blighter won't go down.'

'You could sing her a lullaby. Jessie used to sing them to me.'

'Go on, maestro, you have a go.' Mrs Jackson smiled, waiting for him to sing.

'"Speed, bonnie boat, like a bird on the wing. Onward! the sailors cry . . ."' He began, and then stopped, knowing it wasn't Jessie who'd sung that song but someone else a long time ago and far away, a lady with a face he couldn't quite picture.

'That's lovely, Louie, carry on. She likes that.' But he couldn't because it made him sad.

'I've forgot the rest,' he said, climbing into his bunk, feeling strange.

Jessie came into the cabin very late and kept the light off while she undressed. He thought he heard her crying in her sleep but perhaps he dreamed it.

Next morning, there was a new bustle and shouts of land, and then they sailed up the Sound into Sydney Harbour, seeing the great bridge before them. Word came from the crew that as they were the first of the war brides from England, there would be film cameras to greet them and newspapers wanting interviews.

'Best bib and tucker then,' said Elsie. 'Our friends back home can see us land in style. We must put on a show. Imagine us, film stars on Pathé News cementing the bonds of Empire!'

There was a fussing of putting on make-up, hats and stockings. Dulcie was decked out in a cotton lacy dress and picture bonnet, while he was made to put on his kilt and tie. 'We must fly the flag for Scotland,' Jessie ordered, fixing her grey suit with the tartan lapels.

Big Jim was hovering by the exit doors to say goodbye. He took Desmond aside. 'Now you take care of your aunty, promise me. She's a mighty fine woman and I wish her well, but just in case you ever need a helping hand, here's my address in Adelaide. If you ever pass my door you'll be sure of a warm welcome.' He shook his hand firmly. 'Pleased to meet you, young man, and good luck!'

When he released his hand Desmond found inside a pound note and a piece of paper with an address on it. Embarrassed by such riches, he shoved them in his jacket pocket and made his way out into the sunshine. The crowds were cheering and waving to greet the new arrivals in this bright new world they called Australia Fair.

Aunty Jessie wasn't keen to be in the photographs so they hung back until all the fuss was over, and then went through all the form-filling and checking papers. Desmond noticed his name was written in her passport. He had no papers of his own.

Then they pushed their way through men kissing wives and babies. 'Aw, look at that little kiltie with the curls.' Someone wanted to take a snapshot but Jessie pulled him away quickly. It was going to be hard to find anyone in the crush, and it was very warm.

'Where's Bob hiding?' She laughed, but Desmond saw she looked worried.

He tugged at her sleeve. 'We can find Big Jim. He'll look after us,' he offered. Big Jim was their friend.

'Don't be silly. And it's Mr Boyd to you . . . Bob's here somewhere.' They searched around in circles. 'He must have got the telegram.' Then she stopped, seeing a woman holding a piece of card on which was written, 'Welcome, Jessie Kane.'

'Look! That's us, over there.' She rushed across. 'I'm Jessie . . . where's Bob?'

A woman in a battered straw hat and baggy cotton dress waved back. 'You're here at long last. Welcome, Jessie. You took your time. I'm Bob's sister, Adie Malone. He sends his apologies; poor man's crook again. And who's this smart fella?' Adie eyed him up and down with surprise.

'This is Louie , my nephew. His mother is . . . well, not with us any more. He needed a home so I brought him with me. Bob knows him. He was our pageboy. He'll be no bother.'

Desmond saw Jessie gulping and looking nervous as she pushed him forward for inspection. He smiled and held out his hand. Adie's felt like sandpaper.

'I don't know what Bob'll say about this. Not enough room to swing a cat as it is. Still, he's here now. Can't send him back, now, can we?' She tousled his hair. 'Wasted on a boy are these curls. Bob'll soon get the shears to them. Come on, the truck's parked up.'

'Is it nearby?' Jessie asked.

'The truck's round the corner,' Adie Malone roared. 'The farm's four days' stiff drive so be prepared for a bumpy ride. Let's find somewhere you can take off those fancy things. By the time we hit the dirt, they'll be like rags. Hope you've not brought a lot of stuff like that with you.'

Jessie looked at Desmond, trying to smile, but her eyes were wide and worried. 'Don't worry, no one's going to take any sheep shears to your hair. Just you wait and see, Louie, it's all going to be fine once we get there.'

Desmond was not convinced. How he wished no one had turned up and they could go home with Big Jim Boyd.

32

Callie glanced out of the window as the plane landed at the military airbase. Everything was looking grey and dismal. She'd not slept since that visit to Château Grooten and the news of Ferrand's death. Nothing had turned out well for them. What good had she done these past three years? What could she report that was of any value to the war effort? All she'd done was get herself arrested. What she'd experienced in the camp might be useful in bringing criminals to justice but the very thought of those terrible months made her mind confused and jittery. No one who hadn't been there would ever understand the horrors.

She was processed in the air terminal and told to expect an interview in London at some later stage. No one seemed interested in her story but she told it as best she could to anyone who would listen. It appeared the war was past history and her unit was being disbanded. Everyone was getting on with a new fight with their old allies the Russians. She filled in forms for vouchers and was sent on her way north feeling as if she was of no importance now the war was over. Her uniform was ill-fitting, her hair was unkempt, her skin sallow from her illness. She must look nothing like her old self. The first thing she did was send a telegram to tell Phee she'd landed. Then she headed off from the bus to the station in Oxford.

It was when she saw her reflection in the washroom mirror that she knew she couldn't face them seeing the state of her. On impulse, she headed back into the town to find a hairdresser to put some colour into her grey faded hair. She would've liked to find a dress, but with no clothing coupons there was nothing she could do to smarten up.

They'll have to take me as they find me, she decided. I've been in the wars in more ways than one. She sat in a café on the High Street overlooking the golden stone buildings of the university, feeling numb and listless. What are you doing here wasting precious time? she scolded herself. It was then she recognized that familiar sensation in the pit of her stomach of fear: fear of being unrecognized, fear of being changed, fear that Desmond wouldn't know her, that the world she'd left had moved on without her. It was like coming back from the dead.

Seeing the ruins at Château Grooten had unnerved her, and meeting Karel confirmed to her what she had already sensed in her heart, but this was different. This was coming home. *I want Dalradnor to be as it always was, a haven, my refuge, unchanged by time. I want all the clocks stopped until I return.* Only then could she pick up where she'd left off when Desmond was three. All those months in prison she'd clung to images of Dalradnor for her sanity. Now, procrastinating in this café, she wondered how she'd feel when she saw it for real.

Phoebe dressed with care these days in clothes easy to zip or put on by herself. Suspenders and stockings were difficult so she wore knee socks with garters. The winter chill stiffened her limbs and some of her fingers were useless, but at least she was independent from having to be dressed like a child. Betty came in from the village to fix her hair into a simple chignon. Today, she wanted to look as normal as possible for her daughter's return.

Mima prepared the bedroom with care, finding stems of fragrant daphne to scent her table. They lit fires to air the rooms. Burrell would go to the station to meet her train but say nothing. Caroline must not suspect anything until she was safely home. Phoebe was dreading this encounter and wanted every-thing perfect to offset the moment when she must tell her the awful news. There was game casserole warming in the AGA, and Callie's favourite bramble crumble with custard. Phoebe was trying not to shake but she watched the grandfather clock crawl so slowly around the afternoon hours. The telegram lay in the hall and now there was nothing to do but wait with dread until she returned.

'I'm back!' Callie joked, throwing her service cap through the door. 'Where's everybody?'

Mima smiled. 'Welcome home, Miss Callie. You've been sorely missed. Your mother's having a wee rest. She had a stroke a while back. It's knocked the stuffing out of her, as you will see.'

Callie noted Mima didn't comment on her appearance, which was a relief. The house looked just the same, draughty, quiet, with just the tick of the old clock and a whiff of log smoke.

'Come away in and get the warmth of the fire. I'll call Miss Faye.'

There was no sign of Desmond, no bat and ball or clutter of toy cars, no dog to greet her, but then he wasn't home from school yet. They'd not keep him off lessons just because she was coming home.

Phee came down the stairs slowly, clutching the banister rail, smiling. 'You made it. Did you have a good journey? No kisses or hugs, no fussing, just her usual gracious theatrical entrance, except Phee had aged too. She was still trying to be dignified but clearly struggling, and her shoulders were stooped. 'I have to take my time these days. Let me look at you . . . Oh, my dear, you're so thin, but it suits you. And your hair . . .'

'I'm fine,' Callie said, knowing she looked a mess. 'But you're not. When did this happen?'

Phoebe dismissed her comments, shaking her head. 'I'm much better than I was, stronger each month. It's slowed me down but it could've been worse. Come in. Mima will bring us a sherry.'

'I'm not a visitor. I can fix a drink for myself. When's Desmond back from school? Does he know I'm coming? What have you told him?' There was a pause as Mother shifted into her chair.

'Caroline, there's been a few changes here, my dear. You have to understand I wasn't well enough to see to him, and with Jessie getting married—'

'So you've packed him off to boarding school. I thought you might. Which one did you choose?' Callie replied, feeling flat now she knew Desmond wasn't home to greet her.

'Not exactly. Sit down . . . There's something you should know . . . When Jessie married her airman, he wanted to take her back to Australia and sent for her.'

'You mean the Aussie from Stirling? What's that got to do with Desmond?'

'Quite a lot, as it happens. Now you're not to get upset, but I had this stupid stroke and was in hospital while you were doing whatever you were doing overseas. I thought they'd tell you, but of course with a war on . . .' Phee was garbling and Callie suddenly felt uneasy.

'Spit it out, Phee. What's happened to Desmond? Not an accident? Oh, my God!'

'He's fine. It's just that Jessie offered to have him for a while when I was ill but I said no, of course.' She paused, staring into the fire.

'And then . . .? Tell me!' Callie snapped, her heart racing with suspicion.

'She took him away with her one night behind my back . . .'

'You called the police? Where is she now?' The panic was rising. 'You let her take my son . . .? Where to?' Callie jumped up and began to pace round the room. This was terrible news.

'They sailed for Australia before Christmas to join her husband. I don't know any more than that.'

'But that was ages ago, and you did nothing?' Callie was screaming. 'The police must have done something. I wrote to you telling you I was alive and coming home long before that.'

'We thought you'd died. The first I knew was a telephone call from London. I never got a letter from you. If we had, things wouldn't have . . . I'm so sorry.' Phee began to weep.

'I sent a postcard from Leipzig. The nuns posted it. I was in hospital. I was sick. This is ridiculous. You never informed the police that she'd taken my child without my consent or yours? How could you do such a thing?' Callie spat the words out like bullets at her mother.

'Caroline, don't blame me. I was in bed, unable to speak. I couldn't look after a little boy. Jessie was his nurse. I trusted her. He'll come to no harm with her. She loves him like her own.'

'But he's *my* child, not hers. How could you even think I didn't love my baby?' Callie was weeping too. 'It's not fair. I wrote to you as soon as I got my memory back. We must go to the police right now.'

'But we thought you were dead. No one knew where you were — or if they did, they wouldn't tell me. Don't blame all this on me. You chose to volunteer and join up to have your adventure and leave us,' Phee argued, not looking her in the face.

'And you couldn't wait to off-load my son, could you? What sort of grandparent are you to do such a thing? How dare you call my war work "an adventure"? Did you think I was playing at war games? You have no idea what I've been through . . .'

'I'm a sick woman. I can't be expected to cope, and Jessie loves him. No one would tell me anything about your work.'

'Jessie's his nurse, not his mother.'

'Think how you loved Marthe . . . not me.' Phee was pleading but Callie felt ice cold in her fury.

'I didn't even know you were my mother. How weird was that?'

'At least I protected you. Things were different and your son had a father somewhere.'

'Not any more, he doesn't. The war saw to that.'

'So Toby is dead. He's no loss to the world, is he?' Phee snapped back.

Callie couldn't take any more. She stood looking out of the bay window, deciding what to do, then made up her mind to tell the mother the truth. 'You think I'd let that man father a child? That waste of space is still somewhere out there fleecing the hide off some poor sucker. He's not Desmond's father. Louis-Ferrand van Grooten was. He was shot for his country. I have his medal in my bag. It's all Desmond will ever have of that dear brave man now.'

'And you call me callous? You let us think your husband was his father, but all the time you were having an affair?'

'Louis-Ferrand was more than an affair. We loved each other, we planned to be together. I wanted Desmond to be safe here, out of the war, and he was until you . . . We could all have been happy now. What have you done to me?' Callie screamed. 'What have you done to *us*?' She turned on Phee with burning eyes.

'Don't blame me for your mistakes. This is all your own doing, Caroline, can't you see? You stayed away too long. You put yourself before your boy. Every choice in this world has a price, as I know only too well.' They were facing each other square-on now.

'I only did what you did in the last war. I did my duty for my country. I chose to serve. I thought Desmond would be safe. How wrong I was. I never expected you to betray me like this.'

'You should've learned from my mistake. We're both as bad as each other, so don't keep putting the blame at my door. I won't have you talking to me like this. No woman should leave her child to do such dangerous war work, whatever it was, and I have no desire to know. What's done is done.'

'How do you think this war was won? By ordinary women sitting on their behinds sipping tea? You have no idea how many brave patriots put their family feelings and duties behind them to fight oppression. In every country, women gave their lives. I know, I met hundreds of them in Ravensbrück and many are just dust now. I owe my life to three French women who befriended me. Do you think for one moment I'm letting it rest at this? I have to fetch him home. He doesn't belong to Jessie Dixon. He's mine. If I'd thought this would happen I'd have never left him with you. His place is here, in this house, not across the world with strangers. I have to go to him right now.' Callie made for the door.

'Just calm down. You're distraught. We'll have tea and talk this over. I know it's a shock but we'll think something out. Perhaps take a holiday on a ship and visit them in due course.'

'Are you mad? Do you think I can stay in this place a minute longer, knowing my son is out there with strangers, thinking I'm dead? I have to write to them at once, let them know I'm coming for him. How did she get past the authorities? You must give me every detail.'

'No one's heard from them yet. I have no address, but the Dixons will have one. Calm down, you'll wear out your shoe leather pacing the floor. We'll ring for tea.'

'Stuff your bloody tea.' Callie stormed out for her coat and bag. 'I'm not stopping here without Desmond. I came back for him and I'll not rest until I find him. It was thoughts of him brought me back from the dead. How can I go on living without Ferrand and our child? I could kill you for what you've done to us!'

'Oh, Caroline, don't be foolish. It's getting dark and you're exhausted. Come back and rest!'

'Rest? You can all rest in hell, for all I care. I'll never rest until I see Desmond again. If he's not here then this won't be a home of mine ever again.'

'Caroline, darling, think what you're doing . . .'

Those were the last words thrown at Callie as she rushed out the door and into the night.

'Come away to your bed,' Mima urged Phoebe from her chair in the drawing room. 'She's long gone to a hotel, the poor lassie. I hardly recognized her. You can see she's been through bad times. It's written on her face. It was never going to be easy breaking such news.'

Phoebe stared into the dying embers. 'Things got said in anger that can never be unsaid.'

'Aye, our tongue's a fearsome tool right enough, but she'll come round one day.'

What have I done? Phoebe felt sick with worry. The two of them were like strangers yelling insults to each other. If only there'd been a better way to break the news, but short of lying and delaying the moment . . . And now Caroline was gone. She'd charged in and got it all wrong and made things worse. *Who am I to talk for making things worse?*

Phoebe felt so bone weary, so old and out of touch, helpless as if the world was rushing on, leaving her far behind. Her career was over, her dear friends dead and now her child was abandoning her. But she would never abandon Caroline. While she lived, this place would always be waiting for her daughter and her grandson's return. Whatever comforts she'd gleaned from her success would be all theirs one day, but at this moment she'd gladly give every penny she owned to have her family back by her side. How could she go on living if she never saw either of them again in this life?

She climbed the stairs stiffly, one by one, vowing to make things right. She paused at the top of the stairs, breathless, when an idea came to her. Perhaps Callie's old friend Primrose might step in and help, talk some sense into her daughter before it was too late. She must find out just where Jessie was hiding, inform her lawyers. There had to be a way to restore the child back to his mother. If only she hadn't been ill and feeble, wrapped up in her own worries and careless of her charge. If only she knew how to make amends . . . *If only* – the deepest of her regrets were held in those two little words.

33

'Has that kid wet the bed again?' yelled Bob Kane as Jessie gathered up his sheet, trying to hide it with the rest of the wash. 'Make him wash the bloody thing himself.'

'Oh, Bob, he's still out of sorts with all the changes. Give him time to settle in,' she argued, as Desmond hid behind the door out of sight. There were always arguments over him, ever since he'd walked through the door at Ruby Creek. Bob had taken one look at him and shrieked, 'Crikey, Jess, I wasn't expecting that little runt.'

Adie had delivered the pair of them and left promptly for her own family close to Marree. They were dumped on the doorstep of the farmhouse, miles from anywhere. The sheep farm was surrounded by sheds and cabins and fences, and in the distance was a line of mountains with hundreds of sheep scattered over miles of fields. Bob's leg was still in plaster from his motor-bike accident and, helpless, he shouted orders from a chair. He couldn't use his truck or horse, but he made sure Jess learned to drive him about and do the chores he couldn't manage. He didn't look like the man in uniform she'd married in Dalradnor. He didn't shave and his skin was the colour of burned toffee, he smoked a cheroot and shouted all the time.

'This accident fair shook him up,' Ma Kane explained. 'Banged his head, out cold for a week, he was . . . Nice to have another pair of hands around the place and no mistake.' She was a tubby old lady with skin like leather and wore slippers on her swollen feet.

'You must be quiet around the house,' Jess whispered to Desmond. 'Uncle Bob's father died while he was away and the farm needs a lot of work. This is the worst thing that could happen. We must help him get better.'

'When can I go to school?' Desmond asked.

'I'm not sure. We're too far out of town for you to walk, and they can't spare the petrol, but there's a school on the wireless we can listen to. Just let's get Uncle Bob on his feet.'

Desmond looked out of the window to the far mountains. All the colours of the earth and sky were different from Scotland. There wasn't a loch to swim in, and the creek was dry. There was no one to play with and Jessie was busy cooking meals for the farm men, washing and clearing, while Bob's mother did her farm chores. No one ever sat down from sunrise to sunset. He was expected to see to the chickens and the eggs. He hated being left with Bob, who sat in the porch giving him orders.

One morning when Jessie was busy, Bob called him over. 'I'm sick of potatoes and beef, fancy a plump roast chicken tonight, so bring me a good bird, choose one of the old ladies and be quick.' Desmond wasn't sure which one to choose so he chased them round the yard and caught the one that pecked him. He tucked it proudly under his arm and brought it back to the porch for inspection.

Bob nodded. 'Now kill it,' he ordered. 'Go on, it's about time you earned your keep. Wring its neck.'

Des jumped back, holding onto the bird. 'But she lays good eggs,' he argued.

'We've plenty more where she came from. Just pull and twist.' Bob made a gesture.

'You do it, please,' Des pleaded. He'd never killed a living thing before.

'Do as I tell you, boy. If you live here under my roof, eating my food, you do as you're told. This is not your fancy house in Bonnie Scotland with everyone at your beck and call. This is a working farm, and the sooner you learn how we do things . . . I didn't want a namby-pamby brat foisted on me, so behave. Once Jess has kids of her own, you'll be out on your ear. There are places you can be sent and you'll never see Jess again. Is that what you want? Now do it!'

Des felt the warmth of her feathers, the heartbeat of the trembling bird. He tried to do what was asked but the bird wriggled and he knew he was hurting her. 'I can't,' he cried. 'I don't know how.'

'Oh, give it here, you pansy.' Desmond didn't want to hand it over but he knew he must. In a second, the hen lay dead, its neck stretched, floppy. 'Give it to Ma to pluck and draw and make sure you watch her. Next time it will all be your job.'

'Do we have to stay here?' he asked Jessie that night when it was bedtime. 'I don't like Uncle Bob, he shouts. I don't like this place, either. It smells and the tin roof makes noises. I want to go home.'

'I know, love, but we can't go back, it'd cost too much. When Bob's plaster comes off, he won't be so crotchety. It's the heat and dust and the flies. We're not used to it yet. Now try not to have an accident tonight, it only makes things worse,' she whispered as she tucked him in with a kiss.

He tried to stay awake, not to fall fast asleep, but in the darkness and heat he felt the warm trickle seeping through his pyjamas. It was too late. He ripped off his sheet and hid it under the bed. He felt the tears coming and he didn't know what to do. Perhaps if he wasn't there, Jessie would smile more. If he walked down the track that led to town, he might find his way to Adelaide and Big Jim. He hated being stuck in the middle of nowhere. Perhaps if he ran away now, Bob wouldn't be able to come chasing after him.

Jessie wasn't Jessie any more. She didn't bounce, her curls lay flat on her head, and her face was covered in brown freckles. Her clothes were dusty and she wore a pinny and a frown all the time. They didn't fit in well. The ways of sheep were strange to her, she being more used to cattle on her own farm in Scotland.

Slowly, Bob began to hobble around with a stick and drive the truck with one leg. Once a week they went into town and Jessie insisted she went to church now and then. That was when the good clothes came out of the trunk: Desmond's jacket and shirt, her pretty frock and straw hat. His sandals were polished.

When they both dressed up he thought of the *Stirling Castle* and Big Jim and all the fun they'd had then. It made him think about running away. One Sunday he sat through the service, thinking only that he had a chance right then. Jessie would be better off without him. There was a railroad stop going north and south. He had no luggage, but he did have the pound note for a ticket and Jim's address he knew off by heart. It would be sad to leave Jessie but she'd come looking for him and then she'd stay and they'd all be happy together. The Kanes would be glad to see the back of him. There was nothing for him at the farm but smelly chores.

The summer heat was almost over and everyone was busy with sorting sheep. He wouldn't be missed. 'I'm going to the Men's room,' he told Jessie, trying not to give himself away. He wanted to cling to her but he daren't, so he shot off down the Main Street to the station halt. He dodged an old man sitting whittling wood outside the station and tried to look as if he was waiting for a train to arrive. If anyone asked, he was waiting for visitors. He sat and waited but nothing came either way. The man whittling wood kept staring at him.

'When's the next train south?' Desmond asked him eventually.

'Tomorrow, nothing today, sport. It's Sunday.'

Des stood up, feeling foolish. Now he'd have to go back or hide out all night. He'd have to make up some tale. As he left the station it was his bad luck that Bob was hobbling out of the hotel bar and spotted him.

'What the hell are you doing in this part of town?'

'Says he's waiting for the train south.' The old man laughed. 'Reckon you've got a runaway there, Bob.'

'Like hell I have. Get back up the street.' Bob marched him up the street in view of everyone, grabbing his arm so he burned the skin. 'You little runt, just wait till I get you home, making a fool of me like that.'

'What's he done now?' Jessie was waiting by the truck.

'He's going to learn a lesson he'll never forget when I get him home. And if you know what's good for him, you'll keep your trap shut or it'll be the worse for both of you.'

'I'm sorry, don't move . . .' Jessie was putting ointment on his strap wounds. The weals on his back and legs were stinging, raw from the beating. He lay on his tummy, trying to be brave. The punishment was bad enough, but Bob made Jessie watch it too. Then he demanded the clippers and went for his hair 'I've been wanting to do this since he came. You make a sissy out of this boy.'

'He can't help having curly hair,' Jessie pleaded.

'It's coming off. "Click go the shears, boys, click, click, click,"' Bob sang, clipping his scalp as he pulled chunks and snipped them so close to his head Desmond felt the stabbing sharp edges. He shaved his hair clean off. Des watched the black hair dropping in coils onto the floor. There was blood running down his forehead but he was too shocked to make a sound. He wanted to scream out but he was too afraid to move and make the pain worse. With every snip something inside him shrivelled up. He stared at the stone wall and the fireplace, hearing the sizzle of the hair on the fire.

'Oh, Bob, please stop. He's only a little laddie. What's got into you . . .? Don't take it out on the boy.' His mother was trying to calm him down.

'Shut up, Ma. He has to know who's boss in this house, the sooner the better I'll make a farmer out of him yet.' Jessie was crying, gathering up the hair with her brush. 'Stop snivelling. You only make it worse for him, taking his side.' Bob said, looking pleased at his handiwork.

I hate you, Des thought, and I'm never going to speak to you again.

From now on it was going to be all-out war between them. He would never give into tears while Bob was around. Next time, he'd get right away and he'd make sure he took Jessie with him. She deserved better than Bob Kane, and Desmond knew just who that might be.

34

Callie fell through the door of Primrose McAllister's flat in Sinclair Road. Primrose gathered her into her arms with relief. 'At last! I'm so glad to see you home. I thought we'd never see you again . . . Your mother rang, so I was expecting you. She's so worried. Oh, poor you, you don't deserve all this. Come on, sit down. I've got a bottle of wine. It's so wonderful to have you back.'

Callie collapsed on the sofa, back among familiar surroundings. So much had happened since she'd lived here and yet the place was just the same: the shabby furniture, the pictures on the wall. She wanted to curl up and sleep for a hundred years.

'I've got to do something,' she said.

'Not tonight you don't. You're going nowhere. I'd no idea . . . Get this down you.' Primmy shoved a tumbler of sweet wine into her hand. 'Knock this back. It was just the best news to know you're safe. We heard rumours that some of the overseas girls . . .' she hesitated, seeing the look on Callie's face. 'They didn't make it home. I know where you've been. Stuff gets out, official secrets or not. I gather the outfit has been disbanded now, but I'm so, so sorry about Desmond. Don't worry, he'll be safe enough where he is.'

'I have to bring him home. How could Phee do such a thing to us?'

'I'm not making excuses but she's had a stroke and it can change people, Daddy says.'

'I'm going out on the first ship.' Callie gulped the wine. 'As soon as I find out where they've gone.'

'I think you should rest first and get yourself ready. You've had a terrible experience. Be kind to yourself,' Primmy said gently, sitting down beside her.

'The only thing that kept me alive was the thought that I'd come back to Desmond,' Callie replied fiercely. Primmy must understand the urgency of everything. 'I can't wait to see his face when I turn up. He's bound not to remember me, but children don't forget their mothers, do they?' She was looking to her friend for reassurance.

'Don't expect too much too soon. One of my friends at work, her husband came back from a Jap POW camp last year and her little girl wouldn't have anything to do with him. "Who's that man in your bed? I don't want him there!" she cried every time he came near her. Poor man was distraught.'

'That won't happen to me. Desmond's bound to remember me.'

'It's been an awfully long time to a child, Callie. I'd hate you to be—'

Callie put her hands to her ears. 'Why are you being so negative? I'll get all my papers in order, make sure I get a war pension, sort out a place to live and all that kind of detail. I'm not coming back without him.'

'You must make your peace with Phee. Promise me. I know she feels terrible, and she's not well.'

'I'll never forgive her for what she did.'

'She's your mother, she did her best.'

'She was never the motherly sort. You can't change nature. When we return, time enough to sort her out then.' All Callie was feeling was a burning rage towards her mother now.

Primrose saw that Callie was running only on nervous energy

and she brought out a wodge of cheese and some crackers. 'All that's left of my ration,' she apologized.

'I'm not hungry. Pass the bottle over. This is good stuff.' The wine was warming her stomach and relaxing her panic.

'Ralph procured it for some favour or other. You've not met him yet. We met at work.' Primrose blushed. 'He's the best thing that came out of the war for me. We're getting married so make sure you're back for my wedding. I hope you'll stay here and not rush off tomorrow.'

'I'm going to see my lawyers and see what funds I have. I need to buy a house. I've got some unfinished business to do with you know what. They want me to sign an affidavit about my treatment in Belgium. They've captured some of the guards. I owe it to my friends who were betrayed and all that.' Callie shook her head wearily.

'Can you talk about it?'

'Never . . . Don't ask, please. It's locked up now and I've lost the key. That sort of stuff can never be shared. I don't want to think about any of it. It won't help get Desmond back where he belongs. That's all that matters to me now. I'm just waiting for an address from Jessie Dixon's family. I know she and Desmond were on the passenger list for *Stirling Castle*. As soon as I have that, I'll be writing and demanding to know his whereabouts.'

'Don't rush it, Callie. Send them postcards, things to remind him of you, pictures of Dalradnor.'

'I'm never going back there.' Callie snapped, resenting all Primmy's caution.

'Why not? It was his home and yours. You love it there. Don't be so black and white. You'll have to build a bridge between you both. You chose to leave it all behind when you volunteered. You knew what you were doing – or did you?'

'I thought you were my friend,' Callie cried, not wanting to hear such arguments. 'You're as bad as Phee, telling me what I should or shouldn't do.'

Primmy hugged her. 'I am your friend. I'm on your side. What's the use of friendship if we can't be honest with each other? Tell the truth in love and all that, I was taught. I'm just trying to help. It's all very complicated and emotional for all of you.'

Callie shook her off. 'I'm not listening to this rubbish.' She rose up but the room swam around her. The wine had gone to her knees as well as her head and she fell back onto the sofa.

'Come on, up the wooden hill to Bedfordshire. Time to sleep off all this upset,' Primmy suggested, taking the glasses and empty bottle to the sink. 'We have to plan your campaign step by step. First, Jess and Desmond must know you are alive and well. She must realize you intend to collect him from her. So you need to have a home ready for him here, somewhere you feel you'd both fit in, and that won't be easy now. Then you should give Jessie time to prepare Desmond for your news and visit. He's not a baby now but a young boy with ideas of his own. Tread carefully, Callie, and all will be well. Are you listening?' Primmy turned, shaking her head. Callie was snoring, fast asleep. The wine had done the trick.

35

'Has the runt lost his tongue?' Bob sat at the table, trying to goad Desmond into responding as he chomped on his stew. 'Is he stupid?'

Since the beating months ago, Des had never said a word to Bob, not one. If he asked him anything, he grunted and nodded. He obeyed him and took the occasional clip behind the ears and taunts in silence. He liked to see the puzzled look on Bob's face. It was war between them now and Jessie was taking his side when she could, covering up for his silence with excuses.

'He needs to go to school,' she pleaded. 'It's not right to keep a boy from his lessons.' She always knew how to get round Bob with a smile. 'You and I wouldn't have met if you hadn't passed your exams.'

'You teach him then, if you're so keen. Get him some books.'

Jessie needed no second bidding. The lessons were the highlight of his weekday, when they sat together, poring over reading books and doing sums and making shopping lists for him to add up. There was an old piano in the parlour, out of tune but that didn't stop Jessie playing it, and they sang Scottish songs: 'Loch Lomond', 'Roamin' in the Gloamin'', 'I belong to Glasgow'. That always made Jessie cry and Ma Kane used to come in with her mending and join in.

One Saturday night, they rolled up the carpet rug to practise Scottish reels for the church dance, but before long Bob stormed in as they were singing the music. 'So the boy can sing when he wants to.' Everyone stopped silent at his entrance. 'Go on, don't mind me, let's hear the mute sing for his supper. Don't think I don't know what you get up to behind my back. Sing or else . . .' He pointed Jessie to the piano. 'This is all your doing.'

'Son, they're only having fun. Leave them be!' Ma Kane pleaded, but he slapped her down.

'Shut up. If a man can't be master in his own house . . . Sing, you bloody pommy, sing.'

Jessie sat at the piano, not moving. Des stood by her side, his mouth shut tight in defiance, his throat dry with fear, But it was when he saw Bob lift the fire poker that he knew real panic. He turned to Jessie and nodded. She started to play 'Loch Lomond' and he tried to get the words out but they shrivelled in his mouth and hardly a sound emerged. '"By yon bonnie banks . . .",' was all he could croak.

'You can do better than that.'

Try as he might he couldn't sing a note. Suddenly Jessie stopped playing and looked up at her husband. 'He's scared, Bob.'

Bob slammed the piano lid down hard on her fingers, trapping them, and she screamed out in pain. Des flew at him like a demon, kicking out at Bob's legs as the big man raised the poker and thrashed him, blow after blow, until he fell down in a faint.

He woke up covered in bandages, not knowing where he was. Ma Kane was bathing his brow. 'I'm sorry, Louie. He's gone mad this time. You've got to get out of here before he kills you.' She was crying. 'This isn't my son any more, he's queer in the head.'

'Where's Jessie?' Desmond cried in alarm.

'Resting up. I don't know what devil's got into him, but since his accident . . .' She paused, staring at their wedding picture on the dressing table. 'It can't go on.'

Des couldn't move for the pain in his limbs and in his head. Was this all his fault for coming with Jessie? Was that why Bob got so mad? He knew to keep her safe he'd have to leave but now he was so tired, he couldn't think straight any more. All he knew was he hated Ruby Creek, and Ma Kane would help him if he asked nicely.

'Have you got a stamp and an envelope I could have?' he asked her the next day when he sat in the kitchen, trying to peel potatoes.

She smiled. 'I'll see what I can do, but mum's the word.'

36

Callie sat with her sundowner on the deck of the *Empress*, sunning herself. At long last she was on her way to Australia and would arrive in time to see in the New Year. It had all taken much longer than she'd hoped. There were so many loose ends to tie up, not least trying to find a house in the suburbs when there was such a housing shortage. In the end she'd taken a lease out on a house near Bexhill-on-Sea. Des would love to play on the beach. There were good schools, and it was a place where no one would know their business, a place where she could put all the past behind them and start again.

At last, she'd got a firm address for Jessie Kane, pinned her down to a farm called Ruby Creek near a town called Marree, and sent off the first salvo by way of warning that she was on her way.

This ship was packed with young children starting a new life in a new country, orphans accompanied by nuns and teachers. They were dashing all over the decks, full of beans, their pale city faces blossoming the fresh air. Callie tried to imagine how Desmond would look now, aged seven. She'd sent him a parcel for Christmas with a beautiful Dinky car and a picture of herself in uniform. She'd sent Jessie a letter, enclosing a postcard of the ship for him and she'd also enclosed a picture postcard of her mother in her heyday. It would remind Jessie of her responsibility to the family. Phoebe Faye in her Gaiety Girl glory looked so pretty and formidable. It was a pity her son would never see his grandmother again unless Callie was ready to forgive her, but this would remind them of her importance.

It was good to be on board a ship again. The last time she'd been dreaming of Ferrand, on her way home, carrying his child. How happy they'd been in Cairo with all their future before them. If only they'd known what lay ahead. Even now her dreams were broken by nightmare scenes she couldn't control. Soon she would return with her son and they'd begin new lives together, and nothing and no one would ever separate them again.

It was nearly Christmas and Jessie and Ma Kane were busy shopping in town for provisions. Des begged to go with them or his plan wouldn't work. His bruises were fading but he had a bad scar over his cheek. Bob wouldn't want his injuries to be seen in public so he put on his jacket to hide his arms, despite the heat, and a cap over his shaven head. He wore shorts made from a pair of Bob's denims, and his feet were poking out of his sandals. Bob didn't look at him directly, and no one said anything about that night. Jessie's fingernails were black and her fingers were strapped together so he and Ma took over her chores.

Desmond asked if he might go to the post office. He was clutching his pound note and his precious Christmas card. He wanted to buy Christmas presents and post his special letter to Adelaide. It had been burning a hole in his pocket for weeks. He had written out the message very carefully in his best handwriting.

'Have you been in the wars, again, Louie?' The post mistress looked at his face with concern.

'The horse tossed me again,' he said, not looking at her. He handed over his letter.

'While you're here, there's something for your Aunty Jess from England. Make sure she gets it, sonny.'

Desmond slipped it into his pocket and set off to the store to buy a tin of chocolates and some hankies for Ma, and some tinsel. It was Christmas, after all, and even if it was hot, Jess promised there'd be a Christmas tree to dress. With a bit of luck Bob would drink and fall asleep and leave them all to enjoy themselves listening to the wireless on their own.

Bob had been very sober since that terrible Saturday night. Desmond had heard him pleading with Jessie to forgive him. He took them to church without complaint and promised them a picnic as a treat.

There was no snow, and no Father Christmas in the shops. Jess said it was too far for him to come to Ruby Creek but he would leave presents just the same. Jessie whispered, 'You must be nice to Uncle Bob. He's making an effort. He knows he did wrong.'

'Why do we have to stay?'

'Because I made my vows in church for better or worse,' Jessie replied, looking very sad. 'We have to make the best of things.' He knew she cried if there was no post waiting for them from her family. She was hating the strangeness of this place as much as he.

All Desmond's plans went well until Christmas morning, when the presents appeared under the tinsel tree and he gave out his to Ma and Jessie.

'How did you get the money for those fancy things?' Bob sneered, examining the gifts and aware there was nothing for him.

'It's my own money, I saved it.' Desmond smiled.

'Like hell you did. Have you been stealing in town?'

'No, I haven't. I was given it.'

'See how he changes his story. So who would give you money? Jess, have you been taking it out of our housekeeping?'

Jessie flashed him a look of defiance, shaking her head.

'Don't you lie to me.'

'She doesn't lie,' Ma pleaded. 'It's Christmas Day, leave it off.'

Bob grabbed Des by the shirt collar, making him wince. 'Tell me who gave you money.'

'I was given a pound on the ship when we left.'

'Who was it?' Bob tightened his grip.

'Big Jim gave it to me.'

'Big Jim who?'

'Our friend. He was coming home from the war.'

'A soldier on the ship. Why would he give a runt like you money?'

'Oh, Bob, please. Big Jim was our PT instructor. He was kind, that's all.'

'I bet he was kind, so kind he gave him money to keep quiet. Was he your fancy man?'

'Oh, please, calm down. It was nothing like that. We had a few dances, otherwise we had to dance with other girls. Don't jump to conclusions. He took a shine to Louie, that's all. Let's enjoy the day without any arguments. It's Christmas.'

'So bloody what? It's only a day like any other, nothing special. The stock don't know it's Christmas. That boy has a sly look . . . what are you looking like that for?'

'I forgot something, just a minute.' Des dashed off to find his jacket and dipped in the pocket. 'I forgot this letter. It's for you, Jess, from England.' He held out the letter in strange handwriting. Jess turned to open it and then walked out of the room.

'Bad news?' said Ma, seeing her return, looking serious.

'No, it's just family news. I'll read it later. Where were we?'

'Back where we usually are, arguing over this blighter and his antics,' Bob said.

'Don't keep going on at him.' Jess moved closer to Desmond.

'You always take his side. He's got to go.' Bob stared at them both.

'He's too young to go away to school in a strange country, have a heart. I brought him out here for a better life.' She was busy tidying up the wrapping paper into the hearth.

'It's either him or me, Jess. You weren't like this in Scotland. You were full of fun and ready for anything.'

'And I came across the world to be with you, only to find you are not the man I married. You've changed. Anyone can see that. I didn't come here to be battered black and blue. And you treat your stock better than you treat little Louie here.'

'He's a bad influence on you.' Bob stepped forward and Des instinctively stepped back, waiting for a slap.

'Look at yourself, Bob, and your own faults before you go blaming a child. What sort of example have you given him? Not one kind word has passed your lips since we arrived. I can't take much more.'

'Then you know what you can do then,' he replied with a sneer, his arms folded. But when he saw the determined look on Jessie's face his expression changed.

'That's fine by me. I'm sorry, Ma, but enough is enough,' she said. 'If we can't be civil on Christmas Day, what hope is there for us? Come on, Louie, time to pack. I'm not one to stay where I'm not welcome.'

Desmond couldn't believe what he was hearing. Why had she changed her mind? Could it be true they were really leaving? He raced up the stairs after her, smiling for the first time in weeks as she pulled down the suitcase with all the labels on it, throwing in their clothes, all the town stuff they'd hardly worn. 'We have to leave right away. I'll get one of the farm hands to drive us into town. Though where we'll go, I've no idea.'

'I have.' He smiled, holding out the worn slip of paper he'd saved all these months. 'I've sent him a card. He knows about us. We can go there first. I made him a promise and now we can keep it.'

Jessie turned and smiled back. 'What would I do without you, son?'

Desmond flushed with pride. This change of heart was the best Christmas present ever.

37

Callie felt the strange heat prickling her skin as she gazed from the train out onto the countryside, astonished at the sheer size of the territory at the top end of South Australia , the forests, the expanses of flat land with roadside settlements strung out like something out of a Wild West film. Mile after dusty mile with no sightings of people. What would her son have made of such space? It was a new country for young people, new roads and townships; even the soil was so different from her own.

She alighted at the station halt closest to Ruby Creek, excited but uneasy, an obvious stranger in her London clothes. She booked into the only hotel – little more than a bar with rooms above – and deposited her case. Her first action would be to find the quickest way to the farm. She'd hoped someone would have the courtesy to meet her at the station as she'd sent details of all her travel arrangements to them well in advance. There had been no reply to any of her mail, however, so she made for the store-cum-post office.

The woman behind the counter smiled. 'G'day . . . Can I help?'

'I hope so. How do I get to Ruby Creek?' Callie paused, smiling, aware of her accent. 'To the Kane farm. I'm looking for Jessie Kane. Is it far?'

'You from England?' the woman asked.

Callie nodded.

'Sorry, can't help you there. Jess's been gone a while back,' she whispered. 'There was a bit of trouble. If you ask me, Bob Kane wants his head seeing to, letting a hard worker like her go . . . Still, I reckon his head's not been in the right place since he flew off that motor bike. Took off, sje did, on Christmas Day and only been here five minutes. She had her reasons, so I don't blame her.' She leaned over the counter to make her point.

'So where is she now?' Callie couldn't believe she'd come all this way to hear this.

'I heard they were seen catching the train south. Perhaps they've left for good. I don't think they settled.'

'They?' Callie asked. 'She took the boy with her?'

'Of course. She'd do anything for that kid. He's a funny one. Came in here all secret with a card to post. Lonely kid, shame they cut off all those curls. Now, young Louie did have an address somewhere in Adelaide,' she offered.

'Can you remember where?' Callie asked, wondering why she called him Louis.

'Have a heart, do you think I read all the mail before it's sent? I'm not that memory man on the wireless . . . Though, come to think about it, the little fella was so proud of his handwriting and not many farm boys come in like him, especially one as didn't go to school. Now what was the name . . . Wait, it'll come to me. It was a name I knew . . .' She shut her eyes, trying to concentrate. 'It began with a B . . . Ball was it? Nah . . . I don't know any Balls.'

'Oh, please remember.' Callie was shaking.

'I know . . . Boyd Rankin, he was at school with me in Marree.' She shook her head and smiled. 'It was addressed to a Mr Boyd of Adelaide. That's the best I can do.'

'Do you think they went there?' Callie was desperate.

'Why are you asking me? Ask Ma Kane . . . or perhaps not. Are you a relative or Welfare?' The postmistress was eyeing her with suspicion now.

'A close relative . . . I came all this way to see them and now I'm too late.' She was close to tears and so tired, but she didn't want to give too much away.

'You sit down and rest your feet. You can do me a favour. I have a pile of mail addressed to Jess here somewhere. Wait a sec.' She darted into the back and brought out Callie's Christmas parcel and letters.

'But I sent these for Christmas,' she said wearily.

'The addresses weren't quite right and they went somewhere else. Now you can give them in person. It's worth trying in Adelaide. It's a fine city and this Mr Boyd might help you find them. Good luck . . . I didn't catch your name?'

Callie nodded, saying nothing as she walked out of the shop, trying not to cry with disappointment. She'd built herself up for the reunion here, and now all this. Desmond hadn't got her pictures and presents. Had Jessie fled after receiving that first letter, which Callie saw wasn't in the pile? Was that why they left so quickly?

What she needed now was a stiff drink to soothe her anxiety. She walked across to the hotel but the bar was closed so she lay on her bed thinking that those meagre clues were a thin thread to string her hopes on. But she'd not come all this way to be defeated.

Later that evening, she walked into the bar, flinching to see the men clutching their beers staring at her as if she were from another planet. An unshaven man in dungarees staggered up to her.

'I hear you've been asking after my wife.' She could feel the anger in his voice as he eyed her up and down. The jungle drums had been beating fast. 'I know who you are.'

'And I know who you are, too, Mr Kane, and what must have made Jessie runaway with my son on Christmas Day.'

'Louie's your son?' He stepped back, looking to his mates for support. 'What sort of mother leaves her son in the hands of that whore?'

All her training flared into the instinct to punch him where it hurt, but she drew breath and said loudly, 'One who was captured by Nazis and held in a concentration camp, Mr Kane. Who couldn't make it home in time, like so many of your prisoners of war.' The bar fell silent at her outburst. Everyone was listening. Callie had not spoken of her experience to anyone but she wanted to fell this man at one swoop. He was a bully who needed flattening. 'And if I hear from my son that you harmed him in any way . . . Watch out. I know where you live and, believe me, I was trained to kill, so you'd better tell me what you know about where they've gone.' The steely look in her eye had its effect, but Kane was not about to lose face.

'Where do you think, missus?' he smirked. 'To her fancy man in Adelaide, and good riddance to another whingeing pom.' He turned his back on her in triumph and swaggered to the other side of the room but no one moved with him.

'Thank you, that's all I needed to know,' Callie called after him in defiance. She turned to the barman. 'I need something to take the smell of that rat away . . .'

Desmond sat at the dining table in Maitland Avenue, looking across at Big Jim in admiration. He couldn't believe he'd made his dream come true. They were sitting down for lunch with a white cloth and flowers on the table, with plates of lamb and roast potatoes, in a room with magic carpet rugs and pictures on the wall. Now they were sleeping in a bedroom with pretty curtains and with no smells of sheep and dirt. The Boyd house was a palace made of brick, not wood, with big windows and a garden to play in. It was like being in heaven after that tin shack in Ruby Creek. Jess was smiling at everyone and telling Jim's parents how kind Jim had been on board ship.

Jessie was nervous when they'd knocked on the door but old Mrs Boyd asked them inside and called her son at his workplace on the telephone. 'It's the little Scottish boy who sent you the card from the Outback and his mom . . .'

Jim came rushing back to greet them. 'I read your note and was coming to visit you after Christmas, but you beat me to it. You can stay with my parents until you get sorted.' He was looking at Jessie and smiling. 'I think yer mom needs a rest, by the look of her.' They went into another room to talk.

Des liked it when people called Jess his mom. All he could think of now was being safe from Uncle Bob, safe from being knocked around, safe in a town with proper shops and streets with parks everywhere.

'I'm going to look for work,' Jessie warned. 'And you'll have to go to school.' Des couldn't think of anything better. 'And we can't stay here. It's not proper, so don't expect anything fancy like this. It'll be two rooms for us.'

'I don't mind,' he said. Anything was paradise after Ruby Creek. However, he had some secret plans. He knew Big Jim liked Jessie and she liked him. If they stayed here long enough, then they might get together and be one family.

Jim took Desmond to his building supply depot and he stared up at the great bays of sacks of concrete and sand, and stacks of timber. There were trucks for lifting sacks, special tools and buckets, machinery parked in rows. Cats were darting everywhere. He ran to try to play with them.

'Watch out or they'll bite. They keep the vermin down. All this material is helping building new homes for the soldiers coming home from the war and settling down. Do you like it?'

Des smiled up at him in awe. If Jim hadn't given him his address and he hadn't sent the Christmas card, what then? Now all the dark clouds had melted into sunshine and he could feel the warmth all over him.

Finding the Boyds in Adelaide wasn't too difficult. It was a good Scottish surname and there were plenty listed in the telephone directory in alphabetical order. But it was too hot to visit each one on foot, so Callie decided to sit down and ring round until she found the right family. The man in the hotel desk was helpful, but as she went from one name to the next, it was beginning to look hopeless. 'Keep going,' he encouraged, offering to do some himself for her. They listed all those from whom there'd been no reply and just when Callie was starting to feel despondent she struck lucky.

'I'm looking for a Mrs Jessie Kane and Desmond Lloyd-Jones travelling with her from Ruby Creek to see a Mr Boyd. Have you had any one of that name call recently?' she asked the woman who had answered the telephone.

There was a pause. 'Who's that speaking?'

'This is Mrs Caroline Jones, Desmond's mother.' Callie was trembling.

'I'm sorry, we've no Desmond Jones here,' came the answer, but there was something about her hesitation that made Callie persist.

'His full name is Desmond Louis . . . It's just possible you might know him as—'

'Oh, you mean, Louie.'

'You know him? He and Jessie, they are with you?' Her voice was rising in excitement.

'Not exactly, but I think you'd better explain yourself, Mrs Jones.' The voice was more cautious now. Callie began her story but soon the woman interrupted. 'We can take this matter further in person at our address in Maitland Avenue, perhaps after tea? I presume you have proof of your connections . . .'

'Oh, yes!' Callie staggered with relief, still holding the ear piece in her hand.

'Are you OK?' The man at the desk rushed over, seeing her swaying. 'Bad news?'

'No, I think I've found them in Maitland Avenue. My son's here in the city. Now all I need is a taxi.'

'A nice part of town, madam,' the desk clerk said, but Callie wasn't listening.

He's here and I shall see him soon. I must get changed, look my best, prepare my papers. I can't believe this is happening. She could hardly stand still in the lift up to her room. There was such a lot to do before she made a triumphal appearance at the Boyds' house.

Des ran all the way from school to the building-supply depot as he always did on a Friday night. He stayed there until Jessie got back from working in the baby nursery and mothers collected their children. He loved Fridays, the best night of the week, going out to the pictures and then back to their lodgings in Pitcairn Street for a fish supper, with two whole days of no school to look forward to. Tomorrow, they might go to Elder Park to watch a cricket match while Jessie did their washing. Then he stayed with the Boyds while she and Jim went out alone. He stayed the night for a barbecue and went to church in the morning, to Sunday school. They all went for a walk in the parks and he sailed his yacht.

When he ran through the gates today, however, Jim's dad was looking serious. 'Got to take you home. You've got a visitor,' he said, ushering him into the black saloon car that was always polished to a sheen for the weekend.

It must be an important visitor for Jim to leave early, and who would come to visit them? Then his heart sank. Bob Kane must have traced them here and come to fetch them back. We're never going back there, he thought. They were settled here now. Des liked his school and his mates. He felt himself beginning to tremble all over. He'd tried to block out all those awful times on the farm but sometimes in the night Bob's face jumped out to frighten him and he cried out. Jessie came to hug him better. What if Bob brought a policeman and said they had to go back?

'Who is it?' he asked Jim's dad, and his voice came out squeaky.

'Don't ask me, just got a call to say come back at once.'

Des cowered back in his seat, dreading the moment when he'd come face to face with his sworn enemy.

Callie stepped out of the taxi on the avenue in the Westbourne Park suburb, admiring the line of gracious bungalows set amongst shrubs and parkland. This looked a prosperous household. She walked up to the porch, trying to compose herself. How could she bear to see Jessie Dixon with her son, and what was she going to say to him? Oh, just get on with it, she goaded herself, striding forward to ring the bell.

A woman with iron-grey hair and a bronzed face lined by years of sunshine welcomed her inside. 'Mrs Jones, come in . . . I'm Mrs Boyd and this is my son, Jim.' She smiled, pointing to a tall young man who filled the door frame with his height.

Callie nodded politely as she was led into a large drawing room with huge glass windows with shutters on the outside and a door leading out down a lawn to a wide swimming pool.

'Can I get you something to drink . . . a shandy?'

'Just water, thank you.'

'I'm afraid there's just the two of us here. My husband will bring the boy later, and Jess is at work. It gives us the chance to talk privately. We're curious to know what brought you so far from home.'

'I thought it would be obvious, Mrs Boyd. I've come to collect my son.' Callie saw them look at each other in surprise.

'Your son? But we thought Louie's parents were . . .' Mrs Boyd hesitated. 'We thought they'd passed away in the war. That's why she brought him out with her.'

'But as you can see, I'm here, at long last. Desmond was three when I joined up and went overseas, but he's never been out of my thoughts.'

'That was a very unusual thing for a mother to do.' The criticism was implied but Callie stood firm.

'They were unusual times, as anyone who lived through it
will tell you.' She looked to the son for support. 'I thought I
could be useful to the war effort.'

'But what's taken you so long?'

She was ready for this one, explaining about her capture and
internment, her sickness and the letter that was mislaid. She said
very little about her secret mission abroad.

'And your husband? Did he not have relatives?'

'Mr Jones left us to fend for ourselves before the war . . . I
have no idea where he is now. That's of no concern to me. All
that matters is that Louie, as you keep calling him, knows his
mother is alive and has come for him. Jessie has no claim on him
at all, you must understand that. She was just his nursemaid.'

Jim leaned forward. 'But I think she has. She's the only mom
he knows.'

Callie shook her head, spilling the water on her dress. 'Then
he'll have the advantage of having two mothers to spoil him for
a while.' She smiled but they didn't.

'I don't think it's as easy as you make out,' Jim continued. He
was looking at his watch. 'They won't be long now. Would
you like a turn in the garden with my mother so I can prepare
Jess for this meeting? She's not had things easy herself.'

'As you wish,' Callie replied, feeling uneasy. She must prepare
herself for Jess's appearance and stand firm in her demand to
collect her son, no matter what.

The room was full of grown-ups when Des peered round the
door, searching out the dreaded face, but Uncle Bob wasn't
there, only a lady in a blue dress and jacket, with a hat on, who
smiled at him. He smiled back politely. Jess was standing up with
Big Jim and his parents were on the sofa, all looking at him.

'Say hello to Mrs Jones. Do you know who she is?' Jessie said
in a squeaky voice. He smiled again, shaking his head, and held
out his hand. He'd never seen this lady before.

'Hello, Desmond,' she said. 'I haven't seen you since you were so high.' She lifted her hand up to a space by the mantelpiece.

He looked to Jessie for reassurance. What was he supposed to say next?

'Jessie here looked after you for me while I was in the war. When they thought I wasn't coming back, she kindly brought you with her for a while. Now I've come all the way from Scotland to take you home.'

Des stepped back, not understanding what she was saying, and he saw that Jess was looking sad.

'Your mother was very ill and couldn't get back when the war ended so I took you instead. Now she wants you to go and live with her. What do you think, Louie?' Jess added.

He felt all funny inside. He didn't know this lady and she was making Jessie cry. So he backed slowly out through the open door and fled upstairs into a bedroom away from all the staring eyes. Why had that lady called him Desmond? Who was she? Didn't she know he belonged here? He remembered the ship and Big Jim and the food and dances, but nothing before that. He remembered bits of Ruby Creek and the poker on his legs but nothing else. He buried his head in his hands to make her go away.

The room fell silent at Desmond's sudden exit. Callie's euphoria vanished the instant she saw the blank look on the boy's face. He had no idea who she was. It was agony to see him turn to Jess as a child turns to its mother when afraid. He'd grown into a leggy young boy, his curls straightened, lightened by the sun, his skin suntanned. He was a handsome boy with flashes of Ferrand's dear features in his face.

Now she sat alone with these strangers lined up in their beautiful home. A strong family sitting side by side was something she'd never known. She felt their strength and bond but

she would not be defeated by numbers. They all left the room
so she could talk with Jess and ask for an explanation of how
she'd deceived Phoebe. It was obvious she'd made a disastrous
marriage, but how could she of all people judge her for that?

'It was Louie who rescued us by writing to his shipboard
friend. The Boyds have been kindness itself. I'm sorry but I did
what was best for Louie at the time. Your mother couldn't cope
and you were presumed dead. What else could I do? He's
known me all my life, as you knew Marthe, or have you forgotten how you sang her praises to me?'

'But to bring him all this way, far from his roots, and to pass
yourself off as a relative, that was dishonest,' Callie argued.

'Better that than leave him in some boarding school with
strangers,' Jess snapped back. 'Your mother is in no fit state to
have a child in the house. I stand by what I did. You left him in
my care, and taken care of is what I've done. He doesn't
know you now.'

When the Boyds returned, the atmosphere changed. 'We've
decided that you must stay here,' Mrs Boyd suggested. 'Let
Louie get used to you. You've been a long time apart. We don't
know what else to advise. You can't force a child of his age to
comply like a toddler. Time has no meaning for them.'

Where had Callie heard that before? It was what Primrose
had warned. Once he realized they were flesh and blood, there
would be some recognition of the tie, surely?

'Thank you,' she replied, feeling so weary and sick. 'There's
so much I have to show him and so much he needs to know. He
just needs time. It's not too late for us to change things, is it?'

Nobody spoke; no one smiled or gave her any encouragement. She was on her own against them now; a mother fighting
for her son.

38

Desmond didn't feel like eating very much as they sat round the dining table. He kept staring at the lady across from him. She was pretty, but not like Jessie. She had blue eyes and straight teeth and smelled of flowers. Jess never wore perfume. She kept looking at him when she thought he wasn't looking. Then they were left alone and she brought out a parcel from her shopping bag. 'I went to Ruby Creek Post Office and they gave me back my Christmas parcel. I'm sorry it never arrived on time.'

'That's OK,' he said, peering at the parcel with interest. Inside was a big red car to play with and some pictures of a house and faces he didn't recognized. There was a book about Orlando the Marmalade Cat and some sweets in wrappers. 'Thank you,' he said, remembering his manners.

'Don't you remember this? Here's you with me having a piggy back . . . in the garden at Dalradnor. It was Granny Phee who took this snap.' She shoved the picture in his hand. There was a little boy with curly hair astride a laughing lady. He didn't know them. 'I'm too old for piggy backs now. I'm going to play cricket and Uncle Jim's got me stumps.'

She pushed another picture across to him of a fancy lady with feathers in her hair. 'This is your Granny Phoebe. She was a famous actress on the stage. Isn't she pretty? She was poorly and that's why Jess took you from us and brought you here.'

'She didn't take me, I asked her.'

'So you do remember then?'

'No. I remember the big ship and Uncle Jim and Ruby Creek.'

'I'm sorry it's been such a long time, but now we've got time to start all over again, Desmond.'

'I'm Louie,' he corrected her. He didn't like the name Desmond.

'Yes, your father was Louis-Ferrand, a very brave man. I have his medal for you to keep. He died in the war,'

'That's OK. I have Uncle Jim to look after us.'

'Big Jim is not your family. I am your family now.' Why did she keep saying this?

'What's family?' he asked. He didn't want her family. He had Jim and Jessie.

'We are the people God gives to cherish you and bring you up.'

'God's given me Jim and Jess now.'

'Yes, for the moment, but I am your real family now . . . Louie.' She leaned forward as if she wanted to hug him.

'No you're not . . . I don't know you. Go away!'

Callie sobbed all night at Desmond's rejection of her. He didn't seemed bothered with her gift of the precious medal, just handing it over to Jess to hold with the pictures. He was polite and begged to be excused from the table, rushing out into the garden far from sight. She was angry with him but daren't show it. Jess was hovering around, making excuses, and the Boyds were silent but missed nothing.

She stayed for four days and decided to move back to the Queen's Head to prepare her campaign. Living with the Boyds was too much. There were too many of them, chatting, laughing, watching her, ignoring her. She needed to be alone and think through her strategy. First, she bought tickets for a cricket match and the pictures. She took Desmond around the parks after school but he wouldn't go without Jess. Waiting at the school gate had always been her dream, watching him run smiling into her arms, but it was a silly fantasy. A boy of eight didn't do such things. He ignored her. It was as if he didn't want to be bothered with her. Their visits were an endurance test, not a pleasure to be savoured. She persevered for another week, trying to seduce him by taking an interest in everything he did, with promises of trips to London on an aeroplane. The more she tried the less seemed to bother. It was a stubborn defiance she didn't understand.

It was Jim who broke the stalemate one afternoon when they were alone. 'I know it's not been long but from where I'm sitting, this has gone on long enough. Poor Jess is suffering, you are suffering, and the child doesn't know who he is. You can't force a boy to do what he doesn't want to do. He's been through hell with Bob Kane, enough to last a lifetime. Jess is suing for a divorce on the grounds of cruelty. Heaven knows what all this is doing to him now. I think it's time to let the boy have his say.'

Callie stared at him, horrified. 'You mean let him choose his future? Surely not?'

'Why not? Louie is no ordinary boy; he's old for his age. He's had to be. He blocks out what he doesn't want to think about and he's blocked you out too. I'm sorry but he has. As far as he's concerned Jess is his mom.'

Callie shot out of her seat. 'But I'm his mother. I gave birth to him, fed him at my breast. I want my son back,' she protested.

'But does he want to go with you? That is the real issue here. What is best for Louie is all that matters now. Being a mother is more than just giving birth, as it is for any father in sowing the seed. It's about being there, about sharing trust. You have to let him choose his destiny.'

'That's not fair. He's far too young to know what's best for him,' Callie argued. 'I couldn't help what happened in the war.'

'You don't have to explain to me. I was there too . . . all that death and destruction and separation. I'm sorry, but Louie is a loser too in all this. He was deprived of you because of the war.'

'Are you asking me to let him go?' She paced around the room, staring out of the window in agony.

'I suggest we ask Louie to decide for himself.'

'Then what?'

'I don't know. We take it from there.'

'But he's my child. He must do as I wish. I'm his mother. I have a right to my own flesh and blood,' she argued. 'How can a child know what's best for him? I think you've said enough.' How dare he suggest such a solution? Time to beat a retreat back to her hotel and buy a bottle of wine to help her sleep.

She awoke in a sweat in the early hours of the morning, exhausted by her dream. She was chasing Desmond through a maze of shrubs, trying to catch him, but every corner she turned, he wasn't there. She could hear him laughing, shouting, but the more she searched the tighter the bushes closed in on her until they formed a great jungle wall, barring her way to the laughter.

Since the lady came to visit everything was different. People kept disappearing into the drawing room with the door shut, whispering when they thought he couldn't hear. Jess kept crying into her hanky at night and looking worried. He'd been naughty, fighting in the playground and sent for punishment. He kicked and lashed out at boys who teased him about his pommy accent when he was trying so hard to talk like them.

Why did that lady have to come to the school gate in her pretty frocks that made the other mothers stare at them both? Why did she call him her son? Desmond was her son, the boy in the snapshot, not him. Yet he sort of recognized the sound of the name and the picture of the house with the stone steps. She kept talking about Scotland and him wearing a kilt. That was a skirt and only girls wore skirts. He wanted to shut his ears. She was kind and bought him sweets and toys and played ludo and snakes and ladders, but when she tried to reach out to touch him, he backed off and ran into the garden.

One Sunday after church, the minister came for lunch. The table was squashed with people chattering and eating, and the lady didn't look at him once. Then they crossed the hall into the drawing room and sat down, all except the minister.

'Thank you once again for your wonderful hospitality, but I am aware that I must sing for my supper, as it were,' he coughed. 'You Boyds have been in the congregation for years, in good times and in bad, but this is the most unusual gathering. I've been asked to bear witness to a very strange situation indeed. I've spoken with both parties in private and heard some sad tales. I've seen the birth certificate that makes Louie Mrs Lloyd-Jones's her son. I'm also aware of the terrible privations she suffered as a result of her war service. I've spoken to Mrs Kane and heard why she had to flee her marriage vows. In normal circumstances, there should be only one outcome, but Jim and you all feel that the boy should have his say.'

'He's too young to know his own mind,' the lady butted in.

'I understand your concern, Mrs Lloyd-Jones, but nevertheless, I'm going to ask young Louie some questions in private, if you don't mind.'

Then the minister took him out of the door into the garden, to sit on a bench next to the bush roses. He asked him all about Ruby Creek and why they left. Louie showed him the scars on his legs. The minister shook his head. 'Shocking!' He asked him what he remembered about Scotland and what he wanted to do next. Didn't everyone know what he wanted?

'I want her to go away,' he said.

'Why's that? What has she done wrong?'

'She wants me to go back and I won't . . .' He turned away from the old man as he spoke.

'But she is your real mother. She brought you into this world.'

Louie ignored him. 'Aunt Jess is my mom now. I want to stay with Jess and Jim.'

'You do realize that you will upset Caroline Jones very much if you say no. She's come a long way to find you. She loves you very much.'

'I don't care, make her go away.' He sat on the bench, shaking his head, watching the old man walk back into the room where they were all waiting.

As soon as the Reverend Mitchell came back into the room, the atmosphere was charged with tension and the others left quickly, leaving just Callie and Jess sitting in silence. He stood with his back to the fireplace, looking to each of them in turn. 'Whatever I say now will disappoint one of you. Perhaps we ought to bring a lawyer in to verify the legal situation before we go any further . . . before Louie has his say. He's a solid little chap and knows his mind.'

'What did he say?' Callie couldn't wait a moment longer.

'He'd prefer to stay where he is, I'm afraid. He was most adamant.'

'That's ridiculous. He's my son. He has to come with me. It was the thought of him that kept me sane and helped me survive in the camp. I can't just let him go just because he thinks his place is with her.' She could hardly bear to look at Jessie.

'With respect, Mrs Jones, whose need is being met here, yours or his?' His words lashed her like a whip. 'Do you want him for your own gratification or can you listen to the needs of a little boy who has been from pillar to post with only one fixture in his life, Mrs Kane here?'

'We can share him then . . . I'll come and live here and he can spend time with each of us,' she offered in desperation and renewed hope. 'That's been done before, I'm sure.'

'In the long run, it wouldn't work and you'd still want to take him back to Scotland,' Jess argued.

'It has to work. I'm not letting you have him. You've had him long enough. It's my turn now.' Callie fought her corner, trying not to panic.

'It doesn't work like that . . . an "either her or me" solution,' the minister intervened. 'You both love the child so he comes first and what he wants comes first . . .'

'Are you asking us to choose between ourselves who will let him go?' Jess asked. 'I never set out to take him or love him as my own. He was in my charge. It was my job, but as his nurse-maid, I grew to love him and he, me.' She turned to Callie with a look of sadness. 'You know how that feels . . . I'm sorry you couldn't be there so I took over. I didn't mean to steal your child,' she cried.

'But you did. You stole his heart and I'm a stranger to him and always will be now.'

'Not necessarily. I'm sure there are ways for you to be involved in his future. Be his aunt,' the minister suggested.

He said the wrong thing there. Callie felt her hackles rising. 'Like my mother had to hide that fact by calling herself my aunt? Never! If I go, I go for ever. I won't confuse the issue. Desmond needs stability and I can offer nothing but my love. Even I can see it's not going to be enough for him, but I won't leave without asking him myself, please.' No one spoke. No one called her back. Callie made for the garden door, straightening her crumpled dress. 'Where is he now?'

The minister pointed out into the garden. Slowly, she walked down the veranda steps. The minister's words had wounded her beyond repair. She had come, yes, out of love but also guilt, desperately needing to have Desmond to herself so normality could begin again. His return put all the sacrifices to rights. It would be a healing moment when he said 'Mummy' to her again.

The man was right in pointing out how she needed him more than he wanted her. In his child's mind, there was a

mother and father waiting in the wings in this brash and beautiful young country.

*Must his wish to stay here be sacrificed so I can have the life I always
dreamed of living with him? Do I sacrifice my own happiness so he can
have the life he deserves and knows here? How can anyone ask me to
do this? Is letting go the price I must pay for leaving him? How can I
live if he turns me away again?*

'Louie,' she called. He was kicking a ball around the grass,
ignoring her, pretending he couldn't see her.

'Listen to me, please. I know you've spoken to the minister
but I need to be sure for myself. Would you come back on the
big ship with me, back to our big house where there's horses
and chickens?'

'No. I hate chickens,' he replied, not looking at her.

'So what do you want to do?'

'I want to live with Aunt Jess and Uncle Jim for ever.'

'Why's that?'

'Dunno . . . They are my family now.' He stared at her with
those blue, blue eyes.

'I suppose they are.' Callie sighed, kneeling down to his
height, holding out her hand. 'But that can never stop me being
your mummy. Can I write to you? Will you write back to me?'

He shrugged. 'If you want, but I hate writing.' He carried on
kicking his ball as if she wasn't there, ignoring her outstretched
hands.

'I'd better say goodbye, then.' Callie swallowed back her
tears as she drank in his serious face, wanting to fall at his knees
and beg him to love her. Then the boy held out his hand but
she couldn't take it, turning to flee from the terrible heat of his
rejection with a howl of grief.

When Louie returned to the drawing room, the lady was gone.
He knew she wasn't coming back and he felt important to have
sent her away. Now he'd have Jessie all to himself once more

and no one would ever talk about this again. He just knew it was a secret that wasn't to be shared outside this house. When he went to bed that night, Louie kept hearing that cry the lady made when she ran off and saw the tears in her eyes as she kneeled before him.

He remembered how he cried when Bob killed the little hen, the one he'd had to choose. He could smell the lady's perfume and suddenly saw that garden in the picture, the path where roses tickled his face and he heard her singing in his dream; singing the song that always made him sad. When he woke, the bed was wet and Jess was cross and he couldn't tell her why. All he knew was they'd never talk about that visit again and the sooner he forgot about the lady in the rose garden the better it would be. No one would ever call him Desmond again. From now on, his name was Lou.

39

Callie sat in the bar of the Queen's Head, hugging her drink. She'd lost count of how many she'd downed, but not enough yet to banish the expression on her son's face in the garden. She tried to blot out that look of triumph and defiance in his eyes. *Have I done the right thing in abandoning all right to him? Why have I no fight left to claim him? What are you doing? No proper mother gives up her child to another just like that?* She felt so befuddled by her shifting emotions. *Is it better to give a child a chance of happiness where he feels secure, or to drag him kicking and screaming to a strange country he no longer remembers? How can I do that to him?* Her heart was crying but her mind answered back.

You can't bribe feelings into a child who won't accept them. You have to leave him to get on with his life with those good people, with that strong family unit. How can you stand up to them? Who are you but a wreck thrown on the shore, battered by life's rocks with no one to support you in this decision? You are nothing, a failure at everything you ever did. You chose the wrong husband, if indeed he was one. You made the wrong decision to join a dangerous mission that failed before it even began, and you stayed away too long from your child. You deserve everything . . .

Callie slumped over the bar. 'Another. Make it a double,' she called, but the barman ignored her.

'I think you've had enough, don't you?' said a waitress. 'Better get you a taxi home.'

'There'll never be enough of these to blot out what I've just done,' she snapped. 'A double!'

'Come on, love. "Home, James",' the barman said. 'She's a resident. See her up the stairs, will you?'

Callie was led into her bedroom and flopped on the bed. 'Where's home? Where do I go from here?' she cried into the silence of the night.

Mima was rehanging the Nursery curtains when the letter arrived. They'd had the room redecorated in blue striped wallpaper and bought curtains with ships on them for the windows. All the baby toys were put away and there was a school desk and a bookshelf full of old books. Everything was ready for Desmond's return. Phoebe brought the letter up the stairs to share the news with Mima, but the stamp puzzled her. They must have stopped off somewhere exotic. She sat down to glance through it, but couldn't see much without her spectacles.

'Read it to me, please,' she asked her housekeeper.

As you can see by the pyramid pictures, I am no longer in Australia. I thought I'd better warn you that Desmond will not be returning to Dalradnor now or at any time in the future.

I found them both holed up in Adelaide. The set-up with the Boyds is quite comfortable. Jessie's wartime marriage was a disaster, like so many, I fear, so for the safety of my son she removed them both to the Boyds', whose son she met on the outward journey. They have taken my son under their extensive wing. Desmond is now called Louie and has taken a shine to Jessie's friend. He follows him around like a pet lamb. I have had a few snaps developed. They will be sent on to you in due course.

'Ought I to read on, Miss Faye? It's awful private . . .'

'Read on . . .' she ordered.

It was decided (not by me, of course) to allow my son to choose his future. As everyone warned me, having stayed away from him so long, he prefers to remain where he is with Jessie. He didn't recognize me at first and kept me at arm's length. After so many changes in his young life, who can blame him?

Needless to say, I couldn't stay on there. I have assurances that we will be informed of all his future progress and kept in touch with him. We are free to visit and all correspondence will come to Dalradnor Lodge.

So there you have it. Everything I planned turned to dust in my fingers. I no longer care what the future holds for me. I could stay and make a fuss or accept this fait accompli and disappear. I jumped ship at Port Said. What is there to come back to in Britain but bleak grey weather and rationing? That's why I'm staying with my old friend Monica Battersby in Cairo for the foreseeable future. We've been revisiting old haunts and happier times: a couple of not-so-merry widows. Who knows, one of these nights I may bump into my errant husband in some sleazy bar and have the satisfaction of giving him his rightful due. Perhaps not.

I don't intend to return to Dalradnor without my son, so don't you expect a visit for some time, if ever.

Caroline

'Oh dearie me.' Mima handed Phoebe back the letter.

She clutched it to her heart. 'My poor, poor child,' she cried out. 'What'll become of you now?' Phoebe felt the brittle words searing into her, all those unspoken accusations. She heard the sadness and despair behind them as she collapsed onto the bed, knowing she'd never see her daughter again in this life.

'Miss Faye, are you all right?'

Phoebe didn't move, she could hardly breathe as the icy chill of realization stabbed like a dagger into her chest. 'Caroline . . . I'm sorry.'

They were the last words she could mouth before the darkness overtook her.

Part Three

MELISSA

2002

I know where I'm going
And I know who's going with me
You're the one I love
But the dear knows who I'll marry . . .

Traditional British folk song

40

There was something magical about a Sunday morning in London, thought Melissa Boyd as she kicked the crinkly leaves along the quiet streets on her way to Bloomsbury. She could hear church bells in the damp air, the traffic was light and people were sitting relaxed outside the cafés, their heads in Sunday papers. 'Easy Like Sunday Morning' was the song playing in her head. As she sprang down the gracious streets she was getting to know so well, her heart lifted. That first wave of homesickness for Adelaide was passing.

How could it not when she was settled as a post-grad student into the busy routine of the Royal Academy of Music, a conservatoire steeped in musical history? There was no time to mope around with such an intense repertoire to learn, classes not only in voice performance but in stage movement, Italian pronunciation . . . She was learning to get around the city on buses and the tube, and attending the social events in college organized for international students. What a melting pot of talented artists she was working beside.

Melissa was flung into the deep end when a student didn't show for their first Master Class with a visiting professor, who asked her to sing instead. No chance to chicken out. This was what performance was all about, forgetting the nerves that would cripple her breathing and phrasing in front of the audience, and learning from one of the greatest sopranos in the world as she gently offered criticism and encouragement. There was so much to learn.

The flat she was renting was close to Marylebone High Street, not far from the college and Regent's Park. Walking in the autumn mornings reminded her of all the parks around her home city. If only her parents could know how thrilled she was to be here in a city that never slept. There was only Patty, her best friend in Australia, to email now and she promised to come and visit her.

Her father, Lew's, strange letter was not forgotten, nor his request to find out more about his early years, but life was so busy this first term that it had gone on the back burner. Now, clutching the postcard, she was on her first foray into the world of postcard collecting at a hotel in Bloomsbury where, she'd been told, regular fairs were held for enthusiasts. This would be her starting point, if she ever reached there. Everything in London was further than it looked on her street guide but on such a lovely morning she didn't care.

She wasn't expecting such a crush of stalls and browsers in the exhibition room, many selling only one thing: postcards. After her brisk walk, she was sweltering in the crush as she began to look around for some likely sources of information.

There was every sort of postcard known to man: saucy seaside ones, pictures of old streets and ships in harbours, foreign cities, wartime pictures, hand-tinted shots, embroidered souvenirs and mourning cards, Royalty and ships; all the weird and the wonderful, neatly stacked in boxes, priced and labelled. But where to start? There must be a theatrical specialist somewhere but in the hubbub it was difficult to seek out the right stalls. Soon she was standing in a daze.

'Can I help?' asked one stallholder. She was sitting knitting and eyeing the punters between rows.

'I just want some information about this,' Melissa replied, showing her the picture.

'Ah, you need Mark over there. He does films and early theatricals.' She pointed to a man in shirtsleeves, who was sorting out his stock. 'Come with me.' Melissa was swept along to be introduced.

'Mark, this young lady needs rescuing,' the friendly woman laughed. 'I don't think she's seen anything like this before, not where she's from . . . New Zealand?'

'Australia,' Melissa corrected, smiling. Brits never knew the difference. 'Thanks, but I'm not looking to buy. I'm just a poor student. I wanted someone to take a look at this postcard to point me in the right direction.' She passed it over to the tall young man, who examined the front and back.

'Early twentieth century, she's one of the Gaiety Girls. From the look of her signature . . . Phoebe Faye? Not top of the premier league but definitely a beauty in her day.' He looked at Melissa and then at the photo again. 'Any relation?'

'Flattery will get you everywhere but I'm not here to buy. Haven't got a clue who she is, but my father found it years ago and had a feeling it might be important. I'd like to find out more about her.'

'It won't be her real name, of course. Stage names were carefully chosen. I've got a box of girls somewhere but I don't think I've got anything else of her. They produced hundreds of them for their fans. Not very valuable, I'm afraid.'

'That's not the point,' Melissa said. 'I just promised I'd find out why it was sent, and this one of a ship. The name on the back isn't even his name or at least, it's not the one he used. Desmond's a bit old-fashioned now, isn't it? It's all a bit of a mystery, but thanks for your time.' She turned to move away.'

'Wait,' he called. 'I know someone who knows more about that time. I'm general early theatre stuff, films of the thirties and forties. Would you like a coffee . . .? There's a guy you'll never find if I don't introduce you. I'm Mark Penrose, by the way.'

'Melissa Boyd.' They shook hands warmly. He had kind eyes and a strong face.

'Just have a look in that box under the counter, while I ask Ben to mind my stall. There might be something else. I forget what I have.'

'Is this your job?' Melissa was curious.

'Good Lord, no! It's my hobby, or rather my obsession, ever since I was given Great-gran's postcard scrapbook. I'm a lawyer, for my sins, and you?'

'Post-grad student over here on a scholarship from Adelaide, studying at the RAM.'

'Wow, a musician. You must be good. What instrument?'

'Voice . . . singing.' She found herself blushing at his interest.

'Opera?'

Melissa nodded. 'You like Opera?'

'What's there not to like . . . *Tosca* is my favourite. So why aren't you rehearsing your arias instead of trailing round this madhouse?'

'I'm on a mission for my late father. I promised him to find out who he is . . . was. This postcard is part of a box of clues. I have a gut feeling it's important. I have to find her.'

'Ben, mind my stall . . . I need to take my friend to Humph . . . fifteen mins?' Mark shouted to the man next to him. 'Oh, and watch the guy in the blue anorak . . . blink and he pockets stuff.'

Mark edged her through the crowds to the furthest corner of the room where a stall was covered in theatre programmes, posters, postcards and autographs. A couple sat behind it. 'Humph, this is Melissa. Do you know anything about Phoebe Faye, a Gaiety Girl?'

'I might do for a pint,' he laughed. His wife pushed him up.

'Get rid of him for me while I sort out this clutter. He can't part with anything . . . Go and talk shop for fifteen minutes and let me get on with trying to sell something for a change.'

The three of them found a corner in the cafeteria. Melissa listened as Humph reeled off everything he knew about this musical star.

'She was one of the It girls of her day, one of the Postcard girls, but she did her bit in the Great War with the concert parties that entertained the troops in France. Not much after that, a film or two. She did one with Ivor Novello, I think, or was that Lily Elsie? Now, *she* was a huge star. A signed photo of her is worth a bob or two.' He sipped his coffee and smiled at her. 'I did have one of Phoebe in army uniform but I sold that to a suffragette collector. No one's asked for her in years and now two in the last month.'

The names meant nothing to Melissa. He was talking of nearly a hundred years ago.

'Did she marry?'

'That I can't tell you. You'll need to find her obituary somewhere in the archives. She was a minor player but she must've been good. George Edwardes, the impresario, chose his Gaiety Girls well. Many were from humble stock but they had potential: good looks and good voices. Quite a few of them married into the aristocracy. Does that help you?'

'Thanks, it's a start.' Melissa shook Humph's hand as he stood to return to his stall. 'Where would I find obituaries?' she asked Mark. As she sipped her coffee she felt herself being drawn further into the life of Phoebe Faye.

'You could start with the British Library,' Mark suggested. 'They hold all the newspapers, but we need to know when she died. That will mean a trip to the Family Records Centre for the registry of births and death. She'll be in there somewhere - unless she's still alive,' he added.

Melissa felt daunted and yet excited. Phoebe was becoming real, not just a pretty face in a photograph. 'I don't think I've time to go searching round London. We've got rehearsals soon, but thanks just the same.'

'If you need any help . . .' Mark offered. 'You've got me curious now why a girl comes all the way from down under clutching a postcard of a long-lost relative.'

'We don't know that,' Melissa said, looking at Phoebe more closely.

'I have my suspicions already.' Mark laughed, glancing up at her. 'She was a singer; you're a singer. She was a looker and so are you.'

'Thank you . . .' Melissa flashed him a look and caught interest in his eyes.

'Look, I'm serious. Here's my card and email address. I really am interested so, if you don't follow her up, I will. I'm going to search my collection in case I've missed anything.'

She followed him back to his stall, not sure where to go next in this strange search, but one thing was certain: she'd like to know a bit more about Mark Penrose, opera buff, lawyer and postcard addict.

Melissa was so wrapped up in rehearsals the following week, she was taken aback when a postcard arrived on her mat: 'Let's meet at Patisserie Valerie next Saturday about eleven. I've got news. Mark Penrose.'

She didn't need any persuading to visit the French pastry shop and café on the High Street, having already found a fondness for their *tarte aux framboises*. It was touching that Mark was keeping his promise to search out more postcards, but she hoped he wasn't expecting something more than a cup of coffee.

I'm not in the market for emotional entanglements. Time enough for all that when I've made my mark in the music world. I'm here to further my artistic career and not be distracted, she thought. But it would be nice to see him again.

None of her usual jeans and sweaters suited her that Saturday morning. Her ensembles piled up on the floor as she decided which jeans and top struck the right note: not too scruffy and not looking as if she was making a special effort. The look she was after was what her friends called smart casual, and her aboriginal art earrings added a touch of exotic interest.

So busy preening was she, she was almost late. Saturday on the High Street was always buzzing with weekend shoppers and browsers. She waved to some college friends as she sped along. It was one of those balmy days in late autumn with a hint of bonfire smoke in the air. Her first term at the Academy was rattling along and it was good to feel part of the place.

Mark was sitting at one of the outside tables on the pavement. He stood up, looking stylish in his tweed jacket and jeans. He was taller and better looking than she recalled. 'Hi.' He smiled, ushering her inside. He was carrying a portfolio case, which looked hopeful. They found a corner tucked in the back of the café and ordered. He leaned over and she caught a whiff of expensive aftershave. So he had made an effort too.

'This is good of you. I wasn't expecting such a prompt response seeing as I've not had time to do anything,' she offered.

'No problem, there's lots to get to . . . I've got a rugby match later.'

'Is there no end to your talents? Postcards and rugger – what a combo.' Mel laughed.

'Don't mock. It's only a scratch side but keeps us fit. The secret of life is balance, my grandma used to say and she was right.'

'Was this the gran who got you into postcards? I only knew one of mine and she died when I was ten, and my mom later . . . Families are a mystery to me.' It was still painful to recall her mother's sudden death.

'I'm sorry. Perhaps this will cheer you up. Here . . . what do you make of this obituary?' He handed her a photocopy of something out of the *Daily Telegraph*.

'How did you find this?'

'Oh, we lawyers have ways.' He smiled, and his eyes were grey-green flecked with amber behind his glasses. 'This tells us all we need to know about Phoebe. Her real name was Phoebe Annie Boardman, born in Leeds, and she died in 1948 from a long illness. She didn't marry but was engaged to someone in the Great War. There's a bit about her serving in Lena Ashwell's concert parties . . . her film career . . . but it's the bit at the end that might interest you. She was survived by a niece, Caroline.'

Melissa was speed reading the piece as he spoke. It was headed by the portrait of an elegant woman of about thirty with crimped hair gathered into a chignon at the back.

'Sometimes "niece" was shorthand for a daughter in those days,' Mark continued. 'It covered the embarrassment of having a child out of wedlock. It says Phoebe died in a village near Glasgow. That might yield up some information. What do you think?'

Melissa suddenly recalled her mom saying Granny Boyd was Scottish . . . 'Oh. yes, this is brilliant. Thank you. Are you saying that this Caroline might be the one who sent the post-card? That's a bit of a leap, isn't it?'

'Her birth certificate could be useful. You'd be amazed what can be gleaned from them: place of birth, full name, parents, unless it's a short certificate.' He paused, shaking his head. 'If so, what's being hidden?'

'But we don't know her date of birth . . .'

'You just take a rough point around the 1914-to-'18 war period and look for a Caroline Boardman. If she's legit, then she'll be the child of one of Miss Faye's two brothers. There were no sisters. It's all guesswork, I know, but then with her full name, look for her marriage certificate and perhaps her death certificate. If there isn't one, chances are she's still alive . . . The daughter of Phoebe Faye. She's the key to all this . . . our only lead.'

They sipped their coffee in silence as Mel took in this barrage of facts. It was nice that he said 'our lead', as if he was a part of this.

She wondered if she was really linked to these two women. Could there be another family over here she never knew existed? Finding Phoebe was just an exercise she'd promised to do for Lew but Mark was taking it all seriously. Was he being helpful because he was interested in her? How could she repay him without encouraging too much?

'Look, I've got to thank you for this. Could I give you tickets for our Christmas concert? Perhaps there's someone you can bring along.' She smiled hoping he'd get the hint.

'I'd be delighted. I 'm sure I can drum up support for you but you must keep going on this. These old dears have a habit of popping off and who will answer your questions then? Next job is the Family Records Centre. How about I go with you? Two pairs of hands will get through more searches than one.'

'I'm not sure. I can't take up any more of your time and I'm up to my ears in rehearsals right now. I didn't come to London to play Sherlock Holmes.' She hesitated, sensing how rude that sounded. 'I'm sorry. I really appreciate your help, but this search will have to fit in . . . I get your point about Caroline being very old, but now we have this and the other photos in the box—'

'Now you tell me.'

'Just a snapshot of two schoolgirls with writing on the back, but I've not looked at it closely.'

'Is it in the same handwriting as the card?'

'I'd have to check . . .'

'Do you live nearby? Let's have a look at them both.' He jumped up, looking at his watch. 'There's just time.'

Melissa thought of the state of her flat, all the clothes strewn about. Still, if he had any ideas of seduction, one look at the state of her room would dampen his ardour. 'It's just off Wells Street.'

Mark went to the counter to pay and browse the mouthwatering array of goodies. 'Sarah will love these,' he said as the waitress filled a box with what he'd picked out.

So he had a girlfriend. She was safe, so why did that make her suddenly feel flat? Why had she assumed he was single? Such a good-looking guy wouldn't still be single unless he was gay, and she'd sensed from the start he wasn't. There was a Sarah in his life, another lawyer perhaps.

She wanted to ask but somehow couldn't bring herself to enquire as they walked to her flat. 'Sorry about the mess,' she warned as she put the key in the door. 'I slept in,' she lied. 'Now where the hell did I put Dad's shoe box? It might be still in my case.' She was waffling on, knowing it was shoved under her bed, gathering dust. Cleaning was something she'd not yet built into her routines. 'Here it is.'

They cleared a space on her dining table. She pushed the letter aside – that was not for sharing – and rummaged through the snapshots for the school one. 'There they are . . .'

Mark held up the obituary photo and placed it next to the tall girl with long blonde plaits. 'Those two are definitely related. There's a look across the eyebrow and the shape of the nose. The little one is all hair.' On the back it read, WITH PRIMMY AND ME.

They were both wearing regulation gymslips of the 1930s, and in the background was a castle-like building or a school, perhaps.

'It could be anywhere. I guess Primmy's short for Primula or Primrose. What a name to go through life with . . .' Melissa smiled. 'They look a couple of tearaways.'

'Can you see what it says on their tunic badges?' Mark peered closer with his glasses. 'If we blew that up we might find out which school.'

Melissa laughed. 'Trust a legal eagle to spot that. Their hairstyles could be twenties or thirties. A girls' school could be anywhere.'

'Not with the badge. Can I take this?'

'I can't let you keep doing this. I should be doing it myself,' Melissa replied, reluctant to involve him further but he seemed to have more time than she did.

'Don't worry, you'll have to do all the leg work later in your vacation. Just let me give you a start.' He fingered in the box and picked out the medal. 'This looks like a *Croix de Guerre*. This just gets curiouser and curiouser. What did you father tell you about all this?'

Melissa hesitated for a second. Oh, hell, Mark might as well read the letter; no point in hiding any of it now. 'Read this,' she said, shoving it into his hand, and sat in silence as he read it slowly, pausing to look up at her with concern on his face.

'I'm sorry. This is private,' he said, handing it back to her. 'Thanks for trusting me with this. You must see it through. Your dad's giving you something here, something very important. He loved you.'

'He had a funny way of showing it,' she snapped, feeling the emotion of it all welling up again. 'Why did he have to leave it until he was dying to tell me? It's not fair.'

Mark reached out to hug her. 'I know it's not fair, but look what you've achieved in just a few weeks. You've named the picture and found out about her family. This is all linked in some way to your father, and if you want to find out how and why . . . birth certificates and school badges, the whole shooting match, will bring you closer to your goal.' Mark glanced at his watch. 'Must dash, got a ball to chase.' He made for the door. 'I'll be in touch. Don't be sad, you'll get your answers.' With that he was gone.

'Don't forget Sarah's cakes,' Melissa yelled, following down the stairs with the box.

'Thanks. Enjoy your weekend.' He looked up at her with a grin.

Melissa shut the door, feeling empty now that'd he left and strangely envious of Sarah and her box of cakes.

Three weeks went by before she heard from him again, another of his curious postcards with a cryptic message: 'Look up St Margaret's School for Girls, nr Arbroath, Scotland on the web. Could be useful to contact. Mark.'

She was getting to know her nearest internet café well, emailing to friends back home about her London life, so it was no big deal to pop in and search out the name. Mark was right. Before her eyes was the very castle school in her photo, and an image of the school crest with its motto, 'Onwards and Upwards', plus a potted history. But how could she visit the wilds of Scotland when opera rehearsals were reaching their peak?

There was an address in Cheltenham for the secretary of St Margaret's Alumni Association. An old-girl's network would never fail to find who was where, Melissa hoped. It was worth a try, and at least she could tell Mark she was doing her bit.

Between costume fittings she composed a simple letter asking for details of the whereabouts of two former pupils: Caroline and Primrose, with their rough dates, addressed it to the secretary and sent it off, not expecting to hear before the New Year.

A reply came winging back by return:

Dear Miss Boyd.

Thank you for your recent enquiry. I am coming to town next week. Please could we meet for lunch next Thursday? Your letter is very intriguing and I do have information that might be helpful to you. Shall we say one o'clock in the restaurant at John Lewis, Oxford Street?

Yours sincerely

Mrs Elizabeth Steward

PS. I will be the one with the tartan scarf.

Melissa picked out one of her witty Jacky Fleming postcards to tell Mark of this stroke of luck. Bit by bit perhaps she was edging closer to the truth about Miss Faye and her niece, so what had Mrs Steward got to say that was so urgent she'd needed to reply by return?

41

Melissa pushed her way through the Christmas shoppers and up the escalator where a woman draped in a tartan shawl was peering across at the crowd. She was about fifty, with a shock of curly aubergine-coloured hair.

'Mrs Steward?' Melissa asked, walking up to her slowly.

'Miss Boyd . . . I can't believe this, my goodness . . . I've saved us a table. Melissa — what a beautiful name, and to think you came all this way to find out about Callie . . .'

'Not exactly. I'm here to study.' Melissa didn't want any misunderstanding, trying to explain as they wove their way through the crowded dining area, skirting round shopping bags.

'It's such a coincidence. I gave up being secretary a few months ago but somehow your enquiry was sent to me, not the new secretary. I just had to meet you.' She sat down with relief, plonking her bags on the floor. 'I always come to town for a little Christmas shopping and to see the decorations . . . sad, isn't it? I'm Libby . . .'

'You knew them both then?' Melissa fished in her bag for her postcard and photo. 'A friend of mine managed to find the badge from this picture,' she explained, holding out the photo for her to see. 'I don't know how this came to be in my father's effects after he died, along with this postcard, but I know who Miss Faye is now and this is her niece?'

Libby delved for her glasses and looked at the snapshot with a smile. 'That's my mother.' She sighed. 'Primrose McAllister. The two of them met on their first day at St Maggie's, a couple of horrors, always into scrapes. Callie was her best friend.'

'Was? Are they both . . .?'

'Mummy died five years ago, an amazing woman – well, those wartime women were.' She paused. 'As for Caroline, I don't know. Mummy was a wireless operator at Bletchley Park, very hush-hush, and she married Ralph, my father, after the war. Callie was a bit of a mystery.'

'You think she could be still alive then?' Melissa couldn't believe what she was hearing.

'It's possible, but you'll never find her . . . a strange woman.'

'You met her?' She held her breath.

'Only once, when I was about seven, after she came back from Suez in 1956. I do recall her as tall and very blonde, her skin dark from the sun. She brought my brother a toy camel and an Egyptian doll for me but it was Mummy she came to see. I've brought Mummy's album but there's not much to show you after then.'

They ordered lunch and chatted on about the school as they looked at the album. Libby talked about St Margaret's and her mother's friendship. 'I know she was married at sometime and lived in Cairo, but Mummy never said much. I was too little to understand then. A child sees from a child's height but even I recognized she was very different from Mummy's other friends.'

'How?'

'My dear, she had a scent on her, cigarette smoke and a strange perfume on her breath. I was a little afraid of her as she was so tall and elegant. Mummy said she had been in the war too but I don't think I was very happy when she came to stay.'

'To stay?'

'Oh, yes, to stay . . .'

November 1956

Callie hung over the rails watching the ropes loosening their hold in the Alexandria dock. It was a relief to be making this hurried exit from Egypt after the Suez Crisis erupted and the streets were full of troops. She no longer felt safe in the city, feeling against the British was rising, and Monica Battersby made sure they got a berth back to England at the first opportunity.

Their friendship was strained after the business with Cecil Mason, who was Monica's new escort after Ken died. He soon became Callie's drinking partner. He knew all the best dives by the river, good jazz clubs and night haunts. Monica made a fuss over the noisy crowd they brought back to the bungalow until all hours. She was getting old and cranky, taking Ken's death badly. Cecil was her consolation until Callie caught his eye.

Monica didn't understand why she liked his bright company, noisy bars, lots of chatter – anything to keep her from thinking how Desmond was living without her in Adelaide. The letters she'd written got brief curt replies from Jessie and nothing from her son, not even a proper thank you for Christmas gifts. Then everything stopped and her letters were returned unopened. They'd moved house and left her behind.

Why didn't I insist on my rights? she punished herself over again but she feared it was all too late and too complicated. Money was getting a problem. It seemed to evaporate between the bank and the bars. Monica seemed jealous of her dizzy social life and they hardly met socially. They were not sharing a cabin on the ship home.

Callie peered up at the blue and the heat haze, thinking she'd have to face grey clouds, chilly winters and the emptiness at Dalradnor now Phee was dead. The news arrived too late for her to return even by plane. She had a pile of Phee's private letters that Mima forwarded, not knowing what else to do with them. They were shoved in her hatbox along with a letter from the estate informing her of the will and its contents, but when she looked again it had got mislaid somewhere in the rush to leave.

She wanted nothing from Phoebe, certainly no written excuses for her appalling behaviour. That part of her life was over. She needed no reminders.

As she watched the ship edging slowly out of the port she felt no remorse, no guilt or, indeed, anything much these days. Living in a cocoon of pleasant oblivion in Cairo it was easy to pretend none of the past had happened. Now the idyll was over and she must come back to the harsh reality that she was fair, forty and over the hill.

Only gin hit the spot, took away the fear, the pain and the shame. As long as she had her supplies she could survive, gliding over the surface in an elegant haze. Desmond could be forgotten. He wouldn't recognize her now and that was for the best. What was done was done. And yet . . .

He was there in her dreams, running along the lochside, but then the barracks at the camp loomed up and the great roller coming ever closer to flatten her. She heard the dogs tearing human flesh and saw the frozen corpses hanging from the gallows like blocks of ice. Only death would release her from the pain of those images and that was something she swore on Celine's dear spirit she would never bring about herself. Life was a precious gift for some and an agony for others. She would not take the easy way out, but slowly, slowly, she could poison herself with liquor. She would not make old bones.

Trust Primrose to write and keep an eye on her welfare from a distance, offering her a bed until she found her feet back in London. There was still some private income and a small war pension to keep her fuelled up. Otherwise her prospects were grim. Who would employ a broken war veteran with no qualifications but a secret capacity to hide, dissemble and kill? She was a failure in every department. She couldn't keep a man satisfied in bed. They took her body but never touched her mind. She had no shame because she felt nothing when they coupled, but at least having somebody in her bed was better than the emptiness of waking up solo. She had never once been anywhere in Cairo that reminded her of Ferrand's love.

I can't stand much more of life. If only I could crawl into a quiet corner and find some peace. My heart is an empty sack, a dark empty space.

Midway through the voyage she pulled Phoebe's letters out of the hat box to chuck them overboard in one last act of defiance. If she was to return back to England she wanted no reminders of the past. She stood, arm outstretched, on the deck in the moonlight, ready to scatter them to the four winds, to leave a trail of paper floating in the foamy wake, but then she noticed the handwriting was not her mother's and the envelope had a military stamp. She was curious, and found a lamp and a deck chair to sit down and examine them further.

This was no everyday correspondence but letters from her own father, Arthur Seton-Ross.

Much as she hated her mother's actions, she could not blame him for desertion. She owed it to him to at least read his thoughts. It was all she would ever have of him now.

My darling girl,
    It was a miracle to see you walking towards me in the officers' mess in Boulogne in your uniform, looking just as beautiful as the first time I saw you on stage and fell in love with you there and then. How I wished I could have stayed longer, but

knowing I would see you again in London made all the weariness of a war seem worthwhile.

These past few days lying in your arms, holding you so close
have been wonderful. I cannot believe the Gods have looked
down on me so favourably.

Callie couldn't read any more. She felt she was eavesdrop-
ping on their lovemaking, and his voice was just like Ferrand in
his letters. She reached into her pocket for the next. It was in
her mother's hand.

Thank you for the most wonderful three days and nights. It was
hard to leave you knowing you will be heading to a frozen
dugout while I am warm and comfortable . . . Your precious
ring is safe under my pillow. If I wear it everyone will know and
I will be banned from serving in France. Miss Ashwell and the
YMCA insist only girls with no relatives serving can cross the
Channel but I wanted you to have my photograph taken in our
special uniform. I feel so proud to be wearing it

Please give me a list of things you need: books, ink, warm
clothes. I have only two requests, one for your photograph and
the other that you take no risks. Now I have found you, I
couldn't bear to lose you from my life . . .

Callie stared at the letter and swallowed hard. She would have
written such words to Ferrand herself. Here were two young
people in love in a war, just as they had been. It was so sad. She
couldn't throw their love away. Now she could not tear herself
away from the letters, searching for the dates to read them in order.

15 May 1916

Dearest Heart of my own heart,

I'm sorry this is a brief note to your postcard. I'm afraid
there's not a dog in hell's chance of me getting leave. There's

a big push coming soon (shouldn't say this as I'm censoring my own mail). You sounded worried in your last letter as if something is on your mind. I'm sorry you couldn't cross the Channel as you wished but were sent round the country in a new concert party.

I am glad my sister, Verity, has decided to train as a nurse and knows your friend Kitty. I have been softening up Father to the idea we will get married as soon as I come home. Not heard a dicky bird yet. Would you still marry me if I'm cut off without a penny to my name?

I'm writing by a candle stub I the dugout while my subaltern snores his head off, louder than Big Bertha . . .

Callie curled up on the deck chair, shivering, sensing what was coming next for the doomed lovers. Judging by the date, Phoebe would know she was pregnant by then, and desperate, judging by the crumpled letter that was stamped RETURNED . . .

I am so sorry to burden you with this but I must share what is in my fearful heart. You and I are about to bring new life into the world. The doctor says by late September, we two will become three, God willing.

Oh, do come back so we may share this momentous time together. If God grants me the blessing of a son, he will carry your precious name. He must be born into love, not shame.

Your loving wife and child-to-be

Callie froze, feeling the pain of learning that she'd been born the wrong sex. Was that why Phee had deserted her? At least she'd had the courage to write to her lover, which was more than she had done herself. Ferrand died not knowing he had a son to live for. How can I curse my own mother for something I didn't even do myself? Why did we never talk of these things? There was a small telegram tucked into the envelope, with the

words: 'DARLING GOT NEWS WILL WRITE. ALL WILL
BE WELL. ARTHUR.'

At least he knew about the baby but, why didn't he come?
Gripped by her parents' story, Callie opened the next letter.

. . . I have asked for compassionate leave. Will be returning on
the 19 September so we can marry on the 20th. I've written to
the family and we can make use of our Lodge in Scotland for a
short honeymoon. Dalradnor is my favourite place and I want
to share it with you. It will be a good place for you to stay away
from the smoke of the city. I can think of no better place to rear
our child.

Your news has lifted my spirits. In the midst of such carnage
to think our beautiful child will be born and Pray God will
never know the horror of trench warfare.

Good night, sweetheart.

Callie stared out, watching the blood-red sun rising up out of
the sea like an omen. She could feel tears of relief swelling in
her eyes that Arthur had known about her and she was wanted
by him. What a pity . . . for the first time, she could feel
Phoebe's excitement and then bitter sorrow, left alone to face
the consequences of their love. Dalradnor was her refuge and he
had been right. How she'd loved raising Desmond there.

There were two more letters but she couldn't bear to read
them knowing what was coming. It was almost daylight, she
was shivering and in need of a drink, but some inner strength
refused to budge her from that deck chair. There was a letter
from a stranger explaining Arthur's fate.

. . . We were straightening out a line after a push, mopping up
some stubborn resistance close to the village of Lesboeufs, but
the enemy stuck to their guns, despite all our efforts. Arthur
took a small platoon on forward watch when they were gunned

down, saving our lives by the warning fire at the cost of their own . . .

The men buried him in the field with as much ceremony and tenderness as they could muster, given the danger, and we placed a marker where he fell . . .

Callie remembered the ploughed field in France she'd visited all those years ago with Phee, the empty field with the obelisk. If only she'd known all this then, but at least she knew how brave Arthur had been, and how respected. She was glad he didn't know what a mess her generation had made of the world; that his sacrifice had been short-lived and that she had had to sacrifice her own lover to the dogs of war.

This, however, would have been no comfort to her aunt as she prepared to give birth alone.

Oh, Ferrand, I never knew where you were buried. I have no letters to pass on to your son, just the medal.

Phoebe had clung to these letters all her life and now they were hers and she'd nearly thrown them overboard. How can you throw love overboard? The last letter was in her father's handwriting. She could hardly bear to look, but knew she must. It was all she had left of him now.

. . . If by any misfortune, I do not arrive for our wedding, it will not be because of any change of heart but because fate has robbed us of a chance of happiness together.

I have made provision for just such an event in the only way I know. You will not be left destitute. That is my promise. I feel an urgency in all this for I have felt for some time a heaviness in my mind that things may not go to plan, that I will not live my full span as I would have wished alongside you and our child.

We've had so little time together, so little time to experience the ordinary things of married life in peacetime. War has robbed us of such joys.

Don't be bitter. Live as you have always done, independent and determined. Give my little darling all the opportunities to grow up into a worthy citizen with a kind and brave heart. And in due course find someone for yourself who will give the child a name so there is no stain on either of you. Society can be cruel to unwed women with a child so I trust you will protect our little one in life as I will do in death.

I have never loved anyone but you. Courage, my brave heart. Be happy in your life and tell our child of a father's love . . .

How I wish I could have known this man. Callie wept. How his words pierce me with shame. My mother did her best to protect me the only way she knew and I fought her for the rest of her life. There was a gulf between us, an ocean of misunderstanding, missed opportunities and now it's too late. What a fool I was. Why can't I get anything right? No wonder I am alone. How disappointed Arthur would be if he knew how I'd turned out.

Callie picked up the letters and fled to her cabin to drown her sorrows and sleep.

As the ship eased into Southampton Water, everyone came up on deck to savour the chill of the English morning. There were hoots and horns as if they were all heroes back from the wars, not exiles who'd suffered a humiliating defeat. The bombardment and assaults on Port Said were over before they got started – the Americans and Russians had seen to that – so why all the Dunkirk spirit? Callie's clothes were unsuitable, the silk and cotton suit no match for the wind and rain, marking her as an outsider, but somewhere on the dockside Primrose was waiting to gather her into the fold and she must show her gratitude.

She waved goodbye to Monica, knowing she'd never see her again. Callie had tried to make amends buying her dinner and trying to explain her crass behaviour over the past years. She'd let

Monica down, as she let everyone down, but she thanked her friend for finding her a berth and sticking with her moods. Monica was polite but distant. They made no arrangements to meet.

To Callie's relief, though, Prim was there waiting to greet her, plump as a capon, with her glorious mane faded into pepper-and-salt fuzz under a thick felt hat. They hugged and she felt her hands feeling her bones.

'You need fattening up. What a time you've had of it, all those troops and bombs. It's lovely to see you again. Callie. It's been far too long.'

I need a drink, thought Callie, hoping she didn't reek too much. 'Thanks for the offer of a bed but I must find a hotel.'

'Nonsense, you are coming to us . . .' Prim was clucking. 'You must meet your namesake, Elizabeth Caroline – but she only answers to Libby – and Peter. He's nearly four now. They're dying to meet you.'

The last thing Callie needed was children in the house to remind her of the child who was lost to her now.

'I'm not sure . . . I'm not very good company and children don't seem to take to me.'

Prim looked at her. 'Sorry. I know it must be hard going all that way, but Libby is dying to meet you and we've got so much to catch up on. I did keep in touch with your mother and we went to her funeral. All the old Gaiety chorus girls of yester-year turned up in their furs and glitz. I think Dalradnor had never seen the like. It was a shame you . . . Never mind, you can see where she'd buried for yourself.'

Oh, Prim, you know how to rub it in. I've hardly stepped foot in the country and you remind me of my failings already, Callie sighed, but said nothing as she climbed into Prim's saloon car for the drive to London. Suddenly she was feeling this was going to be a visit to be endured rather than enjoyed.

Prim and Ralph lived on the outskirts of the city, in a mock-Tudor detached house with a large garden in a tree-lined avenue not far from the station. Prim had a daily and a gardener, and spent her time volunteering in the Girl Guides, the WVS, the church. Callie tried to be impressed with their sparkling home and new gadgets but Prim's life was so far removed from Callie's experience. The children were pretty and polite, but Peter unnerved her, being around the age Desmond had been when she last had him to herself. He was inquisitive and lively. It was a good job she had a supply in her suitcases or she'd have gone mad and let the side down. It was terrible to realize she and Prim had outgrown their childhood friendship. Prim was everything she was not: reliable, satisfied with her lot, a bit smug. Ralph was kind and kept out of the way. Callie was bored and tried to make excuses to move on.

'But it's nearly Christmas. You must spend it with us. Give yourself time to acclimatize before you head up to Scotland,' Prim argued one breakfast time.

'Why should I go there?'

'Dalradnor Lodge is your home.'

'Not any more. I told them to rent it out. I couldn't stand the snow up there after Egypt.'

'But you were always so happy there. It seems a pity . . .' Prim realized she'd said too much.

'I don't recall being happy on my last visit, or have you forgotten?'

'That was a terrible mix-up, Phoebe was distraught. She never recovered from the shock. Have you heard from Desmond?'

It was the first time his name had been mentioned. Callie tensed. What could she say?

'Yes, he's fine,' she lied. 'Doing well at school and the Australian air is so bracing for children. They go barefoot . . . His letters are full of sport.' How did she make this up? But cover stories in the SOE were her forte, after all. She hoped what she said was really true for him.

'Are you busy today?' Prim blurted. 'Only, I have to do the flowers in church this afternoon. Would you take Peter to the park and collect Libby from school at four? Take him to play on the swings.'

Callie nodded. It was the least she could do and it would give her a chance to call in for a top-up bottle in the licensed grocer, buy flowers as a thank you, and some cigarettes. Then she must make an exit, find an excuse to leave their cosy coterie.

The December sun was weak but the sky was bright. She was wrapped in one of Prim's tweed jackets. Peter skipped along the path, racing for the slide and turntable. She tried to pretend she was just another mother out with her little boy but with his red hair and freckles he was a miniature of Primrose.

It was good to smell the crisp air after the dust and heat of the desert, but she was thirsty and there was still a whole hour before school came out. Then she spotted a smart hotel at the busy crossroads, with a tea room attached. They could go in out of the chill and have toasted tea cakes and she'd order a snifter to see her through until home time. To be sure of service she went into the residents' lounge.

'I don't suppose I could have a proper beverage?' she asked the waitress.

'It's out of hours but I can ask the manager,' came the reply.

'Be a sweetie. I'm just off the boat from Suez and it's a shock to my bones . . .'

'Oh, how awful. I'll see what I can do, madam.' The other residents smiled at Peter, expressed sympathy about her plight and wanted to know her story. She told them about Nasser and the Arab protest. Somehow the drinks just flowed after that.

Peter tugged at her sleeve, wanting the lavatory. The waitress took him and it was then that Callie looked at her watch. Heavens, it was half-past five and dark outside. She'd forgotten about Libby! Callie jumped up but the room was spinning. She must pay the bill and find a taxi. She was in no state to walk home.

Peter held her hand to guide her down the steps as if she was blind.

A taxi was summoned but she was so confused she couldn't recall the address.

'I live in the house with the green door in Portland Avenue,' Peter told the driver.

When they arrived there was a police car waiting in the drive and Prim flew out, gathering up Peter in her arms. 'Where the hell have you been with my child?'

'I'm sorry.'

'Sorry isn't the half of it. You left Libby at the school gate in tears, and now this. Where did you take him?' She smelled Callie's breath with a look of disgust. 'You're drunk.'

'I'm sorry.'

'You take my little boy into a pub and drink yourself silly, forget the time. How could you do this to me?'

'I'm so sorry. I was talking . . . It wasn't a pub . . . It won't ever happen again.'

'You bet it won't. I can't have you in this house, putting my children at risk. How could you stoop so low? What's got into you? Don't think we haven't noticed you're never sober . . . always sneaking upstairs to top up. Pull yourself together, Callie. No wonder the Boyds wanted Desmond to themselves, if this is what you're capable of.' Prim couldn't have hit her any harder than with that accusation.'

'I said I'm sorry.' She saw Libby staring at her wide-eyed with shock.

'Do you want to press charges, madam?' The policeman had seen it all. 'Being drunk in charge of a minor is an offence.'

'No. No harm's been done this time and there won't be another. Just get her out of my house.' Prim flared up again. 'If you don't watch it, you'll have no friends left. We all have to live with what the war did to our families. I lost my brother. Stop feeling sorry for yourself and do something useful or you'll end up in the gutter at this rate. I'm sorry but you have to leave. I can't let my children be exposed to bad habits.'

Callie packed her suitcases in silence, suddenly sober, wanting to get as far away as she could from this stifling suburb and the look on Prim's face.

The policeman dropped her off at the station and, with a look of concern, asked, 'Have you somewhere to go now, miss?'

'I'll be fine, Officer,' she replied. 'I'll find a hotel for the night.'

'Watch yourself then,' he said with a wave and drove off, leaving Callie to stand in the cold and the dark.

42

Libby closed the album with a sigh. 'Mummy never talked about her again. That was the parting of their ways, I'm afraid. It was all to do with the war and something that happened in Dalradnor, the house in Scotland where she lived with Phoebe. Mummy said it was a happy house in a beautiful setting until war came.' She paused, rubbing her fingers over the leather with a sigh. 'You have to understand how that generation clammed up about their private affairs and kept their feeling bottled up. I must have witnessed that scene, but all I recall is the reek of booze on her clothes and the policeman in uniform. When I asked later, all Mummy would say was, "The heart has its reasons." I didn't understand then and I don't now. I did hope Callie would turn up at Mummy's funeral. It was all in the papers. I tried to spot her from memory but she wasn't there. So I can't help you after that.'

'I'm not sure I want to know any more about this Caroline woman. She sounds a nasty piece of work.'

'Oh, no, you mustn't say that. Mummy did say she suffered in the war in one of those concentration camps so you have to make allowances, and if she is Phoebe's daughter, not just her niece, you must keep searching. She might still be alive.'

'Not if she's an old soak. She'll be long gone by now.' Melissa was feeling uncomfortable around that subject.

'But you don't know that. Remember the saying: never judge a man until you've walked a mile in his shoes . . .'

Melissa slammed her coffee down. 'But I do know what it's like to live with an alcoholic. I know what it did to my parents.'

'It was your father's burden too?'

Melissa nodded. 'They told me the weakness can run in families. I try to be very careful what I drink and anyway it's not good for the voice. I couldn't face all that again.' She'd heard enough from Libby Steward and none of it very encouraging. 'Thank you for meeting up and putting me in the picture, though.'

'I'm not sure I've helped very much, but do keep in touch. We'd love to hear you sing. We often go to recitals in the Wigmore Hall when we're in town. I've had the privilege of hearing some amazing young artists make their debuts there. Perhaps one day soon it will be you.'

Melissa stood up from the table to catch the waiter's eye.

'Don't you dare pay a penny,' Libby insisted. 'This is my treat.' They shook hands, promising to email each other, and Melissa sped back down out of the busy shop in need of fresh air. Confined spaces and too much talk made her throat tight. She would stroll back and enjoy the Christmas lights in the stores and the wonderful displays in Selfridges' windows. Then she turned up through the backstreets, trying to process all the information she'd been given.

Caroline Lloyd-Jones was an alcoholic and so was Lew. Was this purely a coincidence or was there more? At least Melissa now had a married name for her and the address of the house in Scotland. If this woman had a baby her signature would be on the birth certificate and she could match up all three. Was there an old lady out there somewhere who might be a relative, and if so shouldn't she be searching for her?

After what she'd just heard from Libby, she was no longer sure this mission was worth the effort. It was all so confusing. She reached the bottom of the High Street, pausing at the kerb to cross over the road. It was then she felt the strangest sensation, a tingle of recognition, as if she heard her father's voice crystal clear, whispering in her ear: 'Keep going, Mel, keep going.'

43

1965

Callie strolled down a pretty Cotswold lane, enjoying the smell of the brown ploughed earth and noticing the first flush of spring green on the hedgerows. Over the past eight years, she had drifted from city hotel bar to the quietness of country pubs, from permanent to temporary and casual work in remote areas where the clientele were happy to clutch a pie and a pint. She could top up her need when she pulled pints and accepted tips. It was not the life she'd imagined, but it was a living.

Her walk and her reverie were disrupted when the sound of yelling erupting from over the hedge. She could hear cursing and shouting so she ran to the gate and let herself into the field to see what was going on. The farmer, whom she recognized as one of the regulars at the Wagon and Horses, his face red with rage, was beating a sheepdog with a stick. The dog cowered, yelping in pain, its tail between its hind quarters. It was old and very skinny for a working dog.

Callie was immediately incensed. 'What do you think you're doing, Ted Fletcher?' she shouted in her most imperious tone.

'Mind your bloody business. Bugger off back to your bar.'

'Don't you dare treat your dog like that!'

'It's my beast, disobedient bitch!'

'She looks half-starved to me,' Callie continued, drawing nearer. The farmer held his stick in the air to warn her off.

'Don't you come all lah-di-bloody-dah lady of the manor with me, Callie. You're only the bint from the Wagon and Horses. You'll leave well alone if you know what's good for you.'

Callie saw the menace in his eyes. He was one of those barstool gropers, but she'd never given him any encouragement. 'The poor thing looks injured. Let me look at her.'

Callie wasn't afraid of bullyboys like this one; she'd seen too many in a different league wielding sticks in the camp. Suddenly it was as if she was there, back in the exercise yard, defiant yet trying not to move in case she was beaten. It was the scene that for years kept flashing into her eyes as if she were watching it on a film screen. I haven't fought for my freedom to find bullies on my doorstep, she told herself as she tried to examine the cringing creature. Farmer Fletcher stood blocking her way. He was short but stocky, with hair coming out of his ears and nose like pig's bristles.

'Let me pass,' Callie ordered.

'You and whose army?' he mocked. 'This is my land and you are trespassing.' He lifted the stick more as a pose than a threat, but instinct kicked in from those far-off training days in the SOE, and Callie dodged, caught him unaware, grabbed the stick with a strength fuelled by fury, and brought it down on his shoulders with a crash.

'Now *you* see how it feels,' she said, beating him without mercy until he folded up in pain. She felt the power of her anger. He stood for all the bullies, all those guards who crushed their victims under their feet. Down and down went the stick until the man lay curled on the floor. Pausing to catch her breath she realized where she was and what was happening, but she felt nothing but contempt for the whimpering man.

Callie grabbed the dog from under the hedge and left Ted lying there. He was still breathing, panting in pain. He'd live, but never to hurt that trembling dog ever again, if she had anything to do with it.

The dog was light in her arms as she carried her back to the caravan at the back of the pub, which was her summer billet. 'Come on, old girl, let's see the damage.' She looked into eyes of the frightened animal, seeing pain, distrust, fear. 'I know how that feels,' she confided. She found herself crying. How long had this poor thing been subjected to Fletcher's bullying? 'No more of that for you. You are my friend now,' she said, stroking her softly.

The bitch was no more than skin and bone, and covered with fleas and sores. For all this obvious neglect, Callie knew there'd be a battle to keep her. Farmers had rights to working dogs, but this was something else.

'Dolly, that's what I'll call you,' she announced. She put the kettle on to boil. First tend the sores and then give the old girl a clean-up. There'd be a lot of grooming before Dolly was fit to begin her new life.

Dolly showed her appreciation by shitting all over the caravan floor. 'So that's how it is, then? Out you go on a rope so I can clean up. I'm not going to hurt you. I've had enough sticks on my back not to want that for anyone except your owner.'

Three hours later the caravan and the dog smelled cleaner, and Callie was about to get ready for work when there was a loud banging her door. Two policemen stood there, demanding entry. She recognized Constable Harry (two pints and a packet of pork scratchings every week night off duty) and smiled.

'Is this your dog?' the constable asked.

'She is now,' Callie replied, unconcerned. 'I saw Dolly being ill treated in a field. I relieved her from her owner.'

'That's what we're here for.'

'I gave Ted Fletcher a dose of his own medicine, taught him a lesson.'

'You fair bruised him black and blue. You can't take the law into your own hands, Callie,' said the village bobby. 'He's complained you assaulted him.'

'Of course I did, after he took the stick to me. He was knocking this poor thing senseless. Look at her scars, and she's half starved.'

'She's a working dog, not a pet.'

'Dolly's my pet now. I've rescued her and I hope Ted Fletcher will think again how he treats his dumb workers.'

'It's not as simple as that, Callie. He's charging you with assault. You will have to answer questions down at the station and we'll take down a statement. The dog comes with us . . .'

'Back to more cruelty? You know the man – have a heart. I'll buy her off him, if I have to, but she's not going back there. She's an old lady past her best, anyone can see that.'

'That's beside the point. You can't go battering people.'

'Funny, but, in my lifetime, I've seen plenty of people do exactly that.'

'Not in this country, they don't. Come along and we'll get this sorted.'

'Can I bring Dolly as evidence? We can't leave her alone.'

The dog peered up at them as if in agreement. She limped along, such a sorry sight, but kept close to Callie.

'Reckon that thing knows when it's well off,' Constable Harry muttered, giving Callie a wink.

Callie appeared before the magistrate shortly afterwards and pleaded guilty to assaulting the farmer in anger at the sight of his cruelty. 'I wanted him to feel the pain he was inflicting and I'm not sorry,' she admitted.

'You did that in spades, Mrs Jones. He's walking with sticks and he demands his dog back.'

'I demand the RSPCA look at her first.' Callie was in no mood to be defeated now.

No one spoke and then the magistrate addressed her again: 'What puzzles me is how a man that size let a slip of a barmaid beat him into the ground. He said you were in a frenzy of rage, shouting at him in a foreign language.'

'Did I? I'm afraid my memory has got the better of me.' It was time to play the sympathy card. 'The last time I saw men in breeches wielding sticks, they were thrashing women and children to the ground and leaving vicious dogs to finish them off. You don't forget that, ever.'

'Not in this country?' The magistrate leaned forward, all ears.

'No, in a camp they called Ravensbrück, in Germany, and in other camps. Do you want me to go into more detail?'

'You were an internee?'

'I was, and I never want to see such things again. We fought for freedom from such treatment. I didn't expect to find cruelty like that in an English field. They say tyranny begins with little cruelties to which we turn a blind eye. For evil to happen, it only takes good men to do nothing. I heard that somewhere.'

'Precisely,' came the reply. Then there was silence while the magistrate considered his options.

'Caroline Jones, as this is your first offence, I will caution you formally. There has to be no repetition of such violent behaviour, however well-intentioned. Do you understand?'

'Yes, sir. Can I keep Dolly?'

'That's a matter for the RSPCA, not this court. Please don't go rescuing every down-trodden creature that crosses your path. That is all. You can go.'

'Thank you. I'll go and find Dolly.'

She went into the town in search of a pet shop for a new lead and collar, grooming products and flea powder. It was only when she returned to the caravan that she realized she'd not had a drink all day.

The landlord was waiting in the pub with her cards.

'Pack your bags. I can't have you upsetting my regulars with that temper of yours. Clear all those bottles out from under the van – they're a fire hazard – and take that flea-bitten bag of bones with you. Don't go asking for references from me. You're trouble, you are.'

Callie shrugged. 'Come on, Dolly, we know when we are not welcome. I'm sure there's plenty more hostelries that want a good barmaid and a guard dog.' Callie wasn't worried for the future. This was the best day's work she'd done in years.

It wasn't easy to find work locally with a dog in tow. Word spread about her assaulting a customer so pub doors were sometimes closed on her. She couldn't drink and feed a dog, but with Dolly by her side the need to keep topping up began to fade. Her body didn't like this change and at first she would wake shivering and sweating, imagining camp guards were chasing her through the pine forest. Some bed and breakfasts didn't accept Dolly and made her sleep outside all night, but by now it was high summer and, as a working dog she was used to being outside.

They were so hard up before Callie was due to collect her war pension that they slept under the stars and she used the public lavatories to freshen up. Callie realized she was slipping away from settled work with accommodation into a precarious search for regular work, but she must take what she could get. Fortunately, there were plenty of fruit farms in the Worcestershire area offering piece work picking strawberries and soft fruit, and the farmers had no objection to Dolly.

Dolly sat patiently while Callie bent her back with the other pickers and heard from them there were farms needing pickers right into the autumn so she would earn enough to keep them undercover when winter came. This was encouraging and spurred her on, although she secretly wondered how long she could manage the work. It was good to be with these groups of young travellers in their gaudy cheesecloth shirts and skirts, but Callie's back soon ached and her eyes weren't so quick to find the berries on the ground. She needed glasses and without them she was finding it difficult to keep up with the others. Middle age had crept up on her by stealth. She knew she was not fit enough to keep this going for long.

The gang had their own way of living, in old vans and caravans around some makeshift tents they called Sunset Camp. There they sat round a campfire smoking hash and cooking stews of vegetables and anything they could forage. It reminded Callie of her time on the run with Marie and Madeleine. When they realized she was homeless they asked her to join them and she didn't hesitate.

'You look in need of a hearty stew,' laughed a girl who called herself Petal, handing a steaming bowl of food to Callie.

There were other tethered dogs for Dolly to sniff around, and barefoot toddlers with matted hair running all over the camp, minded by young girls with long skirts and wild hair.

The travellers were kind and shared what they had, accepting Callie without question. They talked of their travels and places where they squatted in the bad months: derelict houses far from view, boarded up empty mansions that could be entered and used. Some went to France for the *vendange* – the grape harvest – or north, potato picking. This was a whole new world for Callie to consider, a gypsy-like existence in a caravan of ramshackle vehicles. There were older couples living simple lives, not interested in advancing their careers. They talked of peace and love and meditation, some practised yoga and listened to Indian music, talking of gurus who preached the simple life. She was given a makeshift tent and a rug. Everyone pooled their takings to live and find petrol.

In this shambolic-looking community, for the first time in years, Callie felt safe and, with Dolly as her companion, she never felt alone. Besides, everyone was friendly. There was an order in this society, with rules about privacy and sharing and pulling together. Folk came and went, and there were arguments and personality clashes, but it was just easier to talk them through in a haze of dope smoke.

Callie knew that, for her, life under canvas couldn't last and she'd have to find them somewhere more permanent before winter set in. Yet once she returned to the bar work, she feared temptation would get the better of her. What else was she fit for now?

One morning, she was wrapping up some apples for storage in old newspaper when a headline caught her eye. She unwrapped the apple and straightened out the paper, squinting to focus, unused to reading and still without glasses. A politician called Airey Neave had lobbied Parliament for full compensation for concentration-camp victims. A million pounds had been set aside for survivors by Germany and the MP was making sure people got what was their due. Surely, she would qualify? She folded the newspaper into her pocket to reread later. Maybe she'd ask Petal and the others what they thought.

It was too late for the Celines of this world, but not for her to claim her due, Callie decided. A lump sum would help get her on her feet. But to make her claim she would have to leave the community, the tranquillity of Sunset Camp, and go back into the world of suits and form filling, and register herself in London. She still collected her war pension, but over the years she had drifted away from where she was supposed to collect it. She had her book, however, and that was proof of who she was. Everything else was mislaid or left somewhere. She no longer had a passport. It was as if she hardly existed any more.

Callie didn't need a mirror to know she looked like a tramp, with straggling hair, and wearing makeshift dungarees and headscarf. Her formal clothes were creased and crumpled in a bag, but a good wash might smarten them up enough to pass muster.

How would Dolly feel about being hoicked onto pavements, tied up all day while her mistress found work and a room? Dolly had rescued her from the booze and the bars and given her a new life. Perhaps she'd be better off staying here where the children fussed over her. She was plumper and her coat was glossy. How could Callie take her back into a world where dogs were unwelcome?

Callie sat stroking the old girl, knowing what Dolly had given was precious: her utter loyalty and affection without question, and in return all she needed was respect and sustenance. Dolly had brought her back to life, helped her feel responsible for someone other than herself. This old sheepdog was the nearest thing Callie had to a child, a furry substitute for Desmond. The dog deserved a decent old age, settled, peaceful. She was sleeping a lot lately as if she was slowing down towards her final rest. Tramping streets would be cruel. Years of neglect and cold stone floors had made her arthritic. 'I can't take you away from this, no matter how much I'll miss you,' Callie sobbed. 'If I go, I go alone.'

It was an agonizing choice to make. Part of her knew that it was time to go back into the world again. Perhaps there was still the chance to be useful. Now she was sober she could see things much more clearly. Here, she was just hiding away, licking her wounds as Dolly licked hers. They were two of a kind, but she was still young enough to find some purpose. There was a bit of St Maggie's school discipline inside her heart that would never go away. 'Onwards and Upwards' was their motto. She had life when others she had known now had none. She owed it to them to move on. It was never too late for a second chance, but where and when would depend on this next bit of the journey.

Why do I have to leave behind everything I love? she cried. Why must I always travel alone?

She scrubbed up for the London trip, digging out her black skirt and jacket, old-fashioned now, in the 1950s style, but serviceable enough. Petal dyed her greys into an ash blond tone and then Callie put her hair up into a French pleat. She'd drawn her pension to buy a train ticket and room for the night. She knew she would go to the old War Ministry offices and fill in forms, but as to her return, she wasn't sure.

Taking Dolly for one last walk along the river bank, she tried to explain why she was going away and until she was settled she must live here in the camp. 'I'm coming back for you as soon as I'm settled, I promise,' she whispered. Even as she was speaking, however, she had this feeling that perhaps this was goodbye for good.

Her confidence and resolve lasted all through the journey down from Gloucester, but when she arrived at Paddington, her legs were trembling at the noise and bustle of passengers striding out in front of her. She was sweating, wanting to flee the busy street, the hoot of car horns and roar of engines revving. How could she have forgotten how fast and busy it was here? She felt like a stranger in a foreign land, unnerved by faces all around her. Memories of Leipzig flooded back, disorientating her, making her want to flee.

There was no hurry to make her way to Whitehall. She felt no energy in her limbs to navigate the once familiar streets. What she needed was a little booster. Once she'd sampled a snifter, she'd soon be able to face the world again. Didn't she deserve a reward for all her restraint in the past months? Here, conveniently, was a public house. Callie opened the door and sleepwalked inside.

44

What are you doing here? Melissa was staring over the waters of Dalradnor loch, drinking in the fresh spring air, watching ripples shimmering silver and gold in the sunlight. *What has this place got to do with me? Why have I given up my Easter vacation to come so far north on a whim?* This was the place Libby Steward said might hold the key to Lew's heritage. What a crazy undertaking when she should be studying for her oral examinations.

It was a fee from her last solo performance in *The Creation* that had allowed this extravagance.

Yes, it was a beautiful country, the air was crisp and cool, the scenery stunning, but that was not the point of the visit. She was here to ask questions, but where to start?

She'd been reluctant to set out on this quest. Perhaps it was a mistake to refuse Mark's offer of help yet again, but now she was here she'd better make the expense worthwhile.

One of these days, he'd take the hint and lose interest in her mission, but his persistence was confusing. She wasn't used to having a guy offering to help her out. Cilla and Angie, her friends in college, thought he was cute and had offered to take him off her hands. He was definitely single, Mel had discovered early on. The Sarah he'd mentioned was his big sister, with whom he shared a flat so they could split the bills. How could her friends understand that as much as she liked him, he didn't fit in with her future plans?

'Our courses are so demanding,' she tried to explain to them. 'Then there's rehearsals and performances. I need to have extra tuition.'

'Excuses, excuses . . . He's got under your skin and you're running scared.' Cilla laughed, hitting the nail bang on the head as usual. Why was she compelled to spurn Mark's offer and head up here with only the knowledge that she would find Phoebe Faye's grave, take a look at a house and do a quick tour of the Trossachs with time for little else?

Mark had found her Caroline's shortened form of a birth certificate. What shocked her most was that she'd been born in the next street to her own flat in Marylebone. What a strange coincidence. So how did Phoebe come to be living in the wilds of Scotland?

There was just one post office and general store on the village Main Street. The woman in the shop was not local and knew nothing about Miss Faye but pointed Mel to the Radnor Inn, which nestled among the white painted cottages. There, she ordered a round of sandwiches and a drink.

'And what brings an Aussie lass to these parts?' the landlord said with a wink as he pulled half a pint of cider.

'I'm looking up an old actress called Phoebe Faye and her family for some research. I wondered if anyone might remember them,' Melissa replied.

'Cannae help you with that but I know a man who might . . . Wullie Mackay over there, he's our history man. Hey, Wullie, come and tell the young lassie about yon history books you write.'

From the snug an old man sauntered towards her with a stick and wispy white hair. 'Oh, aye. Now who may you be?' He held out his hand.

'What can you tell me about Dalradnor Lodge and Phoebe Faye?' She might as well be direct.

'It's just a holiday let now. It once belonged to the Seton-Ross estate, used for the shooting season, and then to Miss Faye, after her fiancé was killed in the war. There was a niece but we've not seen sight nor sound of her for years.'

'Would that be Caroline Boardman?'

'The one to be asking about her would be Netta at the farm, the Dixons' old place. They'll be knowing all about her. Have you got a car? I can show you the way.'

Mel swallowed her lunch, offered him a beer and then found herself driving the old man up a farm track, trying to explain to him her tenuous connections to Miss Faye.

'One of the Dixon girls went to Australia to join her husband after the war. She never came home, but few could in those days. Married an airman from there but I dinna ken his name. Netta was the youngest sister, left to see to the farm with her parents and brothers. She'll be the one to ask.'

The farmhouse was a long white building with a milking parlour attached. Dogs barked at their arrival and a woman in an apron came out to greet them.

'Now, Isabel, I've brought Miss Boyd, all the way from Australia. She's trying to find oot about the folks frae Dalradnor Lodge before the war. I think your aunty might be able to fill her in a wee bitty.'

'Netta's full of tales from the past. I never know what's true and what's her romancing,' Isabel replied. 'But come away in and see for yourself, Miss . . .?'

'Melissa Boyd, and thank you'

'You're no' a relation of Jessie, are you?'

'Jess Boyd was my grandmother,' she nodded and smiled. 'But I never knew her.'

'My goodness, wait till I tell Aunt Netta. You'll have to shout, her ears are not what they were, but they can always catch a good crack o' gossip.' They were ushered down a passage to a sitting room-cum-bedroom with a fire in the grate.

'Netta. This lady's from Australia. She knew your sister, Jessie.'

The old lady with white hair fluffed out like a meringue was sitting in a chair crocheting a blanket at great speed. She examined Mel from top to toe. 'She's no' a Dixon, by the look of her. Sit down, you've come a long way, hen.'

Mel tried to explain who she was and how her father died, leaving her a note. She pulled out the famous postcard. 'All I know is Jess kept this hidden and Dad had a notion it was something to do with him, but I don't know who Desmond was.'

Netta stared at the letters on the back. 'Desmond? He was the wee boy Jessie took out with her on the ship. He was an orphan, or so we thought. Jessie was his nurse and when his grandmother fell ill she took it into her head to take him with her. Things didna go well with her marriage and there was a divorce. I think the man took against the boy. Then she settled and married again but she never darkened our door again.'

'And this Desmond came from the village?'

'Oh, my, there was a right mix-up. His mother returned late from the war to find him gone and Miss Faye fair took it bad. They had a falling-out. Folks say the shock killed her.'

'It's Desmond she's asking after, Netta,' Isabel butted in, raising her eyebrows in impatience.

'He belonged at the big house, Miss Callie's wee boy. There was no husband on the scene, as far as we could tell. She'd lived in Egypt for a long time. She went to the war. No one saw her after. Jess didn't write home, just a card at Christmas. I think she was ashamed of being divorced . . . I cannae help you any more. We all felt terrible for Miss Faye. She was a kind soul, right enough. Her niece never showed up at the funeral . . .'

'Have you got any photographs of any of them?' Melissa knew she must seize the moment while Netta was linked to those past times.

Isabel began rummaging in a cupboard fixed into the wall. 'There may be some in the old document box. We keep meaning to sort out her old photos and put names to people on the back before they get forgotten.'

Netta put down her crochet hook and sifted through them with her bony fingers. 'There's Jessie's wedding.'

Mel stared at a bride in a pretty frock and a young man in RAF uniform outside a church porch. There was another of an older woman with hair scraped back standing next to an unmistakable boy in short trousers. Mel blurted out with excitement, 'That must be my Dad!'

On the back was written: LOUIE. RUBY CREEK. CHRISTMAS 1946.

'I'd love to take a copy of this. I've no photos of him as a boy. It's definitely him.' It was the weirdest feeling to be staring at such an innocent roguish grin. She'd known that grin even in his last days. There was a charming innocence in this face, but a toughness too.

'You keep it, Melissa. Fancy you being Louie's daughter. I dinna ken what happened to the Desmond boy,' she sighed, and continued with her knitting.

'Could they be one and the same you were searching for? Sounds mighty fishy to me, but there's one more place you might find out more,' Wullie offered. 'We could always look at the parish records.'

They stayed on for tea, Melissa filling the family in about the Boyds' successful building supplies business in Adelaide. Netta told her what they knew about Miss Faye and the Seton-Ross family.

Then it was back to the village and the manse. Wullie introduced her to the minister, who found the register for them to browse through, pages and pages of old names she didn't know until she came to 1939 and a baptismal entry, a name she'd known the minute Netta Dixon had told her story. Here was the proof in black and white: 'Desmond Louis Lionel Lloyd-Jones. Baptized Easter Sunday 1939. The mother was Caroline Rosslyn Lloyd-Jones. Father Tobias Lloyd-Jones (deceased).'

'I think you've got your answer now,' Wullie smiled.

'I think this deserves a celebration,' Mel replied. 'And a big thank you all round.'

Now she could go back knowing she'd found Lew's real identity, solving the mystery of his rightful family. Now she could get on with her own life. That was as far as she needed to go, surely? But questions kept tumbling around in her mind. What was Caroline doing that made Jess take her son so far away, and why if she was coming to Australia in 1947 did she return home empty-handed? How could she leave her little boy in Australia knowing he belonged with her? Why did no one tell her father who he really was? All these strange questions still needed answering.

It wasn't enough just to know the bare facts. If a job was worth doing and all that . . . No use leaving all these puzzles hanging in the air, she sighed.

It was almost dark when she stood at the gates of Dalradnor Lodge, peering up the driveway to the tall house with the stepped roof. She could hear children shouting as they played out in the twilight and then a voice calling them inside for the night. If this was Caroline's rightful house why had she never returned? Oh, hell! This whirlwind visit was not the end of her quest but, as Churchill had once said, 'the end of the beginning'. To answer all these puzzles, she'd have to find Caroline, if she was still alive.

45

1966

Callie woke up on the bench of a deserted station, not knowing where she was or how she found herself here. She recalled being in London, but where was Dolly? Then she remembered her dog was at Sunset Camp, and safe. She was stiff from sleeping rough, her tongue was furred and her hands were twitching. She could smell the spirits on her lips but the rest was a blur. She felt sick and shaky, unable to focus, her body weak as if she had been crushed. Her skirt was soiled and wet. What had she done now? How could she be in this state and not remember?

There'd been crowds and the traffic and a fear of suffocating . . . Yes, the mist was clearing . . . She'd needed a drink to steady her nerves. The last thing she could remember was sitting in a bar.

Looking around, Callie was flooded with fear, seeing this wasn't anywhere she recognized, but at least her handbag was in her lap. Did she ever get to the Ministry? She recalled the tall white stone buildings towering over her as she stumbled off the bus and up the steps to the foyer. There was a man in uniform who had asked with whom she had an appointment but she'd brushed past him.

'Take me to the bloody traitor who betrayed us . . .' She could hear the echo of her shoes on the stone steps, the hush of officials around her as she was shouting. This must be a bad dream, surely? It was terrifying not to recall another thing. She felt groggy and faint as she rose up gingerly.

'Ah, there you are.' A woman in a tweed suit marched down the platform. 'You're awake and ready to come now?'

Who was this figure looming over her? What had she done? Was she safe?

'Who the hell are you?' Callie demanded.

'Oh, don't start that again. You know who I am, Charlotte,' came the brusque reply.

Why was she calling her Charlotte? 'I'm not Charlotte.'

'You are as far as I'm concerned, and don't look a gift horse in the mouth. We'll get some tea down you and out of those disgusting clothes. You look ridiculous.'

Am I dreaming? Callie thought again, staring up at the woman, a little older than herself, in a trilby hat with a feather perched at the side. There was something familiar about her, though, but she was too befuddled to know where they'd met before.

'Where are we? I don't remember.'

'Little Brierley Halt, our nearest station. We've come off the milk train. Thought you'd better sleep it off before I take you to see the girls. My goodness, Charlotte, you know how to wreck yourself,' she said, holding out a hand. 'Madge Cottesloe, but you'd know me as "Marcelle", for my sins.'

'Marcelle . . . Charlotte . . . Beaulieu Abbey all those years ago. Was this the large army officer who got herself stuck on the net ropes at Arisaig on the survival course?

'Arisaig?'

'Exactly, hole in one . . . You went on to glory and I failed spectacularly . . . They put me out to grass until the war ended. I gather you got the worst of it.'

Callie suddenly felt sheepish and embarrassed about what was coming next.

'You came to HQ, shall we say a little worse for wear. I was told to make sure you survived the traffic. Had a rough ride, I gather. Still, that's all in the past. Thought I'd better find you a billet, judging by the state of you. You're finding civvy street not to your liking? Have you been living rough?'

'Where are you taking me? Am I being kidnapped?' Callie said as she was bundled into an ancient Morris estate wagon.

'Just depends how you look at things. Got to get that poison out of your system and get you *compos mentis*. You can take it from there. It's up to you.'

Callie sat in silence, staring out with half-shut eyes. She was in no state to jump out of the vehicle and the mad woman next to her was ex-SOE so she knew all the tricks. May as well sit back and be resigned to whatever fate had in store.

Madge lived with her companion, Alfie, in a tumbled-down manor house in the middle of nowhere, surrounded by fields, sheds and stables. Alfreda was an ex-army nurse who took one look at the state of the new arrival and bundled her into the bathroom, such as it was, to wash and change into clean clothes: dungarees and a work shirt. They ate a hearty breakfast, which Callie tried to face but managed only toast.

'Now come and meet the girls . . .' Madge ordered, and escorted her out into a field where two ponies and a donkey rushed over to greet them. 'Meet Poll, Nina and little Bella.'

Callie was confused. 'Is this a riding school?'

'Hardly. This is a retirement home for old ladies and gents who've fallen on hard times.' Madge paused, giving her a look. 'A bit like yourself, I reckon. You look as if you need a bit of R and R. An extra pair of hands is all I ask. Alfie's recovering from a big op and can't do heavy work. You can earn your keep but first things first. Do I call you Charlotte?'

'That was my codename. I'm Caroline, Callie. I'd not had a drink for months until I got off that train and went into the city. Sorry, it's all just a blank.'

'Well, there's no booze here. Can't afford it. Everything goes on the horses. You'll have to go cold turkey, I'm afraid. You're as brown as a berry. Doing outside work, by the look of those hands?'

'Just fruit picking, bar work. I'm not afraid of hard work.'

'Good, because the state some of our guests arrive in you'll need all your wits and strength to deal with them. You have worked with horses?'

'A long time ago.'

'Thought you might, but you never forget routines: mucking out, grooming exercising, the usual stuff. Welcome to Animal Comfort Farm,' Madge laughed. 'You just take one day at a time and you'll be fine. You've faced much worse.'

'Dolly might like it here . . .'

'Dolly?'

'My dog.'

'Sorry, no dogs here, not yet. Some of our guests get spooked by them when they arrive. Where's she now?'

'Safe where I left her, in a camp with friends. I'm not about to uproot her.' Callie looked around, uncertain. 'Is there a lot to learn? I'm not a nurse.' What was she letting herself in for here?

'All my girls and boys need is routine care, rest and respect for what they've been through. Our trust has to be earned.'

'I'm sorry if I made an utter fool of myself,' Callie sighed. 'I have no idea what I said.'

'You made your point most eloquently, and with great effect, that the experience of war never ends for some people. You stood at the foot of the stairs yelling for all to hear. "Will some bastard tell me who betrayed my *réseau*? Who was it took down false messages and passed them on as true? Did no one suspect . . .?" They ushered you into a room pretty damn quick after that, but you were on your moral high horse by then. They nearly arrested you.

'"How come when I returned, no one would speak the truth? No one wanted to know about what we'd been through. They took statements but no one asked how it felt to find you had lost your child, your future, your lover. We were left to rot in silence, keeled over like wrecks on the shoreline. How can you compensate us for nightmares and the hidden scars?" Your eloquence was impressive and shook some of those desk johnnies out of their complacency.'

'Oh, dear, that bad, was it?'

'Not at all. Very impressive and to the point. We all sensed you needed help and I just happened to be around. Don't worry, our guests here don't know your CV. Just let them teach you what you need to know.'

Later on that first evening, as she sat by the range with Alfie and Madge sipping cocoa, Callie knew it was a bit of a rum set-up, living with a lesbian couple amongst fields full of rescued horses, but for the first time in months she felt safe. This was a second chance to turn things around once and for all, but it was going to be hard. There was no Dolly to keep her on the straight and narrow, just her own determination to find some purpose and meaning for herself, and a good Samaritan who knew just what she'd been through.

Callie couldn't believe the state of the little donkey they called Jumpy when she came out of the horse box. Her coat was matted, hoofs curled up through lack of cutting. She'd been left in a shed knee high in her own waste, scraping wood to stave off hunger. Madge had a phone call from a vet to come and see for herself. The owners had left her behind to die. Madge and Alfie saw to the worst of it, while Callie looked on with a heavy heart. She prepared a stall with fresh straw bedding, water and a horsey companion nearby, ready to nudge her back to life. The donkey cringed when she touched her, as if expecting to be beaten. She eyed Callie with suspicion, so Alfie taught her how to approach sideways on, speak calmly and not stare. 'Talk to her like a child, in a soothing voice.'

Over the weeks, with her hoofs cut, her fur brushed and a good diet, she was healing physically, but mentally Jumpy was scarred, kicking out and running away. Callie rose to the challenge of winning her trust.

The old pony, Poll, assigned as her companion, began to approach her in the field, sensing her turmoil and, being rebuffed, just sauntered away. Then Jumpy began to tolerate Poll's presence and allowed her closer and closer until she followed her from a distance. Then there was that wonderful morning when Callie saw her trotting behind her new friend. When she shook the bucket Jumpy came to meet her at the field gate. Callie cried as she allowed her to stroke away her fear and on the momentous day when Jumpy nuzzled her with affection. It had taken months but was worth all the effort.

Jumpy was so like her own self, Callie smiled, suspicious, distant, not trusting, and yet together they'd made this mutual victory. It was only then that Callie realized she'd found something worthwhile in her life, that she was no longer a drunken dropout but a useful human being, worthy of respect from her charges.

There were heavy bills to keep the horses and the shelter safe, and she knew she'd have to use her pension and any compensation to help out. They needed to raise more funds and get donations and sponsors or there would soon be nothing left in the kitty.

It was at one of their fundraising open days that she was introduced to the vet, Tom Renard, newly retired but willing to look over their stable of patients for a nominal charge. He'd moved into the area after his wife's death and seemed keen to be involved.

'You're doing a grand job here,' he said, shaking Callie's hand, and she noticed how his arms were piebald, tan and white, mottled as if the sun had missed bits of his skin.

He smiled at her curiosity. 'Just a little gift from the Far East,' he said. 'I was a guest of the Japs at Changi.' He didn't need to say any more. The Japanese prisoner of war camps were notorious. Callie felt here was someone who had lost his freedom but had come through unscathed, and she relaxed, showing him around their buildings.

It was Alfie, always so full of practical ideas, who suggested he came on to their committee. He offered to give talks around the county on their behalf to some of the local business groups and societies to raise funds for the sanctuary. Alfie was relieved because this had been her role for years, but since her operation she wasn't up to travelling all over Herefordshire.

'Callie can go with you, if you like,' she suggested. 'Madge is too busy.'

The thought of talking to a roomful of people was too scary for Callie to contemplate without a large gin in her hand, but that was no longer an option. Tom could stand up and spout without notes, but she needed to write down a speech and rehearse it in front of the mirror. Soon, however, she relaxed and developed a warm and friendly style that charmed her audience. She'd parachuted into Belgium and faced the Nazis – what was there to fear in a roomful of well-heeled businessmen?

One evening, Tom was due to address a ladies' circle, part of the Round Table, but he lost his voice so Callie had to stand up and deliver on her own. She didn't hesitate. Her audience were spellbound by her heartfelt account of little Jumpy's recovery and the need for finance to save more neglected donkeys like her, and the applause was enthusiastic.

'That was bloody good,' Tom said, clapping warmly as Callie descended from the church hall platform. 'You should get that

in print. Send it to a magazine with some pictures. It could do
no harm.'

Madge and Alfie were keen on this new idea. 'Just get on
with it,' said Madge. 'It's not about you, it's about Jumpy and
Poll and all the others.'

Encouraged by their response, Callie reworked her talk and
sent it to the *Lady* magazine. To her amazement it was accepted.
The magazine sent a photographer to take photos of the found-
ers and their girls to illustrate Callie's article. Madge and Alfie
were game for anything that raised the money they so badly
needed and they suggested locations and posed for endless
photographs with their rescued animals.

The magazine was due to be published in two months' time,
and Callie realized she needed a pen name with which to enter
her new literary life: no more Callie Jones or Boardman. She
deliberated for a whole morning, while grooming Nina and
Jumpy and mucking out an entire row of loose boxes. Of
course . . . Using her two first names she became Caroline
Rosslyn, which she felt struck just the right note.

Caroline Rosslyn was free to say what her old self could not,
and Callie soon found plenty she wanted to say.

With Tom's help she began to expand her subject. Soon she
was writing articles about how living with rescued animals
helped her deal with her own turbulent wartime experiences.

'I think,' said Tom, reading through her first such piece, 'that
you're drawing some interesting parallels here. Who knows
where this could lead in the development of therapies for both
humans and animals?'

Callie's subject was taken up by the national press and she
was asked to write a feature about the sanctuary.

All this gave her the courage to write one more time to the
Boyds, demanding to see Desmond and enclosing some of the
articles, hoping this would make him proud of his mother. She
had heard nothing for years but had never given up hope.

The only positive that came out of the silence that greeted her letter was that she recognized she no longer needed to drown her sorrows in gin. Instead, she wrote out all her frustrations into a strong article in the press, which garnered a wealthy sponsor from Birmingham.

46

How could it be a year since her father died, and nearly the end of her course already, Melissa sighed. The months seemed to have sped up until they became a blur of written exams, orals and end-of-term recitals.

Now there was the burning issue of which of her concert dresses to wear for the end-of-year ball. She'd asked Mark to be her partner, owing him for all the research he'd done on the medal, something she'd almost forgotten about until he reminded her over dinner one night.

'I showed it to a medal expert. He's a military historian and appears on the *Antiques Roadshow*. He said it's Belgian and not French, given for bravery, and it could be traced. In fact, he phoned me later to tell me he'd found out it belonged to a Louis-Ferrand van Grooten, a professor executed for being in the Belgian Resistance. He was from a distinguished family near Grooten. So what do you make of that?'

'And the baptism certificate called Lew "Desmond Louis". Could there possibly be a connection here? Libby did mention Caroline went to a finishing school in Belgium. Where's this going to end, Mark?'

'You really ought to find this Caroline while she's still alive. She's well over eighty now. I don't understand your delay.'

'I did what Dad asked. If that woman left him in Adelaide and no one ever mentioned her to him, then there must have been a good reason. I don't think she was a very good person.'

'You don't know that,' Mark argued.

'She was an alcoholic. I've told you Libby's story. If Louis-Ferrand is another link, I'd rather find out about him rather than her. But at this moment I have big decisions to make. Do I audition for an opera company or carry on performing and do some teaching as a back-up to pay for more lessons? One thing's for sure, I'm not ready to go back to Adelaide yet.'

She felt she'd only just got the hang of how England ticked and there was so much of London life she'd not seen yet.

'Perhaps a break would help. Time you saw a bit of Europe. We could have a look at Grooten, ask around, do a few bric-a-brac fairs,' Mark offered. 'We can take the Golf.'

For once, Mel didn't reject this out of hand. Mark would be good company and perhaps it was time she let down her guard a little. They'd drawn closer over the summer and she was finding it hard to resist his advances.

'So this is your excuse to buy in more postcards. Haven't you got enough?' she teased.

'You can never have enough.' He kissed her gently. 'Let's go away, just the two of us, and you can make your decisions when you come back.'

Why not, she thought. It was high summer, about as hot as it ever got in this part of the world, and very pleasant. Perhaps it was time to play for a while, celebrate her exam success; forget all the doubts about Dad's birth mother clouding the horizon. She'd walked out of his life so why waste precious time searching for her now?

1986

'How do you live with all you went through in Changi Prison in the war?' Callie asked Tom one evening as they drove back from one of their fundraising talks. The previous evening they'd both seen some television documentary on Japan since the conflict.

Tom had a key to living she, haunted by guilt and bad dreams, hadn't. She was still bitter at her loss and she longed to know what his secret was.

'How do you forgive your enemies? I don't understand.' Callie sighed. 'I can't forget what was done in the camps to innocent women and children. I will never forget or forgive.'

Tom took a moment to clear the cough that he seemed to have had for weeks. Alfie and Madge had been ill off and on for some time, too. 'Something going round,' Alfie insisted, battling on as only she could.

'Nor will I forget,' Tom answered. 'I'm no saint, but I think all of us are capable of terrible cruelty. We all have hatred inside and we will kill given the right circumstances . . . Look at what we see in the sanctuary, what ordinary people do to animals, the cruelty inflicted on helpless beasts. But I think to live with hatred is to burn ourselves out from the inside, destroy the good in us. We can't live without love and dreams.'

'I wish I knew how to find your peace,' Callie said.

'When I've had a bad night I go out into the garden next morning and look around me,' he smiled. 'I just sit and look and listen and enjoy the moment. Very Zen, don't you think?' He laughed. 'I find it's the little things that surprise: the skylark bubbling in the air, the laughter of children in the park on a swing. Call me a romantic old fool, if you like . . .'

'No, I feel it when Jumpy comes rushing to greet me,' Callie replied. She'd noticed the influence of Tom's acceptance on her in small ways. Sometimes at the end of a shift, she walked through the fields for the joy of naming the wildflowers, as she had done with Marthe all those years ago, and she bought tapes of the swing band music she'd loved, which reminded her of happier days.

'You should make contact with your son, you know, go and seek him out.'

'I can't. It's too late.'

'It's never too late to build bridges.'

'He's never bothered to find me.'

'That's no excuse.'

'I'll think about it,' she replied, knowing he was right, but that was as far as it got . . .

The cough that plagued Tom wouldn't go away. All those years in Changi had weakened his health and suddenly he was really ill. As if that wasn't bad enough, Alfie began to falter – little falls, forgetfulness – and any thought Callie had of leaving England to find Desmond was cast aside with all the extra work she and Madge now had.

'Let the old SOE spirit prevail,' said Madge, as the two of them tackled the mucking out on cold dark mornings.

'Onwards and upwards,' Callie always replied, but her heart sank to see that Madge, too, was getting frail and forgetful. After Alfie and Tom died, Madge limped along bereft, but then her forgetfulness turned into frustration and dementia, and Callie had to find a nursing home to care for her until her death.

It was a terrible blow having to struggle on alone. Callie kept the place going with voluntary help but she was coming to the end of her tether. There was so much red tape and form filling, and human beings got on her nerves with their constant harping on about 'the bottom line'. She knew the shelter was in debt and the house was falling down around her ears. By now, the sanctuary had been her life for over thirty years. Here she was her own boss and slave driver, but it was hard to keep soldiering on.

Yet the beauty of Little Brierley never failed to lift her spirits and the joy of watching those poor creatures come back to life was the biggest reward. The committee who had overseen the charity under which the sanctuary was financed founded the Madge Cottesloe Trust to protect the rescue centre, its house and the fields around, and it was volunteers who saved the day. A forward-thinking probation officer suggested some of those in his charge might benefit from working with animals to help their rehabilitation.

Over the years, Madge had worked miracles with some of those lazy louts, turning them into reliable young men ready to face the world. Look what she'd done for Callie herself all those years ago.

This morning it would be Jodie's turn to muck out and groom her charge. She'd come with a sullen pout and surly lip curl, expecting to ride round the field like the celebrity star Jordan. She had needed a kick up the backside and had felt the lash of Callie's tongue the day she had sneaked off for a fag at the back of the stable, dropping a fag end in the straw.

'Put that out!' Callie yelled. 'If you walk away and the straw burns, what do you think will happen to the little donkey in there? Who will hear his screams as he burns to death? How could you be so stupid? Think of others for a change!' She'd seen the look of horror on Jodie's face as cause and effect clicked into her dozy brain. The result was electric. Now Jodie was turning out to be a star pupil and talked of trying to get work as a groom at a racing stable when she was out of probation.

The sanctuary also had disabled school pupils who came to work with their own assigned horse, and it was wonderful to watch them form a relationship with a living creature that didn't answer back or notice their handicaps but accepted their care and responses. Not all of them coped with a lively horse, but it was only fear that made them back away, causing the ponies to tense up. Callie saw with delight how the fears of the children and the fears of the animals could be overcome by working on both together.

She'd learned so much from this place. It had given her confidence to deal with her own fear, kept her sober, helped with the pain of the past failures and given a rich and full new life, more than she dreamed possible. Now she was on borrowed time. Each morning she woke was a bonus and she wanted to keep on going to the last and secure a future for the Trust.

Callie stood outside the kitchen door with a mug of coffee in her hand listening to the rooks in the high trees, the stillness of the air, drawing strength from the beauty of the green fields and meadow flowers, forcing her limbs into action. It was midsummer and she could smell the roses.

Come on, old girl, shift yourself. Nobody left to do the job but you . . .

47

'This is the life,' Mel murmured smiling across at Mark as she lay back in the massive bedroom of Château Grooten Hotel, looking up at the ornate plasterwork on the ceiling. 'I could get used to this.'

'Dream on, sport. Better start singing for you supper like Katherine Jenkins,' he mocked, aware that one of her contemporaries had signed a mega contract with a record company. He kissed her and she folded into his arms.

Coming away with Mark was proving to be fun. They'd driven into Paris, mooching around the antique stalls so Mark could bargain for French postcards of Josephine Baker and Edith Piaf, ferreting out boxes under tables in search of hidden treasure.

Paris in late summer was everything the guide books said: warm pavement cafés in Montmartre, art galleries, buskers outside l'Opéra. It was here in the Hôtel de Crillon they caught the passion of the city and discovered each other as lovers rather than friends.

They toured Versailles and drove through history into the battlefields of the First War, looking for Phoebe Faye's fiancé, Arthur Seton-Ross, and one of Mark's great-uncles. Then they crossed into Belgium, where they sought out Grooten and found the château restored to glory. It seemed a good idea to splash out on a few four-star nights there so they'd be able to explore the district further.

If this was Louis–Ferrand's former home, there was little of the original left. The hotel stood in front of a beautiful lake. It was now a conference centre and wedding venue, with a gracious dining room. Melissa sent a postcard to Patty to put her in the picture. They visited Bruges, sampled the chocolates, and toured the museum in Brussels where they asked about war heroes of the Resistance and showed the medal to the curator. What they heard about that time shocked them both: escape lines betrayed, agents arrested, torture and then executions. It was a sobering visit, which sent them back to Grooten in silence, wondering how this could possibly be connected to Lew.

'If we find the cemetery perhaps we'll discover more about the van Grooten family,' Mel decided.

One of the hotel maids suggested they talk to an old priest rather than the young one now presiding. 'Father Karel's in a home now. This was once his home too. He can tell you its history. He lost all his family in the war.'

Mel grabbed Mark's hand. 'We have to speak to him, but I don't know any French.'

'Don't look at me, I flunked GCSE four times.'

As always in small places, someone knew someone who could help, and soon they were shown to the *maison de retraite* – the care home – where they were told Father Karel now lived. It was a complex of bungalows around a courtyard and, at its centre, a communal building where they asked to see the priest. The manager spoke good English and offered to translate should it be necessary.

'Father Karel has good days and not so good. His mind wanders into the past now but he loves having visitors.' She led them through a corridor and Mel was reminded of her father's last days in the hospital, with that sick bed smell no air freshener can conceal.

The old man was resting by his bed staring out of the window across the manicured lawn, his fingers playing some music on an imaginary keyboard. The manager explained to him a little about why they had called and their interest in Louis-Ferrand, his brother.

'My poor brother,' he said in good English. 'What is there to say? No finer man ever lived.'

Mark nudged Mel. 'Show him the medal,' he whispered.

She pulled it out of the little wallet. 'I have this.'

Karel's face changed at the sight of it, alert and wary. 'Where did you find this? That doesn't belong to you.' His eyes searched hers, puzzled and fearful.

'It belonged to my father, Lew . . . Louie, in Australia. When he died he gave it to me for safekeeping. He didn't know why it belonged to him.'

'But I gave it to Caroline to give to Louis-Ferrand's son all those years ago when she came to find him . . . And you say it was your father's. Do you have a picture of this Louis?'

Thank goodness the ever-bulging wallet of photographs and information they had gleaned over the past year was safe in her bag. Out came all the postcards, letters and photos, including a family group taken with Sandra, her mother, before she died in the road accident.

Karel snatched them all up. 'Yes, yes, that's him as I remember him. He was the best looking of us boys, so like Maman.' His face was radiant with surprise.

'No, that's my father taken before my mother died in an accident. He looks about forty.'

The old man stared at the photo as if in another world, a past world, in happier times by the smile on his face. 'Little did we know how it would all be destroyed. How is Caroline? She suffered, too, in the war in those terrible camps, lost and forgotten, hoping Ferrand was still alive waiting for her. It was me who had to tell her he was dead and see the light go out of her eyes. Then she gave me hope, telling me of his son, who was safe in England, the son she was hoping to show to him. We wrote for a while and then nothing more. He is so like his father. I would like to meet him.'

Mel felt the tears coming as she swallowed. 'My father passed away last year. He wanted me to find out more about his early life. All I know is he came to Australia with his nursemaid and his mother came after him, but he stayed there. I don't know any more.'

'*Mais oui*, that was the last letter she wrote. She told me he was taken from her. Caroline would never leave her boy. The thought of him kept her alive in the camp. All she wanted was to get back to him so they might be together, but now you have come and kept her promise to return. Thank you – and I didn't even catch your name.'

'Melissa Alexandra Boyd. Louis was my father, but I never knew this Caroline; nor did he.' She could hardly speak for emotion as Karel held out his hand to her.

'Sometimes circles are completed by those who follow after us. I thought we van Grootens were all lost and then I find Caroline has a son and now that lost son has a daughter. That is how the wheel turns, my dear. My circle rolls to its end and yours is just beginning.' He paused as the strain of speaking took its toll. 'Thank you, thank you. You give me peace. Caroline will be very proud to know all this too.'

Mel turned to Mark. How could she tell the old priest that Caroline had played no part in her life, that she'd not even bothered to search her out? 'We are tiring you with all these questions,' she said instead.

Karel turned to Mark with a twinkle in his eye. 'Take care of my great-niece. I see my maman in her beautiful face: stubborn but strong, eh?'

Mark nodded. '*Mais oui, exactement, Monsieur.*'

'You will send me a picture of Caroline and give her my good wishes? I have never forgotten her sad face or her courage. She will be old like me, and the old need the young to help them turn the wheel on its last cycle. Bless you, Melissa, on your journey. May God keep you both safe.'

They left him smiling at his silent benediction.

'You have to find her now if only to tell her you have met Louis's uncle. We must go back over the records and see if she is still alive. Perhaps she's in a home too, but she must be on an electoral role. Pensions, tax returns, we are all traceable these days, and the Web might help us speed up this search.' Mark was talking through the options. 'We're so near and yet so far.'

'What's with the "we"? This is my search, not yours?' Melissa blurted out her resentment.

'Why do you always snap when I offer to help?'

'I'm used to doing things on my own.'

'But isn't it more fun when you love someone to share things together?' He tried to catch her hand but she withdrew it as they marched across the hotel lawn.

'This isn't fun, it's serious now, and I'd rather manage solo. It's my family. Oh, don't look like that . . . I'm really grateful for all you've done but when I get back I've got decisions to make. Do I go for a teaching post or go with the agent and try to make a career here, or back home?'

'What's this got to do with finding Caroline? You have just had the best news about her and now you want to rush back and think about other stuff. I was going to ask if you'd like to move in with me now Sarah's left London.'

'To share expenses? I hope you're not expecting me to do your ironing.' Mel laughed, but Mark was not amused.

'What's got into you? It's only a thought. We've had such a wonderful holiday . . .' Mark stopped in his tracks to challenge her.

'I'm not ready to move in with anybody. I need to stay close to college, find a good accompanist. You don't want to hear me caterwauling night and day. Let's keep things as they are.'

'Am I hearing a "don't ring me, I'll ring you" arrangement? Fine, no strings, no commitments, I get the message. London is expensive to live on your own; I just thought—'

'Oh, don't keep hammering on about it. Let's forget it . . .'

This was not how Mel wanted to end this important day. Why was she always doing this, keeping her lovers at arm's length? Father Karel had given her so much to think about. Perhaps Caroline was not the awful mother she'd assumed. He'd talked about her with such concern and love, about her courage and her loss. Now Mel's mind was buzzing with all the information just as Mark leaped in with his offer.

She knew she ought to be grateful for all his help but all she was feeling was fear. She was too young for a serious live-in relationship. Why couldn't he keep things light-hearted and casual?

As they sat on the terrace with their pre-dinner apéritif, she saw the disappointment in his eyes. Better they had this out now, even if it meant a parting of the ways.

Mel stared out over the dusk towards the lake with a sigh. Had Caroline sat here with her lover? *Was my father conceived here?* When it came to finding her grandmother, she knew it was something she must do for herself, but how would she react now if this woman was no longer alive?

They dined in silence and retired early. Mel couldn't sleep, feeling the first chill of autumn in the air between them, knowing their holiday together was over. Whatever might happen in London was no longer certain. Sometimes, what is not said or done speaks loudest of all. She needed to be alone now to sort out her future plans, which had to include one last effort to locate her grandmother before it was too late.

The search for Caroline drew yet another blank when she tried to find out through the estate agent dealing with the letting of Dalradnor Lodge. He just gave her the name of some

firm of lawyers in London to contact, saying they were the
sole representatives of a trust. She felt like Sherlock Holmes,
trying to discount one false lead after another, and time was
running out. Mel really wished Mark was there to cut corners
for her, but they'd only met once since their holiday, to go to
the theatre with pre-arranged tickets. He'd promised to come
to her first recital out of town but she'd not reminded him and
he wasn't there.

There were new students across the landing from her flat but
she didn't mix with them. Angie had got a place with an orchestra and Cilla was busy auditioning for the chorus of Opera
North. Soon they'd all be scattered. Somehow, Mel had lost
that hunger to be an operatic diva. She found she preferred solo
work with choral societies, but fees were modest and teaching
as well was essential.

Adelaide seemed so far away – too far to go for Christmas –
and she wanted to experience another Dingley Dell winter with
a carol concert, a walk in the park, a pantomime and, of course,
snow. The other Aussies in college would bring a bit of cheer
with their annual party, but it was not the same as back home.

She'd made an appointment with the lawyers, Benson,
Harlow and Ford, after school. All she could offer were verba-
tim anecdotes, photos and a copy of her father's baptism record
with his birth certificate from the General Register Office for
Scotland. This gave her his actual date of birth for the first time.
Jess had made sure he'd celebrated on the right day. Louis
Ferrand was not named as the father but, as in the baptismal
register she'd seen in Scotland, the first husband, Tobias, marked
as deceased.

Having explained her mission to a stern-faced secretary, she
was slotted into an office and told to wait.

'Miss Boardman,' said a young girl carrying a file, who
appeared five minutes later and looked barely old enough to be
out of school, 'or Mrs Lloyd-Jones is, as far as we are aware, the

sole heir to the estate according to the last will of Miss Faye. They were estranged and under the rules of *bona vacantia*, the estate will revert to the Government in due course if the legitimate heir is not found. There is no legal marriage certificate for Caroline Rosslyn Boardman and Tobias Lloyd-Jones but you have shown us evidence of an heir.'

'That's Desmond Louis, my father.'

'Yes, we know this, but you say he is deceased, which makes you . . . but if this Caroline is still alive . . .'

'I didn't come here about moneys. I just want to find her.'

'Wouldn't we all, but she is proving very difficult to trace, even with her unusual second name. There is no evidence she is deceased, from our researches.'

If these experts couldn't find her, how could Mel? Her only chance left was Caroline's war record. Karel had told her she was a camp survivor. There must be army records, but how could she circumnavigate red tape? Mark would have helped in this but she'd let him go. She wasn't going to use him just to get information through the back door. There had to be another way.

It was Cilla who suggested she try the World Wide Web and put in a request online.

It was a revelation just how many surfers responded to her request with some very strange suggestions and offers of personal services that had nothing to do with online heir hunting. There were a couple of gems in the undergrowth suggesting she try the women's armed services: the WAAF, ATS and FANY, but this would prove a mammoth task.

Nobody recognized Caroline Boardman, or Lloyd-Jones even, when she mentioned St Margaret's School. This was getting too much, but she sensed an urgency hard to explain. Her father appeared in her dreams, smiling and waving and beckoning her, but she could never hear what he was saying.

The next choral performance was *Messiah* and she must step up her rehearsals with her voice coach to be ready in time, so she was too busy now to carry on researching. She even thought of hiring a private detective but the fees were way out of her budget. In addition she had an abscess forming under a tooth and the pain quickly became so distracting that she simply had to see the dentist.

As she sat in the dental surgery looking at the other grim-faced patients trying to relax, staring at the gold fish in the tank, she flipped through the dog-eared magazines, all so out of date, curled round the edges, with all the crosswords filled in. There were the usual celebrity mags, the *Field*, *Horse and Hound* and a tatty copy of the *Lady*. She turned the pages just for something to do, but her eye was caught by an article on horse rescue shelters. There were harrowing photographs of before and after ponies and donkeys, an article on animal welfare charities, and one about the Madge Cottesloe Trust in Herefordshire.

Melissa would never know what made her eye glance at the bottom of the appeal advertisement where she caught the name and address of the Appeals Treasurer: Caroline Rosslyn.

'It can't be!' She spoke so loud everyone stared at her as her name was called through the Tannoy. 'Got you!' she whispered, clutching the magazine to her chest with satisfaction. 'This has to be you.'

48

Callie couldn't shake off this cold. It was making her feel weak, tired and out of sorts. It must be the frost and chill of late November and all those dark mornings as she prepared the buckets of feed for the stable. The horses were safe indoors but the water trough was frozen. She piled on her fleece and boots and thick Barbour jacket, but she couldn't get warm.

The AGA had gone out. The oil tank was empty, but she had a kettle to boil up water and a hot plate of sorts, though she didn't feel hungry.

'Be sensible, old girl, and wrap up. Lots of warm drinks, and where's your trilby?' she told herself. She knew all the dangers of hypothermia, but why was any action such an effort?

Animals must come first. Vera and Roger Hayes, who lived in Little Brierley village, would come out later to exercise the horses even if it was just a few circuits round the yard. Then there was the donkey shed to check up in the field. If she was careful she could see to that herself. The fresh air might liven her up and put some feeling in her leaden feet. If only she could get rid of this thumping headache. It was hard to raise herself from her chair.

There might be post to collect from the box at the end of the lane with more donations from their latest appeal. Money trickled in, but not enough to keep things going for much longer. If this shortfall each month carried on, the horses would have to be rehomed elsewhere, but all the rescue shelters she knew were bursting with rejects.

'Don't go worrying about that,' she chided her weary spirit. 'Just get on with your chores, shift yourself. There's no time for lounging about.'

Callie dragged herself across to the kitchen sink, turning the tap on. There was nothing coming through. Damn and blast, the pipes had frozen and she couldn't even make herself a warm drink unless there was some limey water left in the furred-up kettle.

She stared across at the bottle of wine on the dresser shelf. It had stood there gathering dust for years, a reminder that she was only one glass away from a drink if she chose. Even the bottle held no allure at this time of the morning.

'Come on, buck up. What would Madge think to see slackers in the ranks?'

The weight of her thick Barbour and boots seemed to be dragging all the strength out of her legs as she headed out the kitchen door. She took the iron shovel to bang on the surface of the ice in the water trough, but as she lifted it a tight band of pain squeezed her chest like a tourniquet and she doubled up, breathless, shocked at the intensity of such an unexpected attack.

'Oh, hell! Not now, not here,' she cried, but only the horses stirred, hearing her voice as she crawled back towards safety and the phone. It felt like a mile on the cobbles, the longest crawl of her life.

'You've done it now, old girl,' she sighed with relief, but sank helpless onto the doormat as the next wave of pain flooded over her.

49

Mel left London on Friday afternoon, driving west, crawling through the weekend getaway traffic and wondering whether to turn round before she'd even begun. She had her practice CD playing so she could rehearse and not waste the journey to Herefordshire. The forecast was chilly but bright, and she'd studied the road map to find the quickest route to Brierley Abbey.

This was the only free weekend she had so it was now or never. Was she on a wild-goose chase or was the burning instinct that she'd found her quarry more than a coincidence of name? It was just too strong a gut feeling to let go. She felt mean not to have rung Mark with the news but he hadn't kept their last casual catch-up, leaving a message on her answer phone to say he was working away. It ought not to have bothered her but she was peeved so in return she decided to withhold her own amazing news.

She thought of their holiday in Paris and Belgium, and those heady nights when they'd made love. He was quite an athlete, she sighed with a smile, but the timing was not right and she preferred to do this last bit of the quest on her own.

Still, she must admit another driver would've been useful. Why did she keep cutting herself off when she really liked him? All her relationships ended like this, not trusting a guy to follow through. Better to go it alone rather than be let down. It didn't need a therapist to tell her this was all to do with Lew and how he'd let her mother down time after time with his broken promises. So why was she going out of her way to follow his example? Why then had she bothered to trace his history to Scotland and Belgium, and now to the borders of Wales? Why couldn't he have done this himself?

Come on Dad, what's going on here? Why am I sitting in this awful traffic in a strange country on your bloody business, not mine? This is nothing to do with me. Caroline whatever her name now is may be part of my gene pool but that's about as far as it goes.

She argued with her dad mentally as the city turned into suburbs and gave way to stretches of motorway and then onto dual carriageways, then down twisting lanes and byroads. This was not the best use of her weekend, searching out a Travelodge, then trying to sleep over some noisy TV in the next bedroom. She got her revenge next morning, rising early to practise her vocal scales in full voice, scaring her neighbours witless before she dodged out for a quick breakfast and exit before they complained. An operatic voice had its uses.

She was glad of the layers of jumpers and scarf when she arrived in Little Brierley. It was just a hamlet: one street, a post office shop, no street names, a pub and a beautiful golden stone church signposted as Brierley Abbey. Then she saw a notice board pointing to the Madge Cottesloe Horse Sanctuary, and began a tortuous drive up a windy lane with overhanging bare-leaved trees reaching out to scratch the car roof with bony fingers. There was a gate to open and then a track, but she could see a horse box and a car parked in the distance.

She found she was shaking with excitement. In front of her was a beautiful golden stone house with mullion windows and a thatched roof. It looked centuries old. Mission accomplished, she sighed, sitting back in relief to have found this remote place. Then she saw a figure coming out of a large shed-like building in jodhpurs and green wellies. She jumped out of the car with a smile. Now I've got you, she thought.

'Caroline Rosslyn, I presume . . .' She tried to make a witty opening even though she was shaking inside as she strode forward, surprised how young the horsewoman looked for someone over eighty.

'Can I help you? Miss Rosslyn's not here. I'm Vera Hayes. If it's about a horse rehousing . . . I'm sorry we can't take any more at the moment. We may have to move soon.'

Mel felt flat. 'No, no, it was Miss Rosslyn I wanted to see. I've come all the way from London. I'm Melissa Boyd. Where can I find her?'

'I'm afraid you're too late . . .'

'Oh, no, she's not . . . oh, damn, I was hoping to speak to her. I'm sorry.'

'She's in hospital, it's serious. We found her yesterday collapsed . . . She's been neglecting herself. Her heart is unstable so we usually exercise her guests. It was a good job my husband and I were early for once. She's not been up to things for quite some time. Are you wanting to do an article on the Trust?'

Mel shook her head sadly. She'd left it too late, as Mark had warned. 'I'm sorry, of course. It's just a bit of a shock. I was so hoping to meet her. It's a family matter. There's so much I need to ask her.'

'Then come inside, we'll have a coffee. I brought a flask; the water's frozen. It's a bit of a mess inside but Callie was never one for housework.'

There was the proof she needed. Callie – that was the nickname Libby Steward had used for her.

Vera wasn't joking. The large kitchen was a jumble of clothes, horse magazines, a clutter of packets and unwashed pots. There was a smell of hay and horse muck in the air as they sat down gingerly. The room felt cold and damp, no place for an old lady. 'She can't keep doing this to herself but she's so stubborn. What brings you out into the sticks in search of her, then?'

Mel could see she was curious but she didn't want to give too much away. 'My father wanted me to look her up when I came to England. She's not been easy trace. He knew her as Mrs Lloyd-Jones, I think. I've been searching in all the wrong places.'

'Callie is a very private person. She keeps her own counsel. Her life has been rescuing horses and donkeys. All I know is she lived with Madge Cottesloe and her partner long before we moved here. I assumed she was single like them . . .' Vera paused, looking round the room. 'As I said, she never talked about her past but I'm sure she'd want to meet you, especially since you've come all the way from Australia.'

'Actually, I've been studying in London.' She told Vera about the Royal Academy and her career.

'Can you stay around? I can find out if she's up to visitors. I'm afraid the house's not very savoury but I'm sure she'd want to give you hospitality – or you can stay the night with us if this is all too much.'

'If you don't mind, I'll stay here. I can help you out too. I loved riding as a kid. My mother was keen on horses.'

'We'll bring you some bottles of water and light a fire in the other room. The old pipes from the well supply are too near the surface and need digging up and lowering. As for the electrics . . . It's a lovely house for a picture postcard but not for living in the twenty-first century. I don't know how she's made ends meet for all these years on just her pension, and now all the worry about the lease coming to an end. It's been praying on her mind,' Vera added as she took Mel upstairs, showing her a corridor of bedrooms with one shambolic room in use, reeking neglect. But there was another room at the far end under the eaves, musty, untouched, that just needed airing with a hot-water bottle and a duster. It would do for one night.

Together, they tidied up the kitchen and then Vera showed Mel the horses and donkeys. She nipped off home and brought back a flask of thick soup and a loaf of bread with some milk. 'You'll eat with us, tonight, and that's an order. You can tell us more about your father and your musical career.'

Over dinner in their own village cottage down the Main Street, Vera gave Mel some important news.

'I've rung the hospital and told a little fib. They think you are a relative over from Oz so you can visit for fifteen minutes tomorrow afternoon, all being well. Otherwise, it'll just me or the vicar's wife who'll do the honours, and I'm sure she'd much rather see you.'

'You're very kind to her,' Mel said.

'It's no chore. Callie has such a generous heart. She's helped so many others in her time, setting them on the right path, especially some of the young tearaways from the towns. She has a knack of gaining their trust, giving them a second chance in life. Everyone deserves a second chance, don't you think?'

They talked late into the night about the Trust and its history, about Madge and Alfie the strange couple who'd founded the sanctuary, and rumours that Callie had been involved with secret war work.

'She never said a word about her exploits. No one could open her up about her past, but Madge once let slip that she'd been in a concentration camp. I think she's a marvellous woman.'

It was strange sleeping in the ancient house with floorboards that creaked when you walked, windows rattling in the wind, with only night sounds and silence instead of noisy sirens and traffic in the streets. Melissa examined the low-beamed drawing room with its inglenook fireplace and landscape pictures on the walls. It was hard to find clues to this new Caroline. She was proving not to be who Melissa had thought. It looked like she was a reader, judging by the paperbacks on her shelves. Her choice of music was old-fashioned: a few classics but 1940s band music mostly. There were pictures of horses and donkeys and people Mel wouldn't know. The mantelpiece was cluttered with dusty rosettes and certificates going back years. There was a silver-framed picture of two women talking to a young Princess Anne. This was a room never used. Callie seemed to live only in the kitchen and the stables. That made Mel sad. Here was a woman who inspired hope in others but gave no comfort to herself. *What would she make of my arrival tomorrow? Will she send me away or approve?* Suddenly it mattered enormously that when they met they would connect.

50

Lying in a hospital bed was a bore. Callie worried about her girls and whether Vera and Roger had drummed up more support to help them. It was good of them to help out but she didn't want to be a burden. Had the pipes burst with the frost? She felt so tired and weary with wires and drips attached to her arms, all the gadgetry bleeping and glugging as she lay trying to take an interest in the ward full of geriatrics coughing and spluttering, This place was a long way for anyone to visit regularly, so the sooner she got home the better.

Doctors and nurses fluttered past her bed and stopped to ask impertinent questions about her bodily functions. She knew exactly why she'd collapsed. 'I've been run down, not eating enough and it was too cold in the house,' she explained to those who would listen. What she didn't say was that all the scrimping and saving was in a good cause and if they thought they could dump her in some overheated glasshouse of a care home, they had another think coming. She'd rather conk out on the job than give into that sort of ending. She would never fit in to communal living. What was needed was a little help in the house and stables, but without any income she'd just soldier on until she dropped. It wasn't so simple now, though, not with some solicitor breathing down her neck about selling the property.

Her eye caught a young woman hovering by the ward door and the nurse pointing in her direction. The girl with sunlit hair was tall and willowy, smiling as she held a bunch of bright orange and pink daisies, and there was something about her stride that lifted Callie's spirit.

'Miss Rosslyn?' She paused, looking down at her. 'Would you also be known as Caroline Lloyd-Jones?'

'Who's asking?' Callie replied with a flicker of excitement tinged with fear on hearing the Australian accent.

The girl searched for a free chair and sat down.

'My name is Melissa Alexandra Boyd from Adelaide.' She paused as if reluctant to continue. 'My father was Lew Boyd. Desmond Louis Lionel Boyd or Lloyd-Jones, I've only just found out. Am I right in thinking he was your son?'

Callie turned her head away to hide the impact of those names. 'Is he here too?'

'Sadly no, but in spirit perhaps. It was his last wish to find out who sent him this.' She was holding out an old postcard, one Callie recognized so well.

'Good God. He kept that all these years?'

'Not exactly. It's a long story but it's brought me on one hell of a journey. You were hard to find.' The girl smiled and she saw her own mother's eyes reflected back at her.

Callie couldn't smile; she found she was weeping. 'Desmond is dead?'

'Yes, sorry.'

The girl reached out her hand and Callie grabbed it like a drowning swimmer grabs a lifebelt. 'He remembered me then? I wrote many times but no one ever answered.'

'I don't know anything about all that, but he left me these bits and pieces to find you with,' she replied, pulling out a wallet of photographs and Ferrand's *Croix de Guerre*, a picture of Primrose McAllister and Netta's photo of Jessie Boyd with Desmond, one Callie had never seen before. Suddenly her bleeper was making a noise and a nurse came running to check her over.

'You mustn't upset her or you'll have to leave,' the nurse warned.

'No, she must stay. This is my granddaughter.' Callie looked at Mel, hardly believing what was she was saying. 'Are you really his daughter?'

'Yes.' They sat in silence, staring at each other in a moment of recognition, a moment like no other.

'And you came all this way to find me?'

'Only from London. I'm studying there but they think I've come from down under,' she whispered. She told her how she'd recognized her name in the magazine. 'Thank goodness Phoebe Faye gave you an unusual second name.'

'I can't believe this is happening. You won't rush away, will you?' Callie could see the nurse hovering by Melissa. 'Let her stay. We've so much to talk about.'

'Just five more minutes . . .'

'Tell me about your father and mother. How I've longed to know about my son . . .' Callie found she was drifting off even as the girl was speaking.

When she woke again there was no girl. Callie remembered the dream, the pretty girl with the sunlit hair and jazzy pink scarf, who brought news of Desmond and gave her hope. It was a comforting dream for a dying woman, but then she saw the bunch of gawdy daisies on her bedside shelf.

'Did I have a visitor?' she asked a passing orderly.

'You did indeed, and she jolted you back into the land of the living and no mistake. You said she was your granddaughter from Australia.'

'So I did, so I did,' Callie replied. 'So perhaps it's not all over for me yet.'

51

Callie couldn't believe the transformation when she returned from hospital in Vera's car. It was as if a fairy had waved a magic wand and sparkled up her kitchen. The Aga was lit and when she peeped in the drawing room there was a large Christmas tree with lights, and a fire in the grate.

'Who's done this?' She looked at her friend in surprise.

'Oh, it wasn't just me. It was Melissa and some friends. She came down last weekend and did the place over, and one or two helpers gave the room a lick of paint.'

'But I can't repay them . . . and the oil . . .' Callie felt weak at such kindness.

'Don't go worrying about that. It's just a little thank you from the Trust to see you through the winter. You've never taken a penny for yourself. It's about time you did. And the doctor's arranging some help. We've let you do far too much so it's a back seat for you . . .'

'I don't understand how . . .' Callie felt overwhelmed with the brightness of her home.

'Melissa will explain when she comes down this weekend. She wanted to give you a chance to settle back and she's got some ideas for raising funds. She's going to arrange a special recital with some of her musical friends. They'll perform in the Abbey, what do you think of that?'

'Where is she? She never came back to visit me.'

'There's a letter on the mantelpiece. I've persuaded her to come here over Christmas. We have to give your young Aussie a proper English Christmas.'

'But upstairs isn't fit—'

'You just take a peek. Everything's spick and span. I'm so glad to have you back here. It doesn't feel right being empty.' Vera smiled. 'It's such a relief.'

Callie felt herself reaching for her hanky. 'I don't deserve all this fuss – and all this snivelling, it's such bad form.'

'Tears are good . . . they help us heal. But no lifting buckets for you. We've got a rota for feeding time.'

'You're such good friends . . . I don't deserve you.' How could she repay Vera and the village for this support? 'What are we going to do about the sanctuary?'

'You can stop that right now. You've given heart and soul to this place over the years, now it's time to receive for a change, so shut up and drink your tea. Just keep faith. All will be well.'

Callie was exhausted with the return journey and now this surprise makeover of her home. She plonked herself into the old Windsor chair to survey her domain. Everything was the same but different, shiny, tidied up. Goodness knows where she'd find anything, but it all felt fresh and welcoming, a new beginning in many ways. It didn't solve the problem of the Trust, however. How would they survive another winter and where would they go then?

It was then she noticed the letter waiting for her from Melissa, and she rootled for her glasses.

I thought you might like to read the enclosed. It was given to me after my father died. It was Desmond Louis who insisted on me finding out who sent this postcard. I thought you'd like to see it again . . .

She picked up the old postcard of Dalradnor village, the one she'd written to her son all those years ago. How on earth had this survived? She stared at the sepia image with amazement, memories flooding back of the excitement of crossing the world to find her son. She laid it down gently, reaching for Desmond's letter, holding it up to the light.

'Dear Mel . . .' She lingered over every sentence, trying to imagine his voice '. . . it's as if I am peering through a hole in a huge wall at a garden full of flowers . . .' His words brought tears to her eyes. Did he remember the garden at Dalradnor? Oh, why had they never met again? She clutched his words close to her chest.

The house fell silent. She was glad to be alone with her thoughts. So much had happened in the past weeks, events that were turning her life upside down.

She read her son's last words to his daughter and felt the sadness within. He had lost all memory of her and yet the smell of roses had reminded him of something and someone. She wept, recalling the bench in the rose garden where she'd sang the old 'Skye Boat Song' to him and he'd said, 'Sing it again.'

He suffered the same weakness for drink as she did, trying to fight his demons with hard work and success, but the loss of his beloved wife, Sandra, set him back, which she understood only too well. How alike they were. How she would've loved to have known him. Had he sent his daughter to find her, sent her blind into another country in the hope of making his peace with her?

If only she could turn back the clock and not have enlisted, if only she'd pursued her claim on him, if only, if only . . . Callie stared into the fire shaking her head. That was then, this was now. Be grateful for a second chance to make amends, she sighed. Perhaps there was a purpose in this wonderful reunion. She couldn't wait to see Melissa again.

52

'What's got into you?' Mel was chuntering to herself in the car. 'Ever since we left London you've got such a cob on you . . .' I'm just tired, she snapped back at herself, in no mood for argument.

'So you've chucked over Mark like you chucked all the others. He lasted longer than most so what did he do wrong?' Nothing, that's the trouble. He kept wanting to be involved and I just needed to do things my way. 'Now you wish you hadn't.'

'Ring him,' said her heart, 'apologize before some other beaut grabs him.' *Oh, shut up!* she screamed in her head. Mark was free to make his own way and I'm free to go mine.

She glanced into the back, hoping she'd not forgotten all the bumf from the lawyers. Mel had emailed Bensons with Caroline's address. Their reply had given her food for thought but she didn't want to upset her grandmother just yet.

The special recital in the New Year was taking some last-minute organizing. It was going to be a gala night in the Abbey with wine and supper. A packed church would help the Trust funds along. The artists, all friends, were coming for expenses only and she'd arranged a brilliant quartet. Angie would do flute solos and be her accompanist for her own medley of items.

Mel was still getting used to finding Caroline by chance – or had some guiding hand been there all the time? How could her grandparents, Jess and Jim, deliberately have kept Lew in the dark about his birth mother? They'd left him to choose. No one forced him to go back with this stranger and it had broken his mother's heart, causing a rift with Phoebe Faye that had lasted for the rest of their lives. How sad, she thought.

Had her father known deep down what he'd done? Surely he was too young to understand such powerful feelings. She'd always felt there was a sadness at the heart of him even before he lost Sandra. Perhaps that's what turned him to drink, and when Mum died it was the last straw. Meanwhile, Callie kept hoping and drinking. Did he remember more than he was letting on when he wrote that last letter? He had spoken about the lady who came to visit and never came back. Maybe he guessed who she really was.

Mel fixed her eyes on the road ahead with a sigh. She would never know. There was so much she wanted to know about Father Karel's brother, Louis-Ferrand. She must write to Father Karel with all her news. It felt like having a whole new family to discover, thanks to Mark's efforts . . .

Mel found she was smiling. Perhaps it was time to concentrate less on the past and more on the future. She'd done her father's work. Perhaps it was her turn to learn from the mistakes of the past, but was Mark Penrose history or part of her future? Did he deserve a second chance too?

She drove in silence through the gathering gloom of December darkness with eyes glued to the signposts to Little Brierley.

53

It was the strangest of Christmases for Callie having a guest in
the house, a guest who waited on her hand, foot and finger,
bringing her tea in bed, mucking out and grooming, taking
telephone calls, shopping as if she was a helpless invalid. Callie
was not used to all this attention, but when she tried to do her
old chores, she was out of breath.

She loved watching Melissa bustling about her kitchen, practising her scales in the stables when the horses were out. She had
high notes that could shatter glass, a gift of a voice that must
surely come from her own mother, Phoebe. How Phee would
have loved to see this girl, this mirror image of herself in her
prime, so like her old postcard pictures, fair and feisty, graceful
and yet boyish. Callie was dying to see her dressed up. The girls
these days lived in jeans and boots.

Once, in her cups, Melissa whispered that she'd just dumped
her recent beau, the one who had gone out of his way to help
trace her family history and how she was having second thoughts
but was too proud to tell him so. Now who did that remind her
of, Callie mused.

It was hard to believe the difference a year could make.
Christmas last year was a pork chop, TV and a stroll around the
fields. She'd always refused all offers of hospitality. She was
going to miss all this company when it was over. She never tired
of listening to Melissa's stories about Sandra and Lew when

times were good. It cheered her heart. He had tried to be a good father but his struggles with the demon drink got the better of him at times and brought about his final illness.

He had found love and fulfilment in his wife, but it was snatched away from him as it had been from her. It was good to know the truth, both black and white. Yet between them, Sandra and her son had brought this golden girl into the world and brought her back to her own family.

There was the promise of the concert in the Abbey to look forward to. The acoustics there were wonderful but Callie was still worrying about the Trust's future. The anxiety had made her ill. She knew she was on borrowed time but determined now to make the most of what time was left, set her house in order, just as Madge had done all those years ago. How could she forget the kindness of those two strangers in taking her in, wreck that she was, bringing her back to life as Melissa had done by appearing by her bedside only a month ago, and yet it was as if she known this child in her heart all her life.

It was the day after Boxing Day, when she had the evening alone with Melissa by the fire, that the girl brought out a large typed email.

'I've been saving up some news for you, Gran. It's been burning a hole in my bag for days so please read it.' She shoved the sheet into Callie's hand and gave her the spectacles that were stuffed down the chair.

'You know I told you I went to the lawyer in London to find out who you were? Well, he sent me this.'

Callie read the letterhead. 'Goodness, are they still going?'

'Read on.'

With regards to our recent discussion about the estate of the late Phoebe Annie Boardman.

We received notification some time ago from Pettigrew and Copeland, Solicitors in Glasgow that the present tenants of

Dalradnor Lodge in the county of Stirlingshire desire to purchase the property and adjoining lands subject to current valuations, etc. if the Estate is willing to sell the aforesaid property.

Now that we have the current address of Caroline Rosslyn Jones, née Boardman, we enclose a copy of this offer for her consideration.

'Do you realize that if you sell Dalradnor,' Melissa added, 'maybe then you can dispose of the assets and help secure the Cottesloe Trust and make this place more comfortable for yourself: a downstairs loo and shower . . . extra insulation, roof repairs. You could afford permanent help. What do you think?' Melissa was excited at the thought of all these options, her eyes sparkling with enthusiasm.

Callie felt her heart clutch her chest for a second. She breathed deeply to release the pain. 'But Dalradnor has belonged in the family . . . It would be yours one day. I don't need anything at my time of life.'

'It doesn't belong to me. I have no connection to the place. I never even went inside it. What matters is what you want now.' Melissa smiled, poking the fire. 'My father left me quite comfortable so don't worry about me.'

It was wonderful news about the possibility of selling the Lodge, Callie thought, hard to take in, and the timing couldn't have been better. 'I suppose the Madge Cottesloe Sanctuary would then have a secure future. We could take in more horses, better housing, train up local staff. I know I'm not going to be up to much.'

'I gather that Phoebe's estate is more than just the house. You're going to be a wealthy woman.' Melissa seemed excited by this but Callie just shrugged.

'I would give it all back to make my peace with her. Money never buys us happiness, just security and comfort, but not what really matters in life. I can't take anything more from her.'

'Why not? If you don't claim her estate it could all go to the government.'

'Don't push me, young lady. This is too much to absorb – and now it's about time you and I had a little chat on another matter.' It was Callie's turn for some straight talking.

'About what?' There was a defensive look in Melissa's eyes.

'About a certain young man, who played a big part in your detective work. I'd very much like to meet him.'

'There's no point now. It's over between us. You have to understand when you're a musician, there's no time for romance.'

'Rubbish, that's poppycock. Lots of artists have wonderful partners. Learn from my life: don't let what really matters slip through your fingers in a search for what will come to you anyway with luck and hard work. You've got a lifetime ahead for success. I guess searching for me has been distracting but I won't be around for ever. I'd like to thank this Mark for all he's done to help us find each other. It sounds as if he's in love with you or he wouldn't put up with all your song and games for so long.'

'Oh, don't say that. He's not what I planned,' Melissa argued, refusing to catch her grandmother's eye.

'I think he was exactly your destiny the minute my postcard fell into your hands. It brought you both together. It brought us all together. Believe me, I know what it's like to find the special one in your life in the wrong time and the wrong place. It's never convenient, but follow your heart, not just your ambition, Melissa. Look and learn from one who knows what it's like to lose everything. Promise me you'll think about this?'

Callie's wise words were hitting hard by the look on Melissa's face. 'Everyone deserves a second chance, even you, young lady,' Callie added. 'You young have choices we never had. It's all ahead of you. Don't feel guilty about enjoying your musical gift and a lover too. I had a love life but it was shattered by war.

How different would all our lives have been if Ferrand and I could have lived together?' She sighed, shaking her head. 'You, of course, might never have been born. There isn't a day when I don't regret some of my decisions. My losing Desmond Louis created a sort of madness, a grief that never went away. All those years we might have shared, and my mother waiting for a reconciliation that never came. I broke her heart too. Why do we not understand our parents until it is too late? We all find ways to ease our pain. I was lucky because Madge and Alfie gave me a second chance here.

'You have to forgive your father for taking flight from his sorrows in his binges. Alcohol is such a comfort for the lonely and bereaved, a slow suicide for some in their despair. Not all of us can be strong-minded, Melissa. I know he hurt you deeply by his absence. What parents forget sometimes is the most important gift we can give to our children is time together, listening time. I let my son down so badly in so many ways.

'I owe the Cottesloe Sanctuary for giving me a reason to get out of bed. The love and loyalty of a bunch of wounded dumb animals was my reward, and now to be given a sight of you, in whom Desmond and Ferrand had a part, is more than I dared hope for. Don't be afraid of giving your heart in love. It's what makes us the best we can be.'

Mel hadn't slept much after that warning. It was hard to admit her fears. She cared more for Mark, too, than she wanted to admit. These past months had been lonely and empty because of his absence. Still, she decided, mistakes are great signposts and the next time she'd be more thoughtful to a partner. She found she was humming to herself the old folk song 'I Know Where I'm Going'. I only wish I knew where I'm going after all this, she sighed.

She heard the van arriving in the church car park. It was time to check her new dress in the makeshift dressing-room mirror among the cassocks of the vestry. It was a deep magenta velvet, strapless, with a tight bodice and a long-sleeved bolero edged with ribbon. Round her neck was a collar of pearls that Callie had lent her from Phoebe's estate, in a box with matching drop earrings. She felt as glamorous as if she were Maria Callas at La Scala, and nervous in that special way. Time to wish each player 'toi toi', the musicians' secret good-luck wish, each to each other. This may not be Covent Garden but it felt like the most important recital of her life so far.

It was a relief to see the church so full. Callie smiled with satisfaction. The great and the good of the county were assembled in their finery. She'd enjoyed choosing a long black skirt and velvet jacket, having her wispy hair dressed into what Melissa called was an 'up do' and she had squeezed into some heeled shoes. Now her eye kept glancing to the door just in case.

The concert started on time with the string quartet's music soaring up to the rafters. There was beautiful piece for flute, and then Melissa walked onto the chancel steps, magnificent and majestic-looking, so poised and beautiful.

When Melissa's voice soared to the rafters, Callie was stunned by its rich quality. The audience turned to each other, surprised by such power and control. Callie was no expert, but even she could see this girl was a star in the making. *And to think she came from me and mine.*

Melissa was staring across to her, smiling. 'In honour of my Scottish ancestry, I have chosen to sing something from Robert Burns: "O My Love is Like a Red, Red Rose".' How could all this talent come from such love and loss, from Phoebe, Arthur, Ferrand, Desmond and all the messiness of their separations? Here was truly a new beginning. This girl brought such pleasure, pride and meaning back into her life. Callie hoped she could return the favour in some small way. After thunderous applause, Melissa began the haunting 'Shepherds' Song' from

Songs of the Auvergne. Callie reached in her pocket for her hanky as her teary eyes roamed over the audience, young and old, all joined by a love of music.

She had hardly slept since she read the email with the offer to sell Dalradnor Lodge She had sworn never to return there without Desmond. It made such sense to secure the shelter here, but the Trust knew their lease was now up. It was only a matter of time before things must change. The sale would solve all their problems and yet . . . This was not the time to be worrying about the future.

Only one thing was missing. She glanced over the faces, searching around until she spied a tall young man covered in snowflakes edging slowly through the door, his eyes fixed only on Melissa. That looks promising, she smiled to herself. Vera's last-minute invitation had worked . . . Everyone deserved a second chance in life. If only she could be sure she was doing the right thing for the future of the Trust in what she might do next . . .

Finally

Callie sat among the roses in the walled garden of Dalradnor Lodge. The scents were fainter now to her older nostrils but the blossoms still filled her heart with pride: 'Boule de neige', the 'Albertine' climbing over the wall, the edging of lavender, 'Madame Alfred Carrière' arching over the gate. All her ladies were doing fine.

Here she felt close to Phoebe, Arthur and Desmond; all those childhood memories were waiting for her here. Never go back, they say, but sometimes you have to return with older wiser eyes to round the circle of life. Desmond had not forgotten the scent of roses and how she sang to him. Arthur had taken comfort from this in his dugout. She couldn't bring her son back to life but she'd been granted the next best thing, his daughter.

They'd flown up from London after Mel's latest concert. Callie had taken some persuading to join her and Mark for a summer holiday, but she owed it to everyone to make this visit, to thank the villagers who had helped her granddaughter. Besides, she had another motive in returning.

How could she have ever thought of selling off Dalradnor to strangers? It wasn't hers to give away. It must be held in trust for others. She had inspected the old stables with interest, the surrounding fields so perfect for her guests. The Cottesloe would continue but in another place. There were rooms for students, plenty of outbuildings and no landlord breathing down their neck. Everything could be planned for the future. Mark Penrose would organize that for her.

Once she'd been happy and safe here, and just as peaceful as she was feeling now. Arthur Seton-Ross had seen to that when he gave it to Phoebe. Now it would shelter the weary, wretched and broken in life; animals and humans alike.

I've come home and I'm going to stay here for the measure of life left for me, she smiled. There was still time, she prayed, to effect the smooth transfer of the Cottesloe Sanctuary. That decision was instant once she'd stepped back into this blessed space.

It was Ferrand who had once consoled her in Cairo with the old adage that mistakes are pearls to be cherished. What a string of pearls she'd made in life, but what a jewel of a golden girl was linking them all together as she strolled down the path to greet her now.

Acknowledgements

I owe a tremendous debt of gratitude to my agent, Judith Murdoch, my editor, Jessica Leeke, and my copy editor, Yvonne Holland, without whose immediate support and assistance this book might not have been published. They stepped in when I suddenly became ill, and put the final flourishes to the editing process. Thank you so much.

Although my characters are fictitious, I was inspired by the life of Eileen Nearne – special agent, SOE French section – and accounts of her escape from Ravensbrück Women's Concentration Camp gave me a structure for achieving the same for my own hero.

The difficult choice made by Desmond as a boy was not unusual at that time and was based on a true story told to me many years ago.

I must thank my cousins, David and Pat Rodger, for helping me find 'a Dalradnor Lodge' close to Balfron, Stirlingshire.

Finally, to all my friends and family, who rallied round at a difficult time – you lifted my spirits and lightened the load.

Leah Fleming

Leah Fleming

The Captain's Daughter

The secrets in a woman's heart are deeper than the ocean . . .

For May Smith, travelling with her husband and baby girl Ellen,
stepping foot on the *Titanic* marks the start of an incredible
journey, one which is destined to take her from the back streets of
Bolton to the land of opportunity:
the United States.

But when the 'unsinkable' *Titanic* hits an iceberg, May's dreams
are instantly shattered. Jumping from the sinking ship at the last
minute, May loses sight of Joe and Ellen. Distraught, she is pulled
into a lifeboat. Minutes later, Captain Smith swims to the lifeboat
and hands May a baby swaddled in blankets.

Beside herself, May believes the baby to be Ellen. This rescue
is witnessed by fellow survivor, Celeste Parkes. In horror, they
both watch the death throes of the mighty ship; May traumatised,
knowing her husband has drowned, Celeste wishing her
bully of a husband had been on board and out of her life.

As the dawn comes up, and the two women are rescued by the
Carpathia, a friendship is formed, one which is destined to last
a lifetime. Then May makes a shocking discovery and a split-
second decision which will change the lives of so many…

Paperback ISBN 978-0-85720-344-1
eBook ISBN 978-0-85720-343-4

Leah Fleming

The Girl Under the Olive Tree

Love in a time of war is hard when you are on the wrong side…

1938. Penelope George lives a charmed existence preparing
to be a debutante. But it is an empty life – a gilded cage
firmly shut on adventure and independence.

When her sister Evadne needs her help in Athens, Penny
seizes the opportunity to escape the straitjacket of London
society. Arriving in the historic city, she reinvents herself,
finding her true vocation as a Red Cross nurse, just another
stranger among strangers. Until war breaks out.

Stranded on the island of Crete, Penny tends the wounded
and dying as one of the few foreign nurses left on the
battlefield. Forging a dangerous friendship with Yolanda,
a young Jewish nurse, Penny attracts the unwanted
attention of a high-ranking German officer. Little does
she know how this encounter will change her life…

Sixty years later. It is time for Penny to return, to make the
journey she never thought she'd dare to, reliving those final
dark days on the island. It's a pilgrimage which will lead her
to a reunion with someone she thought she has lost forever
– and the truth behind a secret buried deep in the past.

Paperback ISBN 978-0-85720-406-6
eBook ISBN 978-0-85720-407-3

**SIMON &
SCHUSTER**

IF YOU ENJOY GOOD BOOKS,
YOU'LL LOVE OUR GREAT OFFER
25% OFF THE RRP ON ALL
SIMON & SCHUSTER UK TITLES
WITH FREE POSTAGE AND PACKING (UK ONLY)

Simon & Schuster UK is one of the leading general book publishing
companies in the UK, publishing a wide and eclectic mix
of authors ranging across commercial fiction, literary fiction,
general non-fiction, illustrated and children's books.

For exclusive author interviews, features and competitions log onto:
www.simonandschuster.co.uk

*Titles also available in **eBook** format across all digital devices.*

How to buy your books

Credit and debit cards
Telephone Simon & Schuster Cash Sales at **Sparkle Direct** on **01326 569444**

Cheque
Send a cheque payable to *Simon & Schuster Bookshop* to:
Simon & Schuster Bookshop, PO Box 60, Helston, TR13 OTP

Email: sales@sparkledirect.co.uk
Website: www.sparkledirect.com

Prices and availability are subject to change without notice.